THE
LAND OF NEPHI

A MEZO AMERICAN NOVEL

BY
DOUGLAS V. NUFER

This work is based on the text found within The Book of Mormon, specifically in the areas of The Book of Mosiah chapters 7-25. Characters, incidents, and dialog from that source material have been used liberally throughout this work.

Doug Nufer is the author of several novels and short stories. He enjoys speaking on his works, and the topics they address, and can be reached via Peepsock Press, e-mail (info@peepsockpress.com), or at the following website: www.PeepsockPress.com

PEEPSOCK
PRESS
P.O. Box 51082
Provo, UT 84605

Cover photo of Mayan Ruins at Altun Ha in Belize by Doug Nufer.
Peepsock Press logo by Todd Purser.

Printed in the United States of America.

10 9 8 7 6 5 4 3 2

For Abinadi

Acknowledgments
Many thanks to friends, family, and countless others who have helped encourage the research and writing of this work. Appreciation also goes out to the many men and women who have made the bringing forth of The Book of Mormon *possible.*

If this work prompts just one more person to read the original, true accounts of the brave men and women this fictional work depicts, then all of the efforts to bring it to pass will have been worthwhile.

Table of Contents

Chapter 1

The Search

Ammon did his best to ignore the pounding rain. The massive downpour refused to be ignored, however. It turned his view into a gray-blue streak and drowned out all other noise. He knew it would not last more than a few minutes. These downpours never did. What they did do was spur the humidity to a peak and turn the rainforest's floor into thick mud.

Ammon did not really mind the rain, though. It broke up the tedium of their journey. He leaned against a tree trunk and watched the puddles form. His men all did the same. None of them attempted to speak over the din of nature's splashing and thrashing. High above, where no one bothered to look, a family of spider monkeys huddled together in the crook of a branch waiting out the cloudburst. They chattered angrily at the water, but no one could hear their cries.

With the first sign of letting up, Ammon pushed off from the tree and motioned for his men to gather. By the time the powerful travelers had regrouped, the cloudburst was nothing more than a recent memory, reinforced by the sporadic dripping from the leafy, tall trees. They all knew the dripping would continue for hours.

"Ammon, do you know how much farther it should be? I mean, do you have any idea of where we are?" Helem was nearly as large as Ammon, which was an unspoken compliment. No one in the party lacked anything by way of physical stature. Helem's question was posed with curiosity, not irritation. All of the men knew that today marked a milestone in their wandering. It was their fortieth day.

"There is only one thing we can know for certain," Ammon responded.

Even those of his men who had ignored Helem's rhetorical inquiry took note of this turn of events.

"What's that?" Amaleki asked expectantly.

Ammon slowly wiped his face with a cloth as he eyed his comrades. He continued to bear the determined expression of a leader. He knew that his men's morale depended on their following a man who did not waver from his purpose.

"The simple answer," he said, "Is that we are one day closer than we were yesterday. We are one day closer to finding our brethren. One day closer to learning what has become of those we love. Many of us have relations who were brave enough to journey to the land of the Lamanites. We now have the opportunity to see if any yet live. I, for one, am determined to do so."

"And, we are determined to follow!" Shelam, another in their party, declared.

"As am I," Amaleki clarified. "I was simply curious. I'll continue this quest no matter how long it will take."

"I know you will," Ammon said, placing his hand on Amaleki's shoulder. "I have never doubted you."

Sixteen pairs of sandaled feet dug into the mud and fought for traction on a steep incline. Mud clung to their sandals, making the men's feet heavy. Thick roots and branches provided the closest thing to firm footing on the spongy earth. The ground eventually leveled out. The party continued onward.

Ammon swiped away at vines and brush as he literally cut their way through the jungle. It seemed that no man had ever set foot in this portion of the land. Ever. He wondered if they really were any closer or merely wandering on a pointless march. He kept such thoughts to himself, however.

The jungle had thinned only slightly, if at all, when the terrain had topped off and leveled out. The explorers trudged onward for quite some time. The undergrowth grew abnormally thick. Ammon and his men teamed up to strike away at it. They stood three men wide hacking at the vines and brush with their swords.

As the men worked their way forward, they grew increasingly more silent. All chatter between them had stopped. The only noise was the sound of their feet on fallen twigs and leaves, the hacking of their swords on fresh vines, and an occasional bird or monkey.

It was Hem who broke the silence.

"Ammon, do you feel that?"

"Yes, I do," was all he needed to reply.

The men stopped still. Each was all too conscious of what Hem was referring to. There was an ominous tension in the air that was nearly palpable.

"It's a powerful feeling of ill," Sheram observed. "It's as though the wind has shifted and I've walked directly into the smoke of an untended campfire."

"I sense it too, Sheram," Ammon acknowledged. "I fear that something extremely tragic or evil has taken place in this very area."

The men agreed. In relating the tale later, several would speak of how the hairs on their neck prickled at Ammon's words.

"We can't help what has happened in the past," Ammon said. "We can only push on toward our future and the welfare of our people. Let's continue."

The men nodded in agreement and commenced attacking the green jungle that stood between them and their goal. Suddenly, one of the men on the far right slipped out of view and disappeared with a yelp of surprise.

"Ammon! Ammon!" his nearest comrade cried out.

"What?" Ammon shouted back.

"It's Emer! He's fallen!"

"Fallen? Can he not get back up?"

"No, he's disappeared entirely from view!"

Ammon and the rest of his men hurried over to where a very excited Nephite stood.

"I was standing right next to him. We were cutting our way through. I heard him cry out. When I turned to see, he was gone!" Jeshua shouted excitedly.

"Is it some sort of hole...?" Ammon was about to ask, but was interrupted by a disembodied voice coming from below them.

"It's not a hole," the voice announced, with a rather insistent tone. "It's the edge of a cliff. The ground has given way!"

"What? Where are you?"

"I'm down here. And, I suggest you watch your step, or you will be joining me," Emer called up from somewhere beneath them.

Each man took a step back and looked down toward where the voice had emanated. Jeshua, the man who had first called to Ammon, bent low and pulled at some of the loose bushes that had fallen together, blocking all view of Emer's predicament. Amaleki came over and helped. They both carefully tugged at the brush, ensuring that they themselves had firm footing. Finally, an opening began to appear between them.

What they saw was not the black void of a hole. Instead, it was the bright illumination of open territory. Directly below them, Emer clung to a branch on the edge of a steep cliff. His dirtied face peered upward. Sweat streaked his temples and his muddy hands shifted their grip on the branch above his head.

"Throw me a rope!" he called to them, attempting to overcome the indignity of his precarious position.

His fifteen comrades immediately stepped back and looked for firm holds so that no one else joined their hapless companion unexpectedly. Amaleki and his friend lowered a rope and pulled Emer to safety. Moments later, all was calm again and each member of the party stood on firm, level earth.

"I suggest we watch ourselves," Emer explained. "This thick growth is right on the edge of a rather impressive drop."

"Yes, we thank you for finding that out, Emer," Ammon replied.

"Certainly, but you should also know that I saw something as I fell."

"What was it?"

"I couldn't really tell because it was behind me from the way I was hanging there. As far as I could make it out from the corner of my eye, it looked like a city," Emer offered.

The men grew extremely interested. This was the first solid hint that they were heading in the right direction. They gathered closer, each one throwing questions at Emer.

"Is it Nephi?"

"What did you see?"

"Did you see anybody?"

"I told you. It was behind me. I only caught a brief glimpse of it on the way down. And, at that moment I was more concerned about where I was going and how I was going to stop. I didn't dare let go with either hand, and could not quite see it as I hung there. I'm sure it's still there. It's not as if we can't all take a good look."

"Emer is correct," Ammon acknowledged. "We should cut away more of this brush and take a look for ourselves. And, I suggest we watch our steps."

The men approached the brush. They poked the ground with their swords, seeking solid resistance before delicately placing their feet forward. When swords broke through to apparently open air, the men stepped back and nodded to each other. Then they swung their swords with swift determination along the ground until they could see a break.

Next, they swung them directly in front of themselves until they cut a perforation chest high. One man ventured forward to make the final cut. With a gingerliness that his warrior frame was unaccustomed to, he trimmed away the top. With the final hack, the vegetation opened as a door before them and then sank away dropping down into the bright void beneath them. The men crouched down and peered through the opening.

"He's right!"

"I see it!"

"Do you think it's Nephi, or a Lamanite city?"

"Hold on, men. Grab some ropes and we'll all know soon enough," Ammon replied.

Helem stood upright from having peered through the opening. He looked to his leader and spoke his mind.

"Ammon, suppose it *is* a Lamanite city. I don't think it would be wise if we all just walked down there and presented ourselves as prisoners."

"I see your point. Helem, you, Amaleki and Hem come with me. The rest of you wait here. We'll come back for you as soon as we know it's safe. Make yourselves comfortable. You may be here a while."

"We must hope that none of us wanders too far in the night," Emer observed.

"Yes. Now, grab some ropes and get moving," Ammon coaxed.

The men tied a length of rope around the nearest tree trunk and dropped the loose end through the opening. It was not long before four Nephites in turn, dangled the two dozen yards of open space that separated their comrades from the lower landing. Once down, the rope was quickly retracted. The men above silently waved farewell and bid good luck to their leader as they crept back behind the reclusive cover of the underbrush.

Ammon and his trio found themselves on a landing on the hillside with unusually sparse vegetation. All about them, the rainforest encroached on and swallowed the land. On this landing, only a few yards in diameter, they were permitted a limited view into the distance. They turned and could make out the city far below and across a plain.

It was too far to be able to discern who, if anyone, inhabited the city. They could make out the top half of the largest building. Its pyramid-shaped walls were capped by a stone canopy-room with a flat top. Steep stairs dissecting each side of the building were distinctively of Nephite design. Beside the pyramid, was an unusually tall watchtower with peculiarly wide steps circling up to its highest platform. A twelve-foot tall stone wall circled the city, keeping its inhabitants safe from both beasts and invaders. On the outskirts of the ancient city, they could see the tell-tale signs of farms and cattle.

As they surveyed the city, Hem looked northeastward and made another discovery. "Ammon!" he said, nudging his leader. Ammon pulled his gaze away from the southern city and turned to look at Hem. As he did so, he saw what Hem was pointing to. There in a clearing at the edge of the jungle, was another city.

This city was of a similar design, in that it had buildings surrounded by a high wall. But, it was built to a much smaller scale. There was no central pyramid, and no watchtower.

"Interesting!" Ammon commented. "Two cities? This is very interesting."

"Yes, but, which one is Nephi, if either of them is?" Amaleki asked.

"I would think that Nephi would be the larger of the two, wouldn't you?" Ammon suggested.

"It was our capital," Helem acknowledged. "I can't imagine building another city right next to it that would be larger than Nephi. That just wouldn't make sense."

As they pondered the possibilities, they realized that their vantage point not only provided them a limited view of their supposed goal, but also bore the potential of exposing their position to the enemy.

"I suggest we move on and make our way to that larger city," Ammon recommended.

The others agreed. They pressed on and reentered the dense jungle on the lower end of the hill. The remaining descent was relatively uneventful. Within half an hour's time, they had cut their way through the growth to the level plain that separated the city from the jungle. They paused at the jungle's edge.

"Can you make out anybody?" Amaleki asked.

"No, not a soul," Hem responded. "No, wait! Over there, I see about a dozen men coming around the corner, by the city wall! See them?" Hem pointed to the eastern side of the city.

"Yes, I see them," Ammon agreed.

"The question is, are they Nephites or Lamanites?" Helem verbalized everyone's concern.

"It's difficult to tell from this distance," Hem responded.

Ammon stated. "I can't be certain, but I would say it looks like a group of Nephites."

"I think Ammon is right. Look at their gait as they walk. Surely, they're Nephites," Hem said.

"Well, we've come to discover who is here, so I say we find out." Amaleki stepped out of the jungle and into the open.

"Stop! Wait! Amaleki, don't be foolish!" Helem called in a hoarse, shocked whisper.

"No, Amaleki is right," Ammon stated, "We should go, too."

They all emerged from the jungle and joined Amaleki. They quickened their pace across the field, hoping to be noticed before the distant men made it to the city gate. They knew that even if these men were Nephites, there were bound to be Lamanites around somewhere. They would stand a better chance of gaining entry to the city if they entered with someone, than if they had to knock on the city gate.

With only a couple hundred yards to go, the foursome managed to catch the eye of what they hoped were their long-lost brethren. They saw the group nearing the city wall stop and turn. They appeared to hold some form of discussion. Then, one man separated himself from their group and was flanked by two other men as he quickly made his way to the city gate and disappeared into the city proper. The rest of the men turned and raced toward Ammon and his men.

"Well, they're definitely Nephites," Ammon surmised. "And, those are definitely not farming hoes."

"What do we do now?" Hem asked. "Do we run?"

"Run? I don't think so. We came here to find out if there were any Nephites here. Now that we know, we need to find out who these Nephites are," Ammon replied.

The four men stood where they were and allowed the armed Nephites to catch up with them. Within moments they were surrounded and well-guarded. One by one they were bound with strong cords with their wrists tied together behind their backs.

"Move!" a guard ordered and gave Ammon a brusque push from behind.

Ammon's right shoulder lunged forward from the force of the push and the rest of his body jumped and stutter-stepped until it caught up. The others were pushed forward as well, and the party was soon on its way to the unknown Nephite city, under circumstances which they had not anticipated. No one spoke.

The guards marched them at a double-pace until they faced the city gate. The group stopped and a guard called out, "Open the gate!"

The gate opened at a steady pace. Ammon and his men were more than a little curious about what they would find inside. They craned their necks to peer within the widening gap as the gate swung open.

Because of their rough reception, they half expected to see Lamanites marching about in the city square. They were a little surprised to see only Nephites. Again, they were startled from their thoughts by another series of pushes from behind.

"Get moving!" a guard commanded.

The group was physically pushed through the city square. As they marched, they noted the inhabitants. Word of their entry had spread quickly and citizens were gathering to watch the spectacle. Parents kept a tight rein on their children. Ammon saw fathers point at them and speak words he could not overhear into their children's ears. He wondered what tales the parents were spinning and why their reception was so hostile.

The guards continued to push and guide their prisoners through the city square and past several buildings made of stone and wood. They came to one of the larger buildings and were made to wait momentarily as one of their guards opened the door and called inside. From within, an acknowledgment was given that they were ready. Their journey continued deep into the recesses of the building.

To the right of the entry was a large series of stairs carved from solid rock which headed down into unknown chambers. Ammon and the others fought to keep their balance as the guards forced them down the stairway which wound around and down to the lowest chamber.

The stairs led to a long, narrow hallway made of stone. Old torches now offered the only source of flickering light. It took a while for their eyes to adjust to the dim surroundings. For a brief while, the four trudged on in blind bursts of sudden stagger-steps with each push from their captors. They leaned into each other hoping to maintain balance and bearing. There was an odd sense of comfort in knowing that they were all in this together. Before realizing they had entered a cell, they received a final shove that completely took them off balance.

They found themselves lying on their sides and fighting to get up to a kneeling position. The floor was damp and covered with dirty hay which stank of dead rats and droppings. It was dismally apparent that the hay had not seen the light of day for uncounted weeks or months. The cold chill in the stagnant air took their breath away.

Sight was just returning as Ammon made out the face of the guard who slammed their cell's wooden door shut. He heard a spine-shivering scraping noise as the guard slid a heavy block of wood into place to hold the door closed. Ammon noted that the man was a Nephite, but bore a look of hatred and disgust that he had not seen in many a year, if ever. He could not imagine what could drive the man to hate strangers to such a degree as this, especially fellow Nephites.

The men all had a thousand questions spinning through their minds. Rather than depress themselves with all of the potential answers, they decided to first busy themselves with helping each other untie their wrists. It was a clumsy, awkward business, as the knots were painfully tight, and the cell was brutally dark. By all appearances, there was no need to hurry. It seemed that they would be there for quite a while.

Chapter 2
Confinement

It must have been only the second day, though it seemed more like a week. It was difficult to count the hours in the darkness. Their only source of light was a dimly flickering torch which must have been quite a ways down the corridor and around a corner. It offered only a faint impression of inconsistent lighting that crept underneath their cell's door. It was the kind of light that can only be noticed when one has been exposed to utter darkness over a prolonged period of time.

When the light began to increase at a rate that would have been wholly imperceptible under normal circumstances, three of the four captives sprang into a state of alert attentiveness. The fourth, Hem, had managed to fall asleep on a clump of sickly-smelling hay. Amaleki gave him a soft, well-intentioned nudge with his foot. Hem awoke immediately from his restless sleep. He could just make out the silhouette of Amaleki looking down on him. He breathed in the overwhelming odor that permeated the cell. He shook his head, disappointed to find himself in the same state that he had hoped was only a very distressing dream.

Neither Hem nor Amaleki spoke to each other. They did not need to, nor did the other two. All of them turned their focus to the flickering light that they could now make out through gaps at the ends of the great door which held them at bay. The pangs in their near-empty stomachs seemed to tighten and bite harder still at this glimmer of potential release. That anticipation heightened and renewed all of their sensations of discomfort and foreboding. Two days of wordless, cruel neglect will work bitterly on any man's soul.

The light flickered and slowly intensified. Gradually, they could also make out muffled sounds of footsteps and scraping noises of someone traversing the corridor. They heard no speaking, nor had they in virtually the entire time they had been held captive. Even in the field, their captors simply sprang into action and had given them only curt orders. It had been an unfortunately puzzling chain of events.

The foursome waited in silence. They wondered if this visit would bring another unfortunate deposit of poorly-prepared rations, or the offer of parole. They had quickly learned the futility of attempting communication with their captors. Helem still nursed a bruise of unknown dimensions from the staff of one jailer who disapproved of his attempt at civility.

By the time the light under and above the door reached its peak, all four stood as a group in the center of the cell, purposely keeping their distance from the door. They were cautious, but unafraid. More than anything, they were curious as to the cause of their treatment and how they were to bring about a remedy.

They heard the great block scrape the door as it was removed from its locking position. It pounded the stone floor and provided an unnerving echo as it was callously dropped. It seemed to take longer than normal for the door to begin to move. Something was different this time. They sensed it.

Finally, the door was pushed fully open and two blazing torches were forced into the room, flames first. The bright light burned their eyes. They jerked their heads instinctively and jumped back startled, ducking their heads and trying to shade their eyes from the searing change in illumination. Their eyes were still attempting to adjust to the flickering light as the guards grabbed the men by their elbows and brutally pushed them forward toward the door. Ammon and his hapless men did well to avoid falling as they staggered forward and lunged in the direction of the push.

Helem dared to ask what this all meant and received a harsh, one-word reply, "Silence!" accompanied by a stiff jab in the back by a guard's staff. The resulting bruise would take several weeks to heal.

They all took the guard's advice to heart and remained silent. Several guards continued to move in on the men and shoved them until they were all standing with their backs to the door. While one guard stood behind Ammon, holding him securely, another guard went to his front and tightly bound a rope around Ammon's left wrist. He bound the other end of the rope around Ammon's other wrist. There was just enough slack remaining for Ammon to hold his fists up to either side of his chest. That was precisely what the guard forced Ammon to do so quickly that it hurt.

Ammon was confused, until he felt a new, searing pain as another guard stepped into the room. Ammon could not see the man, but he certainly felt it when the guard took one end of a three-foot long pole and shoved it mercilessly into the space between the inside of Ammon's elbows and his back. The guard continued to push on the pole from behind Ammon, while the rope-tying guard in front of Ammon pushed on his fists, forcing them up and into his chest. This also forced Ammon's elbows back just barely enough for the other guard to maneuver the pole across Ammon's back and through his other elbow.

With the pole in place, Ammon stood with an awkward stance, his elbows forced behind him. He slowly clenched and unclenched his fists that were now wedged at the base of his chest, in a vain attempt to get his blood to circulate.

Other guards held Ammon's men, while the hapless Nephites saw the fate that was soon to befall them. Sure enough, as soon as Ammon was secured, the others received the same treatment. Once all of the men were bound, they were each whisked around and shoved through the open door, suffering the indignation of harsh treatment.

The remainder of the journey was no better. Their bare feet felt the cold clamminess of the subterranean stone corridor's floor. They had been deprived of the majority of their belongings during their induction ceremony to the cell. Helem and Hem had even lost their shirts.

Up stairs, through more corridors, up more stairs, they were silently forced to march at a quick pace. They were at ground level by now and began to pass several rooms. Some rooms had open doors. As they were pushed passed these, they managed to peer in and catch glimpses of Nephites sitting at tables, or standing. In each case, the occupants stared back and caught fleeting views of these enemy captives. Ammon wondered what thoughts milled about in their minds. He knew he and the others presented a terrible sight in their ragged clothes and dirty hides with ropes hiding the swelling of their wrists and ankles.

The captives soon found themselves face to face with a large, delicately-engraved double door. It opened. A grand push from behind welcomed them into the throne room. The doors closed behind them. Their prison guards left with the closing of the doors. They were replaced, however, by throne room guards. It was painfully obvious that they were to be well watched.

The throne room guards pushed them forward. Then they hit the backs of their knees with their staffs, forcing the men to kneel. Ammon looked back and glared at his guard a moment, then thought better of objecting. Instead, he turned his focus directly ahead of him, where he hoped to finally find the answer to the far-less-than-pleasant reception that they had so far received.

He saw a stately, ancient throne carved of solid, dark wood. It had gold leafing inlaid over much of the carvings in the wood, which caused it to shine as the torch lights flickered. Curving down the left side, forming the arm rest, across the seat and up the other side, forming the second arm rest, and then curling along the back of the wooden throne was an intricately carved serpent. Its head rose some three feet above the throne. Its long, forked tongue was permanently flicked outward. Its eyes were large and slanted. Its fangs were long and pointed.

Sitting on the throne was an impressive looking Nephite king. His long robe was of finely-trimmed, light brown fur. It appeared to be similar to monkey fur, but no seams could be detected. Six fingers bore regal rings with two stones each, representing the months of the year. More importantly, these acted as a token reminder of the duration of his reign – all year long and forever.

He was of a good build, not fat or slovenly in appearance as one might suspect a man of authority to become. His head bore a stately, but dignified crown. It was large enough to make clear his kingship, but was not flashy or ostentatious. The thing that struck Ammon the most was the impression he had when looking into the king's eyes.

While it was abundantly apparent that the king was displeased with Ammon and his men, and that he approved and quite likely ordered their current, brutal treatment, Ammon did not sense deep-rooted malice in the man. To the contrary, in spite of their unpleasant experience and the gruff expression on the king's face, Ammon sensed a deeper series of emotions and inner consciousness which implied a more tolerable disposition. They all noted that the guards took a more active notice of their presence and retained their spears poised at the prisoners' muscular, yet tender, hides.

The king stirred and regained Ammon and his party's attention. "Behold, I am Limhi, the son of Noah, who was the son of Zeniff, who came up out of the land of Zarahemla to inherit this land which was the land of our fathers and who was made a king by the voice of the people."

The king paused a moment allowing his genealogy to sink in. He eyed his captives to see the impact his words had on them. He shifted and offered in a threateningly benevolent tone, "And now, I desire to know the cause whereby you were so bold as to come near the walls of this city, when I, myself, was with my guards without the gate. This is the only reason that I have suffered that your lives should be spared. Otherwise, I would have had my guards put you to death. You are permitted to speak."

Ammon now knew, as his men did too, that their search was at an end. They had found the long lost Nephites whom they had been seeking. Discounting their wretched state, Ammon fought back a smile. He struggled to his feet. The restraining rod made this more difficult than normal, as he was unable to reach out and steady himself. As he rose to his feet, the guards leaned in with their weapons poised, to gain his attention and assure that he did nothing hostile toward their revered leader. Ammon ignored them and faced the king.

Chapter 3
Origins

Ammon bowed with impressive dignity and then stood erect again. With an eloquence that comes from a lifetime of civil living and serving in positions of leadership, he spoke. "Oh king, I am very thankful before God this day that I am yet alive, and am permitted to speak. I will endeavor to speak with boldness. For I am assured that if you had known me you would not have suffered that I should have worn these bands. For, I am Ammon, and am a descendant of Zarahemla. I have come up out of the land of Zarahemla to inquire concerning our brethren, whom Zeniff brought up out of that land."

Ammon's words had a predictable impact on not only the king, but on all those who were in the throne room. The guards nearly dropped their spears. The king's eyes widened and shone with enthusiasm. He leapt up from his throne and stood. For the sake of the regal office he held, he restrained himself from rushing down and embracing Ammon.

"Now I know of a surety that my brethren who were in the land of Zarahemla are yet alive!" he cried out. "This is marvelous! God be praised! We will all rejoice, and on the morrow I will cause that my people shall rejoice also."

King Limhi's glee was contagious. The room was filled with wide-eyed expectation of unforeseen, yet ever-hoped-for, deliverance. In the midst of their rejoicing, Helem shifted his weight, subtly stretching one of his legs in an attempt to rejuvenate his blood supply. The king took note of the movement, and then noticed the bands with which his deliverers were still bound, as well as the tips of the restraining rods that jutted out from either side of the men.

Limhi's face turned pale as he realized what he had done. He quickly urged his guards to remove the bands. The guards, too, shamefully realized the wrongful state in which Ammon and his party were kept. Ammon's attention was torn from the king to the sensation of the confining rod being slid from behind his back. Each of his men experienced the same action. Sharp knives freed their wrists from their bonds. Each man gingerly rubbed life back into his wrists and hands. The guards backed away apologetically, ensuring that their spears no longer pointed toward their brethren.

"Ammon, I, uh, I am terribly sorry. We had no idea. We thought you were someone else," Limhi stuttered.

"Someone else? Who, may I ask?" Ammon queried, with sincere curiosity and a tone of dignified restraint.

"Yes. Well, it is a long story. I will tell it, but not now," Limhi began. "First, I want to see after you and your men. Surely you did not come all this way with only four men. Am I correct?"

"Yes, King Limhi, you are correct," Ammon smiled. "I see you are a man with great insight."

"Where are your other men?"

"I left them encamped on the large hill north of here."

"The large hill? You must mean the hill near the city of Shilom."

"Ah, so that is its name," Ammon commented.

"Yes. It is our sister city, built to help house the people."

"I see."

King Limhi again turned his focus on the disgraceful state of his would-be rescuers. "We can speak of all this later. First, I wish that my servants will see to your needs and get you cleaned up. Then we would like to retrieve the rest of your men."

*****

Hem and Helem were already standing in the city square waiting for Amaleki to join them. Four of the king's guards stood with them. They passed the time by chatting casually and asking a series of questions about life in Zarahemla. King Limhi stood to the right of the group, smiling and talking with Ammon. Ammon and his men all wore clean clothing, provided by their new hosts. Even their sandals, with the support thongs that entwined their way up their calves, were new.

Amaleki rounded a corner and crossed the square with two more guards. They spoke like old friends as they approached the others. Helem turned and greeted Amaleki.

"You look a far sight better today than you did yesterday," Amaleki responded. "Of course anything would look better than how we looked-"

Amaleki stopped himself short as he saw the look of warning Ammon gave him. It was a quick reminder to keep that experience behind them, lest they offend their hosts who had already spent three hours apologizing.

Hem successfully shifted everyone's attention away from an awkward moment and back to the business at hand.

"So, are we ready to get the others?" he asked.

Ammon stepped forward. "I believe Hem is right. We should go." He turned to King Limhi and respectfully added, "With your leave, your majesty."

"By all means. Go. Retrieve your men. Bring them here quickly," Limhi replied.

"We will," Ammon said.

The city gate was pushed open. As it opened, Ammon and his men looked across the field and saw the hill they had descended in the distance. It had only been a couple of days, but it seemed much longer. They wondered how their comrades had fared during their wait. The unspoken consensus was that it would have been difficult for their wait to have been any worse than their own experience.

King Limhi himself had accompanied Ammon and his men to the city gate. Although he did not intend to follow them, he wanted to wish them well on the final leg of their journey. He sent along several guards to aid their friends from the north.

"We are thrilled to have you here. Please, go get your men and then hurry back," the king said, "I have ordered a feast to be prepared for you and all your men. This is a day to celebrate!" he announced.

*****

Ammon and the others were still several dozen yards away from the hill when they saw their men clambering down a rope through the same opening they had used days earlier. The two groups met at the base of the hill.

"Ammon! We were beginning to wonder if we would ever see you again!" Jeshua declared.

"Yes, we thought you might have forgotten us," another added.

"Well, no, that would not be quite right," Ammon replied. "I'm glad to see you are all still well, though."

"So, is it the right city? Did we find the city of Nephi?" Jeshua asked.

"Yes, yes it is!" Hem confirmed.

"It is, but there's much to be done here," Ammon added.

"Much? What?" Jeshua asked.

"We'll tell you what we can on the way there," Ammon said. "We still don't understand everything ourselves yet. Meanwhile, let's go. I believe there is a feast waiting for us."

"A feast?! That's wonderful. We're famished!" Emer replied with unabashed enthusiasm.

*****

The banquet hall was spacious and grand. Crystal chandeliers were given life and light from compact torches hidden deeply within their crystalline and bejeweled formations. The tables and chairs were made of fine wood and bore carvings of animals and plants native to the surrounding rainforest.

The main wall on the west side of the hall was filled with what looked like ancient, but well-kept wooden pictographs carved into dark wood. Each near-perfect square was the height of a man. They depicted the history of the people of Nephi from the time Nephi and his father, Lehi, had gathered their families and fled the land of Jerusalem just prior to the Babylonian conquest of Israel. Various squares showed their journey through the wilderness, the building of their boat, and their settling in the New World.

One square in particular caught Ammon's eye. It showed a path leading to a large tree with fruit. People were shown eating of the fruit and smiling. Across a chasm was a large building containing many more people. The people in the building were pointing at those at the tree, or traversing the path that led to the tree. Several of those traversing the path were holding onto a long rod that paralleled the path. They were using the rod as a guide. Others had let go and were falling into a river that flowed along the chasm.

Ammon smiled to himself as he looked at this particular piece of art and history. He was very familiar with the story it told. It was intriguing for him to see it depicted in this way.

The final pictograph depicted the building of the city of Nephi in which King Limhi and his people now dwelled in a troubled peace.

The pictographs were overshadowed by impressive wooden carvings of grape vines that were scrawled in between the squares and crawled up the walls and across the ceiling. The dark, wooden vines from every wall met in the center of a spacious ceiling. There they wound around each other and supported an enormous bundle of grapes. The bundle spread across a good third of the ceiling, its center hung down at least half a dozen feet, forming a permanent testament to the fruit's abundance.

The other three walls were donned with pictographs that were newer than those on the west wall. These were decorated with carvings from everyday life. The northern wall seemed to be dedicated to the glory of the harvest, particularly grapes and wines. It showed men toiling heavily to cultivate and reap the grapes, followed by others showing various stages of men transforming the grapes into fine wines. The eastern wall depicted other aspects of everyday life and seemed to include homage to an ever-watchful king. Ammon noted that this king was much larger, and yet less sturdily built than Limhi, and concluded that he must have been a predecessor.

Ammon was most intrigued by the southern wall. While it too showed aspects of Nephite living, it seemed to focus on depictions of women performing various tasks or activities. Several were singing or dancing. He could not help but notice that several pictographs seemed to have been taken down from this particular wall and replaced by others showing families at work or praying together. These family-oriented scenes were clearly of a newer style and substance than those on the other walls. He could not help but wonder what had been removed.

Ammon was to learn that most of the ornate carvings and decorations had been created and supplied by King Limhi's late father, but Limhi still knew when and how to put them to good use. The unfortunate fact was that in all of the years of his reign, he had rarely had a good cause to do so, certainly never a reason as splendid as the arrival of Ammon and his brethren. The hall was filled with smiling, anxious faces.

Each of Limhi's people wanted a good view of these travelers from the north who were destined, they hoped, to free them from the bondage under which they found themselves. It was a bondage of which their sixteen saviors were still unaware.

Other than the king's somewhat cryptic comment to Ammon, all indications were that these were a very happy people living and dwelling in the city of Nephi, thus fulfilling the dream of countless thousands of Nephites. It was a dream that had been perpetuated ever since their fathers were driven out of the city by the dark-skinned Lamanites and forced to abandon their treasured home.

As per King Limhi's decree, Ammon and his men sat at the head table to the king's right and left. Nearest their table were the king's counselors and most trusted advisors. Ammon was permitted to speak freely with Limhi, particularly because Limhi was anxious to learn more about these brave men. The Nephites from the north were equally anxious to learn more about Limhi and his people. They swapped stories throughout the feast. Long after all of the pleasantries were completed and the hall was cleared of participants, on-lookers and servants, the king and the sixteen Nephites continued to speak.

At a fairly early stage in the evening, Ammon perceived that King Limhi both accepted and trusted him. He and his men had left the city of Zarahemla simply to find out what had become of those Nephites who had left that secure city two generations earlier in search of the land of Nephi. He was growing fond of these people and could appreciate their interest in hearing of Zarahemla. But, these people, including the king, seemed to be expecting great things of him. He found this a curious affair.

Although Ammon was determined to find out more about this, he decided he needed to do so in as tactful a manner as possible. He realized the importance of allowing the king to first drain himself of questions before returning in kind. The first hour or two of the evening was spent relating to King Limhi all that had occurred in the city of Zarahemla since Limhi's grandfather led his people on their quest to the south.

Ammon spoke highly of King Mosiah II, who currently reigned in peace and wisdom in Zarahemla. He also spoke of King Benjamin who had preceded his son, Mosiah, on the throne. He related the tale of King Benjamin's battles to obtain and preserve the safety and freedom of the Nephite nation and maintain Zarahemla as a sanctuary where men could serve their fellow men, and their God, without fear of reprisals or oppression.

The enthusiasm in Ammon's voice as he spoke of King Benjamin was inescapable. He told of how King Benjamin climaxed his reign when, as an aging king, he called all of the people together and used his own life of service as an example for all men. He summarized the king's sermon on the importance of working with one's own hands to earn one's keep. King Benjamin's final speech before turning his throne over to his son, Mosiah II, was to teach his people to believe in and anticipate the coming of the great Messiah.

This was a significant aspect of the Nephite's religious beliefs. Ammon added that these righteous and goodly kings had proven to be a great blessing to the Nephite nation to the north. They were then experiencing a degree of peace and prosperity the likes of which they knew previous generations had only dreamed. Ammon noted King Limhi sigh heavily at this point in his description. He paused, allowing King Limhi to comment. The king abstained from comment, however.

Retrieving the lag in the conversation, Ammon continued his story.

"We had such prosperity that we became concerned about our brethren who had left our fair city so many years before. We became anxious to find out how they had fared, and if any of them yet lived. We wearied the king with requests to send a group to find them. My men and I were eventually commissioned by King Mosiah himself to lead that search. We journeyed many days and suffered many things – hunger, thirst and fatigue – but are pleased beyond words to have found you and your noble people. We are especially pleased to find you all doing so well in this chosen land."

King Limhi's face turned sour again. His eyes drifted away from Ammon as another heavy sigh escaped his lips. It was hardly the proper look for a king. Ammon could not let this slip by again. He became determined to learn the meaning of the mysteriously melancholic responses.

"Great king Limhi. I continue to perceive that all is not right with your mood and demeanor. We sit in this fair hall and have enjoyed a bounteous feast with company any man would find appealing. Yet, I have seen a look of dejection and foreboding find its way to your face more than once this evening. You must tell me, what is the cause of these terrible moods, and what can I do to be of service to you?"

"Ammon, I see that you are a man of deep perception. You are correct that all is not right with this people," King Limhi began. "You seem to think that we are a free people, free to live and feast as the seasons bid us. The truth is that this grand hall has been seldom used, for we are a people with infrequent reasons to rejoice. We are in bondage to the Lamanites. We are taxed with a tax which is grievous to be borne, and forced to do their bidding."

Ammon and his men were shocked at this revelation. The words caused them to sit upright and silently exchange questioning looks, wondering if they had heard correctly. Amaleki dared to speak the minds of all his brethren.

"Great king Limhi, am I to understand you correctly? Are you saying that you are enslaved by the Lamanites?"

"Yes, you understand correctly. It is a fact that neither pleases us, nor can we long hide it. You would learn it soon enough," the king lamented.

"But, your Majesty, how can such a thing be?" Ammon queried.

"It is a long and ignoble tale. It is also the cause of the great rejoicing among my people at your arrival."

"And, how is that, oh king?" Ammon asked.

"We believe that with your help, we should be able to escape this place and find sanctuary in Zarahemla, if your king Mosiah will have us. We will gladly be your slaves. For it is better that we be slaves to the Nephites than pay tribute to the king of the Lamanites."

"Great king, please, can you help us understand how this has happened? How have you fallen into such a state? How have you fallen into slavery? Can you tell us this?"

"Yes, I can. It will require you to know of my grandfather, King Zeniff. His tale begins long before he was made king...."

Chapter 4
Zeniff

The old man sat at the wooden table, motionless and contemplative. His aging eyes were gaining the thick residue of cataracts, yet maintained a look of dignified serenity. Wrinkles surrounded those warm eyes. Wrinkles brought on by both age and smiles. His flowing black hair of youth had long ago thinned and grayed. His powerful muscles had atrophied to half their accustomed size, but managed to allow the echo of his former youthful self to linger still.

The etching utensil was poised in his hand. The smooth, blank, metal sheets sat flat upon the table awaiting whatever words he saw fit to imprint upon them. They laid there before him, beckoning him to share his thoughts. For a time, he sat staring blankly at the stone wall before him. His mind drifted easily to a time spent long ago, among a people who had held the same dreams, ideals and vitality which had consumed him. Even those who disagreed with his methods maintained their own version of his same goals.

His flood of memories brought both a tear and a smile to his face. It was so long ago. It seemed so near. The more he thought, the closer it became. Finally, without conscious thought, the etching utensil moved into action. Zeniff began his official memoir with these words:

"I, Zeniff, having been taught in all the language of the Nephites, and having had a knowledge of the land of Nephi, or of the land of our fathers' first inheritance, was sent as a spy among the Lamanites that I might spy out their forces, that our army might come upon them and destroy them–but when I saw that which was good among them I was desirous that they should not be destroyed...."

* * * * *

"Hagoth, surely you can see reason," Zeniff boldly declared. "These are a peaceful people. We should at least try to make a treaty with them."

Many Nephites had maintained a death-grudge against the Lamanites that had festered for generation after generation and dated back long before the Nephites were eventually forced to leave their beloved city and land of Nephi and seek a more remote and protected land farther to the north. Some were able to see beyond the hatred. But, others, such as Hagoth, the leader of this expedition, was a full participant in the most bitter of feelings toward a people who were his sworn enemies. He had not come to see if they could find the city of Nephi, rather, he had come to drive the Lamanites out by sword and purge the land of them.

"These are Lamanites!" Hagoth swore back at his junior officer. "It wasn't enough for them to chase us out of our lands. They have continued to hunt and harass us. I intend to catch them unawares and rid the land of as many as we can! It's my duty as an officer and a Nephite."

"And, I feel it my duty to point out what I've learned," Zeniff retorted. "You sent me as a spy, and I've given my assessment. I have walked their streets, seen their shops, and even spoken with several of them.

"What's more, I found several Nephites still among them. Those who had lingered behind when king Mosiah left, still live there! Or, at least their children do! They were not slaughtered as so many of us feared they had been! It's only the fact of their existence that allowed me to mingle among them and walk about in a city of Lamanites.

"I tell you, these people are not the same ones who drove our fathers out of this land! These are a peaceful people. We owe it to them, we owe it to our Nephite brothers who live among them, and most of all, we owe it to our own sense of honor, to negotiate with them first."

"As to any Nephite you have seen among them, I consider them to be both traitors and cowards, worse than the Lamanites themselves," Hagoth sneered. "And, if we attempt any futile negotiation, we will lose the advantage of surprise. They'll know we're here and they'll know our intentions. They'll prepare themselves to resist us and we'll lose an excellent opportunity to take back what is rightfully ours!"

"If we don't negotiate," Zeniff spit back, unflinching, "we'll lose our self-respect and the edge that makes our society so much greater than theirs. We will have stooped to the very traits that we've despised in the Lamanites all these years – their wanton disregard for life, liberty, and all that is civilized!"

"Those are pretty words, Zeniff, but these are real times. We must attack, and we must attack now!"

"No! I strongly disagree!"

"Duly noted, but we attack nevertheless! They are a wretched people, occupying a land that is by all rights *our* land! We must drive them out by the sword!"

"No! I can't allow this! We should negotiate first! Make a treaty! At least try!" Zeniff turned, keeping his face to his senior officer, placing his body symbolically in between the Nephite forces and the Lamanite inhabited city of Nephi.

"Zeniff, I warn you, you speak treasonous words! Step aside, lest I be forced to move you!" Hagoth drew his sword as a show of his determination.

"I will NOT step aside until I'm certain you intend to negotiate."

"Then I'm bound to cut you aside!" Hagoth's fury was at a pique.

He lunged toward Zeniff, who stood defiantly with his fists on his hips. Seeing Hagoth's charge, he instinctively drew his sword and parried the blow. Soon, the hillside overlooking the city of Nephi was vibrating with slashing swords and dashing feet.

Sides were drawn in that instant. Half the men fought alongside Zeniff, while the others contended on behalf of Hagoth. This miniature battle was far worse than any Lamanite attack, for it was brother fighting brother. These men who sought to return their society to their roots were now seeking each other's very lives. Their emotions outdid the heat of the day as the hand to hand combat continued with unfortunate sincerity.

Several men lay dead or dying on the ground before a loud voice cried out, "Wait! Hold!"

As if shaken from a trance, the warriors ceased their struggle, and turned to see who had called them to their senses. Zeniff stood in the center area with his sword raised straight and high above his head.

"Wait!" he called out again, with a commanding voice. "This fighting must stop! Look at yourselves. We are not the enemy! We have been called to seek out our homeland and see if we can retake it. Instead, we've allowed ourselves to draw swords on our brothers all because of a bloodthirsty and austere man who refuses to negotiate with the Lamanites. Whether or not a treaty with the Lamanites is feasible, this fighting is clearly wrong! It must stop!"

The men stood virtually frozen in position as they listened to Zeniff's words. Gradually, they turned their heads, and saw the drawn swords in their hands. They looked across at the faces of their supposed enemies and again recognized them as their brethren. Hagoth lay among the dead. Swords dropped to the ground or, in some cases, were flung down with anger at having been drawn. The men, who moments before had been engaged in mortal combat, now just stood and stared at each other trying to comprehend what had just happened. Many bitter tears were shed as men fell to their knees and sobbed.

"I think it is time we bury our dead and head back to Zarahemla," Zeniff concluded in dismay. "We'll have to give a report of our findings – and our actions. This is not a proud day for the Nephites."

* * * * *

A somber and depleted Nephite army slowly wended its way up the final bend toward Zarahemla's main gate. The tower guard had noted their approach and had already begun to announce their return. It was an unenthusiastic announcement, as even from a distance the guard had noted the lack of triumph in their gait and the decrease in number from those who had set out several weeks before.

The last hundred yards up the straight road was traversed with hundreds of pairs of eyes peering down from Zarahemla's wall toward the army. Men, women, and children had scaled the wall and stood on its catwalk eagerly hoping to catch a glimpse of the returning party. Fathers lifted the younger children to help them look outward and greet the men.

Their shouts of greeting were stifled in their throats, however, as even the children noted the length of each step the men took. The army's eyes were pointed downward. Their feet dragged along as if weighed down by stone blocks. Their legs strained to go forward. Their minds were heavy with remorseful thoughts. Zeniff had spent nearly five weeks trying to determine how best to explain to the new widows and fatherless what had become of their husbands and fathers so far away, so near to success, when events turned so desperately wrong.

The great gate opened from within and the army continued its procession without interruption. The on-lookers were filled with questions which no one dared ask. All who stared conjured up pictures of a Lamanite ambush and pitied their Nephite brethren for the hardships they had endured at the hands of their bitter enemies. No one could have possibly guessed the truth. This, however, did not prevent each member of the army from suspecting that everyone already knew it.

The men continued to trudge along in a straight line, three men wide, through the city square. The first of the army was nearing the far side of the square, while the last of the army was nearly within the walls. The crowd stood in hushed solitude. Few moved. A most notable exception was a little girl about five years old.

She maintained her enthusiasm and dashed in and out among the crowd until she worked her way free to their edge. She quickly ran across the open area of the city square and approached the slowly advancing army. She ran up to one man after another asking for her papa. With each contact, a disturbed soldier would be pulled from his trance by her tiny tugging hands on his muscular, but limp arm. His face would turn and he would sadly shake his head, unable to speak.

Her excitement turned to confusion as she went from man to man, but her energy did not wane. Instead, it turned into a gradually more consuming quest for her papa. She started towards the front of the army and bounced her way toward the back going from man to man in search of the one face that could dry her teary eyes. Exhausting all that she had seen, she ran for the city gate. She arrived there just as the final soldiers entered the city.

She stood there with confused and frustrated tears in her eyes and forced her way to the gate as the last man continued to enter the city square and the great gate began to close. Through the narrowing gap she searched the path in vain for her father. He was not to be seen. The gate slammed shut with a sudden finality and was latched securely into position.

The tenderhearted girl turned and saw the army walking away from her. She shouted, "Papa!"

The army continued to move. She ran forward and, standing just behind the final men, repeated, "Papa!"

The army continued its wearied walk. She ran toward the center of the square, to the right of the soldiers. She stood about fifteen yards away from the army so she could gain a good view of it, and more importantly, so her papa could see her. The Nephites continued to stand in awed distress. Some nursed silent tears that moistened their cheeks, feeling for the girl's loss, as well as their own.

The girl finally shouted at the top of her infantile lungs, "Papa! Papa! Where are you papa?!"

Zeniff had heard her cry even from the front row. He stopped. The army did as well. He turned and saw her tear-streaked face. Her eyes searched desperately left and right for her friend, mentor, tutor and life's foundation. Zeniff left ranks and slowly walked toward her.

When he was five paces from her, she saw him. He opened his arms and continued his approach, beckoning her to him. She saw him and with nowhere else to turn, started for this unknown man. He crouched low so that his arms and face would be at her level. She came to him and he wrapped his arms lightly around her, offering the best comfort he could.

"Your papa will not be coming home today," he said.

"But, papa! I have to find my papa! Where is my papa!?" she asked, with a sincerity and concern that her years could not grasp.

"Your papa loved you greatly, but I'm afraid he'll not ever be able to come home again," Zeniff said with difficulty, his voice stumbling and cracking with emotion. Few of those within that square would ever forget that unfortunate day. The girl burst into unrelenting sobs as Zeniff held her gingerly, wishing he had the words to comfort her.

*****

Zeniff stood with bold determination in the throne room. King Benjamin sat upon his throne hearing his words. The counselors of the court sat both to Benjamin's left and right listening with equal interest. Over the last three weeks, Zeniff had expressed deep regret for the events on the hill overlooking the city of Nephi. As with the Israelites in the days of Moses, the Nephites had a burning love and yearning for the land of their first inheritance. Zeniff was no exception. He remained undaunted in his requests for permission to resettle their homeland.

"I am certain, your majesty, that these Lamanites gave every indication of civility. Had Hagoth at least attempted a treaty, I believe they would have been reasonable."

"Reasonable? Reasonable Lamanites?" one advisor spat out with surprise.

Zeniff turned and looked directly at the scoffing man, "Yes, sir, I believe so."

Before the advisor could reply, young king Benjamin interceded, "Zeniff, I maintain great trust in you and your opinions. Do you honestly believe it would be safe for our people to venture into that land? After all, it has only been one generation since our people were forced to flee for their lives from that very place."

It was clear to all of those within the room that three weeks of tense debate had just been summed up in one question. Whether they felt they knew the answer or not, each breast held within it the unspoken hope that Nephites, any Nephites, could return to their homeland. These yearnings existed regardless of whether or not the person experiencing them anticipated being a direct participant in that homecoming. The point was that Nephites needed to return to the land of Nephi.

Zeniff swallowed to allow his voice to respond without a crack. He ensured that his face shone with confidence, but not reckless arrogance. He restrained his blinking and stood tall. With deliberate emphasis he responded to his king. "Yes, your Majesty, I do."

For a moment, the room was silent as the echo of his reply faded. King Benjamin wisely scrutinized Zeniff's countenance. He perceived Zeniff's sincere and noble intentions. He knew that if any man among his kingdom could succeed at re-colonizing the land, it would have to be Zeniff. Finally, he uttered his decision.

"Zeniff, I do not speak this lightly or without serious contemplation and prayer. We all know how this people longs to return to a land which is rightfully ours. Many have passed through this life without fulfilling this yearning. Perhaps the time *has* finally come. The Spirit whispers to me that it is so. I must conclude that perhaps the Lamanites' hearts have softened enough to allow this great thing to finally occur. And, perhaps you are the man who can make it be. There is one certain way to find this out. I give you both my permission and my blessing to go down to the land of Nephi and dwell there, if the Lamanites will allow it."

The air finally escaped from Zeniff's lungs. He had held it at bay from the moment he completed his reply. His comprehension on receiving the king's blessing was interrupted by a slow clap which ever so gradually increased its pace. Zeniff turned and saw the scoffing advisor standing before his seat. He was slowly, but loudly and deliberately clapping his hands. With cascading enthusiasm others in the throne room broke with protocol, stood, and joined in. The hall erupted in a show of support. Zeniff had won his first, and most crucial, victory. He felt certain that he could soon call the city of Nephi home.

Chapter 5
Return to Nephi

"We'll camp here tonight. Pass the word along," Zeniff ordered.

"Yes, sir," Shemnah replied. He turned to follow the order, then stopped and turned back. He looked down and then turned toward his leader as he asked, "Sir?"

"Yes, Shemnah, what is it?"

"How much farther do you believe it will be? I mean, do you believe we're even close?"

"Close? Yes, I believe we are closer. To be honest, I thought we would have arrived by now, too. It's odd how the jungle can distort your perception of direction and distance..." Zeniff allowed his words to trail off. He had not intended to verbalize his observation.

"You don't believe we're lost, do you?"

"Lost? Oh, no, certainly not. It's just that it's farther than we thought, that's all. We'll be there soon." Zeniff attempted to cover his misplaced words and nullify the dangerous impact they could hold.

"That's good to hear, sir. The rations are falling very short."

"Yes, I know. We hadn't anticipated so many other families wanting to join us at the last minute. I'm grateful they did. I only wish they would have thought to bring sufficient supplies. Tell the people to set up camp. Also, get the supper detail going. We should get these people fed."

"Yes, sir. Right away, sir."

Shemnah turned to pass on the order. He approached a group of officers who had awaited the results of his discussion with Zeniff.

"All right men, we camp here tonight. Spread the word! And get the food detail going!" he shouted, as he motioned with both arms.

*****

The tall trees of the rainforest were bathed in flickering splashes of light from perhaps a hundred campfires. Their trunks reflected the warm glow, while their tops gave the appearance of tent posts bearing the thick, black fabric of the night. No stars could be seen through the dense foliage which spread above them. Zeniff sat at the southernmost campfire with half a dozen of his key officers.

"Zeniff, the others are beginning to voice concerns," Terantum said.

"Concerns about what?" Zeniff asked, believing he knew the answer, but wanting to hear it verbalized.

"They're concerned about how much longer it will take to find the land of Nephi. We've been on the journey for over six weeks now. No one seems to know if we're any closer, and even though we've been living on half rations for two weeks now, we've only got about a day and half of rations left. That is, unless we want to eat the seeds we have packed along."

"We must save the seeds for planting. Afterall, we're not birds!" Zeniff's attempt to add levity to his response failed miserably. His men simply continued watching him and awaiting a real reply. "Seriously, you men need to be able to relay a sense of confidence to these people. They look to you as the guardians of their dreams. Think of it men, we are the first Nephites to return to the land of Nephi! How many others have lived out their lives wanting, but not even realistically hoping, to see what you will see and be where you soon will be?"

"Yes, but, will we really be there?"

Zeniff reached his hand out and placed it on Terantum's shoulder. He looked him in the eye and in all sincerity said, "Yes, Terantum, we will, and sooner than you fear."

"But, how do you know? We've been wandering for weeks!"

Zeniff leaned back so the firelight would allow each of his officers to see and sense the earnestness and confidence in his face.

"We have not been wandering, we have been journeying. And, we have been journeying southward this entire time. I'm telling you, we're very close."

"But, how close?"

"You're going to have to trust me. This is simply too important for us to give up now. We're nearly there. Trust me."

*****

"Zeniff, I have a very queer feeling! A chill just swept through my back and limbs."

Terantum's steps slowed considerably as he spoke. He looked left and right as he sliced away at the vines and dense underbrush with more care than he had previously taken in blazing their trail. The other soldiers behind him also seemed to sense something was amiss.

"Yes, Terantum, I sense it too. It's as if something terrible once occurred here –"

As Zeniff spoke, Terantum hacked a bush loose. He bent down and pulled it free. He was unable to see the object which had put an abrupt halt to Zeniff's words. Zeniff stood staring as a flood of unfortunate memories filled his consciousness. Terantum hefted the bush to the side and flung it out of his way.

He began to continue his query as he turned from tossing aside the large bush, "What do you suppose is causing this odd...?"

His words died in his throat as he saw the object that held Zeniff's attention. There before the two of them was a mound of dirt with new moss and fledgling bushes beginning to grow on it. At the far end of the mound was a sword shoved point down into the dirt. Covering the hilt of the sword was a Nephite helmet. Exposure to the humidity of the rainforest and the occasional downpours had taken its toll. The brass exterior had already begun to tarnish and the leather underpinning sagged limply from underneath.

Zeniff knelt on one knee as a sign of respect. Terantum followed suit, as did all of those who were near enough to witness the discovery.

"That is Jared's helmet," Zeniff said with a distant air in his voice. "I know a little girl who had wished to see it – and him – earlier."

"This must be the very spot where you battled," Terantum said in a subdued voice.

"Yes, it is. This confirms it. We're very near to Nephi. Any nearer and we would be there." Zeniff looked ahead, trying to see the end of the plateau on which they now stood. His vision could only penetrate a few paces through the dense growth.

"We should have the people set up camp here for the night," he announced.

"Here?"

"Yes, unfortunately, here. If we go any farther, we will be directly in Lamanite territory and be seen. I want to go down with only a small group of men to work out a treaty. I think if we go down with our hundreds, we will not only intimidate them, but may make them think we're invading. I can't see any point backtracking only to come back here again tomorrow. We may as well set up camp here, on this hill."

"I see your point."

"I wonder –" Zeniff said to himself.

"What's that, sir?" Terantum asked.

"Eh? What?" Zeniff said, stirring from his thoughts.

"You started to say something just then," Terantum pointed out.

"Oh, did I?" Zeniff answered, "Oh, well, I was just thinking to myself."

"I see."

"Actually, I was just wondering where their king is right now," he added.

"Where he is? Wouldn't he be in the city there below us?"

"Possibly," Zeniff admitted, "But, possibly not. You see, from what I could tell, the Lamanites were not using Nephi as their main city. They seemed to prefer Shemlon, which is a ways farther south from here. When I spied out the city earlier, their king wasn't in Nephi at all during my time there. I gathered from what I could overhear that he somehow preferred Shemlon to Nephi. In fact, that is part of why I'm so optimistic. If the king does not care to make the city his home, then maybe he doesn't care for it too greatly for it at all."

Zeniff's words drifted off again and he got a pensive look. The firelight continued to cast a wavering shimmer of orange hues on his face and every now and then it put a sparkle in his eye. He stirred again and gave the night's final order to his men. He did so with a very hopeful and encouraging tone, "Clear away the area to the west of here. The graves have all been placed on the eastern side in accordance with tradition. We should be able to spend the night here without disturbing them. Ask the parents to keep their children from straying into this area. Try to focus on the positive news. Tomorrow we should all be in the land of our fathers!"

"Yes, sir, I'll spread the word!"

*****

Between the aura of the hill and the angst for reaching their beloved city, the morning could not come soon enough. The first rays of dawn found Zeniff and his four most-trusted officers crouched around a campfire finishing their morning meal. Each man shifted his weight impatiently, anxious to get on with their task. They each knew they were to wait for word from Zeniff. Asking him about his timing and plans would not alter that. Finally, Zeniff stood.

"I believe our noble neighbors should be plenty awake by now. At least their guards should be able to see us clearly as we approach. The light is now sufficient that we shouldn't look like spies sneaking about," he said. "Take off your swords and follow me."

The men's eyes grew wide. "Take off our swords?" one officer questioned with a strong sense of concern in his voice.

"Yes, take off your swords, your daggers, and your armor. We're going to make a treaty, not a war. We must leave our weapons and all pretenses here or our words will not ring true. This will be a tenuous task. We shouldn't give them any cause to doubt us," Zeniff explained.

"Very well."

The officers disarmed themselves and followed Zeniff away from camp and into the jungle. They had marched only a few dozen paces when they were forced to halt. Here the plateau abruptly subsided and descended. A few small trees clung to its edge, but for the most part it was either bare or only covered with moss. They tied a rope to the base of the thickest tree they could find and threw the loose end down the hill. One by one, the explorers lowered themselves down the hillside and onto level ground.

As they crossed the field that separated the hill from the city, they noted the richness of the earth.

"This would make excellent farming ground," Terantum noted.

"Yes, it would!" Zeniff agreed. "We are seeing the first evidence of why our fathers were so reticent to leave this land." Then, to himself, Zeniff voiced a personal regret, "*I just wish my brother, Amaleki, had agreed to come.*"

The five crossed the open field with heart-pounding enthusiasm. Hidden by the brush, high upon the northern hill, many Nephite eyes peered through the jungle's growth watching their every step with tremendous anticipation and hoping for a good report. Some wished they were a part of the first party of Nephites to willingly venture back into the land of Nephi. Others, aware of the potentially fatal reception they could encounter, gladly lingered behind.

About halfway to the city, Zeniff and his men were able to discern a sight which both surprised and saddened them. The protective wall of the grand city of Nephi was in a terrible state of disarray. The closer they came, the more decay they could see. They also noted that the field they were crossing had vague traces of having once been farmland. It was now cruelly overgrown with weeds and grasses.

"*I hadn't really noticed this before,*" Zeniff thought to himself. "*Of course, coming and going in the night hides many a sight. Then when morning came I was so intent on mingling among the crowds that I guess I never really stopped to look at the state of the city itself....*"

His mind leapt back to snatches of memories from a few months earlier when he had cautiously mingled with the crowds in the busy city square. Given that his task was to spy out the people, he had not bothered to look at the walls and buildings themselves. His only memories were of people walking to and fro selling and buying, talking and carrying on in such a friendly way that he had been out and out surprised. It seemed so like a normal society, yet it was made up of Lamanites, with a few Nephites scattered here and there in their midst.

"What a terrible waste!" Joshum lamented aloud, interrupting Zeniff's thoughts.

"They don't seem to care in the least! It's obvious they don't realize the value of what they have, so they can't appreciate it," Terantum added.

Ignoring his own surprise, and wanting to keep spirits high, Zeniff remarked loudly, "It hurts to see others abuse your dreams, doesn't it? We'll make it aright soon enough!"

Zeniff turned his head, looking for any sign of their comrades hidden in the jungle behind them. He knew their hopes and expectations. A portion of him was glad that they could not make out the details which he and his forward party now beheld. For a while longer, in their minds' eye, the city of Nephi, founded by their beloved forefather, would still be a shining wonderland of hopes, dreams, and prosperity.

For a brief moment, he wished he were among them there on the hillside, still oblivious to the cruel ravages that time and lack of attention had played on their cherished city. As they stood there, Jershon turned to speak to Zeniff again and this time his eye caught sight of something unexpected. He whirled around as he walked backwards to gain a better view and nearly lost his balance.

"My word, what's that?" he said.

The other four, still facing forward, heard him and began to stop while Joshum repeated, "What is that, sir?" Joshum asked, pointing behind them.

They all turned to see where he was pointing. They immediately saw a distinctly visible answer to his question, but the answer itself raised even more questions. For, there to the north, a few hundred paces to the east of the hill, was another city. It too had a wall surrounding it. The city was an impressive and unexpected find, but was not quite as large as their targeted city. For a moment, the five men stood and stared in wonder.

"That?" Zeniff asked, "Well, that is another city, obviously. I didn't catch its name. You can tell by its size that it's not very important." Zeniff concluded.

"Yes, well, I would guess it was built not long after our fathers were driven out of the land, and that few have done much to keep it up," Terantum assessed. "Look carefully at the city wall. You can see gaps and holes in it too. It's obvious they do not seem to care much for their structures."

"You're right. I see it," Joshum added.

"This is better than I had feared," Zeniff stated.

"Better?! How so?" the confused Nephite asked.

"If they don't care for these cities, then parting with them shouldn't be much of an issue. Had we come here and found them as the jewels of their society, we would have a terrible time convincing them to return them to our control without the shedding of much blood. I think our negotiations will be all the easier this way."

"Good point!" Terantum said.

"Come on men, it's time for us to negotiate an arrangement. We must keep moving. I assume by now we have been spotted," Zeniff said.

Zeniff was right on more points than one. They had indeed been spotted, and much sooner than when Zeniff had made his comment. The inner city was already beginning to buzz with news of Nephites in the vicinity. The watch guard had moments earlier shouted his find to a guard down in the city square, near the main gate. He, in turn, had sent word to the inner parts of the city.

Word was eventually brought to the attention of the King's main guards. The captain of the guard returned orders that these new visitors must be watched very carefully and brought directly to the throne room. As fortune would have it, Zeniff's timing was very good. The King was indeed in Nephi that day.

"What are they doing now?" one watch guard asked another while both stood side by side on the city wall's catwalk gazing intently over the gate at the pale visitors.

"I'm not sure. One of them just turned around and must have said something to the others because they all stopped and started looking at Shilom. For a moment, I thought they were going to start heading off in that direction."

"That would not do us any good. King Laman will want them brought to him! We better make sure they come, or he'll hold us accountable."

"Here they come again. It looks like we will be all right, as long as we can get them to come inside the gate. Give word to the gatekeeper."

The other guard shouted down to open the gate. The gatekeeper obeyed. He had overheard word of these intruders and was apprehensively curious to see them. Zeniff and his men were only two dozen yards outside the gate as it opened.

"Well, I would say we have definitely been seen," Terantum surmised.

"Keep walking at a steady pace and show no signs of concern," Zeniff advised. "We want them to know we pose no threat, and that we do not expect to feel any threats ourselves."

"Here is the moment of truth," Jacom announced.

Six Lamanite guards stormed out of the city bearing swords and spears. A leather cloth was girded about their loins and their tops were bare, revealing the dark redness of their skin, thus highlighting the most visible difference between the two societies. Their arms bristled with powerful muscles. King Laman always ensured that his main guards were some of his strongest men. It helped raise the intimidation factor when the encountered trouble, or in this case, unexpected expeditions.

The Nephites continued forward and allowed themselves to be surrounded without question. They held their hands away from their sides, with their palms downward, allowing their captors to see that they were wholly unarmed. Without verbalization, the guards made it clear that they were to follow them and enter the city.

The group was rushed quickly through the city square. Zeniff and his men were at once awestruck with this rarest of opportunities to set foot within the legendary city, while also heart-struck to see how poorly kept it was. Decay and debris reigned on all that they saw. Weeds and vines encroached on the ground and walls. The inner city was no better cared for than the outer wall.

Few Lamanites were in the city square at this early hour. All those who were awake, however, were present. None of them spoke as the pale visitors were whisked before their sight on their way to the throne room. In spite of their treatment so far, Zeniff held out hopes of being able to reason with a king he had never met. They were, after all, still alive.

Buildings of stone and wood passed before their view. Corridors and alleyways came and went just as quickly. Around one corner, there came into view a sight so heart-wrenching that Zeniff let out a cry and stopped cold in his tracks. His Lamanite guard had to push him to get him moving again. Zeniff could not take his eyes off the sight. Before him stood the remains of a once-great temple, built by the hand of Nephi himself. Vines covered its unused entrance. Cracks spread like webs across the walls. It was dingy. A grayish-brown color spoiled its stones. Jungle moss nearly enveloped its roof. It stood dying and neglected as if wholly invisible to the Lamanites.

The group was hustled beyond this painful view and were eventually brought to a large stone building and led inside. The largest room was the throne room. The tallest guard approached its door and carefully knocked four times. The door opened from within and the captives soon found themselves standing within their enemy's Judgment Hall.

Seated on a rickety throne of bamboo and wood was a powerful and stern-looking man who bore a golden crown. Zeniff guessed that the throne, or at least the chair which appeared to be claimed as a throne, was of ancient origin and had been kept in modest working condition over the years. It was painfully apparent that over the years there had been several, crude repair jobs done to it. It seemed to be held together out of the sheer desperation of the ropes which were wrapped around its wooden frame. He wondered why a king would dare to sit on it. However, it seemed a fitting throne for a city of such vast disrepair.

The walls of the room bore the tattered remains of decaying tapestries. Most of these tapestries were thin and threadbare. Some were fading beyond recognition. They seemed to tell the story of a people traveling from one land to another over a vast sea. Zeniff stared at their remains in wonder. Could they also be from the original inhabitants of the city? Zeniff's thoughts were torn away from his musings by a commanding voice.

"Who are you and what are you doing here in my kingdom?" the king demanded. "You there, speak!" King Laman pointed at Zeniff.

"Oh, great king, we are pleased to be in your presence this day and to have the opportunity to speak with you," Zeniff began. "We are but humble Nephites who have come to admire your great kingdom. We know of its history and the beauties which it holds and have desired to come down here and behold them for ourselves."

"You speak well – for a Nephite," King Laman retorted. "What is your full intent?"

"We wish to dwell among you – here – in the wonderful city of Nephi."

"Here, with us? Preposterous!" the king laughed so loudly that the chamber echoed. Several joined in.

"Yes, your majesty, here in this very city, if it pleases you!"

"And what benefit, may I ask, will I and my people gain for having you infest my land?"

"We will till the earth and share a portion of our abundance with you. We will restore the city walls and the buildings to give them new luster. We will share our skills and train your craftsmen according to our talents."

"We have no need of learning under the hands of Nephites!" the king bellowed.

He was about to spit out threats, when a wily advisor, who had stood virtually unnoticed beside him, stepped forward. He leaned toward the king, who cocked his head to hear. No one but the two of them could distinguish their words. The king seemed very pleased. His scowl first turned blank, then a slight grin appeared as his head began to nod in agreement. Within a moment, he had a full smile and his head bobbed up and down with emphatic consent.

"I like you!" he replied to Zeniff, at last. "You have nerve and you seem like honorable men. Do you swear that your only purpose is to come and dwell with us?"

Zeniff knelt on one knee and bowed his head subserviently, "Yes, great king, we swear this!"

"Do you also swear to share of your crops with us?"

"Yes, great king, we so swear!"

"How many are you?"

"Just a few hundred, your majesty." Zeniff bowed, trying to lessen the impact of the number.

"A few hundred?!" The king was startled at first, but his face slowly softened and gave way to a pensive look. He added, "I believe we can possibly allow such a thing. But – " His voice drifted off as he gave the idea more thought.

Zeniff and his men's ears perked up; their interest was at a pique.

"Please, give the word, your majesty, and we will listen."

"My people and your people cannot mix. It simply would not do. Yes, it's true we have allowed a few of your people to stay among us when the rest of you left so suddenly. But, so many...too many! We cannot have so many more living among us. It defiles my people. What I will do is this. We will vacate this 'wonderful city' as you call it, both I and my people. I grow weary of these tedious trips to this pitiful place. I much prefer my Shemlon. We will allow you to inhabit this land. In fact, we will also vacate the city of Shilom to the north. You may have both of these cities. Perhaps you can make something of them. We come and go here, but it is only because we can, only because they are here. To us they are but old and barren places which hold only minor interest. It is true that some have actually made homes here, but for the most of us, we prefer Shemlon. And, perhaps –" King Laman purposely let his sentence die again. He was a skilled negotiator, in his own way.

"Yes, great king, what is it?" Zeniff saw that things were going well and was growing fearful that a false step in protocol might trip up the negotiations. He chose his words carefully and forced himself to appear calm, relaxed, and dignified, while also showing deference to the king and his position of authority.

"I assume that your people have skills beyond being farmers and such. Is that not so?" the king asked.

"Well, yes, your majesty, there are those among us who have been quite successful with their farms far to the north of here, but also in other areas," Zeniff acknowledged.

"Such as sheep and goats, do you tend them as well?" King Laman stroked his scraggly chin as he pursued the matter.

"Yes, certainly. There are also those among us who have done well tending these beasts," Zeniff replied.

"Do you expect that there may be an abundance created from these efforts?" Laman asked, more directly.

"I see," said Zeniff slowly and softly to himself. He tried to hold back a smile, for he believed he truly did see. It appeared that the deal could truly be met if he could agree to be generous.

"If such abundance is made, I would ask that you share not just of your crops and grain, but of these animals and such, to help support my people. Do you see this as fair?"

"Your majesty, I see this as more than fair! We have no other desire than to spend our lives in this land. Living among you and your fine people will be a favorable treat. I thank you this day for your wisdom and benevolence." Zeniff bowed again.

"You may return to your land and bring your people down here," the King announced. "How long before we can expect your arrival?"

"We can be here today, your majesty."

"Today?! How so?"

"My people have come with me. They await our word from the top of the hill to the north."

"They are here already? You certainly are a confident people. Very well, have them come down and camp on the outskirts of the city. My people will have these cities vacated within a fortnight. Messenger! Send the word!"

"Yes, your majesty!" the messenger replied and quickly left the room.

"Thank you, your majesty. This is a wondrous day for both our people!" Zeniff replied and bowed low, proud to have worked out an acceptable treaty so quickly with the king.

He stood again, but took on a pensive look. He appeared on the verge of speaking, but was clearly hesitant. King Laman noted this and eyed him carefully. Just as Zeniff was preparing to excuse himself, the king interrupted.

"Was there something more, Zeniff?" he asked.

"No, your majesty." Zeniff bowed then continued, "Well, actually yes, your majesty. I'm just not certain. You have been so gracious. I do not mean to impose myself or my people upon you any more than I already have."

"What is it? Surely you can share your thoughts with your new friends?" the king shrewdly coaxed.

"Well, you see, your majesty," Zeniff replied, "We have traveled far. It has been long since we last took on supplies. I have many families with me –"

"And, I would venture to guess that your supplies are quite low," the king interrupted, suppressing a smile at his cleverness. "Say no more! My people have more than they can eat in a fortnight and sharing what we have with you will spare us from having to pack it with us to our homes in Shilom.

We would be pleased if you would take of our abundance and use it as you see fit."

Zeniff brightened and smiled graciously and eagerly, "Thank you, your majesty! That is most kind, and most generous!" He bowed again.

"Think nothing of it," Laman smiled in return. "Besides, I'm certain you will more than repay us during your stay in this land!"

A trickle of a feeling in the back of Zeniff's mind hinted that there might have been an alternative meaning to King Laman's reply. He shook the feeling off, pleased with his successful encounter and smiled even more broadly, thanking the king once again.

Chapter 6
Co-Existence

The city of Nephi was nearly unrecognizable to any who had seen it only the year before. The older Nephites had joined themselves to those Zeniff had brought with him. Homes were tidied. Decaying artwork which had hung on drab walls was replaced with new, brightly-colored tapestries depicting life in both the traditional and recently-reoccupied Nephite capital. In some cases, artisans had carved wooden replicas of the tapestries to ensure the longevity of the stories they depicted. Building roofs were patched. Crumbling stairs were repaired. The holes in the city wall were patched and reinforced.

The city was now surrounded by something much more than a sturdy wall. It was now surrounded by acres and acres of lush, finely groomed and highly productive farmland that were tended to with care by both husbands and wives in their various ways. The beautiful farms and orchards yielded massive abundance because of the attention placed on them by their new caretakers. These farms joined those recently cultivated farms to the north which led to and surrounded the city of Shilom.

Shilom was blossoming as well. All the king had exacted from the Nephites as payment for returning these cities to the descendants of their founders was a portion of their crops. The crops yielded so abundantly of the fertile soil that this allotment was gladly given. Life was good. The Lamanites were considered both generous and faithful neighbors who kept out of Nephite affairs with equal diligence, as the Nephites did with the affairs of the Lamanites.

The Nephites had transformed their offshoot society nearly as significantly as they had their beloved city and its surrounding lands. They were no longer worried refugees in search of a land which was as much myth and fable as it was a tangible goal. They were now a proud and happy people, content to re-inhabit the halls which their forefathers had once called home. Each brick laid, each furrow plowed, and each fruit tree planted was done so with pride and honor. They were rebuilding and reliving Nephi's original vision.

Their proudest accomplishment and dearest privilege was the restoration of their temple. When their forefather, Nephi, had founded this once-great city, he had built a temple to the God of Abraham, Isaac, and Jacob. He had built it after the manner or style of King Solomon's temple, but using whatever materials he could substitute from the land in which he now dwelt. He had known and loved Solomon's temple back in his homeland before his departure. Now, Zeniff and his people had taken great pains to rebuild and restore the temple. They were honored to dwell in its shadow once more.

In fact, the restoration of their temple was the first official act. Zeniff was determined to restore the temple into working order as soon as was prudent. His people were thrilled to see it shine once more. They would often enter it to ponder and pray after a long, hard day's labor on their own homes. To them it was the house of the Lord and more sacred and special than words could account.

Zeniff was proud and relieved to learn that men who bore the highest degrees of the holy priesthood had accompanied them on their journey. This assured them that both the authority and knowledge to perform the ordinances of the temple dwelled among them. This fueled their determination to rebuild and restore the sacred edifice to its former beauty. Men tithed their time to work on the temple, dedicating one day in ten to temple restoration efforts instead of focusing their efforts solely on their own home or farm. It soon became a rededicated shrine to their Maker and the pillar of their many beautiful buildings.

The people rejoiced to be there. Never had their society known a more excited and contented people. They met each day with great anticipation. They worked with their children to share the tales of the old days; of Lehi taking his family out of Jerusalem and sailing to the new world so many generations ago; and of Lehi's faithful son, Nephi, leading the people in righteousness after the death of his father. The people endeavored to rekindle an appreciation for Nephi's strong ideals and the opportunity it was for them to reawaken them in the city he had built.

Zeniff was keen to oversee it all. It was his persuasion that had convinced King Benjamin to allow him to take so many people back to this fair land. It was his faith and perseverance that had led them through the wilderness in safety. It was his determination that had made the treaty with the Lamanites a fact when so many said it could not be done. It was his dynamic leadership that was now making their dream a reality. The people rewarded his sincere diligence by crowning him their king.

King Zeniff reigned in peace and prosperity for a dozen and one years. His visits to the temple were more than regular. He found a peace and serenity there that fueled his soul and gave him the inspiration he needed to lead his people in righteousness. Life was good in the new land. It was very good.

There were, however, some in the land who began to fear it was too good. They claimed that the Nephites were beginning to be too prosperous and much too numerous. Their darker-skinned benefactors to the south began to question the wisdom of the treaty they had agreed to so many years earlier. At first, fears began among only a few, but, as in the days of Pharaoh of old, the concerns gradually worked their way into the heart of King Laman himself.

"HOW many acres did you say?!" King Laman leapt to his feet with indignation. His face turned a deeper shade of red, bordering heavily on purple.

"My men estimate that they have cleared another 200 acres of jungle," the officer repeated.

"For what?! More fruit trees? More vineyards? More buildings perhaps?!" Laman spit out.

"For all we know they're laying the foundation for yet another city so they can bring even more of these festering Nephites into your land!" Jobadesh replied.

Jobadesh, the king's advisor, was a Nephite by birth, but a Lamanite by choice. He was descended from those few Nephites who despised King Mosiah for deserting the Land of Nephi. His father, Raehab, had felt that Mosiah was too weak and shortsighted to make a real king. He was glad to see the man go and had encouraged as many of his friends and family as possible to defy the king and remain in the land.

Several of these dissenters lost their lives in battle when the Lamanites overtook the city. A few had survived. Some were punished in unthinkable ways, to serve as "examples" as the Lamanite king had declared. But, a few worked their way into the king's confidence. Raehab was foremost among these. He flattered and supported the king in every way he could. Soon, he was accepted and included among the king's nearest confidants. Eventually, he became the king's advisor.

Sadly for Raehab, he had taken ill with a jungle fever the day before Zeniff arrived. Had he been conscious, he would have not only advised against showing goodwill to the Nephites, but would have pushed for exterminating them, before they had the chance to return to wherever they had come from and bring reinforcements.

As fate would have it, the fever had grown worse day by day. As King Laman prepared to evacuate the city, his trusted advisor fitfully succumbed to his withering sickness and passed away turning, moaning, and sweating on his bed. His teenage son, Jobadesh, somehow blamed the Nephites for his father's demise. He hated and despised them. Like his father before him, he set his course to become the king's advisor. It was natural for the king to learn to seek him out and depend on him, as he had with his father before him. Over the years, Jobadesh had ensured that every conceivable ill word about the Nephites made it to the king's ears, including, and perhaps especially, untrue tidings.

Now was the chance Jobadesh had longed for. He saw the concern and fury growing on his master's face. He would make the most of this latest onslaught of news and ensure the king saw the impending danger it represented.

The king flumped back down onto his wooden throne. The wood creaked under his sudden weight. The lashings groaned and managed to sustain him once again. He shifted fitfully, raising his hand to his chin and then tugging at it amid angry thoughts, as if trying to pull an effective idea from within. He threw his fist down and slammed it against the throne's quivering arm.

"I've been more than tolerant. I let those foul people infest our city for far too long. I agreed to let a few in, not this entire 'society' of theirs!" King Laman swore.

"They grow more numerous with each passing year!" Jobadesh added. "Their provisions continue to mount. Some day, not far from now, they will be too numerous and too prosperous for our own good. Soon, very soon, they will not be content with these cities you've lent to them. They'll come on us and drive us out of our own homes! They'll come after your home, oh King. This Zeniff grows too bold, too proud, too powerful. Soon, he will come after your very throne!"

"What?! My throne? MY THRONE!" the king exclaimed with a fretful mixture of fury and concern.

"Yes, my king. We need to take them down a notch or two before we no longer have the chance," Jobadesh advised.

"Very well! We will show these Nephites who controls this land, and keep them in their place! Gather our men!" the king shouted, and slammed his fist hard upon his wooden throne's arm. As if exasperated by the heated discussion, the throne finally gave way. It crumbled and split as it spilled its regal occupant unceremoniously upon the floor. Laman fell with a shriek and rolled down the three steps that led to the level of those who sought his council. His feathered robes curled around his head and shoulders as he rolled, leaving him blinded and indignantly calling for aid with just the top of his hair sticking out of one end of his bundled robes, his legs and feet were flailing at the other end, and his belly gesticulating in the middle.

The king's officers, who could be described as such in only the most loose of military terms, quickly jumped into action to free their imprisoned leader. Ignoring his shouts and curses, they soon had him in a sitting position and then helped him to his feet. The king spit as he bellowed his final oath that the Nephites would be made to pay for their insolence.

His soldiers ignored his recent peril and were wholly behind their monarch and shouted their approval. These officers bore nothing that even slightly resembled a uniform. In fact, they bore nearly nothing at all from the waist up. Girded about their loins was the traditional Lamanite leather loincloth. Their faces, backs, chests, and shoulders were dabbed with bloody streaks and designs. They had leather and metal bands wrapped around their muscled arms. Several of them had shorn their heads bald.

They swung their spears and swords wildly over their heads in conjunction with their shouts. The weapons looked like toys easily tossed about by their brawny, bulging arms. The men had an appearance which would strike terror in the hearts of most civilized people of any era. Beweaponed and whooping as they were, they formed a terrible scene of impending bloodshed.

* * * * *

The orange glow of the eternal orb was just creeping over the treetops and filling the fields with light as it began its daily ritual. The dewy crops responded in kind and began to raise their heads in imperceptible response to the brilliant warmth. Many dozen Nephite farmers and herdsmen were already tending to their crops and watering their animals, oblivious to nature's reactions, but breathing in the aura of their tranquil life with unspoken appreciation nevertheless.

The mist still gathered and rolled along the rainforest's edge in humid billows. A strange noise of stirring emanated from the mist. Farmer and herdsman alike stopped their chores and turned toward the southern mist. All froze in mid-action, with their eyes affixed on the unknown. All they saw was the mist and the trees beyond. The muffled noises rose in a gradual crescendo. Unsure of the cause for concern, they began to turn to each other, noticing that their partners had also sensed some unseen danger.

Some of them were on the verge of dismissing the phenomenon and turning back to real matters, such as continuing their tilling, as the scream began. It was a soul-numbing scream, the war-cry of the Lamanites. It sounded as if it came from everywhere and nowhere all at once. The only hint of its origin was a trembling flock of multi-colored birds which suddenly took flight from the trees directly to the south.

Nephite eyes shifted quickly from the fleeing and squawking birds, downward toward the base of the trees. The mist began to swirl more violently. Gray shapes began to form. The sound repeated itself, more loudly than before, paralyzing several of the farmers with fright and inaction, when reaction was highly needed. The first wave of three hundred Lamanite warriors emerged from the mist and felled a handful of the nearest farmers before the others fully realized that the peace they had enjoyed for so many years was suddenly at an end.

Hoes and farming implements raised in protection and in modest defense were split in two as they toppled to the earth. They were soon joined by their lifeless former owners. Within a few heartbeats, the dire situation was finally perceived by all. The "pale invaders" as King Laman had sneered in his description to his men, were on the run and desperately making for the southern gate. Their shouts did not fall on deaf ears.

The tower guards, who had never known a useful existence until this day, became eyewitnesses to an horrific slaughter of their hapless brethren. They shouted orders to the gatekeeper, long before the gatekeeper could make out the cries of the panicked farmers and herdsmen who headed his way in absolute desperation. The great gate opened and welcomed sweating and frantic men and women within its safe haven. It was locked shut again just in time to deny access to the swiftest Lamanites. Sadly, many Nephites had no need for re-entry into the city that morning, as they had already entered an eternal kingdom in a most untimely manner and to the dismay of their loved ones.

King Zeniff's tranquil society had been suddenly and horrifically violated. He was faced with the first true crisis of his imperial reign. Lives had been lost and still more were being threatened. It was imperative that he act quickly and decisively. His key advisors were hastily called and were already waiting in the throne room when he arrived. Outside the closed doors, anxious citizens awaited their decision.

They did not have to wait long. The strategy session had scarcely begun when it concluded with the determination to fight and protect their lives, city, flocks, and fields. The throne room doors burst open and officers called for their next in rank. Before long, an assembly of men had gathered near the as-yet-unused, but well-stocked armory. The dusty bolts were removed from the great door and tossed aside.

The quartermaster pushed his way inside and began sending out shields, armor, swords, bows, arrows, and scimitars in succession. Officers oversaw the dispersal of the equipment to ensure it remained expeditious. Men who had received their bundles carried them to the city square and began to don their armor. Archers were the first to receive their full allotment and take their actual positions, while angry Lamanite hordes pounded the city gate and futilely attempted to scale the city's wall.

Nephites trained in hand-to-hand combat continued to tie on their leather underpinnings, upon which rested their brass breastplates and arm and leg plates, helmets and the like. The archers leapt up the ladders to the catwalk. They ran along its narrow, elevated pathway along the city wall, keeping safely below the upper edge of the wall itself. They watched for Lamanite warriors as they ran. They began on the western and eastern sides of the city to ensure that the Lamanites were not attempting to surround them. They were not.

The Lamanites were still clustered in the southern end of the city. Like brutish barbarians they were more intent on pillaging the crops from the fields and running off with their herds than they were in watching for a retaliatory attack. The archers from both sides of the city met at the southern-most point and began to take aim.

A Lamanite stooping to herd a sheep into his greedy arms received the shock of his life when his view of the sheep was momentarily interrupted by a thin streak of brown and a sharp piercing sensation in his abdomen. He remained crouched in that position for a moment, looking at the fine quills in the arrow protruding from his belly, not fully realizing what had just happened. As he reached for the obstruction, his life drained from him and he tumbled to his side, never to move again of his own accord. The startled sheep bleated and trotted off in a panic. Both sides had now joined the battle.

More arrows began to fly as the southern gate opened and allowed a flood of angry Nephites out to defend their rights. The Lamanites first turned in anger to repel their insolent neighbors. As more arrows flew and the onslaught of foot soldiers grew, they slowly realized that this would not be an easy conquest. Undaunted, they welled up their warrior's hatred and engaged their pale-skinned foes, whom they had been taught for generations to hate and distrust. Again, they rang the air with their intimidating war whoop. The hand-to-hand combat was furious and deadly. The Nephites maintained the advantages of their armor and numbers. The Lamanites fought with the vengeance of a people filled with blind hatred. Both sides took heavy casualties. The Nephites called to their God for strength during the heat of the battle. The Lamanites simply called out in threatening, murderous oaths. Slowly, the Lamanites were pushed back.

Eventually, they lost ground entirely. The Nephites continued to pursue them and force them out of their land. The sun had set long before the final blows were swung. The Nephites managed to return to their city victorious, but with the grizzly task of burying some three thousand Lamanite corpses, and with the dread in their hearts that this battle was only the beginning of several. Unbeknownst and unrecognized by the Nephites, the lifeless body of the malicious Jobadesh had been among their dead.

None of the Nephites fooled themselves into thinking that theirs was a permanent victory. But, they contented themselves with the knowledge that fewer than two hundred and eighty of their own people had lost their lives that day. Their armor and their God had truly protected them.

* * * * *

"Oh, great king, I congratulate you for bringing peace again to our people after this terrible act by our neighbors from the land of Shemlon who have now declared themselves our enemies." The Nephite bowed respectfully before his king who sat upon his throne.

Those in the room, be they guard or king's advisor, focused their attention on the well-kept and dignified man. Although Jothan was not an appointed advisor to the king, his opinions were well respected. He bore a highly deserved reputation for one who could see clearly to the heart of issues and present alternatives without putting other's opinions at naught.

"I fear, my king, that this may not be the end of strife, however," Jothan continued. "We should arm ourselves and train our men in the arts of defense and warfare, lest we be caught unawares. I also recommend that we place guards on the outskirts of our land to keep a diligent vigil that will give us a greater warning than we received this time."

"Yes, I'm afraid you are correct," the king lamented. "I do not know why the Lamanites have broken their treaty after so many years of continued peace. We have co-existed for so long without a single strife. It pains me to think that they can no longer be trusted."

Zeniff shook his head sadly and paused a moment with his soul caught up in sincere regret. He wondered if he had been too idealistic. Was it true that the Lamanites could not be trusted after all? Would they need to live with continual strife from this day onward? Zeniff's thoughts returned to one comforting thought: they had managed to live over a dozen years in peace. Surely they could somehow work out an arrangement that could perpetuate their stay in this land of their fathers. Zeniff was willing to risk all to stay within the boundary of the people's blessed city.

"We have managed to live here many years without the fear of retribution. Many of us have sons and daughters who have now known no other home but this. To think that we must give it up now would be premature. I believe we should be able to find a means of remaining here a while longer. If it takes posting permanent guards and training our people in the finer arts of warfare and self defense, then so be it. We will do it so that we may remain in this land which our fathers first settled!"

Those who fretted Zeniff's decision took heart. Some had feared Zeniff's zeal would lead to naiveté and he would leave his people vulnerable to attack. Others feared this attack would trigger the end of their stay in the land. Zeniff's decision put both sets of fears to rest.

Zeniff was strict to keep his word. The following day he doubled the guards on the southern wall. He had three short towers built at the far southern end of their borders, spaced evenly from the two extremes and one in the center. These towers were kept manned day and night.

He also put his craftsmen to work preparing all manner of weapons to arm his people. Mandatory training sessions were instituted. Men and boys from 14 years and up were required to spend a minimum of six hours per week training in some form of specialty, be it sword, sling, or bow. Sessions on strategy also became routine among the schools.

Not wanting to have his people live in absolute paranoia and concern, he also mandated an increase in the pursuit of arts and crafts. The women were taught to spin and weave and make all types of fine linen and cloth. The men spent the majority of their days tilling the ground and raising a multitude of fruits and vegetables. The farms and orchards continued to be well kept. The flocks and herds were well tended. The guards stayed ever vigilant, as they unobtrusively sought to keep their fellows safe.

Aiding in what he felt would be his people's surest defense, Zeniff strongly encouraged fathers to lead their families in prayer and worship, to give thanks and respect to God for his great mercies and innumerable blessings. To his great pleasure, their temple was kept occupied and Zeniff's people were able to live in peace for another prolonged period. As the years passed, the urgency behind the military training diminished. The understanding of the need was kept alive with tales told around campfires to wide-eyed youth who were either too young, or not yet born, during the great skirmish.

*****

In the ninth year following the incident which began in the fields, King Laman died. His people mourned his passing. It was said at his ceremonious cremation on the wooden funeral pyre, that he had led his people well and good. Some among them disagreed with this assessment, however. Among these dissenters was Laman's own son, also named Laman, who had considered Jobadesh among his best friends.

Out of respect for his father, he held his peace throughout the rituals of both the funeral and his own coronation. Once he was officially crowned king of the Lamanites, he unfurled a string of oaths against the Nephites such as had not been heard before.

"These pale invaders from the north sicken me!" he swore. The men assembled in his throne room nodded in agreement. "I was but a tender boy when my father, the king, announced that we would be leaving our city, my home, to make room for these cheating and deceitful Nephites. Even then I questioned the act. I have never understood why he allowed them to move in and overrun our lands. Nor have I understood why he allowed them to continue here for year after year after year. These people are not our friends. They are not welcome, and must not stay! We must rid ourselves of their putrid presence now and for good!"

"Great king, I do not doubt or question your words." Lemach, Laman's childhood companion and closest living friend, was the only one present who dared question his new king while he was in the midst of announcing his first proclamation. "I must seek your wisdom, though. Our spies have reported towers spread across their southern borders. Even after these nine years have passed, the towers are yet manned day and night. How will we be able to take these foul people? Surely the tower guards will give warning to the city and all within its walls will be well protected before we reach its border. Our men will then be at the mercy of their archers."

"That is true, but only true if we come at them from the south." King Laman smiled with a sinister lilt.

"But, of course we would come from the south. Our land is to the south, theirs is to the north. How else would we come?" Lemach was so startled by the king's response that he forgot the rigidities customary with addressing his king.

"We will stay off the main roads, cut through the jungle, circle north toward the city Shilom and come back at them from the northeast. They will never expect us, and their aging king will be no match for my cunning and strength."

Lemach let the strategy sink in. He pictured the Nephites diligently looking southward while they swept in from the north. He smiled, "Brilliant!"

"Of course it's brilliant. Gather the men. It's time we rid our land of these pesky gnats."

*****

King Zeniff's eyes still maintained their zealous sparkle. His hair was now white. Wrinkles permeated his face and brown-speckled hands. His back had begun to stoop, but his eyes still sparkled. Everything else aside, he would be able to live out his life content with the knowledge that he had been the driving factor in helping the Nephites return to the city of Nephi.

He sat upon his throne, listening to affairs of state. Three men representing the farmers were giving their report. The court advisors were attentive but less than enthralled by the news they bore. All attention was torn away from the report by a commotion at the throne room door. A Nephite noisily attempted to push his way through the guards. Although the frantic man managed to enter the room, the guards held their ground and prevented him from approaching the throne.

"Great king, I must be permitted to speak!" the man shouted. "Oh king, I have urgent news which must be heard!"

The guards still attempted to push the man away from the room as Zeniff looked up. He saw the man and his efforts. He determined that the man was in earnest. He raised his hand and let it hover a moment with patience and then motioned in a manner to order calm and silence, as he spoke, "Let the brother enter. I wish to hear his words."

The guards parted and allowed the Nephite to approach his king. The man gathered himself together and adjusted his robe after his tussle with the guards, so that it again covered both shoulders evenly, as he stepped forward. He moved with dignity and ceremony, but also with haste. He continued several paces until he was at the customary place for giving audience before the king. The farm men stepped aside, graciously allowing him to take their space. The man bowed low and then straightened up, knowing and appreciating that he now commanded the undivided attention of all within the throne room.

"Great king, I thank you that I may speak to you this day. I am Samuel and I will speak quickly, as the message I have is both troubling and of utter urgency."

"Please, speak now and share this message," the king urged.

"Thank you, my king. The Lamanites are on the move and, I believe, headed toward this fair city."

"The Lamanites!" King Zeniff was as troubled as he was surprised. "After so many years of peace, they now seek vengeance again! This is indeed troubling. How have you gathered this news when all of my tower guards have remained silent on this?"

"I do not doubt that your guards have remained silent, nor do I fault them for so doing." Samuel bowed, implying deference to their faithful servitude. "They would not have seen the Lamanites at this time, for the Lamanites are not coming from the south where your guards keep their diligent vigil."

"Not coming from the south!? Then from where?" Zeniff queried.

"I am from the city Shilom. I was out hunting well to the east and south of our city. As I neared my prey, I heard voices and hid myself, for they bore an ominous tone. From my hiding place, I looked toward the voices and saw two Lamanite spies. I overheard them speaking with satisfaction of their new king's plan to swing wide of your southern guards and catch you unawares in a snare by approaching from the north. Apparently, this new king intends to completely rid the land of Nephites. If what I heard is true, there will be no mercy."

"How soon will the Lamanites be upon us?"

"I cannot say for certain, but I imagine it will be within two days."

"We must work quickly then!" Zeniff turned to the two advisors who sat to his right. "We must take council and prepare ourselves." He then turned to the guard nearest his throne. "Send for the rest of the advisors. We must meet at once!"

The guard nodded and quickly exited to perform his duty. Zeniff turned back to Samuel.

"This news you bear is far from good," he concluded. "It troubles me greatly, but I appreciate you bringing it to us. You have done well this day."

"I seek only to serve my people." Samuel bowed again.

* * * * *

The throne room was now cleared of all superfluous people. Only the king, his two-dozen advisors and three throne room guards were present. Two guards stood on either side of the entrance, while the third stood near the throne itself. Two rows of six advisors each sat in the council chairs on the king's right, while two more rows of six sat in council chairs on the king's left. The council chairs were on a platform, raised slightly from the floor, but not quite as high as the throne itself. Every man bore a look of concern and all eyes were on the advisor to the king's far left.

"Yes, I realize it sounds as if I'm doubting the strength of our armies, but that is not the point. If they are on a quest to purge the land of Nephites and show no mercy, we have to anticipate that they intend to come with their full force and hit us both hard and fast. We have practiced, but quite frankly, most of these men have never fought. Ever. Those who have, did it so many years ago that our skills simply are not at their peak. If they do penetrate our forces and enter the city, all those within its walls will be trapped. I have a terrible vision of our fair streets lined with the bodies of our women and children, cut down in a most horrendous manner."

There was a momentary pause as all considered his words. Terantum leaned forward and broke the brief silence.

"I must agree with my esteemed counselor," he said. "If they break through and enter the city, it will mean our forces have folded and the

Lamanites will likely seal off all exits. Those within the walls will have no safe haven and nowhere to run. I'm afraid that I must agree. Concealing them in the wilderness to the far west is the only safe alternative for them. If the Lamanites break through our forces and storm the city, our women will have seen this and be able to lead our people farther into the wilderness long before King Laman will have realized that the city has been abandoned. And if we prevail - it will be a small matter to have our families reunited again."

Shaking his head, Zeniff raised his hand and put an end to the debate, cutting two advisors off in mid-word and all others who had been on the verge of speaking.

"We can debate this for weeks. The point is we have two days at best, perhaps less. Now is not the time for words, but for deeds. Send out the orders. The women and children will be sent off until all is well. Have the men assemble in the city square. I want every man that can bear arms, both old and young. We must be prepared with every possible sword. I, too, will join the battle."

"King Zeniff! No, we cannot allow this!"

"Yes, we can. And we will. I want no chance of failure! If I'm asking my men to lay their lives on the line, I intend to be right alongside them. People are more greatly motivated by example than by word. This is our most dire hour and I intend to lead by example! Furthermore, tomorrow will be a day of fasting and prayer!"

* * * * *

King Laman himself was the first to peer out from the jungle's edge. In the distance, he could make out the city of Nephi. A sinister grin covered his shorn head.

"Is it not just as we said?" the first spy offered.

"They have no idea we are here. If you look very carefully, you can just make out the shape of their tower guards far to the south, watching for your arrival," the second spy added.

"Yes, if only they knew we are already here! That would surprise them, but then, we are about to do just that!" King Laman laughed to himself, allowing an excited and undignified snort slip out. He turned to an officer behind him. "Ready the men. It's time!"

The word spread quickly through the evil force. The men wore nothing but a leather loincloth. Each man had shaved his head bare. Wicked designs were painted on their lean backs and bulging shoulders and the colors - whites, yellows, vibrant blues, and reds - were intentionally chosen to contrast with their dark skin. The swords they bore were finely sharpened and forged for strength.

Laman himself began their infamous, heart-splitting war cry. It was quickly taken up by all of his warriors in a frenzied excitement. As he turned to exit the jungle and begin their attack, he was more than slightly surprised to see the city gate open. His first thought was that if they could reach the city while the gate was still open, their slaughter would be all the easier. It was not until he and his men were dashing across the acreage toward the city that he saw it. Not only did the gate remain open, but the Nephites were now pouring out of it. Not just Nephites, but armed Nephites. These were men with swords, shields, and armor.

Laman's war cry died in his throat. As if following their leader in his every deed, the whooping ceased nearly as suddenly as it had begun. The men they saw pouring from the city were neither surprised, nor concerned. Instead they looked angry. Laman continued to lead his men into battle. As he did so, he shook his head as he tried to assess his foe. No, "angry" was not the right word. It was more a look of determination. It was obvious to Laman and his men that not only did the Nephites know of their arrival, but they were well prepared for it and determined to hold their city. Row upon row of armed men continued to flow out of the gate at a frightening pace.

A few hundred yards into their dash, they saw that more Nephites were making their way around the eastern wall. They were apparently coming from the southern gate. Undaunted, Laman let out another horrific war cry. His men followed suit. The jungle stirred and shook at the sound of their war-whelps. They doubled their pace and ran with swords and clubs held high above their heads. Their bronze, painted bodies rushed forward in a frenzied streak.

Even as the two groups of Nephites joined, there was no end in sight to either line. Somehow, *somehow*, the Nephites were aware of their attack, "*But, how?*" Laman spat. He continued the onslaught. Within heartbeats, the two armies met. The clashing of swords was instantaneous and men began to drop as if bouncing off of each other.

The Nephites had allowed their meeting to take place far enough away from their walls to allow maneuverability, but close enough that their archers could take aim. While the two armies clashed, the archers stepped into view. They lined the entire eastern wall, standing on the catwalk and fully loaded with arrows enough to spare. They had nearly two dozen years of stockpiling at their disposal. If necessary, they would use them all to defend their lives and homes.

Those Lamanites with slings and stones quickly learned the fatal lesson of the effectiveness of a well-placed sword in close hand-to-hand combat. The Lamanites began to lose hold of the concept of unquestioned victory like dew at noon. Their war cries dimmed as their concentration shifted to survival. To their shock and horror these mighty bronze men had to fend powerful and accurately wielded blows from young and old Nephites alike. Several went to their graves spitting at the indignity of being cut down by mere boys or old men.

All of the Nephites virtually sang with confidence. As they saw their ability to withhold the attack, they took heart and fought all the more aggressively. Several of them uttered such words of thanks as, "God be praised!" and, "By the strength of the Messiah!" while still in the heat of battle.

The fighting lasted with a duration that exhausted human bodies. Swinging blows began to be as equally exerting as fending them. Many Nephites lay lifeless in the field, but many, many more Lamanites lay beside them and all around. The Nephites had the clear advantage. The Lamanite wall of aggression began to crack and ebb. Once the ebb became distinct, it increased.

The Lamanites found themselves fleeing for their lives, while the Nephites stayed on their tails ensuring they left their land completely. That night, King Laman led a broken, battered and depleted army southward to the land of Shemlon. They were highly discouraged, dismayed and disillusioned from their objective. They had intended to purge the land of Nephites. Instead, they had nearly succeeded in extinguishing themselves.

Farther north, a much different mood prevailed. Husbands, wives, and children were reuniting and returning to their homes content, safe, and grateful for the preserving hand of the Lord and the wisdom of their inspired leaders. Many made pilgrimages to the temple to give thanks.

✶✶✶✶✶

Zeniff sat at the writing table, allowing his mind to wander a moment longer. The memory of the final battle and the peaceful days that followed warmed his heart. The Lord had indeed been kind. The land was good. The people were content. They were in the land of Nephi. He had brought them there and they had raised a generation within its boundaries. It was very good.

Zeniff picked up the etching tool again. It was time to finish his record. He wrote his final words, "And now I, being old, have conferred the kingdom upon one of my sons, Noah. I say no more. May the Lord bless my people. Amen." He laid the utensil down, closed his eyes a moment, and breathed in the warmth that memories of a life well spent provide.

Chapter 7

King Noah

Zeniff's passing and the weeks of official mourning were now distant memories kept alive by only a few. The years had brought many changes. The great king would not have recognized his former utopia. Orchards had been cut and burned to make way for vineyards. Winepresses had long ago replaced armories and altars.

The watch towers to the south were overgrown with vines and weeds. Their bottoms clung loosely to the sides, as the wood rotted and decayed in the humid climate. In the center of the kingdom, not far from the city square, was a new tower, tall and massive. From its peak one could not only see within the walls of Shilom to the north, but could also see over the trees and into the land of Shemlon to the south, home of the Lamanites.

The tower dwarfed the city's temple. This indignity was scant compared to the other disgraces that had been brought upon the building that was once the pearl and centerpiece of the city. This edifice was now guarded more closely than a treasure vault, for in it was kept the main stores of the king's winery. Sacred walls were now smeared with purple stains spilled from baskets of ripe fruit, or barrels of potent liquid. Gone were any physical reminders of sacred or holy offerings or practices, be they tapestries or altars. The building now reeked with the stench of fermented drink that was as corrupted as the people who had allowed this evolution into decadence.

Beyond the walls of the former temple, the throne room had traded dignity for pomp - not just pomp, but gaudy arrogance and avarice. The original throne was long ago replaced by the ornate, stone throne Ammon had found when he appeared before King Limhi. The counselors' seats were also replaced with intricately carved seats of dark wood.

Zeniff's advisors were permanently absent and had long ago been succeeded by two dozen men the new king mockingly referred to as his "priests." Though it was true that they had once been endowed with a form of the priesthood by their predecessors, they had long ago neglected their calls and violated their worthiness to retain these sacred positions. The platform on which they sat now hosted a solid gold banister close to their seats so that the men could lean their lazy arms and bodies upon it as they exacted wicked tolls upon a once-great people.

King Zeniff's offspring sat upon his throne. His stomach bulged and stretched as if attempting to flee from the confines of his bright blue tunic. Purple wine streaked his lips and stained his scraggly beard. Although the room was not excessively warm, and his exertions rarely went beyond reaching for his goblet or shouting filthy orders, beads of sweat gathered and dripped from his forehead. His most favored concubine sat in the far corner of the throne room awaiting his bidding at the day's end.

"Oh, great and powerful king, may the sun shine brightly upon your vineyards and may their juices never dry," the messenger began.

"Yes, yes. What is it that forces you to disturb my day?" King Noah shook his outstretched, pudgy fingers at the man as if waving off a pesky fly.

"Mighty and wise king, I'm compelled to report on the latest incident with the Lamanites from the south," the man stammered.

"What of them? I give you guards. What more do you need?"

"Yes, my king, you give us guards, but I fear they are too few. The Lamanites continue to come upon your people in small bands. Seven more of your loyal subjects now lay dead and their flocks are stolen."

"And, what of my guards then?! Do they not earn the pay with which I endow them?" the king bit out impatiently.

"I cannot say to what degree the pay must be earned, but three of the dead are the guards you sent. You sent no others."

"We just drove them off within a fortnight, yet already they return. Such pathetic parasites," the king slurred out.

"Yes, your majesty, but-"

The man was interrupted by a commotion at the throne room door. Several angry people had gathered. Their muffled voices grew suddenly louder as the throne room door began to open. The king looked up with a scowl on his face. He wondered who dared to interrupt his council session. He saw his guards attempting to block their entry. There were at least five men who moved in and out of view as the commotion continued. It was evident that there were still others beyond the view of the door.

"Pick one or two and let them enter," the king finally commanded. He was both irritated and a little curious.

The guards at the door were in the process of using their spears to hold the crowd at bay. They held them horizontally with one hand on either side of the spear's center and were physically pushing the crowd back. The guard who normally kept vigil at the king's side had left his post and had quickly approached the uproar. He had arrived just as the king's order was given. He turned back to the king and gave a quick nod. Then he turned back to the crowd and pointed to two of the more persistent men.

"You and you, come in! The rest, wait outside!" The others hesitated a moment and the guard repeated forcefully and with an impatience that warned of retribution, "I said, 'Wait outside!'"

The two nodded approvingly and made motions with their hands for the guards to move their makeshift barricade to allow them to enter. The rest of the crowd was silenced for a moment and then, as the men entered the throne room, they picked up where they had left off, protesting their lack of admittance.

"The rest of you leave, or else you will feel the point of my spear and not its shaft!" the king's guard bellowed as he turned his spear toward them.

The other guards did the same. The crowd was frustrated, but finally relented when faced with potential skewering. They slowly backed out of the room, mumbling, and the throne room door was closed again. The two chosen men stood on the inside. The king's guard did an about face to return to his post and act as escort for the two men.

"You two! Advance and approach the king!" he ordered.

The three men marched forward. The guard had a determined quick pace, the other two showed a small degree of hesitation in their steps as they looked about the elaborate throne room. Their eyes caught hold of the golden and bejeweled statuary lining the walls. They saw the carved wooden trim along the ceiling; the luxurious tapestries hanging from both the walls and ceiling. They marveled at the costly apparel on the men who lined either side of the king, and the king himself who sat in all his corpulent splendor.

"Kneel before your king!" the guard commanded the two.

They bumped into each other in nervous awe and then did as they were commanded. While on their knees, they still looked around the room in wonder at both the decor and the inhabitants. This was unmistakably their first visit within the royal chamber. Their eyes eventually rested on the crowned figure in front of them.

He sat slumped diagonally in his seat, resting on his left elbow. The stone throne seemed to groan under his weight. A basket of grapes lay within arm's reach of the king, next to it was a large goblet filled to the brim with the royal wine. A servant continually refilled the cup after each sip or gulp. The king bore an impatient, spoiled expression. His demeanor was that of a man accustomed to power and with getting his way in all dealings.

"I have allowed you to enter. Now what do you want?" he demanded, more than asked.

"Oh, great king, we are honored to be in your presence this day!" the first man began.

"Yes, yes, what do you want of me?" the king repeated impatiently.

"Great king, we are troubled today by an evil man who has come among us," the second man took over their explanation. "He is stirring up the people and spreading lies about you and your honorable counselors!"

Noah gained a sudden interest in what they had to say and moved more quickly than was his custom to an upright, sitting position. He even paused in placing the grape he held, into his mouth.

"What? What man is spreading lies? What lies? Who is this man?" the king demanded.

The two gained confidence now that they were growing accustomed to the environment and the king had now acknowledged a willingness to hear their tale.

"Abinadi! His name is Abinadi!" the first man said and nodded enthusiastically.

"Yes, and he is claiming to be a prophet sent to reclaim this people. Your people," the second man added.

"A prophet?! Reclaim this people? From what? From whom?! This people need no reclaiming," Noah responded.

The priests concurred with the king's assessment. They nodded and mumbled and turned to each other for confirmation that they were all in agreement with their beloved leader and mentor.

"What things has this self-proclaimed prophet said?" the king demanded.

"Lots of 'woe this' and 'woe that' type of stuff about needing to repent and such," the first man said, again nodding his head in an exaggerated manner which he hoped would bring acceptance and appreciation for his simplistic words.

The second man glared at the first with a look that made it clear that he wanted his partner to remain silent and let him tell the story.

"He said his name is Abinadi and that the Lord had spoken to him and commanded him to come among us and call us to repentance. He said the Lord has seen our abominations and if we do not repent, he will 'visit us in his anger,'" the second stated.

"'Visit us in his anger?' That sounds like a threat, your majesty," one of the priests observed. Others nodded agreement.

"There's more," the second Nephite explained. "He said if we do not repent and return to worshiping the Lord God, he will deliver us into the hands of our enemies. That we will be afflicted by our enemies and brought into bondage. That there is none but the Lord Almighty God who will be able to save us."

"This is preposterous! What audacity!" the priests shouted.

"There's more! There's more!" the first man said enthusiastically and turned to his comrade, "Tell him the rest!"

"He said that except we repent and cry mightily to the Lord, He will not hear our prayers and will be slow to ease our burdens, even if we later decide to repent."

"Who is the Lord that will bring such affliction to my people? Who is this Abinadi that I and my people should be judged of him? Where is he now?" the king asked with distinct irritation.

"We were as angry as you are at his words, great king," the second man replied. "When he spoke these slanderous words, we grew angry and sought to take him and stone him. But, he somehow slipped through the crowd. He has disappeared. But, we will keep a constant vigil for him in case he dares to show his face in our city again!"

"Send out a decree that if this Abinadi is found, he is to be bound and brought before me and tried for treason and summarily executed unless he recants his lies and threats!" the king commanded.

* * * * *

Two years passed. King Noah and his priests continued to lead the people as they always had, enjoying their debauched lifestyles to the fullest. The people followed their lead willingly, if not zealously. The golden ideals of King Zeniff had decayed into a slovenly city of sin which would have given Sodom and Gomorrah a run for the title.

A lone, hooded figure arrived at the city's main gate and called for leave to enter. After three turns at knocking and calling out, the gate finally began to swing open. The gate's guard peered out.

"Who is there?"

"I am."

"And, who are you?"

"I am a Nephite merely seeking admittance into the city of Nephi. May I enter?"

The guard was about to turn the man away, when to his own surprise he heard himself respond, "You may. Do so quickly!"

The weathered man entered the city and was well into the town square before the guard had latched the gate closed again. The guard shook his head as if to clear it and looked for the old man, but could not find him among the milling crowd. The next thing he heard was an old, yet powerful voice coming from above him.

He stepped farther into the city proper to gain a vantage point to see above him and saw the old man standing on the wall's catwalk directly above the city gate. The man had cast aside his cloak. His arms were raised in a dramatic fashion as he spoke. The wind blew his long hair and beard. His cloak flowed behind him giving him a surreal aura of divine power. He faced the city square and prepared to address the people.

"Behold! The Lord has commanded me to come and prophesy to all you people, saying, 'Abinadi, go and warn this people, for they have hardened their hearts against my words! They have not repented of their evil doings! Therefore, I will visit them in my anger and woe be to this generation! It shall come to pass that because of their iniquities this generation will be brought into bondage and smitten upon the cheek, driven before men and slain. The vultures of the air and the dogs and wild beasts shall devour their flesh! And the life of King Noah will be valued as a garment in a hot furnace, for he shall know that I am the Lord! All this will come to pass except this people repent!'"

From the first syllable he had uttered, Abinadi's words traveled with clarity to all those within the city square. Merchants immediately stopped plying their wares. Shoppers ceased haggling and bartering. It was as if time itself ceased for a moment from its eternal round. Guards stood transfixed, incapable of rushing this wizened, yet powerful, orator until his discourse was complete.

The words were clear and unmistakable. All of those who heard them would long remember where they were, and what they ceased doing, as they were spoken. The effect was complete, but it was not to Abinadi's personal advantage. He continued to prophesy of terrible afflictions that would plague the people, lest the people change their ways. At the climax of his speech, Abinadi clenched his fist and threw it high toward the heavens as he made his final emphasis of the need for the people to repent. At this moment, all of the people were united as one.

A cry went up from the crowd, which spontaneously fused into a mob. Angry voices shouted.

"He has reviled the king!"

"We have done nothing wrong!"

"Who is this man that he should offend us with his words?!"

"Away with him!"

"Guards! Seize this man and take him to the king!"

"He has spoken treason against our king!"

"Seize him!"

Citizens and guards alike charged up the ladders that led to the catwalk. Abinadi stood still and with resolution. He did not attempt to flee. Within moments, the angry citizenry had hold of him. They bound him and dragged him off of the wall. They whisked him through the city square, holding both of his upper arms tightly. His feet dragged behind him. Men and women chided and berated him as he passed. Several spit and swore at him. He took it all in stride without a reply or even a flinch.

The angry mob was all too pleased to march up to the throne room door and announce to the guards that they had a special prisoner for their king.

"This man Abinadi has returned and reviled the king! We have brought him to the king so that he can pronounce judgment on him!"

"Wait here and I will see if the king will admit you," one guard announced in reply.

The crowd egged on the guard, shouting their indignation at Abinadi's prophecies. Their shouts could be heard from within the throne room. They had raised the room's attention long before the door was opened and the guard stepped through. When the guard reentered the room, the king motioned for him to come forward without the customary gossip-chain passing of the message from guard to guard to the king.

"What's this commotion that disturbs our session?!" Noah demanded.

"The people have captured the man they call 'Abinadi.' They say that he has reviled the king and that they have brought him to be judged of you," the guard replied in a level tone.

"Abinadi? Abinadi? Should I know that name?" the king asked no one in particular.

One of his priests in the seats to his right spoke up, "Yes, my king. This seditious man was here a couple of years back and spouted off all manner of ill-intentioned threats and warnings about you. I am surprised that he has dared to come back."

"Oh, yes, I think I remember him now!" King Noah's face lit up with faint recognition. "Have him enter. This should be interesting."

The guard bowed, turned, and went to retrieve Abinadi. When he returned, he and another guard escorted, or rather dragged, the aged Abinadi into the room and forced him to kneel before the corrupt Nephite king. Abinadi's clothes were now in tatters. His legs were shackled with ropes. His wrists were tied together.

His long white hair and flowing white beard were unkempt from both wind and the mistreatment from the crowd. Still, even while forced to kneel, there was a dignified serenity about the man. His demeanor was far from that of a frightened prisoner ready to beg for his life. Instead, it was of a man at peace with himself and nature. While at the same time, it was clear that he maintained a righteous indignation for the man before whom he now knelt.

"So, Abinadi, my friend, you have returned," the king spoke mockingly. "What brings you back to my fine kingdom? Do you wish to live among us now, or do you prefer the rocks and holes in which you have apparently hidden yourself these many months?"

A voice shouted from the doorway, "He has prophesied evil concerning you, great king!"

"What? What is this? Who dares speak without being bidden?" the king demanded with irritation.

"I do!" a tall, muscular Nephite pushed himself into view from between the guards at the door. "I am Korinor. I speak for those of us gathered outside your throne room, great king."

"Korinor. I do not know you. You may enter, though. Step forward and approach the throne." The king watched him approach.

Korinor walked with pious dignity and stopped beside Abinadi. He was a tall, handsome man, who exuded confidence. He bowed and then knelt respectfully before his king.

"Stand and tell me the accusations which you have against this man," the king commanded.

"This man has prophesied evil against you, saying that your life shall be as a garment in a furnace of fire." Korinor's voice raised with anger the longer he spoke. "He said that you, great king, would be as a dry stalk in a field which is run over by wild beasts and trodden under the foot of men. That you will be like the blossoms of a thistle that when they are ripe they are scattered hither and thither by the wind lest you repent of your iniquities."

The king's face turned into a severe scowl with these graphic analogies at his pending demise. Korinor continued, "He pretends that the Lord has spoken these dreadful words. But, we know that he lies. What great evil have you done, oh King, or what great sins have your people committed that they should be condemned of God or judged by this man? We are guiltless. And you, great King, have not sinned. Therefore, this man has lied and prophesied in vain. We will not be taken captive or put into bondage, for we are a strong people who have prospered well in this land. We have delivered this man into your hands so that you may do with him as seems good to you."

Korinor finished his accusation, bowed again, and then folded his arms and stood with the defiance of a snitch achieving satisfaction in a deed well done. His words were not lost on the king, or on his ill-intentioned priests. They were in an absolute uproar and ready to deal harshly with Abinadi.

The king's face had turned purple with rage. He was so flustered he was incapable of coherent speech. Incapable of giving a complex order, he finally blurted out, "Away with this man! To prison!"

The guards grabbed Abinadi by both triceps and hefted him to his feet. Without having so much as uttered a word to the king, he was whisked out of the room and dragged to the very dungeon which would later house Ammon, Hem, Helem, and Amaleki.

Chapter 8

Abinadi

The slovenly king and his so-called priests sat in council. The topic of discussion was the old man currently rotting in their foul prison. They pondered how to deal with such a man who brought such unpleasant words to their kingdom and people.

"All this talk is well and good, your majesty, but I say we bring him back here that we may question him and see if he will recant his words," a portly priest with a red robe announced.

"Better still, if we question him properly, we may be able to trip him up in his words and find a point of law with which we can accuse him, and rightfully put his meddling to an end!" his counterpart on the opposite side of the hall conjectured.

"Well put, Amulon," King Noah observed. Turning to his guards, he ordered, "Fetch that man and bring him here!"

* * * * *

Noah's priests delighted in exercising their crafty wit in endless debate. They prided themselves in ripping to shreds the logic, stamina, and esteem of those who entered the king's court. Often those who brought issues of dispute before the king for settlement found both parties emotionally worse off for having come, and the disputed item either confiscated or inequitably divided.

When "outsiders," as they called them, were unavailable, the seedy priests would debate and dispute among themselves. Abinadi's presence simply fueled the appetites of these supposed priests for another round of lopsided debate. They actually thrilled at the prospect of questioning him. They intended to cross him, so that they could come upon a point of law for which they could level an accusation against him.

It would quickly become evident, however, that they did not understand the character and power of the man who now stood before them. Not only did he withstand their accusations, but he would soon turn the tables and begin to challenge them at the very core of their authority and responsibilities.

The shifty priest named Amulon, who sat in the first row and closest to the king, was the first to speak. He leaned forward and rested his upper body on the golden bulwark. His smug expression disclosed his intentions.

The other priests repressed smirks as the man prepared to speak. Amulon had a well-earned reputation for being the most formidable and relentless accuser among them. They sat back waiting to witness the master at work.

Amulon looked at Abinadi with contempt and asked, "When our fathers left the land of Jerusalem and set sail for this Promised Land, they took with them the book of the prophets. What do the words mean which are written therein where it reads, 'How beautiful upon the mountains are the feet of him that bringeth good tidings, that publisheth peace, that bringeth good tidings of good, that publisheth salvation, that sayeth unto Zion: Thy God reigneth!' and so forth?"

Amulon sat back and received silent congratulations from his cohorts for having identified what they perceived to be an obscure piece of trivia for which Abinadi would be unable to launch a worthy counter attack. His special friend and comrade in crime, Amaleki, looked over at Amulon and gave him a knowing wicked smile of approval.

Abinadi stood still, silently waiting for more, ignoring the ropes that bound his hands and shackled his feet. His posture continued to exude humble dignity in spite of the tattered clothes that graced him after spending days in the wretched dungeon of a prison cell. When he perceived that this was the extent of the first question, his face took on an incredulous yet somewhat stern look as he asked, "Are you priests, and pretend to teach this people, and to understand the spirit of prophesying, and yet desire to know of me what these things mean? I tell you, woe be unto you for perverting the ways of the Lord! For if you understand these things you have not taught them. Therefore, you have perverted the ways of the Lord. You have not applied your hearts to understanding. By this you have not been wise. What do you teach this people?"

The priests were taken aback by his dogmatic response and confident demeanor. Some whispered quickly among each other. Others sat upright. A handful recognized that this would not be their typical debate.

Amulon took hold of Abinadi's question and offered a distinct, emphatic reply, "We teach the Law of Moses."

"If you teach the Law of Moses then why do you not keep it?" Abinadi demanded. Before any of the shocked priests could reply, Abinadi pummeled them with even more stinging questions, "Why do you set your hearts upon riches? Why do you commit whoredoms and spend your strength with harlots? Why do you entice these fair people to commit sin to such an extent that the Lord has sent me to prophesy against this people?"

Objections were stifled as priests caught in their own guile were dumbfounded at the nerve of this man who so accurately brought their debauchery to the forefront. More than one throne room guard suppressed a smirk at this unprecedented turn of events. They exchanged silent glances at each other as they prepared themselves to hear how the priests would respond. Before the priests could do so, Abinadi continued to expose the blatant error of their ways.

"Do you know of the truth of my words? Yes, you know that I speak the truth. You ought to tremble before God, for the time is soon at hand when you will be smitten for your iniquities."

Abinadi paused, letting his eyes rest on one priest after another. As his eyes shifted from one priest to the next, the priests felt uneasy. He seemed to peer into the depths of their souls. His purity of purpose uncovered feelings they did not wish to reveal. Each in turn caused their gaze to drift away from his.

"You claim you teach the Law of Moses. What do you know concerning the Law of Moses? Tell me this, does salvation come by the Law of Moses? What do you say?"

The priests were silent a moment until one in the back row on the far right corner farthest from the king, who went by the name Alma, spoke up, "Yes, salvation does come by the Law of Moses."

Abinadi looked over at the priest. He noted that the reply actually seemed to be sincere, lacking the arrogance of the other man with whom he had so far conversed. He replied, "I grant you this, I know that if you keep the commandments which God delivered unto Moses on the Mount of Sinai, you will be saved. But, now let me ask you this, have you kept these commandments? I tell you no, you have not. Have you taught this people that they should keep these commandments? Again, I say no, you have not."

This direct affront on their priestly obligations brought their rage to a head. The king himself had heard enough. With anger in his voice and a blazing scowl creasing his bloated face he demanded, "Away with this fellow and slay him! What have we to do with him, for he is mad?!"

Both priests and guards alike stood and attempted to lay their hands on him, but Abinadi withstood them and declared, "Touch me not! For God will smite you if you lay your hands on me! I have not delivered the message which the Lord sent me to deliver. Neither have I told you that which you requested that I should. Therefore, God will not suffer that I will be destroyed at this time. I must fulfill the commandments God has commanded me. And because I have told you the truth, you are angry with me. Because I have spoken the word of God you have judged me to be mad."

As Abinadi spoke these words, the people of King Noah did not dare to lay their hands on him, for the Spirit of the Lord was on him. His face shone with a great luster, even as Moses' did while he was on Mount Sinai speaking with the Lord. Abinadi spoke with power and authority from God.

The men could feel his words vibrate in their chests. Not a man among them could avoid feeling a humbled intimidation.

The king was as shocked as any of his priests. He meant to shout for his guards, but only fumbled out the half-broken command, which came out as more of a plea for protection than a command. "Guards," he said with a cracking voice, then cleared his throat and said more clearly, "Guards!" and gathering strength added, "Seize this man!"

At first, there was no movement from anyone. Abinadi stood tall, stoic and unflinchingly. The king looked around in desperation. "Guards! I said seize this man! Seize him now!"

It was clear that the king feared for his life, as if Abinadi would suddenly charge and overpower him – but, no – it would not be through some sort of physical assault. The king and his court sensed that the power of the man before them was some sort of otherworldly and undeniable power. It was as if they feared he would call down the powers of Heaven itself and cause them to wither before him as dried leaves. Even the jaded Amulon was intimidated.

The king continued to look desperately from left to right trying vainly to urge his guards to action. Finally, he picked up a handful of grapes that lay nearby and threw them at the guard to his right to get his attention and spur him to move, "I said seize him now, or face my wrath!" Noah continued to fear for his life, but could not avoid the threat. Such language and behavior was engrained in his very soul.

The guard barely acknowledged the minute pummeling, although he did stir. He noticed that his spear-bearing arm had slackened and he pulled the spear upright again, but with care. He swallowed hard, and looked over at his king. The king urged him on emphatically. Desperately. He turned his head to the old man.

There was an aura physically surrounding the captive that was wholly overwhelming. Abinadi continued to stare at the king. The guard could feel the prophet's concentration. He hesitated again, but a quick turn to see his king let him know that if he did not act soon, he would not live to see the sunset. He stepped forward to address Abinadi. His movement to action persuaded the other guards in the room to move as well.

The bound Abinadi was surrounded by what could only be described as meek and lowly guards. They pointed their spears at him, but did so in the awkward manner of one who approaches a calm beehive planning to shoo away the inhabitants, but knowing that one false move could result in an angry swarm from which there is no true defense.

With his spear pointed upward, the lead guard again turned to get clarity of duty from his king. The king flicked the puffy fingers of his right hand at the man, urging him to continue. The guard shifted the tip of his spear toward Abinadi, attempting to be threatening, but was clearly apprehensive. He tried to give an order, but although his lips moved, no words were uttered.

Abinadi calmly turned his head toward the guard as the spear approached. As he did so, he let his eyes linger on the king's a moment then turned them to the guard's. The guard felt his soul-piercing gaze and blinked. He flinched and looked down. His spear drooped. He shook his head and looked up toward Abinadi again, but refused to look the man in the eye. He took a firmer hold on his spear and again pointed it at the prisoner.

He delicately pushed it toward Abinadi, obviously fearing any repercussion, but desperate to give a show of authority over the man. His demands fluttered and stumbled out as a repetitive series of "You – you – you –" but any further threat escaped him. His inability began to frustrate and anger himself. This was a man accustomed to bullying. He had been cruel to women and children both. Why should this old man pose any threat? His anger gathered momentum and he finally thrust the spear toward Abinadi in a clear attempt to force the man to obey.

As the spear approached Abinadi's skin, Abinadi's gaze shifted from the guard's eyes to the spear he held so menacingly in his powerful hands. The spear suddenly vibrated violently. There was a loud SNAP! and the spear burst in two. Not just in two, but into splinters. There was little left of the wooden shaft. Even the metal of the finely honed tip was scored. A fine wisp of smoke curled and rose up from the hollow of the spear's metal tip which now gently, harmlessly rolled back and forth on the stone floor. For a few, brief moments, the tinny ringing noise made by the tip was all that could be heard, as everyone remained stunned by what had just transpired.

The guard looked at his emptied palms. They were throbbing and red. With shock and wonder he slowly looked up at Abinadi. There was no malice in Abinadi's eyes. Somehow there was a serenity and a peace that come from singleness of purpose. Had the king been capable of bellowing another order, it would not have mattered. The guard would not have been capable of responding to or obeying it. He bowed his head and then slowly kneeled before this man of God.

The other guards dropped their swords. Most of them bowed as well. One was awestruck and terrified to the point that he backed away as quickly as he could. He stepped backward into the golden armrest of the priests, nearly tripping over it. He caused a goblet to tumble and spill fragrant wine on the priest behind him. He then turned and ran out of the room. No one was capable of stopping him either physically or verbally. They just let him go and sat motionless waiting for Abinadi's next words.

"You see that you have no power to slay me! Therefore, I will finish my message. I perceive that it cuts you to your hearts because I tell you the truth concerning your iniquities. I also see that my words fill you with wonder and amazement – and with anger. But, I will finish my message and then it does not matter what happens to me, so long as I am saved in the heavens. I will tell you this much, though. Whatever you do with me will become a type and a shadow of things to come.

"And now I will repeat to you the commandments of God, for I perceive that they are not written in your hearts. I perceive that instead you have studied and taught iniquity the most part of your lives."

Abinadi recited the Ten Commandments verbatim. After he finished, he asked, "Have you taught this people that they should observe to do all these things and to keep these commandments? I tell you, no. For if you had, the Lord would not have sent me to come and prophesy evil concerning this people."

Again Abinadi let his eyes scan his audience, moving slowly from one man to the next, occasionally holding a priest with his glare, eye to eye, until the beleaguered priest's soul could not tolerate the silent interview any longer and he turned his head aside, shamed.

"You have said that salvation comes by the Law of Moses. I tell you that it is expedient that you should keep the Law of Moses as yet, but the time will come when it will no longer be necessary to keep the Law of Moses. Salvation does not come by the Law alone. It will only come through the Atonement, which the great Messiah will make for the sins and iniquities of His people. Without that, all mankind would unavoidably perish, notwithstanding the Law of Moses.

"Moses prophesied to his people concerning the coming of the Messiah. He said that God should come down and dwell among men and redeem His people. Even all of the prophets who have ever prophesied since the world began have spoken of the coming Messiah and the great and everlasting sacrifice He would make, in plainness and sincerity.

"Yea, even the great prophet Isaiah said, 'Who hath believed our report, and to whom is the arm of the Lord revealed? For he shall grow up before him as a tender plant, and as a root out of dry ground. He hath no form nor comeliness, and when we shall see him there is a no beauty that we should desire him. He is despised and rejected of men; a man of sorrows and acquainted with grief. Surely he has borne our grief and carried our sorrows, yet we did esteem him stricken, smitten of God, and afflicted.

"'But he was wounded for our transgressions, he was bruised for our iniquities, and with his stripes we are healed. All we, like sheep, have gone astray, and the Lord hath laid on him the iniquities of us all. He was oppressed and afflicted, yet he opened not his mouth. He is brought as a lamb to the slaughter, and as a sheep before her shearers is dumb, so he opened not his mouth.

"He made his grave with the wicked, and with the rich in his death, because he had done no evil, neither was any deceit in his mouth. He hath made his soul an offering for sin. He shall see his seed, and the pleasure of the Lord shall prosper in his hand. He shall see the travail of his soul, and shall be satisfied. By his knowledge shall my righteous servant justify many, for he shall bear their iniquities. He was numbered with the transgressors and he bore the sins of many, and made intercession for the transgressors.'"

Upon quoting Isaiah, Abinadi paused a moment and proceeded to explain the prophecies more clearly, "I would that you should understand that God himself shall come down among the children of men and redeem his people. He shall be the Son of God and shall be subjected to the flesh and to the will of the Father. He shall suffer temptation, but not yield to temptation. He shall suffer himself to be mocked, and scourged, and cast out, and disowned by his people."

"After working many mighty miracles among the children of men, he shall be led, yea, even as Isaiah said, as a sheep before the shearer is dumb, so he opened not his mouth. Even so, he shall be led, crucified, and slain, but shall rise again, triumphant. Thus God shall break the bands of death, having gained the victory over death. He shall make an intercession for the children of men, having ascended into heaven, being filled with compassion towards the children of men, taking upon himself their iniquity and their transgressions, having redeemed them, and satisfied the demands of justice.

"And now, who shall declare his generation? Who shall be his seed? Behold I say unto you, that whosoever has heard the words of the prophets and have hearkened unto their words, and believed that the Lord would redeem his people, and have looked forward to that day for a remission of their sins, they are his seed. Or, they are the heirs of the kingdom of God.

"For these are they whose sins he has borne. These are they for whom he has died, to redeem them from their transgressions. Are they not his seed? Are not the prophets, every one that has opened his mouth to prophesy, are they not his seed?" Then, in a direct answer to the question Amulon had posed to him, Abinadi continued and both quoted and explained the passage that had been presented earlier, "These are they who have published peace, who have brought good tidings of good, who have published salvation, and said unto Zion, 'Thy God reigneth!' And, oh, how beautiful upon the mountains are the feet of those that are still publishing peace from this time henceforth and forever! For were it not for the redemption which he hath made for his people, which was prepared from the foundation of the world, all mankind must have perished."

Abinadi continued to preach and teach of the resurrection and the blessings that will come to those who live just lives and receive a righteous reward for their faithful acts and deeds. In this he spoke of mankind as a whole. However, those men sitting before him were not mankind as a whole. They were leaders, and as such, they bore the mantel of responsibility for setting proper examples and, even more, because they were priests, they owned the right and responsibility for teaching their people. Abinadi knew full well that these men were failing, miserably, in meeting the sacred obligations of the offices they held.

His eyes narrowed and his face grew even more serious as he continued to speak. It was not with malicious intent, but to bring added clarity to his words. He pointed first to King Noah, but allowed his arm to slowly sweep to the right and then the left to make it clear that his words were meant for all those men who sat behind the golden railing.

He continued, "But behold, and fear and tremble before God, for ye ought to tremble, for the Lord redeemeth none such that rebel against him and die in their sins! Yea, even all those that have willfully rebelled against God, that have known the commandments of God, and would not keep them. For salvation cometh unto none such, for the Lord hath redeemed none such, neither can the Lord redeem such for he cannot deny himself, for he cannot deny justice when it must have its claim."

After Abinadi had spoken these words, he stretched out his hand and said, "The time will come when all will see the salvation of the Lord. Every nation, kindred, tongue, and people will see eye to eye and confess before God that his judgments are just. Then the wicked will be cast out and will have cause to howl, and weep, and wail, and gnash their teeth. All this because they would not hearken to the voice of the Lord. The Lord will not redeem them, for he that chooses to persist in his own carnal nature and goes on in the ways of sin and rebellion against God, remains in his fallen state and the devil has all power over him. Therefore, he is as though there had been no redemption made.

"Remember the Messiah who shall rise from the dead and break the bands of death that the grave should have no victory and that death should have no sting. He is the light and life of the world; even a light that is endless that can never be darkened. Because of him our mortality shall put on immortality and we shall be brought to stand before the bar of God and be judged of him according to our works – whether they be good or whether they be evil.

"Now, ought you not tremble and repent of your sins, and remember that only in and through the Messiah can you be saved? So, if you teach the Law of Moses, also teach that it is a shadow of those things which are to come. Teach the people that redemption comes through the Messiah, who is the son of the very Eternal Father. Amen."

When Abinadi had finished speaking these words the king was beyond feelings of conscience and in a fit of pique. He commanded in a voice that was loud and shaking with anger, "Seize this insolent, pious wretch and put him to death!"

"Not so, your majesty!" a voice spoke from within the realm of the priests. "I know for myself that this man has spoken the truth. I trust he has spoken truly for many of the rest of you as well. We should do him no harm!"

All eyes within the chamber turned to see who had spoken these words. Even Abinadi looked into the ranks of the priests to see whose heart he had finally reached. On the corner farthest from the king's left sat a young priest in honored garb. It was the Nephite named Alma.

"What did you say?!" the king questioned him with focused anger.

"I said that this man speaks truth, and if we harm him, we will be harming an innocent man of God," Alma responded.

"An 'innocent man of God'? He has reviled the king and spoken evil of the king's priests!" the grand priest Amulon spouted. Abinadi's hold on the consciences of the most hardened priests had seemingly ceased at the conclusion of his sermon.

"I tell you this man has spoken the truth!..."

Alma was interrupted by a voice that echoed throughout the chamber. "Enough!" King Noah bellowed. "This man is an enemy to the people. His supporters are also enemies. Are you foolhardy enough to support this vile man?!"

"I support the truth, and this man has dared to speak truth," Alma bravely retorted. "Something I have not done in far too long! It is high time we all wake up and realize this."

"I have heard more than enough preaching for one day. I see where your allegiances lie. I want no more of this. Remove yourself from my presence, and do so quickly if you know what's best for you!" the king warned.

Alma felt the burning stares of his former comrades. His lip trembled imperceptibly at this public confrontation and threat. He mustered dignity he had not deserved in many a year and stood tall. He reviewed the other priests for his final time as one of them. His eyes sought some sort of companionship or willingness to agree with his position. He was met with hostile stares.

He turned and looked at the wizened prophet who stood bound in the square before the king. The vagrant image of the man's tattered clothing and weathered face disappeared in a sea of radiance and righteous indignation. Alma nodded to the man for whom he had gained a lasting respect. Abinadi nodded in reply. Alma held his gaze a moment and felt as if Abinadi saw into his very soul.

It was a cleansing, marvelous feeling that enveloped him and for a moment removed from him the realization of where he was and what he was doing. Abinadi nodded again, first toward Alma, and then toward the exit. Alma came to a realization of his perilous state. He stepped down from the platform.

"So be it!" he stated as he headed quickly toward the door.

A guard stepped forward with hesitation. He sensed he should block his way, but had not been given the order. He looked to his king and leader. Noah gave no sign, so the guard allowed Alma to pass. He looked the guard in the eye as he did so. The guard ignored Alma's gaze and continued to watch his king. Noah seemed to be playing one of his deadly games. Alma sensed his situation was dire, but gave no outward indication of it. To the contrary, he walked with deliberation, intent on giving the impression that he felt he could safely stroll out of the chamber and return to his home.

The king allowed the charade to continue. When Alma had departed and the throne room door was closed behind him, Noah spoke in a calm, level tone, "Get him. Kill him," was all he said.

The king's guard who had hesitated in blocking the exit now nodded acceptance of the order. He motioned to two other guards and the three marched to the door. The door guards opened the door to allow their exit. As they entered the outer hall, the throne room guards were perplexed. Alma was nowhere to be seen.

The moment the door had closed behind him, Alma had dashed in a silent sprint for safety. Rather than tear out of the chamber building, he turned right and dashed down the hall, deeper into the large building's interior. The guards that Noah sent to apprehend Alma quickly emerged from the throne room. They dashed into the hall and were taken in by the deception. They quick-stepped to the left, toward the building's exterior. Once in open territory, they conscripted the guards who stood watch at the council building's entrance. The group split up and began a massive search throughout the city. The guards at the gate were given explicit instructions to not let Alma leave the city.

Meanwhile, Alma continued his stealthy dash deeper into the chambers of the central building. He found the stairs leading far within to the records vault, grabbed a torch from the wall, and headed down. When he came to the great stone vault, he loosened the locking stone and pushed the stone door open. He replaced the stone from within, effectively sealing himself inside.

He was pleased to see that there was a small shaft for ventilation, but even more pleased with himself for having the foresight to hurriedly bundle up the fruit he had passed as it sat on display in one of the halls. He settled himself down for what could be a long concealment.

He knew how seldom these record chambers were used. Abinadi was right about the priests' lack of understanding the law. It was largely due to their lack of studying it. Alma was determined to record as many of the words of Abinadi as he could recall. He had all of the utensils and supplies he needed at his disposal. He felt unworthy to take on the task, but had a burning, overwhelming desire to do so while Abinadi's words were still fresh on his mind. Besides, he needed something to keep himself occupied and to spend his energies on while he remained concealed.

Far above him in the council chamber, Abinadi was not faring half so well. The moment the guards had left in pursuit of Alma, the king's attention returned to Abinadi. With Alma gone, there remained no one in the chamber who had the least pity or inclination for defending Abinadi and his cause.

The king looked him up and down with a stern, angry glare. Abinadi stood tall and withstood his glare, unflinching and ready to take whatever treatment was in store for him. For a moment, Noah's and Abinadi's eyes caught each other's. A power of wills began. Noah flowed hatred through his stare. Abinadi let the hatred melt beyond him and dissipate without internalizing it. Instead, he stared back, beckoning his enemy to heed his words, change his life, and begin to rule his people with a righteous hand.

Noah tore himself away from the silent war of wills. He shouted to his guards, "Take this man out of my sight! Throw him back into the pit!"

"The pit" was their pet-name for the dungeon-like prison cell in which Abinadi had already spent two wretched nights. When Abinadi was again unceremoniously shoved through the door, he lost his balance and landed on a patch of rotting hay. He heard a couple of the pit's permanent residents scurry off. The door was slammed shut and the locking block put back in place. Virtually all light vanished, leaving the man of God to languish in a most unfitting manner and for an indeterminate amount of time.

Abinadi spent three nights in this untoward prison room. His only visitors were infrequent guards with insufficient provisions of unpalatable food. This is not counting the more frequent visits from the furry fiends who preyed upon themselves and whatever crumbs or leftovers they could steal away from what they felt was an obtrusive cellmate. He could make out the eerie sound of their claws scratching the bare stone as they ran. He made sure to keep his body in the center area of the cell, avoiding the sides and particularly the corners.

The faint light that occasionally flickered underneath the crack in the door was his only earthly companion. Abinadi's mind was not on the things of this world, however. He looked inward and upward with the hope of an eternal rest in a kingdom far better than that in which he now dwelled, with a king more marvelous than any earthly one could dream to be.

Abinadi's thoughts were suddenly brought back to earth when his cell door was jerked open and a blinding flash of torchlight was shoved into his face. His eyes recoiled in pain. Blinded, he relied on his ears to help him discern who had arrived. He could make out the sounds of at least three guards. His arms and wrists felt the harsh ropes wrapped around him afresh and tied off, until the blood was nearly prevented from its routine course to the tips of his appendages.

He was lifted and shoved toward and through the doorway. Each time he regained his balance, he received another quick shove between his shoulder blades. Such was his journey up the stone stairs, through the halls and back into King Noah's royal throne room. Abinadi found himself again kneeling before the unrepentant tyrant.

"Abinadi, we have found an accusation against you," Noah smugly declared. "You are worthy of death. For you have said that God himself should come down among the children of men. For this blasphemy, you will be put to death unless you recall all of the words which you have spoken evil concerning me and my precious people."

"I tell you, I will not recall the words which I have spoken to you concerning this people, for they are true," Abinadi replied, stoically. "It is only to let you know of their surety that I have suffered myself to fall into your hands. I will suffer even until death, but I will not recall my words. They will stand as a testimony against you. If you slay me you will shed innocent blood, and this too will stand as a testimony against you at the last day."

There was something in his words and demeanor that finally pricked the king's conscience. He was on the verge of uttering the words which would set Abinadi free, for he was finally fearful that the judgments of God really would come upon him. His words of pardon were stifled, however, when the chief priest to his right, Amulon, suddenly stood with indignation. He pointed at the captive and shook his finger as he spoke.

"He has reviled the king!" Amulon accused. "He has reviled the king! What more witness do we need?! This treasonous man must be put to death as an example to all those with such treacherous minds and hearts!"

The room soon vibrated with shouts of agreement and anger. The king felt the sweeping fury that now consumed their minds. His men wanted vengeance. They wanted it in his behalf. He did not know how to save face and save this man. He chose to dismiss the man, the feeling he had had, the power of his words, the truths he had been told, and protect his reputation among his peers – no, not his peers, his underlings. His reputation proved to be dearer to him than his very soul. He shouted above the din, "Deliver him to be executed!"

The guards grabbed Abinadi by his shoulders and arms and dragged him through the halls and outside. Abinadi did not struggle. News of the sentence spread rapidly. By the time the guards and royal procession reached the town square, it was filled with onlookers. Sticks, twigs, logs, and boards were hastily gathered and heaped together in the center of the square. The priests created an inner circle, closest to the pile of debris.

Abinadi, already bound from shoulder to ankle, was then tied to a large log which had been placed firmly in the center of the kindling. More kindling was spread around the prophets' feet, knees, and waist as the pile continued to grow. When all of the preparations were complete, the priests parted to allow the king himself to step through their ranks to face his opponent. He strode smugly, sweating from the exertion of the walk. A wicked smile creased his face.

"My life will be valued as a garment in a hot furnace? Is that not what you claimed?" The king smiled wickedly. "I'm afraid I just don't see it, Abinadi. Not today!"

He spat at the prophet. Even this seemed to be too much excursion for the foul man, as a string of spittle clung to and hung from his beard. He took a few steps back and turned toward the torch bearers and nodded for them to step forward. He raised his hand, signaling that they should wait before lighting the wood. Noah then turned back to face the milling crowd. He spoke in a loud, commanding voice.

"This man, this self-supposed prophet, has dared come to our peaceable kingdom and stir up strife. He has mocked myself, your chosen priests, and you fine people. We will now show you what becomes of such evil men who dare to pervert the ways of our fine society!"

Turning to the torch bearers, he commanded in a level tone, "Light it!"

The flames took to the dry wood with deliverance. Rapidly growing flames quickly engulfed the base level of the pyre. King Noah added one final taunt, "What say you now, Abinadi? What do you think of this God who allows such calamities to befall his chosen prophets?"

As the flames began to scorch him, Abinadi responded calmly, matter-of-factly, yet loudly enough to be heard above the crackling fire, and without any hint of pain or fear, "Behold, even as you have done to me, so will it be that your seed will cause that many shall suffer the pains that I suffer, even the pains of death by fire! And, this will be because they believe in the salvation of the Lord their God. You will be afflicted because of your iniquities. You will be driven, scattered, and hunted as a wild animal and taken by the hand of your enemies. Your people will be burdened with tasks grievous to behold. And you, King Noah, shall suffer as I suffer, the pains of death by fire. Thus God executes vengeance on those who destroy his people."

Through all this, Abinadi remained remarkably calm. The words had been spoken as a foretelling or prediction, rather than as a curse or threat. Noah appeared a little unnerved at these words, but quickly shrugged it off. Abinadi looked up toward the heavens and cried out, "Oh, God, receive my soul." With these words his head suddenly fell forward and his entire body went limp, never to move of its own accord again. Perhaps what Noah found most distressing was the look of tranquility and peace that remained on Abinadi's face, even in death.

Chapter 9

Alma

Alma sensed that something was amiss. He put down his writing utensil and gathered the metal plates he had engraved. He quickly put them into the bag which had contained the fruit. He added to it other plates he had previously chosen from the shelves of the vault. No sound could be heard through the thick stone door. Still, he leaned against it and placed his ear on the cold rock, just to be certain.

Stooping, he then pulled the locking stone from its place and gave the door a push. It moved under his weight with a muffled scraping noise. Alma paused a second at that sound, hoping no other ears had detected it. With the door only partially open, he listened again. The only sounds he could discern were the wispy flickers of his torch's flame.

He pushed the door open more, enough to squeeze through with his bag of written treasure. Once out, he closed the door again and replaced the locking stone from without. He wanted to ensure that no one would find the door ajar and guess why it was so, or who had stayed within.

He followed the passage toward the carved stone stairwell. Once at its base, he doused his light, not wanting to pre-announce his movements. Pausing to listen again, he determined it was safe to ascend. Stone stairs never creak, so he was able to move quickly. As he neared the top from his subterranean hideout, he could feel the warm, humid jungle air he had previously taken for granted. The scent of flowers and foliage which it bore brought a welcome relief to him. He breathed in deeply to replace the stagnant, stale air he had suffered through for three days.

Sensing he was still in the clear, he proceeded out of the stairwell and into the hall. Looking both ways, he could see and sense no persons. He considered this to be both puzzling and fortunate. He made his way through the passageways to the back entrance of the city's grand, central building. Finally, he emerged into the open air.

He knew his life was now a precious commodity. To his knowledge, he and Abinadi were the only two living souls who had ever dared to defy the king. Others had defied him over the years, but they were no longer living. In all cases, the king's wrath had been keen and complete. His murderous orders were always quickly and swiftly obeyed by guards who did not want attention focused on them for hesitating. Alma fully recognized the need for stealth and secrecy on his own part now.

He took care to advance without being seen. Although he was pleased with his good fortune, he was surprised at the lack of people he encountered. He had gone a considerable distance and still had not seen a single soul. He made his way to the west side of the city. He knew that the jungle encroached closest on the west.

Once there, he found a ladder and clambered up onto the wall's catwalk. He quickly glanced in both directions to ensure he was not seen. As he looked north, his eye caught hold of something that made him do a double-take. Smoke. Smoke was not so extraordinary in and of itself, but this seemed to be quite a large amount. He found himself drawn to it, in spite of the danger. He found he could not leap over the wall and dash to the rainforest until he discovered why his very soul seemed moved to this billowing phenomenon.

He kept low and quickly darted along the catwalk, recognizing that he was attempting a very foolhardy move. He reasoned that if he were seen, he could be quick enough to dart over the side and dash toward the jungle before any guards would be able to stop him. He continued circling the city toward the town's square on the northern end.

For the first time, he began to see people. They were running forward, also in the direction of the smoke. No one noticed him, as they were too intent on reaching the city square. He raced along above their heads on the catwalk, continuing onward and beyond the dense crowd. He was getting ever closer to a view of the base of the telltale trail of smoke.

When he finally lunged forward beyond the final building which blocked his view, he stopped cold. There was the heart of the crowd, gathered in the city square, held back by a circle of priests and guards. There was King Noah standing forward facing the source of the smoke. And, there was Abinadi helplessly bound to a burning pillar. Alma nearly shouted, "No!" but forced the word to die in his throat. He could just make out Abinadi's final words, "Oh, God, receive my soul!" as the prophet's body went limp.

Alma was torn to pieces within himself. He desperately wanted to free the man whom he barely knew, but loved and admired in a way he could not yet understand. A voice within him spoke reason to his racing mind and told him that now was the time to disappear. He found himself on the outer side of the wall, letting himself down with a rope, without consciously realizing where he had found the rope, or when he had tied it off.

He hit the ground running and was in the rainforest before the crowd's focus had shifted away from the king's "example." Once within the shadows of the jungle, Alma did not stop running. He continued onward and onward in a straight course. His mind sped even faster than his feet.

"What does it all mean? How can Abinadi be dead? Who will take up his cause? How will Noah be brought down to justice? Will he be brought down at all? Surely, he must! The Lord has to have had a purpose in this. Who will carry on the work?"

He was sweating profusely, and panting heavily. His lungs burned within him, but not half so much as his heart and soul. Dozens of urgent questions and fretful thoughts continued to pummel his mind as he raced. Alma finally sat to rest on a boulder by the edge of a large pool of pure water at the base of some hills.

He was so caught up in what he had witnessed over the past few days, that he was wholly oblivious to the beauty of the area he had entered. A small waterfall cascaded into the pool, offering a serene, constant rushing sound that soothed his nerves. With his mind and body throbbing, he placed his sandaled feet into the waters. The water's cooling effect sent tingles through his vibrating body. He looked at his feet, still submerged in the clear liquid.

He marveled at the peaceful and calming effect the water brought throughout his entire body, although only his feet rested within it. As he pondered this impact, it dawned on him what needed to happen next. Abinadi had brought cooling, cleansing water to a parched city. He was only one man, but he had already affected another. Alma realized that it was now some other man's turn to bring the water, or the serenity that it represented, to the people.

He sensed that he now had a critical mission to fulfill. But, he felt so unworthy. His life had been caught up in the evils that Noah had professed. He knew all too well the iniquities he himself had committed. His was a tarnished soul. Surely the Lord would not want such a vile servant as he had been. Surely there would be someone else to succeed Abinadi!

He stepped from the water and knelt by the large rock, collapsing in anguish as he did so. He cried bitter tears and pled with the Lord to forgive him of his many transgressions. He sought the forgiveness and redemption of which Abinadi had spoken. The very thought of his playing any sort of role in freeing these people from the bondage of sin and iniquity with which they had allowed themselves to be bound, burned, and scoffed at him. He knew his sins, and he knew the Lord knew them too.

He thought of his dear young wife, whom he had betrayed far too often in seeking the acceptance of his King and the other priests. He thought of his tender, infant son whom he had vainly named after himself and realized the wicked course his example was plotting for the boy's life. He was ashamed, embarrassed. He was also angry with himself. During his soul-searching, he had gained an entirely new perspective on what his wife and young child meant to him.

More importantly, perhaps, he had begun to gain a perspective of what he, and his influence, meant to them. He realized for the first time that as a husband and father he had a sacred obligation to these two people that no other person could fill. And, he realized with self-bitterness that he had failed miserably in his role.

Unavoidable questions began to pummel him like a heavy rain. Why did he allow himself to do things he knew were wrong? Why did he persist? Why did it take another man to wake him from his state of guile? How could he ever face his wife and look her in the eye again? How could anyone, especially the Lord, ever want to associate with him again? How could he possibly return to the Lord's good graces? Was it even possible?

Abinadi had said it was. Or, had he? Had he truly said such a thing? Surely not. Surely that was too great a thing to believe. Alma picked up the bag of metal plates he had borne, almost absentmindedly, with him on his hectic journey. He carefully pulled out the record of Abinadi. He read it again and again, slowly, thoroughly, thoughtfully, longingly. He poured over the words with the earnestness of his soul; pondering, studying, seeking, yearning in a way he had never done so before.

It became unmistakable. It was unbelievably true. It was nothing short of miraculous and merciful. Truly, Abinadi had said it was possible for even a wretch as he was to return to the Lord's side. Abinadi had made it clear that teaching such forgiveness, as the result of sincere repentance, was not only his own mission, but that of the promised Messiah. Abinadi had further explained that he had come to call the king and his court to repentance. If this was so, should that not include him? Should not the mercies of God be able to extent to such a wretch as himself? It was too much to believe. It was too great a thing to even hope for.

But, surely it must be true. He had felt his heart burn in the presence of Abinadi. It was not just the burning of shame and guilt. He knew it was the burning that comes from being in the presence of a man of God, of feeling the Spirit of the Lord work upon him. If he could feel the Spirit, should that not mean that the Spirit was trying to reach him? To help him? To cleanse him?

As unworthy as he felt, he earnestly sought for the Lord's forgiveness and direction. He knew his life needed changing and he knew he needed the Lord's help to make a lasting change. He also knew this would not be easy. But, he earnestly, sincerely, and aggressively sought for the Lord's loving mercy to help bring him back to a spiritually and morally sound life.

The sun rose and set at least twice before Alma finished his prayers. All the while, he held the plates close to him. They had truly become a sacred record and guide for him.

*****

The curtains did their best, but patches of torchlight still crept through tiny gaps and played on the walls of the building across the alleyway. Alma crept up to the window and listened intently to the hushed voices that debated within. His suspicions were quickly confirmed.

"I'm telling you, the king has gone too far! He was an innocent man!" a deep voice stated.

"I'll never forget how his body just went limp at the very moment he cried out!" another added.

"But, what can we do? He's the king!" a third pointed out.

From out in the street, Alma spoke into the window, "I have an idea," he said.

All of those within the room jumped with a start, filled with fear. "Who said that?" the deep voiced queried.

"I did," Alma replied from outside the house.

Those in the room were more than a little concerned when they saw the door begin to open. One of them ran to it, intending to hold it in place. He was silently stopped by a warning shake of the head by the muscular, deep-voiced man. If they were to be discovered this night, it had already occurred. If not, then perhaps this would be a new friend to their cause. The man backed up and let the door swing open, while everyone held their breath.

Alma's head appeared from behind the swinging obstruction and he entered the room. Air was let out in gasps.

"Alma! Is it truly you?" the deep-voiced man asked in surprise.

"Yes, Helam, it is," the fugitive replied.

"We have heard all sorts of stories. We were certain you were dead, but no one could account for when and where!" Helam said with excitement.

"I can. And, I assure you I that am not dead, though I believe the king wishes it so. As to the 'where,' I found a place with a pool of clear water not far from here. I have been spending my time there trying to gather my wits and determine what we should do next."

"Do next? That is precisely what we are trying to figure out," Helam said.

"I gathered that. Are you open to some opinions?"

"We're open to leadership," Helam admitted. "We've only heard snatches of what Abinadi preached to the king. If it is at all similar to what he said on the city wall, it must have been awfully impressive!"

"It was. That it was," Alma said with a tinge of sadness. "The world has lost a truly great man. One we need desperately right now."

"I fear for the Nephite people at this time," Helam said. "He did much to wake us up to the arrogance we have displayed before God. The Lord has been patient with us. But, I do not know how much longer his patience will last."

"I was there, you know. Right there in the court. I heard it all," Alma said with a touch of melancholy. "I tried to stop them. I told the king to let him be, but then they came after me. I'm certain if I'm found I'm as good as dead."

"Yes, you are!" Shadra confirmed. "The king's guards have been going through the city specifically asking for you. Anyone who knows your whereabouts is to report it directly to the king's guards. Anyone caught harboring you or withholding information about you can be put to death – without a trial. They're very anxious to make an example of you. Our lives are in danger simply because you are here."

"I feared as much, and I am sorry."

"Don't be," a man named Ezra corrected. "We need you. We've been searching for you ourselves. We've allowed ourselves to become enslaved to our own base desires, and have given honor to a man not worthy of being called a man, let alone 'king.' We need you to lead us back to truth."

"I appreciate your vote of confidence." Alma put his hand on Ezra's shoulder, then he turned back to the rest. "Truly, I never planned this. Yet, I feel the Spirit guiding me. When I fled the king's court I dashed down and hid myself in the record chamber."

"The record chamber! So, that's where!" Shadra could not help himself. The grand mystery had been solved.

"Yes, I stayed there for three days. While there, I wrote down everything I could recall Abinadi speak to the king and his priests. I could feel the Spirit with me. It was as if I was listening to the entire discussion again. I feel as though I must have written it word for word. While I was there I also had plenty of time to peruse the records. They were far too dusty and stiff from lack of use. I took the liberty of collecting what I believed to be the most critical records. It is time for this people to be taught the word of the Lord again."

"With all that we have witnessed these past few days, we have to wholly agree with you, Alma," Helam said, shaking his head slowly in agreement.

"It's plain that we can't teach within the city, not for long, anyway. We are bound to be discovered," Alma observed. "I know a place where I believe we will be safe. It's a bit of a hike west of here. I don't think the king will suspect. We should be safe there, and be able to speak openly. I'll share with you the words of Abinadi, but also the words from the other ancient prophets that have been left unspoken for far too long. It's time this people began to learn of the Messiah and the great and everlasting atonement He will make for this people and all mankind. You need to spread the word and have all who earnestly want to learn come and meet with us. But, beware of spies. We can't be too careful."

Then, he turned to Helam to ask him something more personal, "Helam, you are my oldest and most trusted friend."

Helam nodded, and asked, "What is it, Alma? I sense you need something important."

"I do. What can you tell me of Naomi?"

"She is well," Helam responded. His face remained serious. "Well enough, considering. At least, no harm has come to her yet."

Alma was visibly relieved to hear this. "Thank goodness," he said. "I have been terribly worried about her and young Alma's safety these many days. Noah knows where I lived – where they live. I was afraid he would take out his anger towards me, on them!"

"He very nearly did," Helam confirmed. "When they failed to find you, he sent his guards to your house. They nearly tore the walls down searching for you. They made a shambles of the place. Then they grabbed Naomi and the baby and hauled them before the king. He was about to have them put to death, when one of the other priests spoke up in their behalf. I believe it was Amulon."

"Amulon!" Alma said with surprise. "He spoke up for them? Of all people, I would never expect Amulon to save them from –"

"Don't be too grateful, Alma," Helam interrupted. "He was doing nothing out of mercy or kindness. He couldn't care less for their safety. He simply pointed out to Noah that if you were to return, it's possible you would seek them out. He suggested that they would have a better chance of finding you if Naomi and little Alma were returned to their home and allowed to go about life as normal. Of course, he has guards and spies stationed all around that area. If you even set foot near your home, you will be spotted and pounced upon like a hungry jaguar seizes its prey!"

"I suspected as much," Alma sighed. "That is why I came here first. I didn't want to risk going home. Not yet, anyway."

"I suggest you don't risk it ever," Helam stressed. "Besides, there's no need to."

"What? What do you mean?" Alma asked, clearly confused.

"It was on market day, just two days ago," Helam explained, "That we decided to free Naomi from her prison. She had taken little Alma with her, as she must, and had gone to the market. Guards followed her as always. But, as you can imagine, the guards had to stay back a ways, lest you see them and stop from contacting her. We knew this, and planned our little scheme accordingly."

"Little scheme? What little scheme?" Alma asked with renewed interest.

"Shadra and Ezra worked out the details," Helam smiled. "I should let them tell you this part."

"I had a hand-wagon loaded higher than my head with baskets," Shadra said rather gleefully.

"And, I had a table full of bags of grain," Ezra added.

"You know how crowded the square is on market day," Shadra hinted.

"Yes? Yes?" Alma coaxed.

"Well, I just pushed my overloaded wagon through the crowd, just as innocently as I could," Shadra explained. He held his arms out as he talked, pantomiming a recreation of the event. "I looked left and right, calling out to anyone interested in purchasing them. Of course, I ignored anyone who showed interest and just kept moving along. I made sure I was headed straight for Ezra's grain, but first I wanted to make sure Naomi passed between us. Just as she did, I closed the gap, all the while, I had to make it look as if I had no idea Ezra was there."

"Oh, but when he plowed into my table and spilled my precious grain, EVERYONE knew I was there!" Ezra said with an even bigger grin.

"We made quite a fuss!" Shadra admitted.

"You have never heard two men squabble that loudly!" Ezra said. "We went at it tooth and nail. We called each other every name we could and even made up a few. Meanwhile, Shadra made a pretense of trying to pick up his scattered baskets, while I kept scooping up handfuls of grain and dumping it back onto my table. Of course, it kept spilling off like a waterfall, so I was able to keep at it for quite some time. All the while I angrily shouted threats and accusations at Shadra."

"Which I enthusiastically reciprocated," Shadra pointed out.

"By the time it was all over, Naomi and her baby were far away and quite safe," Helam concluded.

"But, how?" Alma asked.

"While these two went at each other's throats," Helam continued. "I and a couple others grabbed Naomi and the child. I hushed her and let her see me. She was startled, but when she recognized me, she quickly realized something was afoot. We had her duck her head and put on a different shawl as we quickly pulled her through the crowd and toward the nearest alleyway.

The guards were so flustered with the baskets and grain that they couldn't see what was happening."

"They kept trying to get around us, but I'm afraid our argument was quite animated," Ezra admitted.

"We just kept moving around, pretending to pick up our goods while innocently arguing. We made sure that we blocked the guards at every pass," Shadra said.

"They got quite frustrated," Ezra observed. "Finally, they just pushed us both over. Shadra still has a mark on his forehead from where his head hit my table."

Shadra pulled up his bangs and let the bruise be seen. Alma winced at the palm-sized wound. "It was more than worth it," Shadra confided.

"Once we had her in the alleyway, the rest was easy," Helam said. "I led her to my home, while another of us grabbed the baby and came by a different way, just in case."

"You led her to your home?" Alma asked. "You mean here? Is she here now?!"

"I certainly am!" Naomi said from the hallway.

"Naomi!" Alma said, running to her. "I've been so worried! Are you all right?" he said, hugging and kissing her. She did the same, repeating his name and crying for joy. After a moment, he suddenly stopped, realization striking his soul. He held her arms and stepped back from her and in all seriousness said, "I've been such a fool! I've been terrible to you, and to little Alma. I'm so, so sorry," he said shamefully.

"I know," she replied. "I know, but I'm just so happy to see you're safe. I feared the worst!"

"Those days are gone now, sweetheart," Alma committed. "I swear to you, those days are gone. It seems like so long ago now –" his voice drifted off again, but he quickly recovered and added, "I've changed. That man, that wonderful brave man, Abinadi, has brought a change to me. His words struck me like no other words could. I've finally actually studied the word of the Lord. I've prayed. I've begged and pleaded for the Lord's forgiveness. I feel He has seen fit to grant it. But, now I must beg for your forgiveness." Alma fell to his knees holding Naomi's hands in his. "I'm terribly, terribly sorry for all of the pain and suffering I've put you through. I can't imagine what it must have been like. I promise you, those days are over. I'm now ready to be yours and yours alone forever and always. Can you ever, possibly forgive me?"

Alma let go of his wife's hands, his hed bowed low. He honestly didn't know what to expect by way of reply. He knew all too well what a sinful past he was trying to bury. Naomi had every right to turn her back and walk away from him. He half expected her to. He desperately hoped that she wouldn't. He had no idea what he would do if she did. But, he was sincere in his repentance, bitterly, eternally sincere. He was a changed man in both heart and soul.

She would have no way of knowing this, but he did. He knew his own sins in a way he had never known them before. He was appalled and abhorred by them. He could not fathom how he had been able to pursue them previously. He could not see how he could have even tolerated them, let alone sought after them so completely, even gleefully. Now that he had fully tasted of the love and instruction of the Lord, never again would he allow such base behavior to enter into his heart and soul.

But, how would Naomi react to his claims of renewal and commitment? She had nothing to go on, but his word. And, his word to her had been broken so many times before. Alma searched her eyes, longing to hear a merciful reply. The seconds seemed like lifetimes as he waited. To the others in the room, her answer seemed immediate.

"Oh, Alma, of course I forgive you!" she said pulling him to his feet, tears trickling down her fair cheeks. "I have always known you had a good heart. I've just been waiting – longing for – and praying that one day you would come to your senses!"

Alma was beside himself with relief and joy, "Oh, Naomi! I will be yours forever!" he said as they embraced once more.

Chapter 10
The Waters of Mormon

Not too far west of the land of Nephi was a place which was called Mormon. The king had named this land Mormon because it was occasionally infested with wild beasts. Be this as it may, there were no wild beasts in the land at this time of year. The land was far from uninhabited, however, at least not in recent days. In this tranquil land there was a large pool of pure water, fed by a cascading waterfall that flowed down from the nearby foothills. It was here that Alma had fled after the burning of Abinadi. And, it was here he repeatedly returned to with his followers to preach the gospel and allow them to feel a burning in their bosoms.

What began with a few dozen had grown over the weeks to be a couple hundred souls. They had gathered again at the water's edge in the wilderness. Alma had finished reviewing the words of Abinadi several weeks previously and had spent a great deal of time teaching from the "book of the prophets" the words of Moses, Isaiah, Jeremiah, and other great men whose words were written in the sacred records their forefathers had taken with them on their voyage to the Promised Land.

This particular day's sermon had been on the covenants which one must enter into to show their God that they have humbled themselves before Him and are willing to show an outward token of their obedience. In particular, he taught of the covenant of baptism.

"Behold, here there is much water." Alma gave a wide sweeping gesture toward the clear, renewing pool of water with his arm as he spoke. "And now I know that you are desirous to come into the fold of God, and to be called His people. I know that you are willing to bear one another's burdens, that they may be light, and to mourn with those who mourn, and comfort those that stand in need of comfort. I also know that you wish to stand as witnesses of God at all times and in all things, and in all places that you may be in, even until death, that you may be redeemed of God, and receive eternal life. Now, if this is the desire of your hearts, what have you against being baptized in the name of the Lord, as a witness before Him that you have entered into a covenant with Him that you will serve Him and keep His commandments, that He may pour out His Spirit more abundantly upon you?"

When the people heard these words, they clapped their hands for joy, and shouted, "This IS the desire of our hearts!"

Alma took Helam by the hand. They waded into the water and stood before the congregation. Alma held Helam's wrist firmly with his left hand and raised his right arm to the square behind Helam's back. He then spoke with a loud voice saying, "Oh, Lord, pour out thy Spirit upon thy servant, that he may do this work with holiness of heart."

The Spirit of the Lord came upon Alma in a most powerful manner. His face radiated a peaceful glow. Alma continued and said, "Helam, I baptize you, having authority from the Almighty God, as a testimony that you have entered into a covenant to serve him until you are dead as to the mortal body. May the Spirit of the Lord be poured out upon you. May he grant unto you eternal life, through the redemption of the Messiah whom He has prepared from the foundation of the world. Amen."

Upon this, Alma buried Helam, and himself, in the water and brought them both up again. He allowed himself to be baptized with Helam, in essence, as a sign of his own humility and acceptance of the Call and authority he had received from the Lord. They both came out of the crystal-clear water praising God and rejoicing. Alma reached his hand out for another soul. Ezra entered the water with him and was also baptized. Only this time, Alma buried only Ezra in the water, and remained above the surface himself. That day Alma baptized some two hundred and four souls.

Of all the souls that gave him pleasure to see enter into this eternal covenant with their Lord, no soul gave him greater joy than that of his beloved wife. He was pleased, honored, and humbled to take her by the hand and lead her into the waters of baptism. Tears of gratitude filled both their eyes as he pronounced the baptismal prayer and then sacredly lowered her under the waters. After he raised her up again, she hugged her husband with love and thankfulness for the change he had brought – not only on himself – but on so many of their dear friends and neighbors as well.

After this great act, they formed themselves into an official church and called it the Church of God. Alma ordained priests to help preside over and teach the members of the church, ordaining one priest for every fifty members. He instructed the priests to teach the people only those things which had been spoken by the mouth of the holy prophets, which was repentance and faith in the redeeming power of the coming Messiah.

He also commanded them that there should be no contention with each other, but that they should look forward with one eye, having one faith and one baptism, having their hearts knit together in unity and in love one towards another. He commanded that they should teach and live by the commandments given to Moses on Mount Sinai, as well as many other great and wise principles. He also made it a point that the priests should work for their living and not rely on the bounties of the congregation, knowing that this practice had been a contributor to the laziness and idolatry of the priests of King Noah.

* * * * *

This fledgling church, reborn from the ashes of iniquity, continued to prosper and grow in spite of its need for public anonymity and secrecy. The king's men continued to hunt for Alma. Noah's anger continued to grow at the frequent reports of sightings of, and close encounters of nearly catching, Alma. What angered him even more were the rumors of a movement among the people. He had his guards search the city in vain for any possible meeting places. In all cases, their attempts resulted in not a single capture.

"Give me your report!" Noah demanded of his officer.

"Your majesty, I fear I do not bear news worthy of reporting."

"Give me whatever news you bear!" the king roared.

"My men continue to hear of this Messiah movement, but they have yet to gather any tangible evidence of its existence, or any distinct witnesses of the so-called believers."

"This is preposterous!" the king bellowed, spilling his goblet of wine. "We have been searching for these people for months! And all you can tell me is that they seem to exist!"

The officer held his peace. The priests did likewise. None of them wanted to draw attention to themselves, lest they become the focus of the king's wrath. Noah shifted in his stately seat, tugging at his beard. Finally, he stopped his fidgeting and pointed a pudgy finger to his officer again.

"Your men have been going out in uniform, have they not?"

"Certainly, your majesty! They represent the king!"

"Not anymore. Have them go about privately in the garb of ordinary citizens. Perhaps we can smoke them out with a more casual approach. Have your men feign as if they would join this 'movement.' Perhaps then we can find their meeting place and take them all."

"A marvelous idea, your majesty!" the king's right-hand priest, Amulon, responded.

"Of course it is!" Noah replied. Turning his attention back to his officer, he rudely commanded, "Now, go and do as I have said!"

* * * * *

Six weeks later, it was a much cheerier officer kneeling before his king.

"Report," the king commanded.

"Oh, great and wise king. We have done just as you have commanded. I sent my men about the people. For weeks, nothing new was discovered. Recently, however, one of my men came across a small group discussing matters in the marketplace. He edged in and voiced an interest in their discussion. They spoke of the Messiah. He said he yearned to know more of this prophecy. He said their faces lit up. They asked what he knew and he shared those fables that are commonly known among us all. He asked if they knew more and how he could be taught. He spent the morning in discussion with them. These discussions continued for over the course of several days. Finally, they announced that there would be a meeting later that day and asked if he cared to join them."

The king and his court maintained an avid interest in this news. The officer beamed with pride at being able to give this report of a successful infiltration.

"He said it would do his soul good to do so. That afternoon, he met the group at the south gate of the city. They hurried north close along the west wall so that the tower guards could not see them. They continued until they reached the portion of the wall where the jungle is nearest. Then they dashed across the plain to the trees. They began a journey through the jungle to the designated meeting place. All the while, they encountered other groups of travelers also bent on attending this meeting of traitors."

"And, how far was it?!" the king demanded.

"It was only a couple hours' march. He attended the meeting long enough to get a feel for the size of the group, then sneaked off, excusing himself, to return and give his report to me."

"How big was their group?" Amulon asked.

"He estimated only a few hundred persons."

"Does your soldier know the way back to the site?" the king asked.

"Certainly, your majesty! There would have been no point in his going otherwise."

"Marvelous. We have them now! Send word. Tomorrow we will rid ourselves of this insurrection once and for all!" the king declared with glee.

* * * * *

"Alma! Alma! I've just come from the king's throne room. I have terrible news!" the guard announced.

Alma ceased speaking to the multitude and listened to the report.

"We've been found out. The king sent a spy. He knows this place. Your lives are in danger! You must leave quickly!"

"Thank you, Enorum, we knew this would happen eventually. It was good of you to maintain your position in silence for so long."

"I came as soon as my shift ended."

Alma turned to the outdoor congregation. "We have been discovered. The king will take us if he can. Now is the time to take the possessions we have stored and make our journey into the wilderness. We can't return here again. Go and gather your families, tents, and provisions. We will meet north of here, as we have spoken of so often in the past, at nightfall. Hurry!"

*****

"I'm telling you, this is the place, the very place!" the soldier swore. "They were here, you can tell. Look at how the grass is matted down. You can tell that many people have been right here!" He motioned emphatically to the ground with both hands. "They said they would be here by now."

"Well, whether they were or not, they're certainly not here now," the officer responded.

"Maybe we beat them here and they'll arrive any moment! We should wait," the soldier suggested.

"Yes, well, I tell you what, you wait for them. I have a report to make to the king. I give you credit that it looks like we have indeed found their gathering place, but I suspect that now that we've shown up here they're not likely to return. The king's not going to like this. Not at all!"

*****

"What?! What do you mean, 'It looks like they have left'?!" the king demanded.

"It's just as I've said," the officer replied, trying to remain calm. "It was evident that a large group of people had been there, but they were gone. The tracks seemed no more than a day or so old. We couldn't have missed them by much. I sent out search parties to comb the area, but the only tracks we could find headed back here. My guess is they must have returned to the city."

"They're here?! In the city?!" the king's eyes grew wide.

"Well, I wouldn't say that exactly -"

"What do you mean you would not say that? You just did!"

"No, sir, your majesty. I said they likely returned, I do not believe they're still here. They probably returned, gathered their things, and then left for good. I do not think you will have to worry about them any more."

"I'm not interested in your opinion of what I need to worry about!" the king roared, causing the officer to cringe. "I wanted those traitors back to face justice! I can't believe you let them slip through your fingers!"

"With all due respect, your majesty, each year you have forced more and more of my men out of service by refusing to provide them with any means of sustenance from which to survive. You have done this for so many years now that my forces are too far depleted to be of much affect. The wilderness is a large area. We just do not have the resources to cover all of it adequately."

"I do not care about your excuses! I wanted those people back! If you can't do this, then perhaps I need an officer who can!"

"Perhaps so, your majesty, but I seriously doubt you would be able to find one."

"Why you insolent miscreant! How dare you mock me?"

"Sir, I meant no disrespect, I simply do not know of any man, officer, or existing army, that would be able to track people in this wilderness," the officer bowed low, hoping he had managed to pull his life out of jeopardy. "Your majesty, I believe you should be more concerned about your other subjects."

"What do you mean?! Speak plainly!"

"While you have your army off searching the wilderness for dissenters who will not be found, your remaining subjects are gathering and plotting their own rebellions. Word among them is that they are no longer citizens, but prisoners. They say that your efforts to stop Alma and his followers from leaving is proof of this. They say they have no intention of letting themselves be held captive by a lazy and idolatrous king. It appears Abinadi has had a bigger impact on your people than you thought."

The king fumed throughout the officer's discourse. Finally, in a pique of frustration and a loss for words, he merely shouted "Aah! Be gone!" and waved his flabby arm at the man.

The officer bowed briefly then quickly exited, thanking his lucky stars that he would live to breathe another day. Noah threw his wine goblet as the door closed behind the officer. It smashed against the wooden door and splattered sweet and rich-smelling liquid on the inner guards. Neither guard flinched or dared to move. They simply allowed the wine to drip down their cheeks, as they stared blindly forward, hoping this would be the only taste of the king's wrath that they would feel.

*****

"Gideon, it's just as you feared," a Nephite stated. "The king is on a rampage. He is planning on 'purging the city of these rebellious traitors' as he put it. I fear no man will be safe. We already know what he did to Abinadi."

"Someone must put a stop to this!" Gideon declared. "I'm tired of waiting for others to wake up to truth and need. I still regret how I blindly sat by and allowed him to destroy Abinadi. I don't think I will ever be able to live with myself for not at least trying to prevent that travesty. No more!" He drew his sword and swore, "Too many god-fearing men have already died! The king must be stopped and I will do it myself if I have to! This I swear!"

Chapter 11

Gideon

Alma and his followers moved surprisingly quickly through the trees and brush. Even their flocks moved quickly and avoided dallying at waterholes. Rather than complain about the long journey, the children were among the lead, racing to the tops of hills and challenging the others to match their speed. It was as if God himself were speeding them on their way.

They covered ground at twice the pace that Alma had feared they would. Somehow they maintained the pace for a week and a day. Just before Alma had intended to give the command to stop for lunch on the eighth day, Helam, who led the advance party, came bounding back toward Alma and the others. His face was glowing with excitement.

"Alma! Alma! We've found it! Surely we've found it!" he shouted.

"Found it?! What do you mean?" Alma asked incredulously.

"The land in which God intends us to live! I have never felt so inspired by a land's beauty as by this!"

"Is it far?"

"No! Just through those trees!" Helam pointed his muscular arm to a group of trees some twenty yards straight ahead.

Naomi turned to Alma. She said nothing, but the sparkle in her eyes told him that she was hoping the same thing he was. Perhaps they would soon be able to start their new lives in a new home and put all of the bitter memories from their past behind them, where they belonged. She smiled and Alma put his arm around her and pulled her to him.

Little Alma was carefully bundled in his wraps. His father cradled with a firm, yet delicate, grip with his left arm. As his parents lovingly embraced, the tiny baby stirred, blinked his eyes, squirmed his head left and right and then looked up into his father's deep brown eyes. The infant smiled brightly, causing both parents to laugh.

"It looks like little Alma already approves of this land, Helam," he said to his friend.

Alma led his people onward. Those nearest him could not have helped but hear Helam's enthusiastic report. Word spread quickly to the others. By the time Alma and the forward party had reached the trees to which Helam had pointed, everyone was anxiously aware of what may lay beyond them. Their spirits were very high.

Alma paused at the edge of the trees, perceiving an unusually warm feeling come over him. He sensed that Helam's words were on the verge of coming true. Without conscious intent, he took a large breath as he raised his sword and pushed aside the draping vines that concealed his future home from sight.

As the vines moved aside, bright sunlight caught the metal of his blade and blinded him momentarily. He tilted the sword away and freed his eyes to gaze ahead. He saw an unusually large clearing in the jungle. As he scanned its expanse, a large group of beautiful multi-colored birds stirred in the center, took to flight, and then circled the area before disappearing westward over the tree tops.

Alma's breath left him. The northern edge of the plain butted up against a steep hill. A cascading waterfall split the hill in two. Its river flowed southward then split into two smaller rivers with one feeding the western area, and the other flowing farther east where it also formed, filled, and continuously refilled a large body of crystal clear water. The plain itself was covered with lush, green grasses and flowers of a dozen colors.

"I would have to say that Helam is right!" Alma managed to say at last. "We should set up camp over there," he said, pointing toward the natural pool. He turned back toward those who were pressing forward and emerging from the trees in slowly increasing numbers, he exclaimed, "It looks like we have found our new home!"

His pronouncement was met with exuberant shouts of praise, enthusiasm and relief. It was not long before many tired feet found rest and relief by soaking in the burbling waters that flowed out of the pool. Their first tests of the water revealed the hoped-for absence of any piranha or "devil fish" as they were more commonly referred to. The ground took little urging from their shovels to reveal a rich, dark, and fertile soil. It appeared that they had found a bit of paradise.

Alma pointed to the far western end of the field. He said in a loud voice, "We will build our homes and shops there. The Lord willing, our efforts will turn this into a beautiful city and a land of peace." Turning to his smiling wife, he added in a more subdued tone to her alone, "We have found a place where we can raise our children to learn to love and serve the Lord." Both parents embraced as they thought warmly of the possibilities for their future together.

✳ ✳ ✳ ✳ ✳

Gideon leaned against the post and waited silently. He knew that the king would pass by at any moment. He stood just under the shade of the fruit vendor's canopy, ignoring the milling crowd of those who bought and sold. He knew the king enjoyed observing the Nephites' wives from afar as they went about shopping on market day. Soon, the king would emerge from his protected sanctuary and into the open. Gideon fingered the hilt of his sword waiting with expectation. Soon, the city would be freed from the oppressions inflicted on them by "his obesity," as Gideon mockingly referred to his despised leader.

He watched the walkway leading to the city square from the central building which housed the throne room and protected the monarch. He kept a steady gaze, ignoring the soft, warm breeze which carried the fragrant smells of lush jungle flowers throughout the city. The vendor had to repeat himself three times before Gideon became aware of the request to either buy something or move on.

He turned and verbally defended himself with the impatient businessman as he moved to a different spot. As he leaned against a wall on the opposite side of the walkway, he kept his eyes staring down toward the exit with unblinking diligence. It seemed it had already grown too late. The peak shopping hour was already in full swing. Surely the king would normally have been in position by now.

He looked back toward the square to confirm again that it was in fact already full. As he began to turn back toward his vigilant study of the walkway, something caught his eye. It was a group of people, or some such. He turned back and took a better look. It was the king! He was milling personally among the people! How had he gotten out there? Why was he in the square itself, instead of in his chair on the flat-roofed inn? He must have come out the other exit. Why?

No matter. Now that he had located him, Gideon would make his move. The king was busily talking to two women. His two guards were on either side of him, keeping the push of the crowd back. Gideon tunneled his way through the crowd making a subtle approach. He did not want to give away his intent and decided to swing wide to the east and then turn and come in from the north. He kept his eyes away from the king, to avert any suspicion of his intent.

The square was unusually full this day. His progress was slowed. He looked toward the king and was shocked to not see him. Panic gripped his heart. Where had he gone? He quickly looked right, but could not see his prey. He turned to look left and walked right into a lady named Hannah, knocking her baskets to the ground.

"I'm terribly sorry," he apologized, "I didn't see you!"

"That's all right. It happens all too often, I'm afraid," Hannah responded in a good-natured tone. This seemed to her to be an unusual method for this handsome stranger to choose to meet her. Gideon was too preoccupied to notice her deep brown eyes and dimpled smile as she stooped and began to gather her things.

Gideon leaned down to help her, but as he did so, his eyes scanned left, searching. He paused suddenly in mid-stoop. There, not more than a dozen yards away was the king! He stood up straight again. The king's eyes met Gideon's. Gideon knew it would give himself away, but he could not help it. As he looked at the king, his eyes narrowed threateningly. Noah seemed to sense their intent and a flush filled his cheeks. The woman's voice interrupted Gideon's thoughts.

"If it's not too much trouble, I could use a bit of a hand, before my goods are trampled," Hannah called up from below.

Gideon looked down between the milling pairs of legs. He saw her desperately trying to gather her wares. Three baskets lay on their sides. Grain had spilled from one and was under the serious threat of being trodden upon. Grain was one of their most basic and necessary staples. Hannah was scooping it together with her bare hands back into her basket.

Gideon looked back toward Noah briefly as he bent down to help. Noah was no longer facing him. Gideon was in an even greater hurry than before. He dropped down and began quickly scooping the grain into the basket.

"I appreciate your enthusiasm, but I would really only like the grain, not the street too!" Hannah teased, assuming this was a chance to get to know this handsome stranger.

"Oh, I'm sorry, I'm – uh – here." Gideon was heavily distracted.

He continued to scoop the grain and dirt together. The basket was quickly filled and Gideon grabbed the other two and essentially pushed them into the woman's open arms. She was surprised and flustered.

"Here! Here, good as new!" he declared while trying to pull away from the incident.

"Well, thank you, but I –" she tried to protest, all the while maintaining her good nature, but was admittedly confused.

"Yes, no need for thanks. I must be gone." Hannah stood back, bewildered. This handsome man was going to just run away, leaving her with her wares in disarray and somehow he seemed to think he had done her a favor. She could think of no reply to give him. As flustered as she was, she had to admit that there was more than just a hint of longing as she watched this dashing stranger scurry about with an evident purpose that she did not understand.

Gideon handled the hilt of his sword again and looked for the king. He was completely out of sight. Gideon began to push his way through the crowd, bumping several, quickly-irritated shoppers. He looked from one vendor to another. He saw groups of people here and there. He scanned each quickly and moved about trying to survey every head and face for the king's. It soon became evident that he had utterly lost Noah.

He knew that he would never have another chance like this. He knew he had given himself away to Noah and that as soon as Noah was back in his throne room, he would send out orders to seize him. Angry and frustrated, he kicked the ground and then started off to the right of the square. Far beyond it, his eye caught sight of movement down the way. He looked again, only to sense that something had just disappeared beyond a distant corner. He forced his way through the final ten yards of the crowd, leaving an angry trail of jostled on-lookers in his wake.

With effort, he eventually managed to break free of the crowd. He charged down the stone-paved street. He ignored the houses with large clay pots outside each doorstep as he ran. Nor did he notice the young children at play as he dashed passed them. Finally, he rounded the corner he had seen the shape pass beyond. His suspicion was gratified. Far ahead, he saw the king and his two guards hustling away.

The king huffed and puffed, unable to remember a time in which he had moved so quickly or so far in so short a time. The two guards stayed by either side. Either one could have easily outdistanced the king, but that was not their intent. They intended to stay by his side and ensure that his majesty was safe. Gideon perceived that he would be able to catch and overtake them long before they would reach the sanctuary of the city's central building.

A smile overtook his face. He quickened his pace. The king looked back and saw his worst fears realized. The rumors he had dismissed were true. An assassin was hot on his trail, and he was as exposed as a plump snail out of its shell. The king stumbled as he looked back. An alert guard grabbed his arm and forced his majesty back into step.

"Hurry, your majesty! You must hurry! That is Gideon, I've heard he is quite the swordsman! We must get you back to the throne room," the guard ordered.

"No! Look! – The – tower! The – tower!" the king panted as he spoke.

"Yes, your majesty! Brilliant!" the second guard acknowledged.

The trio was only a few paces from the city's watchtower. King Noah had built it years earlier as a means of overseeing his kingdom. In a way, it was also a tower of spite, not just arrogance. From its peak he could see beyond the jungle that separated the land of Nephi from the land of Shemlon, and thus peer into the realm of the Lamanites. In recent years, the structure was seldom used. But it still towered over the city.

Gideon was mildly surprised to see the king veer right. At first he could not understand the course correction. The reason was made plain soon enough, however, when the king began his climb. The steps were wide and flat. They wound around the tower in a spiral designed so as to require the least amount of effort possible. In this way, the portly monarch was able to ascend to its top without exerting himself too greatly. That, however, was under normal circumstances. These were not normal circumstances. The king ran, or awkwardly trotted, as quickly as he could up their ever-increasing altitude.

Gideon charged toward the tower. The two guards stopped at the base and turned to face their foe. Gideon was undeterred. He raised his sword and shouted bravely as he charged the men. The first stepped forward with his own sword drawn. Gideon's sword was held high and proudly. He raised it even higher as he charged, as if to prepare for a massive downward blow as he quickly closed in on him.

The guard raised his to a peak in preparation of fending the oncoming blow. Both of the soon-to-be warriors knew that Gideon's forward momentum gave him an advantage and that the guard would need a steady arm to deflect such a blow as now zeroed in on him. The guard gritted his teeth and flexed his muscles into an iron grip on his weapon of defense.

Just as the anticipated blow was to land, Gideon deftly swung his sword outward, down, then inward. It took the evil king's henchman completely off guard. It landed on his tender midsection, disarming the man. The second guard leaped into the fray. Gideon spun around and countered a blow that was intended to catch him in the back. Higher and higher above, the king continued to puff his way to the top of the tower.

Gideon was pushed backward and bumped into the guard he had just disarmed. The bump actually helped him retain his balance. He sidestepped as the guard charged forward and ran into his comrade. Gideon turned again and swung at the second guard, slicing through his tunic. Angered, the guard swung back, but Gideon dodged the blow. For a few exasperating moments the two parried blows back and forth.

Gideon found himself standing on the tower's lower steps, with his back facing upward and his sword facing his adversary. The guard lunged forward and Gideon twisted his sword in such a way as to fling the guard's sword aside. A quick flick and Gideon landed a blow on the man's fighting arm, incapacitating him. Rather than finish him off, Gideon raised his leg and gave the guard a hearty push with his foot, forcing the man to fall backward onto his injured comrade. Both men lay on the ground groaning. Gideon had ensured that they were now wholly unable to hinder him further, while at the same time, he was careful to ensure that their wounds were not too grave.

Before either guard had the chance to bind their wounds, Gideon turned and charged up the wide, winding steps. He could hear Noah plodding desperately along far above him. Round and round he ran on the gradual slope, closing the gap. To his surprise, Noah was considerably higher up than he had anticipated him capable of clearing. It seemed to Gideon that he could actually see a trail of sweat left behind by the frantic king. Gideon had charged nearly to the very top of the tower and still had not caught his prey.

Gideon could hear the wheezing long before he closed in on the man. As it grew louder, he knew he was nearing his goal. There was no way out for the despicable despot. The tower was a foolhardy means of escape. Soon, the souls of an uncounted number of tortured and murdered Nephites would have justice. Gideon led with his sword hand as he charged around the final corners.

Noah knew his life had only seconds left. He looked about frantically, seeking some means of escape. The tower provided none. He looked around him, realizing his guards could never reach him in time. Then, in the distance, he saw a glimmer of hope – an excuse to use that even Gideon would have to acknowledge as valid. He stopped and pointed as he shouted.

"Gideon, stop! Look! The Lamanites are on the move! The city is in peril!"

"What?! What game is this?!"

"No game! No game! Look for yourself! The Lamanites are on the move!"

Gideon looked in the direction indicated by the bulging, quivering index finger. Beyond the city wall, beyond the rich fields of grain, beyond the orchards, beyond the jungle which separated their land from that of Shemlon, Gideon could make out the distant, tiny, yet unmistakable images of a Lamanite army on the move. There was no time to spare. The people needed to be warned quickly if they were going to be able to have any form of a plan of defense.

The king saw his pursuer's shoulders cave in momentarily, with the realization of what he was now being forced to do. He took full advantage of his only hope to save his puffy, pink skin.

"Gideon, regardless of the differences between us, the people need me now! I have to go back and lead them to victory! You know this to be true!"

Gideon paused, unable to respond. He clenched his teeth and closed his eyes in frustration. He raised his sword and then held it frozen in the air. Noah sweated and cowered, nearly crying. Gideon's sword arm moved in for the kill, then backed up. His fingers shifted position on his grip. His face suddenly twisted as he made his decision.

"Alright, Noah, I will spare you for the sake of the people. But, I promise you, this is not yet over!"

Noah nodded and began to work his way around his assailant. "I know. I know. But, you have chosen what's best for the people. I will see to it that they survive this attack."

Gideon at first let him pass, then, seeing the rotund ruler slowly waddling his way down the tower steps, he shook his head in disgust and charged beyond him. "Out of my way, man! Let me get down there to warn my people!"

Gideon hustled the rest of the way down the winding tower. The two guards stood at the base applying their bandages. Each winced in pain as Gideon brushed passed them in disgust and hurry. He was on the flat and just starting to run to warn his fellow citizens when he heard an all-too-familiar voice shrieking from above him. It was Noah.

"Hear me, people! Hear me! The Lamanites are upon us! We must flee into the wilderness! Save yourselves! Run with all haste! Flee into the wilderness!"

"Why that cowardly fool!" Gideon spit out in disgust. "Save his people! He has absolutely no intention of saving them. He's just going to run! I should have known."

Gideon thought of returning to Noah, then thought the better of it. Noah had just made it clear that the city had absolutely no defenses in place. The people were going to need someone with a clear head and a fast mind if they were going to survive the day. He dashed off toward his men.

Noah completed his descent from the tower. The two guards greeted him respectfully at the base. He slapped them both.

"What use are you?!" he shouted as he pushed his way beyond them.

The two looked at each other in distress and shrugged as the king hurried on his way, shouting to the people.

"Hurry! Run to the wilderness! The Lamanites are upon us!"

* * * * *

The Lamanites broke through the southern jungle and quickly overcame the hapless farmers who had no forewarning of their danger. The enemy army of dark-skinned warriors did not even slow their stride as they cut them down. They passed by the long-abandoned watchtowers without paying them any heed. The rotting floors quivered as they dangled in the breeze and vibrations as the enemy swept passed them. The Lamanites knew that they would soon be within range of the city's archers, but charged the city in spite of the danger. To their surprise, no arrows pierced the air to hinder their advance.

As they ran along the city's eastern border, they learned the reason why. It appeared to them that the entire city was emptying and heading directly into the wilderness north of the city and west of the great hill. By the time the Lamanites cleared the city's north wall, the last of the Nephites was already disappearing into the wilderness. The great city gate was left wide open, leaving the city vulnerable to occupation as a lasting testimony of the lack of leadership possessed by Zeniff's eldest son.

The Nephites' flight consisted of anything but organization. The only common thread among them was the fact that they all stayed essentially in one group and ran in a common direction – the one farthest from the pursuing Lamanites. Their hasty migration was hindered by the density of the jungle's terrain. They were also hindered by the number of women and children among their ranks.

King Noah, plodding as he was, managed to stay near the lead, because of the slowness of those trying to keep their families together.

"Sir! Your majesty!" an officer shouted.

Noah did not reply. He was too terrified. He ran with sloppy abandon, sweat pouring off his vibrating body.

"Sir!" he repeated and moved himself to trot before his majesty. "The Lamanites will soon overtake us. We can't possibly keep ahead of them at this pace. We must prepare to fight!"

"No! No! Not that! Run! Run!" the frantic monarch retorted.

"But, sir! The army is nearly upon us! We must fight!" the officer said.

"What's slowing us down are all of these blasted children and their dithering mothers," Amulon retorted. "We would move much more quickly without them!"

"Yes! Amulon is right, as always!" Noah acknowledged in a panic. "It is these women and children's fault."

He stopped and turned to face his people, intent on giving a distinct order. The people needed leadership and looked to him for the desperately needed answer to their dire situation.

He stood there drenched in sweat, his chest heaving for air. At last he managed to shout out in quick gasps, "You people! You move too slowly!" The people knew this. Now they wanted to know what help their king would offer. He continued, "The Lamanites are nearly upon us because of you! All you men stop bothering yourselves with these women and children. They do nothing but slow you down. They will drag you down to your death if you let them! Leave them! Leave them now! You must, or you will perish! Now run! Run!"

The king's order was met with pandemonium. Many simply could not believe they had heard him properly. Panicked others perceived wisdom in his point and left their families without so much as a backward glance. Wives and children wept at being abandoned by their husbands and fathers at the very moment in their lives when they needed them most.

Several groups stood and argued the merits and atrocities of the king's order. The king himself could not have been less interested. He had already hurried on his way with Amulon and the other priests and a surprisingly large number of men who had not hesitated in following his final order to his society.

The remaining Nephites huddled together in a massive group. Their cries and shouts filled the jungle and overpowered the sounds of the jungle animals and the war cries of the approaching enemy. Gideon found Limhi, Noah's eldest son, among the men in the lead.

"Limhi! Limhi! We need a plan, what should we do?!" Gideon called out.

"Do? I'm – I'm not sure. I just can't get over – I mean, I can't believe – It's just that I have never been more ashamed of my father as I am at this time!" Limhi said with unproductive honesty.

"I agree, but this is no time for lamenting pathetic fathers! We need a plan, NOW!" Gideon retorted.

Just then the multitude pushed into them like a floodwater seeking lower ground. The Lamanites had caught the farther end of their group. A massive slaughter had begun and the rest of the citizens were seeking some form of safe haven.

"We can't fight them off, not without our army!" Limhi noted. "The best we can do is appeal to their moral integrity!"

"Their what?!" Gideon asked incredulously.

"Their moral –" Limhi stopped himself and put it in other words. "We should send our daughters out to plead for our lives! Surely they won't kill our daughters!"

"Now I understand! Good plan!"

The daughters were not so complimentary about the prince's plan when they were asked to come away from their families and directed toward the scene of the slaughter. A brave and noble daughter caught onto the idea, however, and tried to calm her Nephite sisters.

"Sisters! Sisters!" Esther said, "This is our gift to our people. If we die, we die! But, I believe we will live and because of us, our people will live!

Now is the time for us to plead for the lives of our people. If we don't, our families will surely die!"

The quivering mass of fair daughters huddled together a few yards back from where others contended with the front ranks of the Lamanite invaders. The girls held their ground, while the rest of the city's populace retreated a little farther into the wilderness to seclude themselves. Mothers, fathers, and brothers prayed earnestly to the Lord that the young women's efforts would succeed.

There was one among them, a girl in her early twenties named Hannah, whose greatest concern only moments before was of gathering a mass of spilled grains from the city square. She also understood both the danger and the proposed solution. She took heart in Esther's words and was among those willing to sacrifice her own life for her people. She stepped forward to join her sisters. At the last moment, however, as the girls gathered in the clearing, she stepped back. She hid herself behind a tree and cowered in shame, trying desperately not to sob.

It was not long before the Lamanites advanced beyond the hapless few Nephites who had been the slowest to leave their city. They lunged forward ready to take on more of their cowardly enemies. They were staggered with surprise to find themselves running into the gathering of beautiful, young women kneeling as a group and raising their hands pleadingly.

"Spare us! Please, spare us!" Esther and the others begged. "Spare our people! Please!"

An angry Lamanite raised his bloodied sword high above his head and then brought it racing downward in a crushing deathblow. His swing was stopped short by another bloodied sword, however, that was thrust out just in time to save the girl. The clang of metal on metal as the swords met echoed through the wood and the girls twinged at the sound. The intended victim had instinctively bowed her head and kept her eyes closed.

The attacker turned to face the man who had stopped him. The fellow Lamanite held his ground.

"What's the meaning of this?" the attacker shouted.

"What do you think? We don't attack unarmed children!" The warrior did not admit it aloud, but his heart had been touched by the beauty of the young women, but even more by the nobleness of heart of their pleas and potential life-offering sacrifice.

"We attack Nephites! At least that is what I have been ordered to do!"

"We have been ordered to take the city! We've done that! They have given it to us! But, we do not attack children or girls! We have done enough this day! We've won! Let the killing stop."

To the surprise of the hidden on-lookers and the great relief of their daughters, the marauding Lamanites agreed with the outspoken swordsman. He turned to the girl.

"We will spare you," he said as the girl sighed in sincere relief and steadied herself. "But, we will only do this on the condition that you and your people surrender yourselves to us." He looked up and shouted to the trees. "Do you hear?! Surrender yourselves and we will spare your lives!"

For a moment nothing happened. Then a man stepped into view. He continued to walk toward the Lamanites and the group of young women. He held his empty hands in front of him, palms facing downward, making it clear he carried no weapon. Just as it seemed he would be the only one to surrender, a wall of Nephites emerged from their seclusion. They continued to pour out of the wood and gather before the Lamanites. They all kept their arms in front of them, showing their lack of weaponry.

"Who is your leader?!" the Lamanite demanded.

He looked among the passive, pale group that now kneeled before him. A tall man stood. It was Limhi. He simply stood, allowing himself to be seen and identified as their leader. The Lamanite motioned for him to step forward. The kneeling captives awkwardly parted and allowed Limhi to walk toward his counterpart.

"So, you are the leader of these cowardly people?" the Lamanite sneered insultingly.

"I am now," Limhi replied. "Our former leader appears to still be running on ahead."

The Lamanites laughed heartily and loudly at this carefully placed word of self-deprecation. Limhi hoped it would help their cause.

"Those of us who remain here with you do not wish to fight, either. We wish to remain among you in this land as your neighbors and brothers."

"As 'our neighbors and brothers'? I don't think so. But, I believe we can let you live among us – for a price!" the Lamanite responded.

"And what price might that be?" Limhi asked.

"What price would you put on your own heads? On your safety? On your lives?"

Limhi knew the questions were rhetorical and withheld a reply. He also sensed that a peace agreement was only going to come at a steep price.

"What do you have in mind?" he asked.

"That would be for our king to decide. Now, prepare your people for their return! Gather them up so that we may escort them home!"

Limhi nodded and turned to the massive group before him. The people had held still and silent, hoping to eavesdrop on the negotiations. Still, only those nearest were able to hear any details. However, everyone was soon to learn what was to happen next as Limhi addressed the gathering.

"People, hear me! We will return to Nephi! Gather closely together so that the Lamanites can place their guards around us!" Limhi raised both arms as he spoke in a powerful voice and motioned with them to gain their attention. Limhi's eyes met Gideon's. Gideon slowly closed his eyes tightly and grimaced in frustration. He questioned his decision on the tower. However, he had to concede that even that would have been far too late an act. It would not have changed their current circumstances. He should have acted much, much sooner. Why had he waited? Why had the people waited? Why did they let themselves get into this horrible situation? How could such a fair people allow hateful leaders lead them into such dire straits like ravenous wolves among a flock of mindless sheep?

When he opened his eyes again, Limhi was still looking at him. Gideon was frustrated, but recognized that they had no other recourse. He nodded his head slightly, letting Limhi know he had his support.

Limhi again spoke to the people, "Come, let us return to our homes!" The people continued to cluster together and turned back to return to their beloved city, under Lamanite guard.

Chapter 12
Limhi

The captive Nephites marched toward their former homes in silence. The victorious Lamanites boasted and bragged of their bravado the entire way, occasionally jostling one of the captives as they marched them forward at the point of the sword.

It was not a long journey, for they had not fled far when the Lamanites had overtaken them. The Lamanite leader was met by his king at the city's entrance. He reported the victory to his ruler. The king then ordered the captives to enter through the still-open city gate and gather in the city square.

It was an odd sensation. Their former utopian quest had suddenly taken on the aura of a prison. The entrance through the gate which had formerly represented entering into a sanctuary of safety from the dangers of the outside world, now seemed to be an entrance to an enlarged cell.

The Lamanite king himself climbed up and stood proudly on the catwalk above the city gate. He was flanked by his soldiers on either side. They stood nearly shoulder to shoulder along the catwalk and wholly surrounded the city square from three sides.

Once the last Nephite had entered, he ordered the gate closed and locked with a great block of wood. This ceremonious containment added to the Nephites' feelings of claustrophobic confinement. They mingled in uneasy, unnerved silence, awaiting the king's words.

He smiled in a way that sent shivers down the people's spines. It was clear he had accomplished a goal he had held for many years. He was surprised and pleased with the ease at which he had accomplished it. Little did he know how fortuitous his timing had been.

These people had set themselves up for their own fall and fortune had smiled brightly on the conquering king's plans. Soon, this formerly favored society would learn the consequences of ignoring their morality, supporting idolatrous leadership, and drastically dropping their guard.

"You people!" the king began. Every eye turned toward him. His henchmen stood by his side, grinning and scanning the crowd eagerly as he spoke. "You Nephites have learned the power of the Lamanite army this day! You have also learned of our mercy and good-natured generosity! The fact that you now stand here within the walls of your fine city – alive – is proof of this. Is it not?"

He ignored the absence of agreement from the crowd, smiled – or rather gloated – more broadly, and added, "Now, as with all things, such generosity comes at a price!"

This was it. They knew there would be a catch. What was the king planning? What fiendish plot or condition was he about to impose?

"It really is not such a large price, not when you weigh it against the value of your lives or the fact that we will allow you to continue to live in this fine and beautiful city! I will spare your lives on the following conditions. First, should your illustrious king ever return to you, you must deliver him up to me. Second, you will deliver up one half of all your possessions to me. That is one half of your gold, your silver, your jewels, and your other precious things!"

A significant series of murmurs escaped the lips of the crowd.

"Is this too great a cost – for your lives?!" the king reiterated.

With this, he motioned with his arm and his soldiers each drew an arrow into their bows and pointed them directly down toward the captives. The king's point was made all too clear. The murmuring took a different tone.

"It's not too great a cost, is it?" the king repeated.

Several muttered, "No." with their heads hung in miserable despair.

"Is it?!" the king shouted again, verbally whipping the people into submission.

"NO!" several shouted back looking up suddenly at his sharp query.

"I did not think so," the king responded with a reestablished, devious smile. "Now, as the final condition, you will deliver up one half of *all* your possessions and you will pay a tribute to me each year at harvest. One half of your crops and fruits will be delivered up to my servants to bring to me. After all, we have seen how abundantly your fields produce and would simply hate for any of it to go to waste!"

The crowd murmured again, but looked at the archers and voluntarily stifled themselves.

The king was not quite finished. "I understand your trustworthy king has shown his bravery by running wildly into the woods and leaving the rest of you to your fate. What a fine example of manly leadership! I assume you will find a worthy replacement for him. Perhaps you have a fruit vendor who is now looking for a job!" The king laughed and his men laughed with him. The Nephites' faces flushed with anger and embarrassment.

"No matter. Whoever you get, I'm certain he can do an equally credible job! I further assume that he is here among you, listening to my voice." Limhi shifted uneasily. "I want him to clearly understand that my conditions are not optional. I expect each one to be met fully. If not, I will send my men to reign terror down upon you and your sweet city in such a way as you have never known! Understood?!" King Laman eyed the crowd with a look of fierce determination. No one doubted him.

Most of the crowd just stood and stared in a depressed shock as the king and his men sneered and gathered themselves and prepared to leave the city square. Gideon was angry and frustrated. He cursed inwardly, admitting to himself that he was not able to place all of his blame on Noah. He knew that he and the people bore a strong share of the responsibility for their predicament by allowing a sinful ruler to reign for so long. He wisely held his peace as his conquerors made their way through the gate.

He shifted in place, wanting to run and fight, but holding himself still enough to keep from drawing undo and perhaps deadly attention to himself. He knew that if he started a row now, he could not possibly succeed and would most likely make things much worse for himself and his people. He began to pace, preoccupied. His thoughts were abruptly disturbed as he bumped into a young lady about his age.

"Oh! Excuse me!" he stammered.

"That is quite all right," Hannah responded, not looking up. "I'm getting used to it." She was scared and uneasy, but managed to keep a good humor about her.

"Huh?" was all Gideon could manage in reply.

"It is just that earlier today –" as she began her trivial explanation of an earlier incident, she looked up and recognized the man. "Why it's you!" she said.

"Me?" Gideon queried.

"Yes, you, the one who wants me to eat dirty bread." A twinkle had entered her eye and she managed a smile, a feat which, only moments before, she thought she would never manage again.

"Dirty bread? – " Gideon remained confused.

"Yes. Don't tell me you don't remember?" she asked. "Oh, perhaps if I did this." She dropped to her knees and began scooping the loose earth into small heaps.

"What in the world are you doing?" Gideon was thoroughly perplexed. Then, as he heard a soft laugh begin to come up from this strange, but attractive, person crouched on the ground, he experienced the sudden dawning of realization. "Why, you're the young lady I ran into!" he exclaimed.

"Apparently, that has become a habit for you," she replied with an even bigger laugh than before.

"I'm still terribly sorry!" he exclaimed. "I felt awful leaving you that way, it's just that I was in such a hurry." His voice trailed off and his gaze turned distant as he thought of Noah. What seemed to him to have taken place years ago, was only a few hours earlier.

"I gathered as much," she said, holding up her hand for assistance. Gideon had enough wits about him this time to gingerly, but firmly, take her hand in his and gallantly help her to her feet. He even managed a smile, but the pain that racked his soul was not wholly hidden.

Hannah could sense there was something terribly serious hidden behind Gideon's deep brown eyes. She was hesitant to ask, but decided to pursue anyway. She tried to take on a bit of a light-hearted tone as she asked, "Just what was it that kept you so distracted, anyway?"

"I was, uh –" he was confused about how much to tell her. He felt he could not possibly tell her his whole intent. But then again, he sensed deep within himself, that he also did not want to deceive her. "To be quite honest, I was looking for King Noah," he said at last.

"King Noah!" she said, inadvertently recoiling. "What on earth for?"

"I had a matter to discuss with him. It was an urgent matter." Hannah eyed him apprehensively, curiously, and sensing that this was no typical matter, she went quiet, choosing to not interrupt. Gideon felt her gaze even as he looked away. He cocked his head to the left, struggling with the words and trying not to grimace. His eyes glanced upward as his head slowly turned back toward her and he fought for just the right words. He still could not manage to look her in the eye yet. Looking downward, he began, "You see, I wanted to let him know that I, uh – disagreed – with him on a certain matter." He now looked her straight in the eye and finished, "Actually, I wanted to let him know that I *strongly* disagreed with him." He could not help but frown, and did not notice how tightly he grabbed the hilt of his sheathed sword.

Hannah noticed, however. She saw the blood vessels in his hand and forearm bulge as he squeezed the handle. "I see," was all she said. She decided it would be best to leave the full explanation for another day, and suddenly realized that she earnestly hoped that there would be another day – with this intriguing man. "Why, I don't even know your name," she said.

"My name?" Gideon was again surprised and shaken from his thoughts. "Why, I am Gideon, son of Joshua." he replied and bowed slightly as he did so.

"And, I'm Hannah, daughter of Jothan," she answered, with a bit of a curtsy.

"I am very pleased to meet you, Hannah, daughter of Jothan," Gideon said with sincerity.

"I'm glad," Hannah said. "I think we should make good friends," she added, somewhat surprised at her own boldness.

"You do?" Gideon flushed slightly. "Well, now so do I. So do I."

Life was sometimes brief among the Nephites, especially when times were troubled. It certainly looked like they had entered into some troubled times. Both of these new friends realized it could not possibly hurt to let down on pretenses and rigidness and admit to themselves that it could be very comforting to endure these troubled times with a new friend by their side.

"I was wondering," Gideon began, "if you would care to have supper with me."

"I was wondering," Hannah replied with a smile, "if you would allow me to fix you your supper."

"I would be honored," Gideon answered, "uh – as long as you promise not to put any dirt on my plate!"

"That will all depend on whether or not you help me!" she said teasingly.

The two had entered the city square tense, worried, and alone. They were concerned about what had just happened in the jungle and even more fearful of what the Lamanites were going to do next. Their dire situation had not changed. They both knew that the next few weeks, months, and perhaps even years, were going to be difficult at best. But, they found much needed comfort in knowing that they had found a new friend, and suspected that it could grow into something much more than friendship. The one thing they knew for certain was that although tensions and worries would persist, they were no longer alone.

*****

Among the Nephites as a whole, it all seemed like a dreadfully long bad dream. The Lamanites finally withdrew and left the Nephites to recuperate from their defeat. The first issue of business was to resolve the very point their enemy's king had highlighted. Who would now rule over them?

The choice was made obvious when Limhi was identified among the crowd. He, being the king's eldest son, was the natural successor. As evil as Noah was, the people still demanded a king. Further, they demanded that he succeed his father. Besides, he had, after all, been the one to negotiate with the Lamanites in the woods. Within the hour, the coronation had transpired and Limhi sat on his new throne, giving audience to several self-appointed advisors. The priests had fled with their former king, so their entire political system needed replacement. Gideon was among the observers in the throne room watching as the leaders debated their next moves. He himself had been appointed a captain in the king's army.

"I know their conditions are harsh, but we have no choice!" the new king responded to an angry Nephite with resolve and patience.

Limhi was a handsome man with a strong build. His only physical resemblance to his father was his dark, wavy hair and piercing brown eyes. Years of toiling in the fields with others had not only taught him the value of work, but had given him a physique wholly foreign to Noah's rotund frame. There was a seriousness in Limhi's tone and gaze, but one could also detect kindness in his demeanor and a wisdom that extended beyond his years.

"And, what of the old king?" the angry Nephite continued.

"What do you mean?" Limhi asked.

"The Lamanites want him. What do we do if he comes back?"

"I know he came up lacking in more ways than I care to number, but I'm not interested in throwing him to the Lamanites to abuse and destroy," Limhi responded.

"What do you propose, then?"

"I propose waiting to decide that when - and if - he ever returns. That is all."

Gideon noted that Limhi spoke with a finality that made it clear he was not interested in having the matter pursued any further. His face twisted into a pensive scowl. "He'll not get off that easily," he muttered under his breath.

"Eh, what was that?" the man standing nearest him queried.

"Nothing. Nothing at all," Gideon lied, and left the throne room.

He made his way through the hallway quickly, but without giving the appearance of hurrying. He wanted to make certain that he did not attract any attention. Once outside, he made his way through streets and alleys until he arrived at a small, stone building with a wooden door frame and a log roof. He slipped in without hesitation and quickly closed the door behind him.

"What did you learn, Gideon?" one of a dozen men asked him in earnest.

"It is as we suspected. King Limhi has no intention of tracking down Noah and bringing him to justice," Gideon replied. "In a way, I don't blame him. It's bad enough he has to live with the stigma of being his son."

"But, we can't let Noah wander about freely!"

"Agreed," Gideon responded. "As a captain in the army, it is my duty to seek out and put an end to all traitors and enemies of this people. I can think of no greater traitor or enemy than King Noah himself. Who knows what damage he and his priests will cause if they're not stopped? We will have to take care of them on our own. Are you prepared to go?"

"You just give the word and we are on our way."

"Good. I will keep my post in the throne room to keep abreast of the latest events here," Gideon reached out and held his companion's arm. "Do not fail us."

* * * * *

Deep in the jungle, the men awoke with a start on the third morning. The faint sound was indiscernible, but growing. Gideon's dozen leaped into position, crouching and secluding themselves from view. They waited. The sound grew louder and more distinct. It was soon clear that several men were approaching and locked in tense conversation. They were not just oblivious to being overheard, but evidently not concerned about such an eventuality. As the men approached, their conversation grew louder and more distinct, until it became clear enough for Gideon's men to make out their words.

"...I agree. Nothing could have been worse," a voice stated with a tone mixed with resolve and irritation.

"Soon we will be able to -" the second voice was cut short by Gideon's chief man, Himni.

"Halt where you are!" Himni shouted from his secluded perch.

The group of three dozen or so Nephite travelers froze in their tracks. They were taken entirely off their guard. Several of the men looked around frantically in a vain attempt to find the source of the order.

"Drop your weapons or we will stick you full of arrows," a second man, Teomni, ordered.

The group quickly turned their heads in unison in the other direction. So far as they could tell, they were now surrounded. Whether it was Nephites or Lamanites, they could not say, but they knew they would be wise to obey. One by one, they dropped their belongings. Their "weapons" were the meager items they had picked up when fleeing Nephi. Some had actual swords, others knives. Most had nothing more than glorified walking sticks.

"We hear you! We have obeyed. Now spare us! We are only trying to get back to our families!" a tall Nephite in the front area called out.

"Stand still with your hands outward!" Himni ordered.

The group obeyed. Himni stepped into view. The Nephites turned to see him to their right. They breathed a sigh of relief at the sight of his white skin. "*At least he's not a Lamanite*," several thought to themselves.

"Who are you people?" Himni demanded.

"We are Nephites, like yourself."

"I can see that!" Himni bit out. The rest of his men cautiously moved into view. They came from all directions, keeping the group surrounded. "I asked who you are!"

"My name is Zoram. We come from the city of Nephi. We fled with the king when the Lamanites attacked. Now we're returning to find our families."

"Is the king or his priests among you?"

"No. They most certainly are not!" Zoram replied.

"What?! Where is the king then?!"

"The king is dead," a voice responded with more than just a hint of righteous indignation.

"Dead?! How?" Teomni asked with surprise.

"We killed him," a short Nephite said in a flat, disgusted tone.

"Killed him? How?" Himni asked with a shocked and somewhat irritated lilt to his own voice.

"When the Lamanites attacked, Noah ordered us to flee. You know this. You were probably among us," Zoram explained.

"Yes, unfortunately we were. Go on."

"Then you may be aware that when the king felt we were moving too slowly, he ordered us to abandon our wives and children and run off without them," Zoram continued.

"Yes, we're aware of that, as well," Teomni said with disdain.

"Well, we're not proud to say that we listened to the king. We left our wives and children to be slaughtered by our enemies, while we ran ahead to save our own skins. It was a cowardly act, for which we are greatly ashamed," Zoram's voice tapered off. He was unable to continue. Several others would take turns finishing the tale.

The first to pick up in his place added, "When we felt we were safe, the gravity and cowardice of what we'd done sunk in. When we fully realized what we'd done, we swore that we would return and try to rescue our families. If we were to die in the effort, then so be it. We deserve such a fate."

"But, the king would not have any of it," a third chimed in. "He forbade us to return. He said it would mean certain death. He didn't care a fig's pit for our families. We insisted that we must return, but he ordered us to stay."

"To keep the story short, an intense argument ensued, pitting the king and his priests against us. They picked the wrong time to argue. We had recognized our error and were determined to set things right. The more he spoke, the more we realized how many great evils we had allowed him to perpetrate against our people."

"Our anger grew intense. We grabbed him and bound him to a tree."

"And, we set fire to it. He died a bitter and fitting death, squealing and cursing."

"The priests tried to stop us. That was when we turned on them. They thought they could talk us out of it. We shouted that they were equally guilty with the king. That was when they ran off. We chased them, but they got away. Who knows where they are now?"

"We gave up the chase and realized it was more important to return and save our families, if we were not already too late."

This created a reminder and a realization among the fugitives that the men with whom they now spoke would surely know the outcome of the battle with the Lamanites. And, it was also possible that they could know what had become of the Nephites in general which would imply they may also know what had become of their families.

With earnest hopefulness, Zoram asked, "We are not too late, are we? Do our families yet live?" The group searched the eyes of Gideon's dozen, hoping for a positive response.

"Yes, your families are still alive. We worked out a truce with the Lamanites. They will let us live in peace, so long as we pay a tribute of half we own."

The group knelt and praised the Lord at this news. "Thank the heavens!"

"Come!" Himni ordered. "It's time for you to be reunited with your families."

The men stepped forward and began following Himni back toward Nephi, little realizing the deeper significance of their actions. They had unwittingly fulfilled one of the first of Abinadi's many prophesies. They had caused King Noah, the man who claimed he had no need for God, to be put to death in the same manner as Abinadi had been. This was just as Abinadi had said it would be.

At the time the prophecy had been spoken, Noah had felt certain that it had no chance of fulfillment. But, those were different times. Abinadi had also spoken other words which had not yet been fulfilled. Conditions had now changed dramatically enough, that it was now becoming quite likely that they could be.

Chapter 13

Daughters

It is at times surprising what one can become accustomed to within a two-year period. Limhi and his people had become familiar with the many Lamanite guards who patrolled the outskirts of their land. The monthly and annual tributes were already routine. The Nephites had even learned to feel somewhat content under Limhi's reign. Granted, they were not oblivious to their oppressive situation, but they were learning to live with it.

Amulon and the other priests of the now-deceased King Noah, however, were not quite so content. Two years on the run made them tired and left them longing for some feminine companionship. They knew they could never return to their own families. The business with King Noah getting burned at the stake had made that pointedly clear. Devoid of Nephite companionship, they eventually wandered southward toward the land of Shemlon, deep in the heart of Lamanite territory.

While in a secluded part of the country, Amulon and his cohorts became witness to a sight that prompted actions with ever-mounting consequences. Several dozen young and beautiful Lamanite women in their late teens and early twenties had gathered to sing and dance. It was the sound of their melodious voices that first captured the evil priests' attention.

"Eh, what was that?" Amulon asked.

"More trees and monkeys," a fellow priest observed.

"Not that!" Amulon responded with disgust. "That sound!"

"It sounds like – singing," another the priest observed.

"I can tell it's singing. Who is making it?" Amulon bit out.

"I don't know."

"We should find out."

Amulon and the others kept low as they approached the sound. The jungle was dense, so staying secluded was not difficult. The trick was avoiding stepping on twigs or leaves in such a way that would give away their presence. The singing and laughter grew to a peak as they approached an area with thick brush. They peered through the brush and saw their prey.

"It's women!"

"Lots of them!"

"Enough for us all!"

"Yes, enough for us all," Amulon said with an evil sneer. "An opportunity like this doesn't present itself too often, as we are painfully aware."

Amulon backed away from the brush and motioned to the men to do the same. Some were reluctant at first to stop watching, but relented when they saw the anger in Amulon's face at their hesitancy, which was followed by even more violent hand gestures.

"What? What do you want?" they asked in hushed tones.

"I want to do more than just watch a few dances," Amulon responded. "We need a plan."

The others were pleased with whatever plot Amulon seemed to be hatching.

"This is quite a find. From the looks of things, this is not the first time they have been here. I think we should spend some time in this area. If we charge in now, we are way outnumbered and someone is bound to make it back to the Lamanites and reveal our secret. I have a feeling that if we wait long enough, we'll find an appropriate opportunity to solve our loneliness without bringing any suspicions our way."

*****

Their patience eventually paid off. On a warm, cloudless day a number of dancers equal to the number of priests, entered the woods. The young women who frequented the area had always taken care to keep the spot secluded and secret from their parents, who disapproved of their frivolity. They were unaware that in spite of their precautions, their carefree play was being carefully observed.

With the suddenness of a cloud burst, the men dashed toward the girls from all directions. The merry singing shifted abruptly to shouts of fear. Unfortunately for the girls, none but the priests of Noah had ever heard their singing. Therefore, no one but their charging captors now heard their screams. Each man grabbed a girl and held her tightly. The girls were gagged, bound, and carried away, kicking and struggling in vain.

The men took them deeper and deeper into the woods, grinning and snickering at their struggling bounty. When they were certain they were well beyond earshot of any Lamanite guards, they let the young women down. They each sat angrily on the ground with their ankles and wrists tied together. Several managed to worm their way next to each other in an attempt to gain comfort and a sense of safety by huddling in a group. They were frightened and worried. Most were crying.

The Nephite priests looked at the youthful, dark-skinned women with lust and satisfaction. They were pleased to have accomplished such a devilish feat with such ease. The priests stood surrounding the girls, looking down on them, grinning. Amulon stepped forward to address the kidnapped group.

"We mean you no harm! You are now far from your homes. You need not worry yourselves with returning there. We will provide you with all that you need. We offer you safety. We offer you provisions." Amulon took off his leather cap and knelt, attempting to feign sincerity. "We have seen you dance and you have stolen our hearts. We knew that had we tried to talk with you, you would have fled at the sight of us and we would forever mourn out our days with broken hearts and unfulfilled longing. We know that what we have done has been brutish and frightening, but we knew no other way. We offer you our hearts. Please, take them. We wish only to make you happy."

Amulon's men were again impressed with the old wordsmith. He had gained an unparalleled reputation for debate in the king's chambers. He was now proving he could con the heart of a woman with equal subtlety. He paused and bowed his head.

Looking up, his eyes caught those of the tallest of the bunch. She did not recoil at his gaze. He sensed he may be catching her attention. He rose and approached her, then knelt directly before her.

"You, most of all, have caught my eye as well as my heart. If I should live one hundred years, I do not believe I should ever see such a beautiful face."

The girl blushed, in spite of her gag and bindings. Amulon reached for them as he spoke.

"Such a face should not be hidden behind such unsightly cloth. Here, please, let me remove it."

He removed the gag and she did not scream. She continued to watch him carefully. He reached around her for her hands.

"And, such tender hands should not be held in such tight bonds. Please, let me loose them."

He untied her hands. She rubbed her wrists gingerly, but did not attempt to push him away.

"And, such graceful feet should not be bound so awkwardly. Please, let me free them."

He untied her ankles. She shifted her legs to rejuvenate their blood supply, but did not attempt to run.

"Such a beautiful woman should not be alone. Please, won't you stay with me?"

She neither spoke nor moved. She simply stared back into his dark eyes. Her youthful heart swelled with the thought of mystery and romance come to life.

*****

"Where is Fatina?" her mother, Rebekah, asked.

"How would I know? She comes and goes as she pleases," her father, Hamoth, answered.

"Supper is nearly ready. I'm worried," Rebekah added.

"Go and see if she is with Saroni. But, wait until after we eat," Hamoth said.

Just then there was a knock at their door.

"What now?!" Hamoth replied and threw down his wooden spoon.

His wife rose and went to the door. It was Saroni's parents. She opened the door widely and invited them in.

"Have you seen Saroni? She has been out since midday. It's nearly dark. I'm terribly worried," Saroni's mother said as she entered.

Fatina's father, Hamoth, entered the room and approached Saroni's father.

"Lemuel, it's good to see you. What's this about Saroni?" he asked.

"She is missing and so are several other girls. We came here to see if maybe you knew anything," he replied.

"No, we were just planning on coming and asking you the same thing. This is most peculiar."

"I fear something dreadful has happened!" Rebekah said with tears welling up in her eyes. "Please, go and tell the king. Something has happened!"

*****

Two dozen concerned fathers stood before the Lamanite king, pleading their cause. The king sat with a distressed, concerned look. He grew more agitated the longer they spoke.

"We've searched the city. No one has any knowledge of where our daughters are. We found some of their friends. They told us of a place where they would go to dance. We went to the place and found it empty. We also found many tracks on the ground and the brush torn toward the northwestern area of the clearing. We believe they have been abducted."

"Abducted! By whom?" King Laman shouted.

"Who else?! The Nephites!" Hamoth shouted back with equal indignation. "They must be made to pay!"

The throne room soon erupted with shouts of agreement. A war of revenge was receiving both fuel and fire.

*****

Limhi had made it a practice to ascend the tower and survey the kingdom. He always looked to the north first. He knew it would be a fruitless view, but inwardly he ever longed to see Nephites coming from the north bringing with them the hope of freedom from the dangerous entanglement he inherited from his foolish father.

As expected, the north held only the sight of a vast field with trees covering the prominent hill to the north by the city of Shimlon. He looked eastward and saw another field covered with grain. It would be a good harvest. To the south, more farmers were busily tilling the soil. The branches of the fruit trees to the far south were becoming heavily laden with bounty.

Something caught his eye in the far distance beyond the jungle that separated his land from King Laman's. There was an unusual amount of activity in the Lamanite city. He stood and watched longer. His brow furrowed with concern. It was clear that whatever was happening was not good.

He could make out several Lamanites gathering. Soon, there was a tremendous number. Others appeared to be running to join the group. They milled about some, then began progressing to the north, toward the jungle that separated their cities. He now felt certain. The Lamanites were on the move.

He grabbed the warning horn he had placed at the tower's top, hoping never to use. He gave three quick blasts followed by two long blasts. He repeated the signal three times. Soon, he could hear the confirmation coming from the watch towers at the four corners of the city. The city was now alerted. He knew he needed to hurry to get to the city square before panic ensued.

As he stood over the city gate on the catwalk, the citizens looked to him for an explanation.

"The Lamanites are on the move!" he shouted. "We have little time. Open the weaponry. We should seclude our men in the woods to the south. If we can cut them off there, then our women and children will not need to see the battle or feel its piercing daggers!"

The men shouted a unifying cry and did as their king had commanded.

*****

The enraged Lamanites quickly advanced upon their foe. They were swelled with a burning indignation. The front ranks included twenty-four fathers bent on securing the return of their daughters and vowing vengeance on any who may have harmed them. Most of the other men were fathers themselves who swore in their hearts to not only return their comrades' offspring, but set an example that would make the Nephites think twice before repeating such a reprehensible deed. The king himself was at the forefront of the march.

They forced their way through the jungle in as silent an approach as possible. They wanted to be able to hit the Nephites without revealing their intent. In this way, they hoped to be able to overpower the city gate and break through the walls that protected the city.

As they neared the jungle's edge, the king raised his arm for them to halt. He peered out across the farmland. Not a soul was in sight. So far, their plan was proving successful. He grinned and nodded to his closest men. He raised his sword high above his head to give the signal that they should dash across the field and assault their enemy's lair.

Before he could lower his arm, however, the air was filled from all directions with a hideous war-cry. Taken completely off guard, the king was struck in the side with a massive blow that sent him sprawling. He never knew from where it came. The ensuing battle was intense.

Nephites leapt upon the Lamanites from all directions. The Lamanite army was taken wholly unawares. They were absolutely surrounded. The hand-to-hand combat was awful. The Nephites fought to protect their wives and children. Unbeknownst to them, the Lamanites did likewise. Both sides fought with the strength of dragons. Men fell, bled, and died.

The fighting was most fierce from among the Nephites, who also had the upper hand, given their surprise assault. The Lamanite army began to collapse. It turned as one and focused on its rear. The southern-most forces broke free. As the Nephites saw their enemy's intent, they allowed the retreat to commence. They continued to shout and threaten with their swords as the fleeing Lamanites passed through their gauntlet.

The air rang with Nephite victory cries as the Lamanites returned in a hasty defeat to their own land. The Nephite warriors congratulated themselves on protecting their territory and families. They hugged each other and clanged their swords together victoriously.

When the celebration abated, a grizzly task lay before them. There on the floor of the rainforest lay the dead and dying bodies of their enemies. One Nephite, toward the northern edge of the jungle noticed movement from one of the dead. He shouted to his nearest comrades.

"It's their king! The king himself!" he said.

"We should take him back to Limhi," another suggested.

"Yes! We can make an example of him. Bind up his wounds and we will bring him to the king!"

Chapter 14

King Laman

King Limhi sat on his throne awaiting word from the battle. He had lingered behind with a select group of men in case the battle went poorly and the Lamanites broke through. They would have proved to be the people's last defense. Most of the officers and men had already returned from the battle. Those who lingered behind were those who were responsible for finding and tending to the wounded. Theirs was a grizzly, but compassionate service which truly saved lives.

Women and children hoped and prayed to see their husband or father march home of his own accord. If he did not, then their prayers turned to the hope that he would be carried in among the wounded, and not buried among the dead. It was a tense and emotionally wrenching time for all, including those whose assignment it was to bring the foul news of fallen heroes, to anxious loved ones. Because these men were the last to leave the battlefield, they were known as the Last Battalion. Some had said that the name was also derived from the fact that they represented the last hope that a loved one would return home.

It was the tower guard on the southeastern corner of the wall who spotted the Last Battalion returning. They bore several stretchers and also aided those who could still walk, on what seemed like a long trek across the final fields toward the city. The guard sent word to the king that all appeared to have gone fairly well, as he did not see too many injured. At least, it was not as many as several had feared it would be. Limhi awaited the official report.

A knock on the throne room door announced the end of that wait. Limhi motioned for the door to be opened. The throne room guard pulled the door open and two sweaty and dirty Nephite officers escorted a bandaged and wincing Lamanite king into the room. Even in spite of the pain and discomfort, the king managed to hobble forward with an air of stubborn dignity.

"Oh, great King Limhi, we have been successful!" the officer reported triumphantly. "The Lamanites have been pushed back to their lands!"

"Yes, yes," King Limhi replied. "I was pleased to hear this from my officers. What can you tell me of the dead and wounded? Have we paid a terrible price for this victory?"

"I'm sorry to report that many of our brethren to the south, the Lamanites, have fallen by the sword," the officer replied. "However, I'm relieved to report that only a few of our own men have fallen." The officer bowed and looked sincerely gratified. He then turned to the doorway and beckoned with a long sweep of his arm. As he did so, two of his men brought in a wounded and bandaged man of considerable darker skin than their own. He wore no shirt, his head was shaved bare, and he had war paint smeared on his face, chest and shouldered that was now smudged and mingled with swear and blood.

The officer continued, "And, here is their king! He was wounded and left for dead. We have brought him before you so that you may judge him and slay him!"

"This is a fine report," King Limhi responded. "I am pleased with your success. But, I do not wish to slay their king. I wish to speak with him. Bring him closer."

They did as their monarch commanded. The Lamanite king worked his way forward and stood before his captor. He shook off the obligatorily helping hands of those beside him, insisting that he stand of his own accord. He looked about himself, seeing the anger in the eyes of the guards and officers who surrounded him. He ignored their piercing gazes and looked directly at Limhi.

"Why have you come against my people?" Limhi asked. "Why do you wage war? We have not broken our oath to you. Why have you broken your oath to me and my people?"

"I have broken the oath because your people have carried away the daughters of my people!" King Laman replied in a stern tone. "We consider our daughters as treasures and will not sit by and let them be stolen. For this vile deed I have led my people to war against your people!"

"What?!" Limhi shouted rhetorically. "What's this he says? Who has stolen their daughters?!" Turning back to the Lamanite king, Limhi replied, "I will search among my people and whoever has done this will perish! I swear this to you!" Turning back to his guards, he commanded, "Let a search be made! Whoever has done this thing will be brought before me and dealt with severely!"

As the order was given and the guards were turning to carry it out, the Lamanite king was impressed with his counterpart's response. The tension eased somewhat. Many of the men surrounding him were also fathers and, in spite of their animosity, they understood the enraged fury which had led to the battle.

There was one within the room, however, who called attention to himself. Gideon, a captain in Limhi's army who had distinguished himself on the field of battle, had previously given his own report on the battle. He again stepped forward and bowed.

"Great king, I beg of you to listen to me before you begin this search," he said.

Limhi took note of Gideon and turned to him, "Why, what have you to say?"

"My king, I mean no disrespect to you, but do not search the people or lay this to their charge. I believe your people are innocent of this act."

Gideon had the court's full attention and that of the Lamanite king, as well.

"Your majesty, do you not remember the priests of your father? When your father was destroyed, the priests fled and eluded capture. Surely they are still out there plotting evil deeds. Would *they* not be the ones who have stolen the daughters of the Lamanites? You must tell this great king of all of the things these priests have done and why they are most likely the ones who have committed this awful act as well."

"Gideon, you speak wisely," Limhi replied.

"What's this that your man says?" King Laman asked.

"He speaks of evil deeds done by reprehensible men," King Limhi responded. "My father, Noah, was king before me. He was a wicked man who delighted in drinking much wine and consorting with many women. He had two dozen priests who supported and joined him in his riotous living. When your people last attacked us and drove us from the city, our people revolted against our own King Noah."

Limhi paused a moment. It was unclear if he was second-guessing whether or not to reveal the second portion of his tale, if he was touched with emotion at the loss of his father, or if he was simply embarrassed by the legacy he had to now overcome. Revealing the weaknesses of one's own society was never an easy thing. For one king to do it before another was harder still.

"Deep in the jungle, King Noah was found, taken, and put to death. When they tried to take his priests, they all fled and escaped. They're out there still, wandering the wilderness. If anyone has stolen your daughters it makes sense that it would have been these priests, not my people."

"Your tale leaves me speechless," King Laman replied. "It's too odd to be a lie. You seem sincere, so I have to judge it as the truth. If so, I will agree with you that these priests of your father must have done this thing, in which case my people have done a great injustice to your people – a terrible one. I – I must ask for your pardon. I had no way of knowing otherwise."

"I understand," Limhi replied. "Until Gideon reminded me, I myself could see no other possibility." Turning to Gideon he added, "We must thank you for pointing this out."

"I accept your thanks, my king, I live but to serve." Gideon bowed. "Meanwhile, I am certain our friends, the Lamanites, are planning another attack. I fear we will not fare so well the second time, as we have lost the element of surprise and they significantly outnumber us. We will do better to renew our oath and continue to live under the previous agreement, than to die at the hands of this army."

"If I may," King Laman said to Limhi, "I agree with your fine servant. If you will allow me to go out before your army, I will speak with my men and let them know that this fighting must come to an end."

"Will that work?" Limhi inadvertently asked aloud.

"I'm their king! They must listen! I swear to you with an oath that if we go before my people without arms, they will not slay your people."

"Yes, very well. Let it be so," Limhi stated. "We will care for you until you are well enough to return to your land under your own strength."

* * * * *

Not too many days following, the anticipated warning horn was sounded. Kings Limhi and Laman both left the throne room in a hurry. At the southern gate, they met the officers who had been pre-selected for this mission. Gideon was among them. Few words were exchanged, as they had already rehearsed their actions and knew that if this were to succeed they had little time to get into the field before the Lamanites commenced their attack.

They ensured that none of them carried any arms of any sort, then, with the kings from both nations in their lead, they exited the safety of their city and entered the vulnerability of the open, southern field. They crossed it with determination. As they reached the center area, the Lamanites were just emerging from the jungle. The Lamanites began to charge with a war cry, but the cry stumbled and died in their throats as they saw the relatively small group continue toward them without faltering.

The group held their arms extended before them with their palms facing downward in a token display of disarmament. This was noted immediately, but what shook the advancing army the most was the tall, dignified, bandaged, dark-skinned man in their lead. They recognized their king with mixed feelings of shock and surprise. They stopped in their tracks and stood, watching the party advance.

They came within a few paces and the Nephites stopped and bowed. The king continued forward and met his men. The forward officer knelt and bowed. The king reached out and put his right hand on the man's shoulder and raised him, as was their custom. Limhi and his group were not privy to the discussion they held, but it was obvious what messages were being delivered.

Finally, without looking back to Limhi and his men, the Lamanite king and his army turned south and returned to their own land. As relieved as Limhi was that the war had been averted, he was slightly puzzled by that final act. He did not know what he had expected, but he could not shake the feeling that he had at least expected his counterpart to turn and acknowledge him in some way prior to leaving.

"*Was he just seeking his own release? If so, why did not his people turn and attack? Was he just trying to return home and rest his wounds first?*" Limhi's mind queried. "*Ah! You worry too much, Limhi. You should thank the Lord that he has seen fit to deliver your people from more warfare today,*" he finally chided himself as he and his men returned to their city.

Chapter 15

For Freedom

Enough days passed that Limhi decided he was unduly concerned over his parting with King Laman. Peace had finally been restored. He eagerly prepared himself to live out his days in the same degree of solitude and contentment that his grandfather had enjoyed in the land. Life among the Nephites would finally be a good thing.

The people's attention returned to their fields and their crops. Artisans began to focus on intricate pottery designs and complex weaving. Many felt it was surprising how a lack of care had allowed their fair city to fall into disrepair. Noah had never given any focus to such things. Dilapidated buildings were patched and repaired. As the city began to shine again, the people found themselves taking more pride in their work and feeling a sense of enlightenment which brought the emotional well-being of their society to a higher plain.

Through it all, however, the Lamanite encroachment gradually increased. The number of guards surrounding their land subtlety grew. Interaction between guards and Nephites also increased. For the most part, the Nephites ignored their presence. They were in a state of declared peace and managed to forget their troubles and taxation by focusing on renovating and improving their city, crops, and families.

They even took special care to fumigate and renovate their temple. Gideon had eagerly volunteered for, and was granted, the responsibility of leading the work at the temple. The stores of wines were removed. The grape-stained walls were washed and painted. The stench of alcohol was burned out by the fragrant smoke of special woods. The decorations of the temple were restored. But, the people were saddened to admit that there was no one among them with the authority or knowledge to perform any of the sacred ordinances that were at one time performed there daily.

The cleansing of the temple took many weeks. Hannah had also been certain to volunteer for this duty. She took the opportunity to work as closely to Gideon as she could. Gideon did not mind. In fact, he found himself searching her out and calling her to assist with various duties. While Gideon helped the men move large barrels or crates from rooms, Hannah led the women in sweeping and tidying. Much of the time, they found it necessary to scrub the stone floors in attempts to remove the dark, red stains left behind by the wines.

At times, the stains were simply too deep to be scrubbed clean and Gideon would bring in stone masons to hack at and then polish the floor stones. The smaller sections were removed entirely and replaced with fresh stones, quarried from the same quarry their father Nephi had used centuries before. Weeks of labor gradually drifted into months. The people were, however relentless in their efforts. They persisted in revering their temple as a symbol of their penitence and yearning to return to the ways of their God.

After a long day's toil, Gideon would escort Hannah to her home. It became a common practice for Hannah to invite Gideon in for supper. It was so common, in fact, that Gideon became concerned that Hannah was being made to bear the brunt of the expenses for meals that the two of them seemed destined to share. He did not wish to usurp her meager wages and proposed a solution.

"I've been thinking, dear Hannah," he said one evening.

Hannah's eyes lit up. She was anxious to hear his next words.

"I've been thinking that it's not fair that you alone should bear the cost of these wondrous meals. Perhaps -" Gideon paused a moment, concerned that he may be stepping out of bounds, but deciding that he and Hannah had truly become good friends, he decided to continue.

"Yes?" Hannah repeated, expectantly.

"I was thinking that perhaps, I should buy the food that you cook. That way we both bear a responsibility and neither should feel overly burdened to the other."

"'Overly burdened?'" Hannah's face twisted and her anxious smile drooped and then vanished. "Overly burdened?'" she repeated, incredulous.

"Yes," Gideon confirmed. "You see, I want to help -" his thought was cut off as he looked at her. "Why, whatever is wrong?" he asked sincerely.

"Oh, it's nothing," Hannah replied, looking down and turning away.

"No, it *is* something," Gideon astutely observed. "Please tell me what it is."

He stood up and walked to her, putting his hands on her shoulders and lightly nudged them, suggesting that she face him. She turned to him, but continued to look down. He put his hand under her chin and pressed it upward. Her face met his, but her eyes were turned away. Her lips were quivering and Gideon saw a tear or two lightly drip down her cheek.

"Hannah!" he said with deep concern, "What is it? Please, tell me what's wrong!"

"It's just -" She paused, blinked hard, then looked up into his deep, brown, inquiring eyes. She felt a shiver go through her as she did so. She was so in love with the man, why could he not see it? She continued, "It's just that when you said you wanted to not let me bear the burden 'alone,' I thought you were going to suggest something more than merely paying for the food."

"You want me to help cook?" Gideon asked suddenly, without engaging his mind.

Hannah could not help but laugh, "No," she said, "That wasn't quite what I was thinking."

"Then what? –" this time Gideon's pause was brought on by a sudden realization of what his dear, sweet friend might be hinting at. "Oh!" he said, inadvertently stepping back. "I think I know what you are referring to."

Seeing him step back, and trying hard not to take offense, Hannah observed, "Yes, it looks like you do." She found herself turning away from him.

As her long-lashed eyes moved away from his own, Gideon felt his heart yearn to see them again, staring back into his own. He realized the seriousness of the moment. He knew that a false step here could result in the end of their relationship, or at least a very serious setback. The man who advised the king, found himself in want of advice himself. He kicked himself inwardly for his ineptitude and wished he had handled things better.

"Hannah," he said, reaching for her elbow. "Please don't let the idle wanderings of a blank mind come between us. I very much enjoy our time together. I find myself drawn to you and longing to be with you."

These were words much closer to what Hannah had hoped to hear. She continued facing away from Gideon, but was beginning to turn toward him. He had her attention, and she was now hoping he would continue in the right direction.

Gideon paused again, unsure of himself, but fearing to end this poorly, "Would you?" he began, "Would you at least come with me for a walk?"

"A walk?" Hannah asked. It was not quite what she was hoping to be asked, but it had potential and was certainly better than sending him away. "I would love to," she added confidently.

"Grand!" Gideon returned. "Shall we?"

He held out his elbow and she took it, smiling. He led her to and through the door. The street was beginning to empty. Most of the city's inhabitants were already in their homes enjoying their evening meal. They walked arm in arm along the alley toward the city square. As they passed by homes, they could hear snippets of conversations.

In some, mothers were asking their children for help with setting the places at the family table. In others, fathers were telling their sons of farming or hunting experiences. They came by one home where children were singing. They could hear the friendly, deep voice of their father joining in. In the homes were happy, harmonious sounds of life and constancy.

Gideon led Hannah into the city courtyard. It was deserted, except for a friendly, white dog that wandered through. It saw Gideon and its ears perked up. It trotted over to him. He bent down and patted its head, then rubbed its ears until its tail wagged furiously. Gideon could not help but smile. He patted the dog's side and sent it on its way.

"A friend of yours?" Hannah asked.

"Never seen him before," Gideon replied.

"Hmm, you seem to have a way with animals," she observed, "and people," she added looking back at him.

Gideon reached out his hand and she held it. "Come with me," he said, "I want to show you something."

They walked through the square and over to the city gate. The guard nodded warmly, "It's good to see you, sir," he said.

"Yes, Micah, it's good to see you, too. How is the city tonight?" he asked.

"Safe and sound," Micah replied, "Safe and sound, sir."

"Fine. Do you mind?" Gideon asked, gesturing to the ladder that led to the catwalk on the city gate.

"Not at all, sir," Micah smiled. "Should be quite a sight tonight!"

Gideon walked to the ladder and turned for Hannah. She smiled and began her climb. Gideon followed behind her. The ladder was only a gradual angle and poked up through an opening in the catwalk. It was almost like climbing stairs. It was only a dozen rungs to the top and an easy matter to step off and onto the catwalk. Hannah stepped aside and waited for Gideon to join her.

"This way," he said, again taking her hand.

They made their way to the west wall. There was a special area, wider than most with a rail for leaning on. It was used for observing across the field and toward the jungle that led to the area that housed the Waters of Mormon. They paused here and Gideon put his arm around Hannah as they leaned on the wall's rail.

"Look over there!" he pointed.

"Where?" she asked.

"In the grass, toward the trees. Do you see them?" Gideon continued to point.

"Oh, yes! I do now!" Hannah laughed as she saw two large spider monkeys running along, with their tails in the air.

"You don't normally see them on the ground," Gideon observed.

True enough, the monkeys leapt into the first tree they could reach and clambered up and out of sight.

"It's almost time," Gideon mused.

"Time? Time for what?" she asked.

"Time to show you what I brought you up here for," he said with a smile. "Just watch – over there," he continued to point westward.

The sun was now sinking slowly into the treetops. It was huge and orange. It gave off a marvelous flare of red, yellow and orange. The trees essentially glowed.

"It's beautiful!" Hannah exclaimed.

"Keep watching," Gideon coaxed. "Over there, directly west. Watch the tallest trees."

The sun was now almost perfectly framed in the trees. Suddenly, the top fell out of sight. At that moment, beams of light shot out through the branches and spread out over the rest of the jungle, bathing the area in light and warmth. And, in an instant, the beams died down just as suddenly and allowed the sun to set.

"Oh, my!" Hannah breathed out, "I have never seen anything like that!"

"I've always wanted to share that with someone special," Gideon replied, putting his arm around her.

She snuggled up to him, closed her eyes and breathed in deeply, basking in the scent of a thousand flowers that the warm jungle breeze carried caressingly into the city. They remained there for a while, not talking, not moving, just enjoying each other's company. The sunset was long gone and the darkness of night was falling onto the land of Nephi before the stirred.

At last, Gideon said, "I think it's time."

"Time, time for what?" she asked, wondering what more this mysterious man had planned for her.

"You will see soon enough," he said with a smile and a wink. "Follow me."

As he stepped away, he again took her hand and led her back to the area with the ladder. "Let me go first, just in case," he said, not wanting her to stumble.

He reached the ground and waited for her to descend. She soon joined him and asked, "Now, where are we off to?"

"You will see, just follow me," he said, still grinning.

They walked back to the city courtyard. They were about halfway across when Gideon suddenly stopped.

"I think it was about here," he observed, looking around carefully and then appearing satisfied.

"About here, what?" Hannah asked.

"About here that we first met," Gideon responded. "Do you not remember? You were down here, scooping up grain that some callous soldier had caused you to spill." Gideon knelt down on the spot and scooped the dirt into little heaps, with his hand.

"Yes, such a rude solider that was!" Hannah chided him with a big smile.

"And, who would have thought that that very same soldier would one day ask you something," Gideon added.

"Ask me what?" she pried.

Gideon shifted his crouching position so that he was now on one knee, he reached out his hand to her and said, "Ask you to marry me,"

Hannah's heart leapt. She threw her arms open wide and wrapped them around her handsome courter. Gideon lost his balance and the two of them fell to the earth. Hannah repeated over and over, "Yes! Yes! Yes!" On the farthest edge of the courtyard, Micah had heard a sound and turned to see the two of them rolling in the dust. He smiled, knowingly.

"We seem to be destined to be dirty!" Gideon laughed as the two of them finally sat up.

Hannah pulled her hair from her eyes, smiling and giddy, "As long as we're together, I don't mind!"

Torches were being lit around the perimeter of the square. Couples who had finished their evening meals were now entering the area for their evening stroll. Gideon, and his newly betrothed, wished them well as they walked, arm-in-arm from the square, just to wander for a few more hours together.

* * * * *

Not everyone appreciated the freedoms that the Nephites seemed to be able to enjoy in the Land of Nephi. The Lamanites would not be ignored. While they respected the oath of peace and thus refrained from deadly acts of violence, as time went on, they found more means of harassing their pale-skinned neighbors. King Limhi, the unanticipated early heir to the empire, would soon learn of such altercations.

As he sat upon his throne receiving an update on the new cistern being dug in the city square, the guards at the throne room door became aware of people seeking an audience with his majesty. The taller guard listened to a hastily given request that bordered more on a demand. With others in the throne room who had overheard the disturbance, including Limhi, watching him, the tall guard walked over to the throne guard.

He whispered the request to the guard, who nodded in reply. The door guard returned to his position as the throne guard turned and faced his king. He stood wordlessly awaiting acknowledgment from the king.

"What is it?" Limhi asked patiently.

"Several citizens have a complaint they wish to levy against the Lamanites, your majesty."

"The Lamanites? What sort of complaint?"

"Apparently, they feel abused, your majesty. They seek an audience with you to explain, sir."

"Well, what –? Very well, have them enter," Limhi stated, deciding to save his questions for those more directly involved in whatever incident had apparently occurred.

A group of five men entered the throne room. They huddled together, looking about them as they reverently approached their king. They knew enough to bow before him, once the guard led them to where they were to stand.

"What is this abuse I hear that you have suffered at the hands of our benefactors?" Limhi asked.

"Benefactors! Ha! Our guards, you mean!" one of the Nephites sputtered.

Limhi's brow furrowed and one of the guards quickly shot the man a warning look to be careful how he addressed the king.

"We've made a truce with the Lamanites. They have permitted us to continue to live in their land, but we must also allow them to keep an eye on how we treat their land," Limhi replied, trying to avoid any exposition or revelation on his personal feelings about the situation. "What has happened to bring you here today?"

No one in the group spoke at first. They all looked back and forth at each other and continued to huddle close together. Finally, one of them nudged a man whose nose showed signs of having recently bled.

"Tell him!" his insistent friend urged.

The king's attention turned to the wounded man.

"Yes, tell me."

The man took a step forward, breaking away from the group.

"Your majesty – uh – your majesty. We have had problems," the man stammered, then paused.

"Yes, I gathered that," Limhi said, filling the silence. In a more benevolent, almost fatherly tone, he added, "Please, tell me what has happened. How can I help?"

"I'm a farmer. We – we are all farmers. We work in the eastern field. For several weeks now, the Lamanite guards have been coming around and taunting us. They haven't done much. We think they just want to intimidate us. Recently, it has gotten worse, though. They have begun to push us around while we are trying to hoe. They will knock our tools down and laugh. As we pick them up, they knock them down again."

Limhi's face grew more concerned the more he heard of the predictable behavior.

"We have asked them to leave us at peace, but they refuse. They return in greater numbers and taunt us all the more. They pushed my friend here and caused him to fall in the mud. I spoke up against them and they slapped me."

"They slapped him several times, until his nose bled and we all had to plead for them to stop," his friend added.

"I was afraid of this," Limhi unintentionally let slip out. "Please, go back to your fields and do your best to avoid the Lamanites. Do not disrupt the peace or give them any excuses that might provoke them."

"Avoid them?! With all due respect," a third voice from the group spoke up, "That is what we have been trying to do! They hunt us down and torment us like a cruel master would mistreat a lazy dog!"

"Nevertheless, do your best to keep in their good graces," Limhi replied.

"That's it?! That is all you can say?! How will this help? How will we end this?"

"That is all I will say for now. My advisors and I will see about a more fitting solution," Limhi said.

"A fitting solution would be to fight back and rid ourselves of these Lamanites!" one of the group said.

"Yes. Well, we will see what we can do," was all Limhi replied.

He motioned to have the men removed. His guards obeyed. When they had the throne room to themselves again, an advisor sitting in the traditional priests' seats gave a look toward the door, then turned to his king.

"It's just as I said. They increase in numbers daily. These incidents are only going to grow worse. We must find a way of freeing ourselves from this oppression," he predicted.

"I agree. But, what can be done? They hopelessly outnumber us. Fighting would be genocide. I cannot condone it," Limhi replied emphatically.

"It's genocide only if we do not adequately prepare ourselves! If we are properly armed, we will have the upper hand. They come to battle nearly bare all over. If we were to put on armor to protect ourselves, surely we could compensate for our smaller number!" another advisor added.

"Maybe, but we just are not prepared for this now," Limhi cautioned,

"Then maybe we should begin to prepare for this," the first advisor suggested.

* * * * *

Several months passed. As predicted, the incidents grew in frequency and intensity. The people wearied the king with constant complaints of minor abuses. The advisors, too, wearied him with constant prodding of going to war.

"All right," Limhi said after a group of women left his throne room teary-eyed over a pushing incident while they were picking fruit. "I believe it's time. Call out the armory, assemble the men. It's time to drive the Lamanites out of the land of Nephi!"

Limhi spoke boldly and the room erupted in applause at his words. News spread quickly and the city square was filled to capacity with men the next day. They were eager to go to battle and rid themselves of the scourge that infested their homeland. The men checked each other's armor and slapped each other's shoulders as a token vote of good luck in the battle.

* * * * *

The black was just beginning to tear away from the sky, leaving a dark blueness in its wake. The soldiers' leather-sandaled feet were soon soggy from the heavy dew on the thick grass. They continued southward, ignoring their surroundings. The sun was beginning to crest over the trees as they entered the southern jungle. They continued forward, hacking their way through the thick undergrowth, but speaking no words.

Their intent was well known among them all. No words were necessary. They were bent on catching their oppressors off guard and breaking the hold they held on their society. If they could reach their borders unannounced, the advantage would be theirs. If all went well, they would return home victorious. If –

Gideon's head was the first to peer through the southern fringe of the jungle. The open field was devoid of human life. Far to his right, he could see the Lamanite city of Shemlon. Other than the wispy remains of a few smoldering camp fires, the city appeared to remain asleep. Perhaps this would be the day for which they had longed.

He turned and motioned for the troops to advance. The field rapidly filled with Nephite invaders on a stealth attack. They moved quickly and with precision. Shemlon's wooden city wall was only a hundred yards distant. It was not half as imposing as the stone one that surrounded the city of Nephi. The hatchet men gripped their weapons in anticipation. Its thick wood would surely be no match for their finely honed tools.

All attention was focused forward, on their target. This added to their confusion when the blasts of horns came from their right, to the north. Some of the men nearly stumbled in mid-trot as they looked toward the trees. Not a soul could be seen, but the horn blasted a second warning. Its message was unmistakable.

Gideon vainly tried to urge his men on at a greater speed. He saw it as his solemn duty to protect his new bride and was anxious to see that his mission succeed. In spite of his efforts, the advancing army slowed, then stopped. Hope sank. Some of the men debated retreating even before the arrows were sighted. Men dropped suddenly left and right as arrows managed to find their targets on the fringes of the armor. Another wave of arrows could be seen soaring over the city wall and arching directly toward them.

Just as the arrows let loose, the western gate burst open. Lamanite warriors poured out of the city screaming a hideous challenge. Their faces were painted. Their heads were shorn bald. Their dark chests, arms, and legs were bare. They approached unafraid. More warriors charged from around the outer side of the southern wall. Still more hastily emerged from the jungle to the north. It was painfully, brutally clear that the Nephite advancement was not a surprise to the Lamanites. Not by a long shot.

A scattering of Nephites were just dropping from the latest onslaught of arrows as the rest realized that somehow their attack was not just anticipated, but well prepared for. Their mood had significantly shifted from the moment earlier when they thought they were on the verge of releasing themselves from their burdensome oppressors. Now, they found themselves nearly completely surrounded, with little hope of ever seeing their loved ones again.

Gideon tried to rally his troops to stand and fight. Unfortunately, his example of valor was quickly countered and undone by countless examples of morally defeated Nephites as they simply turned and fled at full speed back the way they had come.

The charging Lamanites laughed out loud as they closed in on their prey. Unfortunately, those who remained for the engagement were those who were the slowest to retreat or the few bold souls who were determined to make a stand. In either case, they were hopelessly outnumbered by a ferocious people who delighted in such sport as this.

The Nephite armor merely delayed the inevitable. Outnumbered seven to one, the remaining Nephites could not possibly hold out for long. The fighting lasted less than a quarter of an hour. The Nephites were soundly defeated, while the Lamanites' taste for a good fight was just barely whetted.

Gideon had been knocked unconscious by a blow which struck him while he had turned to shout rallying orders to his men. When he came to, the slaughter was over. While coming to, first thoughts were of his lovely Hannah. They had been married for only a few, short weeks. King Limhi himself had agreed to perform the ceremony. The temple was sparkling that day. Gideon had never been so happy. Hannah had never looked so beautiful.

Now, he found himself fallen on the field of battle, still within the enemy's grasp. He knew he would somehow make it home. He had to. He kept his wits about him and remained motionless and horizontal. He could see that the Lamanites were beginning to come and search among the dead and wounded. If he was to survive, or at least keep from being taken captive, he would need to be gone before they got to him.

Carefully looking in all directions, he verified that he was unobserved. No one was near, other than the bloodied, lifeless forms of his former comrades who had lost their lives in a fruitless effort. He gathered his feet below him and turned to face the nearest woods, still crouching low. Taking a sprinter's stance, shifting his weight to rest on his fingertips and toes, he took one final look about him and then took off at a tremendous pace toward the woods and hoped-for freedom. His wounded head pounded painfully with each step.

He had gone only a dozen yards when a Lamanite saw him and alerted his comrades. Some shouted scornfully. Some considered charging after him. Others simply laughed. They did not feel that he was worth their bother. An archer decided to test his skill and slowly took aim. Gideon continued racing forward. The archer's arrow was let loose and soared toward its target. It zeroed in on Gideon's streaking form with precision.

Just as Gideon would have entered the wood, the arrow came down on target. Gideon, perhaps by instinct, shifted his direction suddenly to the right. The arrow came down on cue, but missed Gideon by a mere two feet, sinking threateningly into the rich soil. He noted its fall and quickly dashed into the hidden sanctuary the rainforest provided. A fellow Lamanite slapped the archer in the back of the head, jostling him teasingly. The archer smiled and shrugged. Gideon continued homeward at a steady pace.

Chapter 16
Alternatives

The crying and lamenting seemed to have no end. Mothers continued to mourn for lost sons, wives for slain husbands, and children for fallen fathers. Hannah's initial exultation and relief upon Gideon's return – even after the Last Battalion had returned – was tempered and soured by the pains of friends and neighbors who would never know the same miracle of relief she had experienced.

Even the king lamented the loss of a good portion of his best men. The only ones who had actually engaged the Lamanites had been those few valiant souls who chose fight over flight. Gideon and only a handful of other seasoned soldiers were among the very few of these soldiers who managed to returned to Nephi. They were unable to retrieve the fallen. Sadly, their bodies laid still and silent on the plains of Shemlon for the birds and wild animals to care for.

Surprisingly, there were no direct reprisals for the skirmish. Perhaps King Laman felt that a solid defeat was punishment enough. The most tangible difference was that the abusive antics of the Lamanite guards picked up in severity and frequency. The Nephites found themselves living in a most oppressive condition. The prophecies of Abinadi were being fulfilled in an all-too-literal manner. The mood among the Nephite nation was now dismal at best. Their poorly-tended crops began to wilt and wane as equally as their spirits.

Hunger, fatigue, loneliness, and fear plagued the city. Far too many new widows wandered the city seeking sustenance which, until recently, their husbands would have provided. The cries continued and eventually found their way to the king. Limhi was at a loss as to how to rebuild his people. The attempt to free them had only deepened the slavery in which they found themselves.

Day after day after day their trials began to wear down each soul. Fear gave way to frustration which led to indignation and then blended into anger. Gradually, the people forgot the slaughter which came of their futile battle and merely focused on their anger. Words of revenge and retribution began to spill out upon the streets. The hostile words took root among the disenchanted and became a cause.

The people sent a delegation to the king, demanding that the army be reassembled for another attack. The king gave audience to a dozen emotional men.

"These Lamanites must be dealt with now and with severity!" the tallest delegate, Zoram, demanded.

"Yes, but by what means?" the king asked with more of an attempt to point out the futility of a forceful approach than as a sincere request for guidance.

"By force! By arms! By warfare!" Zoram declared.

"By force? By arms? By warfare?" Limhi questioned. "Have you forgotten the slaying of our noble brethren? They were cut down without so much as drawing their own swords in attack!"

"Yes, I remember. But, they were poorly led and ill prepared. We now know that such a sneak attack is fruitless. We have other plans now!" Zoram responded.

"Other plans? And what, pray tell, might they be?"

"We will draw the Lamanites out directly. If we can bring them into the field of battle and fight them with honor, we will prevail!" Zoram pounded his fists together and then quickly thrust his clenched hand out in front of him to emphasize his determination.

"I have my doubts," was all the king replied as he slowly shook his frustrated head and brought his hand to his temple to caress another painful throb in his head.

"You may doubt, but we will win! We will rid these Lamanites from our backs and return to our peaceful lives!" Zoram said emphatically gesticulating with emotional charge.

"I have difficulty seeing how you will succeed–" Limhi began, but was cut off by thunderous shouting.

The rest of the delegates each spoke rapidly and with intense enthusiasm in support of the attack. The throne room echoed and shook at the intensity of the shouting. Disorder was taking over. Limhi's anger grew with equal velocity. He stood, stamping his royal staff as he did so. Its piercing thumping was heard over the din.

"Enough! Enough!!" Limhi shouted. "Need I have you forcibly removed?!" Gradually, the arguing subsided and the king was able to speak. "As I was saying, I have difficulty seeing how you will succeed, but I do not know of any other way to seek peace for our people. Gather your armies and attack our oppressors. That is all I will say at this time. Now out!"

The angered king motioned for them to leave and then sat down with an angry thump upon his throne. His guards stepped forward to ensure the king's order to leave was obeyed quickly.

Gideon stood in the far corner of the throne room with a frustrated look on his face. The cheering dozen left the throne room in search of their army. Gideon paused, allowing his eyes and thoughts to drift away from their exit. He then silently and quickly made his way out of the room. He was intent on catching Zoram privately and talking some sense into him. He felt that outside of the public spotlight, where Zoram sought to protect his standing with the king, he could be made to see reason.

He caught up with Zoram and his entourage on the fringes of the city square. He was hoping to pull Zoram away from his men, so they could talk privately, "Zoram! Zoram!" Gideon called out, but Zoram refused to slow his pace or even acknowledge Gideon's voice. The rest of his men were waiting for him in the center of the square. They sat at tables under canopies drinking and waiting for word from their leader.

Gideon refused to be ignored. He ran up to Zoram and grabbed him by the arm, just as Zoram was nearing the first table. Feeling Gideon's firm grip on his arm, Zoram stopped and turned to look at Gideon with irritation. He glared back at him and demanded, "Take your hand off me!"

The men who had been walking with Zoram stopped and surrounded Gideon with menacing looks in their eyes. The men at the table shifted and prepared to stand up and defend their mentor. Gideon ignored them all. He tightened his grip and leaned in closer to Zoram and spoke directly into his ear, still trying to keep this a private matter.

"Zoram," Gideon insisted, "Don't do this! It can't work! It will not help!"

Zoram twisted free and waved his hand by his head to flick Gideon away like he was some sort of nasty fly, "Get out of here! Stop whispering to me!"

"Zoram," Gideon continued. He could see that Zoram was not going to allow this to be a private matter. He also refused to back down. He now spoke loud enough for those closest to them to hear, but still did not raise his voice. "Do not do this! We have enough widows and orphans already. We will do better to raise our families than to raise our arms in a futile fight. We cannot beat them. Not yet, anyway. Not like this. We need more time."

"Time? Time?!" Zoram was preparing to make a public display of his own pomp and bravado. He knew his men were going to hang on his every word and watch to see how he handled this impudent man who dared to question his abilities to succeed. He raised his voice, and waved his arms as he spoke, "We have no time to waste! We must strike and strike now. We must be bold and unafraid to show these Lamanites that we will not roll over and let them dictate to us how we will live our lives!"

Several of his men cheered and clapped, encouraging their leader to continue.

Gideon remained undeterred, "Zoram, do you not see! They outnumber us. Yes, we have got better weapons and shields, but they by far outnumber us! We can't take on so many and expect to persevere!"

Gideon again leaned forward and lowered his voice. He added the following in a hushed way that only Zoram would hear it, in hopes of getting through to the man, "Your wife and children lost you once. Do not make them lose you again!"

Zoram knew painfully well that Gideon was referring to his having abandoned his family to flee along with King Noah. It was shame and disgrace that had eventually brought Zoram, and several of those who now shared the city square with him, to return to Nephi. In fact, it was this same shame and disgrace that now prodded him to action. He was determined to overcome his previous inactions by a show of force and determination against the enemy that had once caused him to run.

Zoram pushed Gideon back, "Whisper not to me, you cowardly buffoon!"

Zoram put on a strong front, but Gideon felt he had struck the right nerve. He did not want to manipulate or torment the man. He just wanted to bring him to his senses.

"Zoram," he continued, "There are better ways. This is a fight we can't win! Not yet, anyway."

"You mean this is a fight you dare not attempt!" Zoram bit back. "Not all of us are cowards, Gideon! Nor are we traitors, bent on depriving this beautiful city and these fine people of the only hope they have of liberty and freedom!"

His men again cheered and pumped Zoram's ego. "You may be afraid to defend your city, but we are not! And, if you continue to stand in our way, we will have to move you out of our way – permanently!" With this, Zoram made a fist with his thumb extended and brought it in a slow sweeping motion across his throat. "Now be off with you! We men have plans to make! You run off home to your wife, or your child, or whatever it is spineless little men like you run off to when real men have duties to fulfill!"

Gideon was about to reply when two men on either side of Zoram stepped toward him and gave him a powerful shove. "Yes! Be off, coward!" They pushed him again, and Gideon stumbled backward and tripped on a basket. The men laughed him to scorn. He stood again and tried to get back to Zoram, but the men continued to taunt and harass him. They had now surrounded Zoram to the point that Gideon could not even see him.

He tried several times to push his way into the throng, but the men just pushed back all the more, shouting and threatening him. One of them finally said with what actually sounded like a touch of genuine concern, "Gideon, just leave!"

Reluctantly, Gideon was forced to do just that. He left with a heavy heart, ignoring the din and jeers that still filled the square and echoed down the streets. He was not so much sorry for himself, as he was frustrated and concerned about the welfare of his people. He knew deep inside that this campaign would not go well.

He later voiced his concern to his wife. She shook her head sadly, and asked what he would do. He turned to her and said simply, "The only thing I can do."

*****

The sun was nearly perfectly overhead as the Nephites stormed out of the southern gate and into the farmland. The Lamanite guards were both surprised and amused by this change in pace. The Nephites marched boldly southward. The guards who had been lingering in the field anticipating the day's prey, headed in the same general direction, but by a separate course. The Nephites moved quickly, but their army was unable to keep pace with their solitary guards who dashed ahead of them, through the thick jungle that separated their two lands.

The army was just emerging from the southern side of the jungle as the Lamanites came upon them. The fighting was again intense. Swords clanged with an unholy, heart-wrenching sound. Too often that sound was followed by the dying shout of a Nephite struck with a mortal blow. Again outnumbered, they fought for their lives.

The tide of the battle never once favored the Nephites. Their armor only slowed their deaths. It did not prevent them. In spite of the metal shielding, there remained too many vulnerable, exposed areas. A Lamanite sword against a bare Nephite forearm quickly left the adversary with no recourse. Death soon followed.

Not too many minutes passed before even the most dogmatic men from the north had to admit defeat and flee for their lives. Soon, the entire Nephite army was again overcome and routed. They turned in disarray and frantically fled. The Lamanites followed only long enough to taunt them some more. The last sounds the Nephites heard as they tore through the brush and frantically ran northward were the groans of the dying and the laughing of their mortal enemies.

Gideon had observed it all. He took it all in and shook his head. He had managed only token support on the fringes of the battle. He had known that their cause was futile, but he had to do what he could to defend his nation. Zoram had made it painfully clear that his presence was far from welcome on "his" battlefield. Still, Gideon had come to offer what support he could and to observe the events so as to learn anything of value from them. What he learned from his observations did nothing to cheer his weary heart. Once again, his thoughts drifted back to the prophecies of Abinadi. The people were truly being driven as that martyred prophet had foreseen.

* * * * *

Due to the speed and preemptive timing of their flight, the self-promoted military leaders had reached the throne room ahead of Gideon. They were in mid-debate as Gideon was given leave by the throne room guards to enter.

"Mighty king, these heathen beasts must be taught a lesson!" Zoram bit out. "Let us return one more time and we will put them in their places! They defy us as a people and you as our king!"

"What do you mean they defy us?" Limhi asked.

"As our men were cut down in the cruelest manner, they laughed and taunted us!"

"What?!" the king was enraged at the triviality they had made of their valiant sacrifices.

"I insist we attack again tomorrow!" Zoram said.

"Do as you will," the king responded in an exasperated tone. "Do as you will. Just leave me now."

"We will conquer!" Zoram vowed stoically.

"Very well. Fine. Just leave me now."

Zoram bowed with exaggerated reverence, then straightened and turned quickly. As he marched through the room and toward the doorway, Gideon was just entering. They bumped shoulders and Zoram stopped for a moment and eyed Gideon sternly. He about gave an insulting remark, but thought the better of it and instead snubbed his nose at him and continued out with his entourage of officers. Gideon felt more sorrow than contempt for the man. He wished that he would have listened to reason, but knew he was too caught up in making this a personal matter.

Gideon continued farther into the throne room. Limhi sat upon a troubled throne. He sat sideways, laying his forehead in his fingertips, his right elbow resting on the arm of the stone serpentine throne, as he lamented over the frustrating loss.

"We will never be free again," Limhi mournfully whispered to himself.

"Great king," Gideon began, trying to draw attention to himself and gain an audience with his majesty. "Great king," he repeated. "Please, do not send these people into battle again."

Limhi turned to see who was speaking to him. He saw Gideon, respectfully standing before him. "What?"

"I beg of you, my king, do not send these people to battle against the Lamanites."

"Why?"

"Because they cannot win."

"And why not?"

"I have watched this people. I have fought the Lamanites myself. I have seen their forces. We are too few in number. Our people lack the skills of swordsmanship. The Lamanites do not just outnumber us, but they're more deft and quicker than our people. They are a brutal people, yes, but they are wise to the ways of the sword. Most of our greatest swordsmen died in the first encounter. Those remaining are simply too few in number or too unskilled in the ways of war to do much more than to offer up their lives in your service. I pray you, please, do not send these people to battle again."

"Gideon, I appreciate your words, but the people must be made free. We cannot continue to live in this land with such oppression. The Lamanites grow increasingly harsh. Our farmers fear tending their flocks and fields. Without their harvest, we will slowly starve. Something must be done to ease our burdens!"

"I am reminded, your majesty, of a man who stood where I now stand, so many years ago. He warned your father of such events. He warned him that if this people did not repent and return to God, we would be driven as a beast of burden, abused, and miserable," Gideon spoke.

"Yes," Limhi acknowledged. "It seems Abinadi was right. So very right." He paused, and then asked, "So, how do we free ourselves from such bondage?"

"First, we do as Abinadi warned and return our hearts to God. It's time we offer up our prayers to the Lord that He will deliver us from our bondage. But, I believe there's more we can do."

"What is that?"

"You said yourself that we cannot live in this land under such conditions. Perhaps it's time we left this land." The king was not the only one in the throne room to look up at Gideon suddenly at this suggestion. "Perhaps it's time we returned to Zarahemla," he concluded.

"Return to Zarahemla?!" The king pondered the implications. "Return to Zarahemla? Give up the land of Nephi and return? –"

"I am afraid, your majesty," Gideon offered, "that it's not so much to give up at this time. Our people are not happy here. They're not safe. They cannot thrive. I fear they will all die. I can see no other alternative."

"Yes, but leave the land of Nephi?"

"Yes, your majesty, I believe we must."

"But, it's been so many years. There is no one alive in this city that has ever even been to Zarahemla. How will we find the way?"

"I propose sending a small group of men to explore the northern territory to find Zarahemla. Once found, these men can return and lead the people north to rejoin the rest of the Nephites and live again in peace and prosperity."

"I see your point. I regret its necessity. Yes, your plan is sound. Choose men whom you trust and leave immediately!" the king commanded.

"Me?!" Gideon exclaimed. Then realizing the inevitability of the decision and the opportunity it offered him to perform a true and lasting service to his country, his face mellowed and he replied, "Yes, your majesty, it will be an honor."

He bowed and left the throne room to gather his men and provisions. Once he was gone, Limhi said to himself, "Meanwhile, let us hope Zoram is successful tomorrow. If not, we will surely have to follow Gideon north."

Chapter 17
Decisions and Confessions

Zoram spent the evening rousing his men and calling them to arms. He gave a passionate speech in the city square calling for every able-bodied man to aid in the quest to free the city from their Lamanite oppressors. Zoram was determined to verbally whip and emotionally batter the men until they would agree to make one final attempt to undermine a more powerful army.

Gideon, on the other hand, had a quieter objective. He visited six of his closest friends and delivered word that they were to meet him at the old courtyard on the southwestern corner of the city at sunset. They were asked to each bring six of their most trusted allies and were told they would receive further instructions at that time. The appointed hour arrived and forty-three level-headed Nephites gathered in a seldom-used section of the city.

"What's this all about, Gideon?" Micah asked.

"We are going to find a way out of here," Gideon replied.

"'A way out'? What do you mean?" Micah asked, with a deeper look of puzzlement growing on his face.

"We are going to find the way back to Zarahemla. If we can find the way back, we can get these people out of here and live in freedom again," Gideon said.

"But, that would mean leaving the land of Nephi!" Josiah said with shock.

"Yes, it would. Tell me, what is there about this land that makes it habitable?" Gideon asked.

"It's the land of Nephi!" Josiah said.

"And, we are dying here!" Gideon pointed out with clarity.

"Zoram's about to lead the attack to free –" Josiah began, but was cut off.

"Zoram's about to lead too many men to a certain death," Gideon countered. "I know it and you know it."

The room was silent for a moment as each man had to agree with Gideon's point.

"And, if we do not find some other way of saving this people, we will be more vulnerable to Lamanite persecution than we have ever been. With each attack we lose more and more good men – the true and valiant ones willing to stand up for our rights. In the end, the only ones left will be those who are first to retreat. What sort of protection will they offer the city, and its ever-growing population of widows and fatherless? If our people are to survive, it's going to have to be in some other land. Not here. Not now."

"You're right, of course, Gideon," Josiah responded. "I guess I just didn't want to admit it. I didn't want to lose the dream."

"It's not the dream that went bad, Josiah," Gideon stressed. "It was the people. We should never have let King Noah and his so-called 'priests' gain so much control over us. When the leaders fall, it's just too easy for the people to tumble down alongside them. It's as if we believe their bad example is a justified excuse for our not making moral decisions on our own."

Gideon's fist unconsciously tightened its grip on his sword as he thought of the slovenly King Noah and the figurative pit that he had dug and then used to bury the people's morals. The thought of raising his family in captivity, or worse still, under the evil reign of someone such as King Noah, made his heart burn. He would do everything in his power to find a better home.

"We need to get these people away from here. The only sanctuary I know of is Zarahemla. I cannot do this alone. I need men I can trust to go with me. Good men. You. Will you do this?"

The men all rose and took a step or two toward Gideon. Micah went right up to him and put his hand on Gideon's shoulder. He spoke on everyone's behalf.

"We are with you Gideon. What's the plan?"

Gideon smiled and nodded. "Thanks. I knew that I would be able to count on you. Each of you." After they had all shaken hands in token agreement of their pact to seek the land northward, Gideon added, "Our first trick will be getting out of the city without being seen."

"We will have to pick a time when the Lamanite guards are not paying attention."

"I was not just referring to the Lamanites. I do not trust Zoram. I think he is too focused on leading a lost cause and gaining some sort of misdirected glory for himself. I also think if he catches us, there will be trouble."

"What sort of trouble?"

"I'm not sure. I just do not trust him. I think we need to be careful."

"We should leave tonight, then," Josiah said.

"Tonight?"

"Certainly, his mind's focused on the morning's battle. We should be able to sneak over this west wall while he is busy in the main city square."

"I see your point. Can everyone do this?" Gideon asked.

"Give us an hour. We will be here."

"Good. See you then. This should be a long trek, so pack accordingly."

"How long do you think?" Micah asked.

"The records say it took Zeniff something over forty days to travel here from Zarahemla. We'll take at least that and then some to find our way back. I think we should plan on at least sixty days up, a week there among the people to prepare them for receiving our people, and then another forty days back. At least."

"Good point. All right. We will meet back here just after sunset."

*****

Hannah watched her husband pack. She was grim and silent. In their short time together, she had already seen him go off to battle more times than she cared for. This time was different. This time he was heading off to the unknown. The land was unknown. The way was unknown. The dangers were unknown.

In some ways, this bothered her even more than his going to battle against the Lamanites. At least they knew what to expect with the Lamanites. With a journey that was planned to take several months into uncharted territory, there was no guarantee that they would even be able to find their way back. She was concerned and deep in thought.

Gideon continued to pack. He sensed his wife's concern and tried to make small-talk. What he did not know was the depth of her thoughts. She had something weighing on her mind that had been there from the day they had first met. It gnawed at her and begged to be brought out into the open. For some reason that she could not explain, she did not want her husband to leave – once again – on a trek that could be his last, without first finally revealing her secret.

She was ignorant of Gideon's talk. To her it seemed as just more background noise. Suddenly, she sensed that it had ceased. She had been looking down, blankly, at the bed that held Gideon's pack. She could see Gideon's hand in it and followed his arm with her eyes, upward until she looked into her husband's face.

"Hannah? Hannah?" Gideon was repeating. "Are you all right?"

"Huh? What?" Hannah responded, dazed. She shook her head to clear it. "Oh, uh, I was just thinking."

"I have been calling your name for several minutes, it seems," Gideon said. "What's wrong?"

"I was thinking," she repeated.

Gideon did not press her. His patient, loving heart told him that she was thinking of something serious and wanted to give her all of the time she needed to find the words to express whatever it was that was on her mind.

"Gideon," Hannah said meekly, pulling her gaze away from her husband and looking downward, focusing on nothing.

"Yes?" he said.

"I – I have something to tell you. Something I'm not proud of."

Gideon's face suddenly flushed. He suddenly felt nervous and a little afraid. His mind raced, trying to come up with a possibility for what she could have done. Try as he might, he simply could not come up with even a hint. She was that good of a person. Sensing she was waiting for him to speak, he said the only thing that came to mind, "What is it?"

"Do you remember that day – the day we all fled into the jungle with King Noah?"

Gideon had relived that day a thousand times. On nights when he could not sleep, he would lie on his bed and relive his chase after King Noah up the tower. He would vividly see each and every step in his mind. He could feel his sword in his hand and the sweat as it streamed from his hair as he rounded the spiraling corners and pounded the next step, lurching forward to catch up with the obscene monarch.

Always he would see each nuance of the chase in such great detail, that it would take three to four times longer to relive it than it actually took in real life. It was as if everything he saw was so full of detail that his mind would study each detail and slow down the events for him, so that he could grasp them all. Each time, he would feel himself raise his sword, ready to strike and then hear Noah's voice call for clemency in light of the approaching Lamanites.

Even though his passion would scream against it, each time he would agree to spare the king for the sake of the people. This would be followed by the inevitable anger and disgust as Noah would do nothing to save the people, but would instead flee into the jungles. Always, he would clench his eyes and fists at this. He could never decide if he had done the right thing by letting Noah go.

Certainly, Noah had received his just desserts, but would it have been so wrong for him to have stopped Noah on the tower? Was it Divine Intervention that forced Gideon to allow Noah to go? Why? WHY was it that each time he relived the day, he could never bring himself to cut Noah down? Why did he always – ALWAYS – spare Noah?

"Gideon?" Hannah asked, stirring Gideon from his thoughts, "Do you remember?"

Gideon shook his head and brought himself back to the present. He loosened his fists which he had subconsciously clenched, and turned his wandering gaze back to his wife, "Yes, my dear, I remember. I remember it well," he said. He then added to himself, "– perhaps too well."

"You know that when we saw that we would be overtaken by the Lamanites, it was suggested that the young and beautiful girls among our people should stop and bow down before the Lamanites and cry for mercy. It was hoped that their hearts would be touched by their fair beauty and the lives of the people would be spared."

"Yes, I know all this as well," Gideon said, he had to stop himself from pointing out that every child in the land of Nephi knew of this. This noble act of self-sacrifice was well respected among the people of Limhi. It was one of the tales that the people agreed to relate to the children – often – so that it would always be remembered. He wondered why she should be trying to remind him of such a well known deed. What was the point she was trying to make?

"Well, there's something that you do not know."

He continued to listen quietly, choosing to not interrupt.

"I – I was one of those girls. At least, I was among them."

Now, this was truly something he did NOT know. She had never spoken of it before. He was truly surprised by this revelation, and quite intrigued to find out how this related to what she was trying to tell him.

"I was there. I heard the plan. I heard Sarah's reply. I knew that they were right. I knew it would be dangerous, but I also knew it would be our only hope. We could hear the Lamanites coming. We could hear the cries of those they were slaughtering – being cut down as they begged for mercy. I wanted – with all of my heart – to do whatever I could to stop the slaughter.

"The men and women all hid themselves. The girls all stepped forward, bravely facing whatever fate the Lamanites would give them. We could hear them approach – they were very close. I stepped forward, too. But, just before the Lamanites arrived in the clearing, I jumped back and hid myself behind a tree!" She burst into tears. "I'm so ashamed!" She sobbed.

"Ashamed?" Gideon said, coming to her and putting his arm around her quivering body. "There's nothing to be ashamed of. You were in the midst of terrible danger. You were frightened. You did what many have done in such a situation."

Hannah cut him off – not in a rude way, but in an effort to allow full disclosure of the truth, "I did not jump back because I was afraid of being killed. I went back because I thought of what they had said. They had said that if the Lamanites were touched by our youth and beauty, they might spare the people. As I stepped forward, I realized that I am NOT beautiful and I did not want my presence to spoil the plan. I did not want the people killed because of me – because of my being vain enough to think that I was beautiful enough to stop their army!"

She pulled away from Gideon and flung herself down upon the bed, sobbing even more greatly. Gideon was at a complete loss for words. He prayed to find the words to comfort his beloved wife.

"My dear, sweet, lovely Hannah," he said, gently putting his powerful hands upon her shoulders. She jerked ever so slightly as if wanting to pull away, but overcoming that urge with the desire to be comforted. "I am so thankful that you have told me this."

Hannah's crying abated a moment. She put her hand down from her face and tried to look up at Gideon. She softly asked in a confused tone, "Thankful?"

"Yes, thankful," Gideon confirmed. "I can see that this was very difficult for you to say. I imagine it has been troubling you a great deal. And, I'm thankful that you trust me enough to share this great secret with me."

Hannah's tears had now fully stopped and she was able to look Gideon in the face. His eyes were deep brown and inviting. They were surrounded by smile lines that were growing deeper as he spoke in a loving, honest tone to her.

"I'm so very thankful that you can share this with me," he repeated. "It confirms that you have the same kind of trust and love for me that I feel for you."

Hannah managed a slight smile at this. Her heart beat just a little faster and she felt the color coming back to her face as the man she truly loved and admired continued to speak words of comfort to her troubled soul.

"I love you, Hannah. I always have, and I always will."

He opened his arms and invited her to him. Before she had the chance to come, he approached her and wrapped his arms around her gently, then firmly. She smiled deeply and closed her eyes with relief.

As they embraced, Gideon whispered into her ear, "As far as I'm concerned, you are the most beautiful Nephite in all the land of Nephi, both inside and out."

Hannah hugged her husband all the more. She shed more tears, but these were tears of joy and gratitude. She had never been so relieved nor felt so blessed in all her life. She was just so grateful to have such and kind and loving man take such care and interest in her and her feelings. She hoped that life with him would go on forever.

Then, she remembered. She was so caught up in the telling of her secret that she had forgotten for a moment that her dear husband was preparing to leave. He was not just preparing to leave, but to go off into the great unknown wilderness. She trusted him. If anyone could possibly find his way out and back again, it would surely be this remarkable man of hers. But, still, she was concerned, and already felt lonely.

"Do you really think you can find Zarahemla?" she asked.

"With the Lord's help, all things are possible." Gideon replied. "Will you be all right?"

"Yes, Gideon, I will be fine," she said with a smile, trying to put back on her strong self so as to reassure him and stop him from worrying more about her than he already had.

"You're certain?" he asked.

"Yes! Now, you better get packing, or you will be late for your own meeting!" she said insistently.

He smiled and stepped back to his gear. He stuffed his bedroll down into his pack.

"I'll be back before you know it," he said. "Besides," he added, turning to her and gingerly rubbing her expectant tummy, "I have to. I don't want us raising our children in a place where they're not free to roam the trees and fields without our fearing for their very lives."

He wrapped his arms around his sweetheart again and gave her a warm embrace.

Hannah whispered her lament, "But, it's just so far! No one knows the way!"

"We will be fine," Gideon comforted her. "We'll head as due north as we can. Zarahemla is supposed to be a very large city. Surely, there are other settlements surrounding it. Even if we don't find it ourselves, we're bound to run into at least *somebody* who is either from Zarahemla, or can tell us how to find it."

"Yes, but what if those people you run into are Lamanites?" Hannah pointed out with a flat, matter-of-fact tone.

"The Lamanites are to the south. Anyone north of here will be Nephites, and our friends." Gideon said this in a way that he almost made himself believe it, too.

"What if -" Gideon raised his hand and lightly touched his wife's lips with his fingertips.

"We will be fine. The Lord will be with us." He reassured her.

"It's just that I thought I lost you once," Hannah was almost quivering, "I don't want to lose you for real."

"I know. I will be careful. And," he looked into her deep, brown eyes showing as much confidence, love and reassurance as he could, "I

WILL be coming back." He paused, holding her gaze with his own, trying to will his confidence into her. "Now, where is little Simon?" he asked.

Gideon knew that little Simon was standing in the doorway, watching and waiting. The boy knew this was his cue to come forward. He ran up to his father, holding his arms up as far as they could reach. Gideon picked up his young son and raised him high above his head. As he reached the apex, he tossed him up into the air. The boy laughed as he flew freely for a moment and then quickly fell back into his father's strong hands.

"You're getting too big for this!" Gideon chided his son. "Soon you will be as big as I am!"

Simon laughed and hugged his father so tightly around the neck that Gideon had to pull at him to free himself, "Ah! That is quite a 'Simon hug' you're giving me. I haven't had one of those in a long time!"

Gideon pulled his son farther away from himself until the boy's grip was lost and his hands flung apart. They both laughed. "Come back here for a papa's hug," Gideon said as he pulled the boy warmly too him again.

He let his son back down onto the floor and put his hand on his shoulder. He knelt down to talk eye to eye with his son, "I'm going away for a while, Simon."

"Why can't I come?" Simon asked for the umpteenth time.

"You know why. It's much too far," Gideon answered for his umpteenth time. "While I'm gone, you're going to be the man of the family. I need you to watch over your mama and help take care of her. Can you do that?"

"Does that mean I have to do the dishes?" he asked.

"Yes, and sweep the floor, and make up your bed, and rake the dirt, and plant the seeds, and weed our garden..." Gideon teased. "You know it means you just need to be a big help with whatever mama needs. Can you do that?"

"I'll try," Simon said, looking down.

"That's fine," Gideon said. "I'm happy if you will just try. Because I know that when you try, you do very well." He picked up his son and held him so that he could sit in his arm. He raised his other arm to invite Hannah closer. She moved in and he gave her another embrace. For a moment, the little family stood there in a tender moment.

"I'll be back as soon as I can," Gideon whispered. "And, I'll bring back word of our new home in Zarahemla."

"I hope so," she said. "This is no place to raise our children." She looked her husband in the eye one more time and then leaned her head against his chest and hugged him deeply as she closed her eyes and whispered again, "I just hope so."

Chapter 18
The Land Northward

Forty three cloaked men gathered from different directions by the west wall. Each bore a small, but full leather pack bearing lengths of rope, a bed roll, a couple changes of clothes, a knife, and provisions for a day or two. All of the men realized they should be able to hunt more provisions on the way. As such, they planned to live off the land. A few had bows and arrows, or spears. Each man's sword hung from his side. These were needed not just for defense, but also to help cut their way through the dense, rarely traversed undergrowth of the northern rainforest.

They scaled the wall without verbally greeting each other. Within a moment, they had dropped silently to the ground on the outside of the great city wall. Looking about and ensuring they were still unseen, they dashed for the nearest jungle, which stuck out like an arboreal peninsula, a bit northwest of where they had scaled the wall. Without realizing it, they were heading for the same patch of jungle that Alma had sought a few years earlier.

Once they were secured behind the confines of the dense trees, they stopped and turned to look back. They could see the city wall across the black field behind them. Campfires and torches within the city square formed a wavering glow over the top of the wall, making the black sky directly beyond the city seem even more pitch.

They could still hear some of the shouts and talk of Zoram and his men, though they could not make out any of the words.

Gideon turned to his men and said, "Again, I thank you all for coming. We had better get moving. We should put quite some distance between us and Nephi before we make camp."

The men shouldered their packs and followed Gideon into the night. The going was difficult in the dark. The tall slender trees were bathed with thick undergrowth. They had agreed to not light their torches until they were well out of sight of the city, for fear of being spotted. They knew full well that even the smallest spark could be spotted from several hundred yards on a black, moonless night such as this.

After less than an hour's journey, however, they assessed that the brush was thick enough to wholly block any light. They paused and Gideon knelt. He pulled his flint out of his pack. Micah offered some kindling he had quickly gathered while Gideon had searched his pack.

The men stood in a circle around Gideon, trying to block the light, warm breeze. Gideon struck his knife hard against the flint. It both sparked and barked. With the first sounds of Gideon's strikes, Zerom, a broad-shouldered, youthful member of their party, instinctively looked back toward Nephi. Josiah looked at him, but said nothing.

"I'm sure we're far enough away by now," Zerom announced. He was consoling himself, as much as reassuring anyone else.

"Yes, quite," Gideon said as he struck the flint a few more times.

Finally, the sparks caught hold of the tinder. The first flame would have been barely discernible in daylight. In the blackness of the night, it was nearly blinding. The men watched it burn expectantly. Gideon bowed lower and carefully blew on the infantile flame, coaxing it to grow. When he felt certain it was going to successfully engulf Micah's offering, he reached quickly for a torch.

Hemnon, who had been assigned to bring several torches, handed one to him and passed out the remainder among the men. Gideon took it without turning his attention from the flames. He held it over the tinder and let it take fire. It caught quickly and wholly overpowered the view of its mother flame. Gideon stood, smiled, and proudly watched the torch burn. He stamped out the remainder of the dying embers that had given it birth.

When Gideon looked up, he saw two glowing lights above and beyond his men. It gave him a bit of a start at first, but when they moved in tandem, left and then right, he realized what it was and smiled.

"It looks like we have a visitor after all," he said as he held his torch up high above his head.

The men heard a monkey chatter and chide Gideon as it scampered off into the darkness of the trees. The others laughed and then held out their torches and lit them as well. Soon, the whole party had light. They looked around them. The flickering flames sporadically lit the trees and limbs above them, casting swaying and dancing shadows all about them. The glow cast by the torches had a peculiar affect on the jungle. It seemed to transform the men from traveling through an empty, outward-reaching void that consumed and devoured their presence, to a sense of being in a glowing bubble with the unknown void shying away just outside of the reach of their torches' glow.

Gideon waved his torch to the right and walked a few paces. The others followed. After only a dozen paces or so, he stopped and smiled. He held his torch high above his head. Its flicker bounced off and revealed underbrush that not only covered the ground at their level, but continued upward as far as his light could reveal. It was a hillside.

"It's just as I had hoped. We're on the right track. Unless I miss my guess, this is a portion of that hill that lies north of Nephi and west of Shilom. That means we're traveling due north."

"That's an incredible feat and a good sign, considering we have no stars to steer by," Micah acknowledged.

"It certainly is. And, I'll take all the good signs I can." Gideon smiled. "We should keep moving."

The band continued northward for another two hours. As they marched, they noticed the hill to their right gradually decline and eventually disappear. They had grown accustomed to walking beside this wall of earth. They had not noticed the sense of security it provided them until it was gone. As they walked beyond its reaches, they noticed that it opened up a fourth direction of an open, endless void of the jungle.

Though no one would confess this, they noted a sense of becoming vulnerable from their right where security had once reigned. This new vulnerability heightened the lack of protection from the other three sides. The occasional hiss of jungle snakes and growling of night animals on the prowl suddenly seemed more frequent and close.

"We should camp here," Gideon eventually announced. "We've gone far enough for our first night."

"Agreed," Josiah replied. "I'll stand the first watch. The rest of you can, well, just enjoy your rest."

"Excellent idea," Micah smiled as he pulled out his bedroll.

It was not long before all of the explorers, except Josiah, were resting peacefully.

*****

"Shh! Zerom, move over to the right more, or we'll lose them!" Gideon said in a hushed tone.

Zerom obeyed and crept stealthily to the right. He moved sideways, keeping his eyes focused forward and taking very broad side steps. He crouched low, enabling his legs to spread more widely, thus cutting down on the number of steps he had to take to cover the distance. As he felt for new footing with his searching right foot, he made sure he avoided stepping on any twigs or leaves that might reveal his position. He moved remarkably quickly, considering the care he took. His nimble, youthful frame gave him an advantage.

"Josiah, move more to the south!" Gideon ordered, keeping his voice low.

Josiah moved with equal deftness, though not quite as quickly as Zerom. He managed to get into place, nonetheless. Gideon looked to his men, then back at their prey. The herd of about a dozen tiny pudu deer stood still, drinking from the stream. The men were pleasantly surprised to find a herd of these elusive animals, and knew the deer would soon be done and then head instinctively to a denser section of the jungle for safety.

Gideon moved closer. Just as he drew his bow, the lead deer had its fill and looked up. Gideon let fly just as one of the deer turned to the north and started to bound off. His arrow missed, but the deer was caught in mid-flight of its second hop by another arrow. Zerom exhaled triumphantly as the deer fell dead by the side of the stream.

"Got him!" he cried out. "Got him!" and he ran toward his prize.

"Yes, you did!" Gideon acknowledged. He could not help but be a little amused at Zerom's youthful exuberance. "And now we need to get some more. Hurry, before they scatter!"

A host of arrows flew. Presently, several of the little deer were taken in a similar manner. The largest of the deer was only a little over two feet long. They were quickly cared for and converted into provisions, allowing the men to feast well on venison for breakfast and ensuring that they would not be hungry for several days. So far, the journey seemed to be highly favored.

The men were just repacking their gear after clearing up their breakfast when Gideon sensed something. He was not quite certain if it was just a matter of sensing something, or if it was that he had heard something. He had the vague sense in the back of his mind of having heard a twig snap. This was not too odd in and of itself. Twigs were snapping all over the camp as the men milled about gathering their gear and chatting good-naturedly as they did so.

Perhaps what caused Gideon to pause was the location of the snap he had heard. It seemed to come from the east side of the camp. So far as he could account for, none of his men were off in that direction. In fact – although he had not made any conscious effort to cause this to be the case – he was the easternmost person in their party.

He did a quick scan of the area and an unofficial, hurried headcount. Yes, he was certain of it. None of the men were over in the area where he thought he had heard a noise. Perhaps that was all there was to it. Perhaps he only *thought* he had heard something. By now, several moments had passed and there was no further noise. Perhaps it was just an echo, or his imagination.

But, no! There it was again. It was the faintest sound of leaves being carefully pressed upon other leaves, with a twig snapping under some form of shifting weight. He was certain he heard it now. Pretty certain, that is.

He cocked his head the way one does when trying to focus, even if it has no real affect on the senses. He scanned the trees carefully trying to see something – anything – whatever it was that had made the noise. He stood there, motionless. Listening. Watching. Breathing carefully, he was trying to not make the slightest noise that would prevent him from hearing it again. He needed to better triangulate the position.

Josiah happened to look over and see Gideon standing there in his awkward stance, holding his pack partly off the ground, frozen in mid-motion. He had no idea what was going on and asked, "Say, Gideon, what are you –"

"Shh!" Gideon hushed him immediately, raising a warning finger from his free hand to his lips.

Josiah understood without further explanation that some sort of imminent danger lurked nearby. Was it Lamanites? Had they been tracked and followed? Was it Zoram?! Would Zoram have bothered to follow them all this way? Why would Zoram be that determined?

Josiah's thoughts were interrupted by a sudden shift in Gideon's stance. "There, I heard it again!" Gideon said, pointing.

Josiah followed Gideon's arm and peered into the general direction he was pointing. Gideon himself stared and stared into the jungle trying to see whatever it was that he himself was pointing at. It did him no good. Vines hung from trees and simply dangled as they seemingly had for generations. Brush and small trees covered with leaves and fallen branches filled the jungle floor. There simply was not anything there.

"Wait," Gideon thought to himself, not daring to speak aloud, "What was that?"

He had seen the vaguest bit of movement. Yes, surely, something had moved and was moving again. It was more of a shadow than a "something," however. It was a blackness that moved in the shadowy blackness of the recesses of the thick jungle. It was nothing discernible, but it had definitely moved.

He saw it – and in some ways merely sensed it – move again. Slowly. Carefully. Steadily. Almost as if stalking.

Gideon looked ahead of the moving shadow. Several yards farther ahead, on the outskirts of their camp, Micah was stooped packing up the last of the pudu deer provisions into his pack. His back was towards the shadow. He was working carefully and steadily and wholly oblivious to anything that might be behind him. He was talking casually with Zerom, as both were still basking in their good fortune and preparing for their day's journey.

Gideon looked back, seeking the shadow. Josiah had crept up beside him now.

"What do you see?" Josiah whispered.

"I'm not certain," Gideon replied, barely audibly. "I haven't been able to make out anything more than just –"

His voice fell silent. The shadow had momentarily moved between two tall, slender trees that had an unusually large gap between them. In the space, the shadow revealed itself.

"My word!" Josiah gasped. "I haven't seen one that large before!"

"And, certainly never at this time of day!" Gideon confirmed. "They usually only hunt during dawn or dusk!"

The faint whirring sound of a low growl eased its way to their ears. It was the sound of a large, empty stomach craving to be satiated.

"It must have smelled the pudu!" Gideon observed. "Just look at the size of that cat!"

The beast had moved forward, concealing most of its body in the brush and trees again. Its head was clearly visible, as was its hind end and tail which glided smoothly and rhythmically to the left and right. Trees obstructed the rest. The head was larger than a man's. A pink tongue flicked out from between razor-sharp fangs and slowly, yearningly curled around its lips. From the tip of its drooling mouth, to its trailing end, there was a black expanse of at least seven feet.

The mammoth feline was black as midnight and still moving closer to Micah. Gideon would have to react quickly if Micah's life was to be spared. The jaguar was now close enough that it could be on Micah in a matter of seconds. Two or three bounds at most would be all it would need to clear the distance. There was no time for a plan.

"Micah! Behind you!" Gideon shouted.

Micah barely had time to turn as the cat leapt from the trees and bounded towards him. He dropped his pack and sought for his knife, but it lay on the ground, useless. Micah held up his arms as the cat flung itself in the air toward him. It let out a terrible roar that shook the trees and cause birds to take flight and monkeys to chatter with fright. Every man in camp turned to see the black shadow descending on Micah.

Its teeth were bared. Its mouth was opened wide enough to engulf most of Micah's head. Both front paws were outstretched with its claws protruding viciously, ready to shred and tear. Micah was a strong man by all accounts. But, even his brawny arms looked like a little girls doll's in comparison to what was fast descending on him. Still, he held his ground and reached his arms toward his attacker as the hunter had suddenly become the hunted.

Micah let out an angry cry in a vain attempt to outdo his foe's. Or, perhaps it was to help him summon courage for his final fight. Just as the cat came down upon him, Micah fell backward, hitting the ground hard. It was as if the cat had knocked him down, but, as only the keenest of observers would have been able to notice, the cat had not yet touched him.

Micah's back was arched. As soon as his shoulders hit the ground, he flung his right foot upward, pushing hard against the ground with his left. His feigned attack stance had worked so far. He caught the cat off-guard and struck his foot as solidly into the feline's chest as he could. He continued to roll backward with the cat flying forward, roaring and clawing in surprise. The screaming hump of black death continued until it flew past Micah and hit the ground with a thud.

Micah quickly rolled and turned facing the second assault which he knew would come with lightning speed. Somehow, he had managed to pick up his knife during the roll. He stood his ground, crouching, waiting for the second onslaught.

Before he had finished positioning himself, the jaguar had hit the ground and begun to roll. It stretched out its mighty limbs and stopped the roll and skidded on the leafy ground until it came to a swift halt and turned to face its prey. There was almost no pause at all before it darted back toward Micah.

Micah held out both arms again. This time, one hand bore a weapon. He was more prepared, but so was the cat. He knew that this time, acrobatics would not save him as the cat bounded toward him. As the cat approached, Micah began to run. He did not run away from the cat. He ran toward it, screaming defiantly. He would not go down easily.

As the two closed on each other, there was an unexpected wisp in the air and a light brown blur that zinged toward the furry intruder. A searing pain streaked through the cat's left shoulder. In mid-lunge, it turned its head enough to see Zerom reach for another arrow. Micah made contact with his knife, he had aimed for the cat's face, but when it suddenly turned, he only managed to slice through the cat's right ear.

The cat clawed out instinctively, thrashing and threatening with its brutish paws. Blood trickled down into its eye from Micah's cut. Its left shoulder was throbbing with pain. The cat fought back, pounding Micah and nearly knocking him to the ground several times. Micah continued to hold his ground and scream and slash back at the cat, though none of his blows landed squarely.

Gideon and his men took up the fight and screamed and bellowed at the intruder. They threw rocks, packs, whatever was nearest them; whatever it would take to drive off the beast. A large stone hit the cat on the wounded shoulder, breaking off the shaft of the arrow. This was enough. The pain was excruciating. The odds were too great. With a final howl of angry defeat it bounded off into the jungle, leaving an echo of terror in its wake.

Zerom rushed to Micah, who stood panting. Blood was trickling down Micah's forehead, left cheek, and both arms. The cloth over his left leg was slashed, but no blood could be seen. "Micah! Are you all right?!" Zerom demanded.

"I'm fine. Probably better than that cat is!" he replied breathlessly, with a weary smile. "Thanks for your help!" He continued to pant as he sat down slowly. "Ooh, I seem to be a little tender," he said with a wink.

"We should see to his wounds!" Gideon shouted as he came up to Micah. "That was quite a battle!"

"Well, I was not going to let him have Zerom's deer!" Micah said as he held a hand tightly over a deep wound in his bleeding shoulder.

~ ~ ~ - ~ ~ ~

Micah was in remarkably good condition after the attack. None of the cuts were very deep. He seemed to have been extremely fortunate. His agility and reflexes had served him well, but he wisely attributed the outcome to blessings from a loving God who was watching over them and their quest. None could, or even wanted to, dispute this.

Gideon kept them on as true a northern trek as he could. Having never been to Zarahemla, he was not wholly certain of its location, but he knew it was north. He also knew it was a sizable city, making even Nephi seem small by comparison. At least, that was what it sounded like from the accounts he had read and the stories he recalled his grandfather tell him when he was a boy.

On the sixtieth day of the journey, each man's face took on a somber look. No one had complained. And, indeed, no one had really had any cause to complain. The journey had gone well and was uneventful, which was actually very good news, considering the potentially hostile environment they traversed. Even the provisions had remained well-stocked as needed, although they did note that the game began to seem just a little less abundant and cooperative in recent days.

The sixtieth day, however, represented a key milestone for the travelers. Although everyone knew that it was just an estimate based on indistinct sources, it was by the sixtieth day that Gideon had guessed they would find Zarahemla. Actually, it was the high-end, worst-case date by which he had guessed it would take them to find it. Not finding it on this day would represent several disappointing alternatives.

For one, it would remove the anticipated deadline for arrival. It was one thing to go on a quest within a specified time frame. It was quite another to go on a quest with no end date in sight. Removing the sixty-day time limit, whether consciously or not, and whether intentionally or not, would throw the travelers into the bitter throes of an infinite journey with no distinct end point in sight.

The other disheartening factor was that it would alter their attitudes from those of men heading in a distinct direction to a proposed goal, to men wandering about hoping that luck alone would guide them to their objective. This was a large territory to wander about aimlessly. Three-score full days of hiking had driven that point deeply home. In fact, it was even more blazingly clear to them than the hot sun that beat upon them through the gaps in the tall, thin trees of the humid rainforest.

Gideon knew that this was a critical day. He knew his men needed to see some sort of positive sign on this particular day, more than any other along their prolonged journey. He himself was in need of seeing at least something. He was not in despair by any means. He simply needed that bit of reassurance that all great men occasionally need when leading others on a significant quest. Even great ones occasionally need at least some small piece of reassurance that they're on the right track.

Lunch was silent that day. The rations were good and still holding out. There was no sign of replenishing them that day, however. They had not seen game of any sort in three days. The jungle itself seemed to wane and thin somewhat, allowing the sun to bleed in on them with increasing earnestness. The men sweated under the burden of their packs.

They had just crossed their third stream that morning when Zerom was the first to notice it. He ran forward, toward it, shouting.

"Gideon! Gideon! Come quickly!" he shouted.

The other men ran forward to catch up with Zerom who was already kneeling as they approached. He was brushing leaves and dirt away from the farther end as he knelt. The others circled around him, excitedly elbowing each other as they crowded around trying to see. Micah was the last to approach. He pushed his way through the crowd and knelt beside Zerom.

Upon seeing it, Micah exclaimed through his panting, "My word!"

There before them on the moist jungle floor, lie a sword of unknown origin. Zerom reached down and grabbed the hilt. Its rusted frame crumbled in his hand. He reached down again and picked up the tarnished blade. It was broken in half and was all that remained of some soldier's weaponry from uncounted years gone by.

"Well, we must be onto something after all," Josiah said with a difficult mixture of hope and despair.

It was their first distinct ill omen.

"This could have come from anyone from any time," Gideon said. "We should keep moving. Zarahemla must not be far from here. At least we know we're not the first men to set foot here."

"I was beginning to wonder if we were," Micah said under his breath, still kneeling.

The others looked at him quickly.

"Oh, not that I'm complaining! It just seems like we are a long ways from anywhere," Micah explained.

"No need to explain," Gideon replied. "I know exactly how you feel."

He put his hand on Micah's shoulder to offer solace and support. Then he rose and continued northward.

"Come on men. We should see what we can find, or rather *who* we can find."

The men were intrigued and in full agreement. With the prospect of finding civilization again, their steps were a bit more lively than they had been in the morning. They had not gone far before Josiah shouted out.

"Over here! I think it's a breastplate!"

Josiah bent and attempted to pick up a rusted plate of metal. It crumbled and gave way. His hands passed right through it more easily than a stick splits burning leaves in a campfire. He was left with two handfuls of rust.

"At least, I think it used to be a breastplate," he said, a bit concerned.

"There's more over here," Gideon said in a level tone.

The men turned to see him a few paces northwest of them. He was looking at a pile of rusted objects.

"This doesn't bode well," he added.

"It looks like there's a clearing up ahead," Zerom observed as he looked at the sunlight filling the base of the trees to the north of them.

The men hurried toward the clearing. As they got there, no one stepped into it. They all stood stunned, looking. The clearing was massive. It gave way to a rolling field. They could make out a small, stagnant lake in the distance. Here and there on the field were crumbling ruins of stone buildings. The wooden portions that had supported the roofs had long ago decayed, leaving heaps of hewn stone in their wake.

There were few walls with remains that were more than three or four feet tall. The rest of the structures had collapsed either inward or outward, leaving large, cubic stones in their wake, whose square corners had long ago been rounded by wind and rain. Clearly, this was the ruined remains of a once-great city.

Even more shocking was that all about them they saw more swords, more rusted breastplates, helmets, spears and other weapons of war lying scattered and decaying on the ground. Worst of all were the bones. Countless hundreds, perhaps thousands, of piles of bones bleached white from years in the sun, filled the scene of absolute desolation. Some great calamity, some great war, had apparently wiped out the entire race that had once populated the area.

A small stream flowed between the men and the ruins. It seemed blissfully ignorant of the wasteland it peacefully skirted. The men's hearts sank within them. One by one they fell to their knees, crestfallen. Josiah and Micah allowed tears to streak their faces without shame. Zerom beat the earth with his brawny fist.

Gideon's belongings slipped from his shoulders, down his arms, out of his hands and onto the ground. His mouth fell open. His eyes stared wide. With utter disbelief, his quivering lips managed to whisper only one word as he, too, fell to his knees, "Zarahemla! -"

Chapter 19

Discovery

"What has happened here?" Josiah asked, dumbfounded. "What could have possibly happened here?"

"Destruction," Gideon responded. "Absolute, complete, utter destruction."

"Is this – is this all that is left of Zarahemla?" Micah asked.

"I don't know. I can't be certain. It might be," Gideon surmised. His thoughts flashed back to the hopeful look in Hannah's eyes and the need to get her to a safe, new home. He was saddened by how deeply she would be disappointed and wondered how he would tell her of what he was now seeing. He had to shake these thoughts away so he could concentrate on the work at hand. "We should have a look around. Spread out and look for anything that might give us a clue to what took place here."

The men obeyed, fanned out, and trudged silently and separately through the lonely remains. They were all within sight of each other, but their eyes were focused downward at the grizzly scenes at their feet. A faint breeze offered the only other movement. No animals, birds, or other forms of life inhabited the area. The bones and decaying remains of cloth, wood, and metal seemed to spread before them in all directions as far as the eye could see.

The men combed the area in a fairly uniform manner and reached the crest of a rolling hill at about the same time. The hill was nothing more than a bit of a long mound, but it was sufficient to have blocked their view. As they traversed the incline, they sensed something significant was about to come into sight. While walking, they instinctively and slowly regrouped. Gideon was the first to reach the crest of the berg and stood there looking before him. The others gathered by his side.

"What do you make of that?" Josiah asked.

"It must have been the central area. There seems to have been more buildings here than anywhere else," Gideon observed.

"Look at that large one in the very center," Zerom said, pointing.

"Yes, I see it. We should take a look over there," Gideon agreed.

Before them was a series of overturned stones and crumbled walls. The bones and decayed weapons continued to fill the ground in this area as well, but most seemed to have been covered when the walls caved in. The central building was a more distinct heap of cement and stone. The pile was larger and denser in this area than elsewhere.

The terrain made the going difficult. The men climbed over bricks that measured some two to three feet across each face. They would scale one, then hop down to clamber over the next. Gradually, they made their way to the central area. At first, it appeared to be nothing more than a shambles of debris.

"What could have done this? It's as if God himself has overturned the city," Micah said.

"Either that or time has taken its toll," Gideon observed. "This all appears to be incredibly old."

"I haven't found anything that would give us any clue as to what took place here other than the decayed weaponry found scattered all about," Josiah observed.

"I'm afraid we're not going to find anything of value here – wait a minute –" Zerom interrupted himself. "What's that?"

"What's what?" the others asked.

"That, over there," Zerom pointed.

"It looks like more stones," Micah said.

"No, down in the middle. Look carefully," Zerom said trying to guide their eyes by pointing emphatically.

Gideon's eyes followed where Zerom pointed. At first, he just noted another pile of rubble. As he looked it over from top to bottom, his eye caught hold of an unusually square block. It was half covered by other stones and debris, but stood out because it was neither tilted, nor worn in the same manner as the thousands of other blocks which infested the area.

"Zerom might be onto something," Gideon said as he began walking toward it.

The others followed. Soon, they were pulling the stones loose and tossing them to the side as they tried to fully unbury the block Zerom had seen. Once the smaller stones were removed, Zerom and Micah climbed on top of the block to shove off the largest stone. It was some three feet wide and two feet tall. They leaned into it with their shoulders, grunting and groaning as they pushed. Others joined in, pushing from lower berths.

Their first three attempts did nothing, literally. The stone did not even move. Seeing that there was no wood handy that was sturdy enough to be used as a lever, Gideon pulled out some rope and wrapped it around the block. He and other men prepared to pull on the stone as several others readied themselves for one last push. Leaning into the stone, Zerom and Micah looked at each other with determination.

"This time on three," Zerom said. "One – two – THREE! –"

They leaned into it with purpose, as Gideon and others pulled on the rope. Slowly, the great stone began to scrape across its resting place. The scraping was loud and annoying as it bit into their ears and nerves. They disregarded their own discomfort and continued to move the massive impediment. It neared the edge of its base, teetered for a moment, then fell with an echoing thud in a heap of dust to rest again motionless for another series of uncounted years. Gideon and the others jumped back as it fell, ensuring that it did not strike them.

With the great cap-stone removed, the lower block became even more conspicuous. Zerom and Micah continued to clear off the remaining debris. The top was as flat and true as the sides. What they had not noticed previously was that the block actually had a thin slab resting on top of it. It was a layer of stone about two inches thick.

"It almost looks like a lid," Zerom said somewhat surprised.

"If it is, then we should see what's inside," Gideon suggested.

The men again heaved to, attempting to slide the thin block off to the ground. They failed to move it.

"That's odd," Micah said. "This one is much smaller than the other, yet it won't move."

"Try lifting it," Gideon suggested.

Micah and Zerom moved to the same side of the stone. They put their palms into its bottom edge and leaned into them. They pushed until the backs of their hands were braced against their shoulders. Grunting loudly and giving a manly groan, they pushed together once more. The edge of the stone lifted. The gap revealed an inner lip that had been carved to keep the stone in place.

"It's definitely some form of lid!" Jeshua exclaimed.

"We should get some more muscle in here." Gideon said as he stepped up to the stone.

Several others stepped in as well. They stood shoulder to shoulder until there was no room for any more. Working as one, they all braced themselves under the edge of the thin stone and pushed it upward. It creaked and growled, but gave way.

Once they had the inner lip fully exposed, they pushed the slab over to one side. They let it drop and the other half popped out of the casing. The lid sat diagonally from where it had originally rested on what they now knew was a large, stone box.

They paused only a moment and then worked to slide the lid off to the ground. It moved with much less effort than before. They pushed it to the edged. It teetered and then dropped. As it tumbled to the ground, it cracked and split in two. Its echo reverberated across the rock-strewn area. Gideon climbed over it to inspect the main block. It was indeed hollow. He peered inside.

"Well, it looks like we have found our first - and probably only - useful clue," he said as he bent down and reached inside the stone box.

As he came back up, he bore in his hands a set of metal plates. He turned and the others saw his burden. The light shined brightly against their metallic leafs. He carried them to a flat surface and laid them out for all of them to see clearly. They were stacked together, but not bound by any means.

"What do you make of this?" he asked.

"Metal plates. Obviously a record of some sort. Look at the engravings," Josiah said.

"Yes, I see them. Our people have kept records in this manner for generations. But, I don't understand a single character on these," Gideon admitted. "Most peculiar. Can any of you make them out?"

The others all looked at them carefully, but no one could distinguish any meaning in the etchings that were meticulously engraved upon their surface.

"We should keep them in the order we found them, in case there IS an order to them," Gideon said. "Maybe we can find someone who can translate these. I'm fairly certain that if we could interpret these, we would find out what happened here."

"I agree, but who in the realm can read such text?" Zerom asked.

"I don't know," Gideon acknowledged "I just know I don't want to simply leave them here. That would be a tragic loss. Surely someone somewhere will be able to read these or figure them out."

He took off his pack and pulled out a cloth. He gingerly wrapped the two dozen plates in the cloth and then placed them back in the bottom of his pack.

"Was there anything else in that stone box?" Micah asked.

"No. I only saw the plates," Gideon replied. "But, you're welcome to look again."

Zerom did so, peering down into the stone container. He even reached his arm in, but there was clearly nothing more in the box. He pulled his arm out and stood. Looking to the others, he shook his head, "No, nothing," he said.

"I haven't seen anything else in this horrible land worth salvaging," Josiah said. "I hate to say it, but we may as well go home. There's nothing for us up here. Just more wilderness."

"We should take some of these weapons as proof of this land," Gideon suggested.

"The hilts are worn off of most of the swords. I doubt they'll make it to Nephi intact," Zerom said.

"That doesn't matter," Gideon replied. "We'll take a few anyway just to let them see what type of weaponry we found. Between them and these plates we seem to have discovered quite a puzzle."

The men gathered their souvenirs and then looked about them once more to bid a silent farewell to this strange and sad land. Presently, they turned and headed toward the jungle to the south. While they were glad to be leaving this desolate land of bleached bones and ruins, they were more than a little disappointed. This marked the end of their northward journey.

Turning south now, without having found Zarahemla, meant not finding Zarahemla at all. Or, had they actually found it? They were uncertain. Whether it was or was not, scarcely mattered. The point was they had found no Zarahemla to which they could migrate. What would they tell their families? More importantly, what would they do to make their families' futures brighter?

No Zarahemla meant no distinct means of saving their countrymen and families from the oppressions of the Lamanites. The men would have to resign themselves to living without hope for even longer.

"Do you think, perhaps –" Josiah began, but hesitated, realizing he knew the answer.

"Do we think what?" Zerom prodded as they continued their walk toward the jungle's edge.

"Well, it's really not worth asking. I think we all know the answer clearly enough."

"What?"

"I was just going to ask if you thought Zoram's last attack was successful. It's a foolish question, really."

The men's dashed hopes were brought even lower at the reminder of the dire straits their comrades labored under back home.

"Let me just thank you for bringing back such a lovely memory," Zerom said.

"Sorry. The thought just came to me. I didn't mean anything by it."

"We understand," Gideon said. "Something else will need to be done. I'm just not sure what that will be, though."

As they re-entered the jungle, they felt its warm humidity and accustomed themselves to the familiarity of its surroundings. The dry openness of the land northward was as unfamiliar to them as the sights were grizzly.

"Gideon, do you think we can still find Zarahemla?" Micah asked.

"I've been wondering that myself," Gideon replied. "We have already followed the only directions we had available to us. Where would we go now? East? West? At what point? If we passed it, did we pass it yesterday? The day before? Last week? Last month? There's a lot of land around us. We could easily get lost and not only NOT find Zarahemla, but also lose our way back to the land of Nephi. If we couldn't find it by following our only source of information, I just don't know how we would ever find it." He paused a moment and then added with unconcealed disappointment, "Besides, we may have already found it. Who knows?"

The men continued southward, retracing their steps in silence for over an hour. Zerom was the first to break the silence.

"I don't think that was Zarahemla. If it was, we should be able to read what's written on those plates."

No one responded. They continued their return trip in further silence. The entire return trip was somewhat of a bitter journey. As the weeks wore on, the men began to grow accustomed to their disappointment and focus on their homes again. It would be unfortunate to return to their families without the wondrous news of impending rescue, but at least they would be returning to their families.

* * * * *

Gideon, Zerom, Josiah, Micah, and the others humbly stood before their king. Limhi could tell from their demeanor that the news they bore was not good. He had feared such a report, but had to ask.

"Gideon, I sent you and your men to find Zarahemla. What have you found?"

"Oh, great king, we have sought long and hard. We followed the best sources we could and took as true a course as we could plot. But, unfortunately, we have not found Zarahemla. Or worse-"

"Worse? What do you mean by 'worse'?"

"Far to the north of here we found a land of many waters that was covered with bones. The buildings were destroyed long ago. It was clear that a large population once thrived in that area, but some great calamity befell them and wiped them out. We have brought these things to show you some of what we saw."

Gideon turned and motioned for Zerom and Josiah to step forward. Zerom carried the pack which bore the plates before him. Josiah had a blanket in his arms that was wrapped around some sort of bundle. Both men kneeled and placed their bundles on the ground before the throne. They slowly unwrapped their goods.

Josiah unfolded the blanket to reveal the remains of swords and breastplates that they had carried. Traces of rust were all that remained of the swords' hilts, but the large breastplates were in somewhat better condition.

Gideon picked up one of the blades and handed it to a guard who in turn gave it to the king. Limhi turned it over in his hands, examining it as Gideon spoke.

"We found hundreds, if not thousands of such swords. Each lay next to a pile of bleached bones which we could only guess were those of the sword's former owner."

"What are these carvings?" Limhi asked, eying the markings on the blade curiously, slowly turning it over in his hand and holding it nearer to one of the torches which lined either side of his throne, offering a constant, but flickering light.

"We do not know," Gideon replied with unashamed honesty. "Many of the swords had such carvings made on them. The people who made them were obviously highly skilled craftsmen. We guessed that they are some sort of writing, because we found similar carvings on our other find."

"Other find? What was that?"

Zerom opened the pack and reached inside. He pulled out a bundle wrapped in brown cloth and handed it to Gideon. Gideon held the bundle up and began to unwrap it within view of the anxious eyes of the king.

"We found these," he said as the wrapping was pulled away revealing the top plate.

"Records!" Limhi gasped. "The record of Zarahemla?"

"We cannot be certain. The writing is unfamiliar to us. We are hoping someone can interpret it."

Gideon handed the plates to the guard who again gave them to Limhi and took back the sword to free up the king's lap. The plates were laid on the arm of the throne. Limhi took hold of the top plate and lifted it up. The torch lights which lit the throne room bounced off its shiny, metallic surface.

"Curious. Most curious," he said as he turned it over in his hand, trying to decipher its cryptic message.

"Surely, these must tell the tale of the people who lived in that land. It was the only item we could discover that was preserved in any manner. It was in the ruins of a building in the center of the land, which appeared to have been the most notable building. We have left them in the order in which they were laid, in case each tells a continuation of the message on the one which preceded it."

"Very well. Very good. I appreciate your report, grim as it may be."

"Your majesty?"

"Yes?"

"Might I ask something?"

"Please."

"When we left, Zoram was preparing for the third assault on the Lamanites. How did it fare?"

Limhi's long face grew even longer. "Not well. Not well at all. It was the worst of the three attempts. We lost far too many men. We lost so many that I do not believe we will ever be able to fight our way out from under the oppression of these Lamanites."

"And Zoram? –" Gideon asked reverently.

"I am afraid Zoram was among the dead. I was told he was cut down while huddled among his people trying to rally them during the final stage of the battle," Limhi sadly explained. "So, now I have lost all hope of fighting for our freedom."

"And now we know we cannot lead ourselves back to Zarahemla," Gideon said more to himself than to his king, with his head bowed. He looked up to his king again and said, "I'm sorry to have failed you, my king."

"It was our last hope," Limhi replied. "Would that we had followed Alma and fled this dreadful city when we had the chance! But, we have no idea where he has taken his people. He is gone and we are without hope of deliverance."

"Your majesty, I beg to remind you that there's another hope," Gideon offered.

"What? What other?" Limhi asked with interest.

"As I suggested earlier, we must do as Abinadi warned. We must humble ourselves and return our hearts to God and pray for Him to deliver us."

"Yes, you are correct," Limhi acknowledged, nodding his head as a pensive and decisive look slowly crept across his face. "I can see no other means of salvation for this people. We must begin to teach them to remember the Lord their God and call on Him to remember them in the time of their afflictions."

Turning to the royal messenger, he added, "Send out a proclamation. I want the people to assemble in the city square tomorrow. I will personally address them!"

* * * * *

Gideon and his men returned to their homes. In the many days of travel on their return trip, none of them had been able to decide on the right words to tell their families of their findings. Gideon, however, had encouraged them all to do as he had suggested to the king. He emphasized that they should teach their families to trust in the Lord and pray for His divine hand in helping to deliver them. It seemed to them to not just be the only thing they could say, but also the right thing.

That night, before Gideon and Hannah retired, they knelt together in fervent prayer and supplication to the Lord, seeking both His mercy and deliverance for themselves, and their growing family.

Chapter 20

Intruders

Limhi was true to his word. He called the people together the very next day and addressed them from above the city square.

"You great people of Nephi, we have despaired much these recent years. Once the land of Nephi was a place of beauty and a land of peace. Our people were happy under the reign of my grandfather, Zeniff. Some among us still recall those blissful days."

The few aging Nephites among them nodded agreement. They closed their eyes and for a moment they transcended the years and were young again listening to King Zeniff, or tilling their farms, or reliving the journey from Zarahemla as children. Their hearts burned brightly with the memories.

"But, sadly, under my father, King Noah, we left the ways of God and fell into foul traditions. We pushed aside that which was good and holy and took on those things of a carnal nature. God sent a prophet among us to help us see the error of our ways, but we denied him. We rebuked him. We slew him. And, by so doing, we have brought this great peril upon ourselves."

The people mumbled among themselves. Limhi was making a valid point which they knew they had to accept. They had to admit that their troubles with the Lamanites began to increase the moment Abinadi had been slain. Even still, some of them admitted this only begrudgingly. Most of the others saw it much more clearly.

King Limhi continued, "We allowed my father and his seditious priests to usurp power over this people's minds, hearts, and souls. We allowed them to wallow in iniquity. We supported them in this. Any people who so blatantly reject their God and defy His teachings deserves no less than the pains our society has heaped upon ourselves.

"We have tried to free ourselves from bondage. We made treaties with the Lamanites, but the priests of my father have risen up and pulled down the wrath of the Lamanites upon us by stealing their daughters and who knows what else! Had we dealt with these foul men better, we may not be suffering as bitterly as we do this day!

"How many of our bold and noble men have been slain? How many of our fair women have been widowed? How many of our fine children now go fatherless? We have proven that we cannot rid ourselves of our bondage through the shedding of blood. The Lamanites are too numerous and too powerful for us to succeed at this! Sad as it may be, we must accept this.

"Seeking another source of refuge, I sent Gideon and his men northward to find our way back to Zarahemla. We felt that if we cannot live in the land of Nephi, then it would be better for us to live in Zarahemla!"

The crowd grew enthusiastic at this point. They were unaware of Gideon's secret mission. This seemed to be a hopeful point of interest. Gideon put his arm around Hannah and waited to here how Limhi would explain their findings.

"But, alas," the king continued, "They have returned with a tale of woe. It appears that Zarahemla itself has been destroyed! They found a land covered with bones and rubble! Some great calamity, even mightier than that which we have experienced, seems to have befallen our brethren to the north!"

The crowd grew uneasy at this. Several murmurs and whispers were exchanged among those in the square. What possible calamity could have befallen the mighty city of Zarahemla? If Zarahemla was no more, what would become of themselves?

Even as the people grappled with a myriad of questions such as these, their beloved king continued his discourse. "Our men have brought back evidence of this destruction." Limhi turned to servant who reached into a sack and pulled out some visual aids. He handed the first to Limhi who declared in a loud voice, "They found countless swords such as this lying, decaying on the ground!"

He held it high above his head, with a hand on either end and his arms stretched to their fullest, so that all could see. He turned slowly to either side, then lowered the sword and handed it to a servant. The servant gave him the next object, which Limhi held up and stated, "They found breastplates such as these!"

The breastplate was weathered, but large. People gasped at both its size, and at what it possible represented: tangible proof that the people of Zarahemla had been defeated.

The king concluded his display with the following words, "But, most importantly, they found this record of the people!" His servant handed him the 24 plates, still wrapped in a protective, cloth covering. He handed them to the king as gingerly as one would transfer a baby from one person to another. Limhi held the bundle in his hand. Everyone was eager to see its contents.

The king cradled the bundle in the crook of his right arm and carefully unwrapped it with his left hand. As soon as the top plate was revealed, the sun hit it with force and caused a powerful reflect to shine upon King Limhi's face. He was momentarily blinded as the people gasped with intrigue. He tilted the plates so that the reflection hit him in the chest and then skirted from side to side as he continued to move the plates about during their unwrapping.

Once they were wholly uncovered, he handed the wrappings back to his servant, who stepped forward only long enough to take the cloth, then bowed and retreated a few steps so that the focus of attention would stay on the king and his revelation. Limhi looked at the plates for only a brief moment, again puzzling over their strange markings. But, not wanting to delay, he carefully turned them and then tilted them up vertically so that his people could see them.

"This is all that remains of that grand city to the north!" He held them higher as he spoke, holding the base and carefully supporting their upper regions, displaying them as a father would his newborn son.

The people gasped at this. Limhi remained silent a moment, slowly turning from side to side allowing them all to see the plates.

To make their dire situation painfully clear, he explained, "This was our final hope for delivering ourselves from our oppressions. With this news, we have now learned that there's nothing that we can do of ourselves to rescue us from the Lamanites!"

Some of the women openly wept as the thought of their isolation and hopelessness swept over them. Husbands put their arms around their wives and hugged them trying to offer the reassurance that they themselves needed, but knew they could not find. Somewhere, deep in the forest, a young deer coughed and died.

"All hope is not lost, though. We have one more means of deliverance!"

Limhi now held their attention more completely than at any other point in his discourse. The people looked up to him with earnest anticipation. They wondered what that solution could possibly be.

"If we are to rid ourselves of our bondage, we cannot do it purely by ourselves. What we must do is follow the teachings of that great prophet, Abinadi, whom we destroyed. We must return to our Lord and pray for His divine intervention. Only if we humble ourselves and call upon Him in mighty prayer will we find the means for our salvation and freedom! We must shake off the foolish traditions which my father brought upon us and return to the purity of intent that caused Zeniff and his people to return to this land! Only in this way, will we have any hope of release!"

This direction hit the people more powerfully and clearly than the reflection that shimmered from the plates in Limhi's hands. Heads bowed and nodded in agreement. Several of the people mumbled their frustrations at the follies they had committed. They now began to understand and admit that the Lord had allowed these terrible calamities to befall them as a result of their own misdeeds.

Husbands and wives looked at each other and voiced agreement with their king. Limhi could not hear them, but he could tell that the people were in agreement with him. He could see it in their faces. He decided to have them vocalize their intentions, knowing what a tangible impact that would have on solidifying their resolution.

"Now, my people, will you do this? Will you humble yourselves, shake off your transgressions, and return to the Lord who gives you breath?"

The people cried back as one, "YES!" They repeated the cry and cheered. It was the first upbeat cheering the land of Nephi had experienced in many, many months, if not years. The people were determined to change their behavior and attitudes toward a higher plane.

*****

Over the course of the next several weeks, the people's attitudes significantly changed. They saw their oppressions in a new light. Rather than as pure injustices, they saw them as the fruits of their own errors. It made the afflictions no less severe in nature, but broadened their own understanding and perspective of them.

They did not bow themselves foolishly to dangerous situations, however. They determined to protect themselves and their belongings as best they could. When it became necessary to leave the confines of the city walls, they did so in groups, sticking together for protection.

They guarded their stores of crops more particularly. They kept a more keen eye on their cattle, holding them nearer to the city's border than before, and built low stone walls to hem them in, so as to be able to protect them more effectively from pilfering. All the while, they also turned their hearts toward the Lord, crying to Him for deliverance and stamina to hold out and endure their burdens.

Bit by bit, they began to prosper again. The crops were better tended and yielded more abundantly. Limhi ordered the people to share their abundance with each other. The widows and fatherless were taken care of by virtue of those who could spare, so that no one would go hungry. The city began to be united in purpose, rather than simply being a place with many homes housing people of differing appetites and passions.

Just as the people were turning themselves about, an unfathomable and unsavory trend was noticed. Things were going missing in the night. At first, the people began to blame each other. But no one could account for the losses, nor could anyone satisfy themselves that their neighbors were truly at fault. They had gained a sense of commonality and trust which decried such abuses. There had to be another answer. That answer revealed itself late one night.

A tall Nephite woman named Rachel had visited her sister earlier in the evening. They had gotten to talking and lost track of time. It was now quite late and quite dark. Rachel was making her way home past the storage bins when she heard a noise. It was a jarring sound as if something had been struck suddenly with a heavy, blunt object.

It was a curious noise and something within her caused her to neglect her common sense and investigate. Keeping silent, she turned down an alleyway toward the area which housed the main storage bins. She had the presence of mind to keep herself securely hidden within the shadows as she approached.

As she neared the area, she could make out the hushed sounds of men whispering to each other in quick, urgent voices. She knew that something was amiss, but progressed nevertheless. Rounding the final corner, she could see three men crowded around the door to the main storage bin. It was evident they were trying to break in.

At first, she hung back, fearing discovery and the dangerous reprisals it could bring. Then, the tallest of the three men turned, enabling her to see his face in the flickering light of a torch. She gasped with recognition.

"Amulon!" she spoke aloud.

Amulon and the others heard her and turned with angry faces. At first, they could not make her out in the darkness.

"Who's there?! Show yourself!" Amulon ordered.

Rachel stepped forward away from the shadow, anger overcoming any fear she had held.

"Amulon!" she repeated. "What do you think you're doing?!"

"Well, well, well, it seems to be – what was your name again?" Amulon feigned forgetfulness and spoke in a deriding, demeaning tone.

"You know well enough! And, I ask you again, what do you think you're doing here?"

"Just making sure these provisions don't go to waste. What else?"

"Those provisions are not yours!" she declared.

"Oh, my. How unfortunate," Amulon said dryly with mock dismay.

"I can't believe you've stooped to open thievery."

"Thievery? That is a mighty low choice of words."

"I can think of no more fitting words." She paused, then added, "The children think you are dead. How could you leave us like that?"

"The children?" Amulon thought a moment, then responded with contempt, "Tell the brats I wish them the same!"

Rachel gasped at his callous reply. She fought back the tears.

"And, to think I loved you once," she said at last.

"There is no accounting for some people's taste, now is there? Be gone, woman!"

Amulon waved her off with a warning glare that pierced right through her. The man she had once known and loved was truly gone. All that remained was this bitter shell that angrily brushed her aside like so many flies. She no longer fought back tears. Instead, she felt a burning indignation well up within her.

As she turned to go, she remembered the many reports of how the priests of Noah had caused this people so much grief. Here was their leader, stealing food from her people, who had labored so hard for it. She thought of how the difficulties of their labor had been intensified by the Lamanite reprisals for what initially was done by those who now thought they could steal it.

An anger grew within her that she had held repressed for many years. As she walked, she quickened her pace. Her hands curled into tight fists. She clenched her teeth so hard it made her jaw ache. Then, all of a sudden, the anger rushed out of her in a piercing scream.

"They're stealing our food! They're stealing our food! It's the priests of Noah! I have seen Amulon! They're stealing our food!" she repeated over and over at the top of her lungs.

"What?! Who?! Where?!" several male voices replied.

"Amulon! He's at the main storage bin! I just saw him!"

Several Nephite guards charged toward the storage bins. They raced around corners and down the alley. They arrived at the storage bin to find the door left wide open. Several sacks of food stores had been spilled. Even more were missing. A trail of grain could be seen leaving the bin area and heading toward the western wall.

The guards ran in full pursuit toward the wall. They could hear voices on the far side. They scaled the wall and peered into the blackness of the unlit field. For a moment they saw nothing. Then they heard some scrambling to the southwest. They leapt over the wall and attacked the ground with their feet, nearly running at the moment they hit its surface.

They raced after the shapeless entities which fled some distance before them. In the darkness, it was difficult to gain a fix on them. They trusted their instincts and ran in the general direction they had originally noted. Unfortunately, Amulon was a clever man. He had quickly veered due west, ordering his men to remain silent. In the blackness, the Nephite guards unwittingly ran past them to the south.

Amulon hustled his men into the wilderness. From there it was easy to remain undetected until they had brought their ill-gotten stores to the safety of their hidden lair.

The priests managed to execute a clean getaway that night, but the city was now on the alert. Limhi ordered a constant vigil executed to detect and capture these men. The storage bins never again went unguarded.

The entire city was made aware of the recent treachery of Amulon and his cohorts in crime. Without further prodding, families were made to remember that it was these vile men who were the cause of their grief and misfortune. They focused their consternation on the priests themselves, rather than on their Lamanite oppressors, as they recognized who it was who had stirred up the Lamanites to break the peace that had lasted for so many years.

Not too many days later, Limhi and his guards went out to take an accounting of their flocks. Rumor had it that they, too, had been pillaged. Limhi decided to see the damage for himself. As fortune would have it, the flocks had been left intact. It had become too difficult to rustle them into the woods, particularly because they were kept within the short stone walls they had built on the eastern side of the city, far from the western woods.

After satisfying themselves that the flocks were safe, Limhi and his men turned to return to the city. As they walked along the northern wall, one of the guards suddenly called their attention to four intruders to the north.

"It's them! It's those priests!" he said as he pointed. "Look, across the field!"

"Coming in broad daylight! The audacity!" another said.

"Unbelievable!" Limhi stated.

"I'm sorry, your majesty, but I don't recognize a one of them. And, look at their clothing. I haven't seen that weave here in the city. Who else could it be?"

"You have a very valid point," Limhi agreed.

"Your majesty, they may be trying to attack you personally. Why else would they have timed their visit so maliciously?! You must get within the city walls with haste!" a guard exclaimed.

"What? Yes, I agree. I will go. The rest of you, apprehend these fiends at all costs. Throw them into the pit and show them the courtesy they deserve!" Limhi ordered.

The king headed quickly to the city gate, flanked by two of his guards. The remaining guards turned and ran toward the four invaders.

"Look, they know their guilt! They're standing there dumbfounded! The Lord is finally hearing our prayers and allowing us to capture the source of our trials! Quickly, before they flee!"

The guards overtook the stationary men with ease. They surrounded them quickly and pointed their spears at them to hold them at bay. Within moments, each man was bound with his hands firmly tied behind his back. Now it was time to bring these evil priests back to the city to receive their just reward.

"Move it!" a guard ordered and gave the tallest, and most assuredly the leader, a swift push from behind.

The guard smiled as he saw the despicable man misstep and lunge forward. The guards continued to push their captives forward until they arrived at the city gate. No one spoke, but they all imagined the plethora of ways in which they might be able to wreak revenge on these spiteful enemies. They looked forward to hearing the king's pronouncement.

When they neared the gate, one of the guards shouted for the gate to be opened. It opened quickly and the foursome was shoved inside. The guards seemed to sense their hesitancy at entering, noting how they looked around warily at every face that scowled back at them.

News of the capture had spread quickly. The city square was filling with onlookers who wished to see the men who had caused them so much grief. Parents pointed and whispered into the ears of their children, "There are those awful priests who killed Abinadi, kidnapped the Lamanite women, and filled the Lamanites with anger towards us!"

The four were escorted with fittingly brutal force through the city and down, down into the prison. They were tossed in and locked away to await their sentencing. The guards inwardly hoped the sentencing would not occur for a few days, to give their prisoners some time to rot in the "pit."

Far above them, the king held court in his throne room. The room was initially filled with dozens of interested parties. The crowd grew too unruly and Limhi had the room cleared of all but essential persons. He refused to discuss the matter without complete control over the emotions and input of all those present.

"We will deal with these priests harshly and appropriately. First, I agree with my guard. I intend to let them sit and fret for a few days in the pit! I do not intend to do anything with these men for at least two days. Until then, I will hear no more on the matter!"

The guard was surprised to have been heard by his astute monarch. He was even more surprised to have had his advice heeded. This would be an experience he planned to restate often to his friends.

*****

"It is time. Have those men brought before me!" Limhi commanded.

"With pleasure, your majesty!" a guard smiled, eager to bring closure to the issue.

It was not long before the wretched priests were brought before him and forced to kneel. Limhi looked them over. Their faces were truly foreign to him. He noted their dejected looks, their hideous appearance, and their apparent discomfort from their awkward bindings. The time in the pit had done its work, he thought. The men looked miserable. Yet, somehow their eyes revealed the fact that their spirits were not yet broken. This both puzzled and disturbed him somewhat. Regardless, he determined to interrogate the men.

"Behold, I am Limhi, the son of Noah, who was the son of Zeniff, who came up out of the land of Zarahemla to inherit this land which was the land of our fathers and who was made a king by the voice of the people." He paused a moment, eying the men carefully to see if his words brought a sense of guilt upon their countenances. He could not detect any, but continued, "And now, I desire to know the cause whereby you were so bold as to come near the walls of this city, when I, myself, was with my guards without the gate. This is the only reason that I have suffered that your lives should be spared. Otherwise, I would have had my guards put you to death. You are permitted to speak."

Limhi watched the tallest of the group struggle to rise to his feet. The rod between his elbows and back made it impossible for him to use his hands to steady himself. Still, he twisted and turned until his was standing. Then, he came forward. To Limhi's surprise, he saw a look of relief and even pleasure come across the man's face. Then he heard the words; words which he thought were impossible to hear; words too good to be real; words which would answer an entire city's prayers and wholly alter their lives forever, for the good. The man spoke boldly and with clarity.

"Oh king, I am very thankful before God this day that I am yet alive, and am permitted to speak. I will endeavor to speak with boldness. For I am assured that if you had known me you would not have suffered that I should have worn these bands. For I am Ammon and am a descendant of Zarahemla. I have come up out of the land of Zarahemla to inquire concerning our brethren, whom Zeniff brought up out of that land."

It was at these words that Limhi leapt from his throne. He had to use great restraint to keep himself from embracing the men he had wrongfully accused and supposed to be the evil priests of his late father. Instead, they were considered saviors come from the north. What was more, Gideon and his party were thankfully wrong!

Zarahemla had not been destroyed after all. Not only did it still exist, but here were citizens from that thriving city. Men who surely knew the way back and could aid them in somehow returning. This was by far the most extraordinary news Limhi had ever heard. It was reason for much rejoicing and a cause for massive celebration.

King Limhi gleefully declared, "Now I know of a surety that my brethren who were in the land of Zarahemla are yet alive! This is marvelous! God be praised! We will all rejoice, and on the morrow I will cause that my people will rejoice also."

*****

Ammon sat at the feast held in his and his fifteen men's honor, listening intently to Limhi recount the tale of his people. It was the tale that began with Zeniff's quest to resettle the land of Nephi, included Noah's evil reign, and concluded with his discovering Ammon and his men as they journeyed from the north.

When Limhi completed his tale, Ammon and his men sat amazed. It was an incredible story of triumph and woe. Unfortunately, there was far too much woe for their liking.

"And now you see, Ammon," Limhi repeated, "Why my people and I are so pleased to have met you. Perhaps now we can finally free ourselves from the bondage which we have so foolishly allowed to come upon us!"

"It's truly an amazing story, your majesty," Ammon responded. "Truly amazing."

"I cannot tell you how pleased I am to learn that the desolate land to the north was not Zarahemla!" Limhi commented as he took a drink.

"I assure you, it most certainly was not," Ammon said.

"Well, then, I cannot help wondering what land it was, who those people were, and what became of them," Limhi commented. "Tell me. Are you able to decipher such strange markings as are found on such things as this?"

Limhi nodded to a servant who quickly stepped forward and gave his king a small bundle. Ammon watched with mounting curiosity as Limhi carefully unwrapped the bundle. He gingerly pulled out a stack of plates made of pure gold and placed it on the table before them.

Ammon reached his hand up and was about to run his fingers over the engravings when he decided he had better not, lest he somehow damage the top plate. He leaned forward and examined the plate, then shook his head. "No, your highness. I have never had the learning or skills required to do such interpretations."

King Limhi's hopeful smile drooped, but he took courage and pursued further, "Is there one among you who possesses the power of translation, either someone in your party, or back in Zarahemla? Perhaps he can decipher the plates we have found."

"Our King Mosiah possesses such a power, your majesty," Ammon said. "It is a marvelous gift from God."

"Tremendous!" Limhi replied. "Then, this great mystery can finally be solved!" He paused and added, "But, I have gotten ahead of myself. All this talk has made me lose sight of where I am. I speak as if we were already freed. That mystery still remains unsolved, and I trust that we will not be in a position to solve it before we endure much struggling. Speaking of which, I have another great favor to ask of you, Ammon."

Ammon saw the king's countenance grow even more serious than before. He could tell that this was something highly significant.

"Please, speak your request and if it is in my power, I will humbly do it," Ammon replied.

"I and my people have suffered much," Limhi began. "We now believe that much - if not all - of this suffering we have brought upon ourselves. We did so by forgetting our God and seeking after the fleeting, carnal pleasures of the flesh. We have come to understand the teaching of Abinadi and the need for repentance. We have also come to understand the importance of not just obeying the word and will of God, but of covenanting with Him to show that we truly believe His words and desire to keep and hold them the remainder of our days. We have a strong desire to enter into this covenant by being baptized. Would you be willing to baptize me and my people?"

Limhi looked eagerly at Ammon. Ammon's face grew somber. He fidgeted a moment, evidently seeking words of reply. Limhi's heart pounded heavily, now fearing Ammon's response.

At last, Ammon spoke, "I can see that you are sincere in this request. I sense that you are even worthy of entering into this great and everlasting covenant. It would please me to no end to see that this takes place. But, I'm afraid, dear king, that I am not the man who can do this great deed for you. Would that I could, but I have not the authorization to perform such an ordinance. I'm truly sorry." Ammon bowed his head, regrettably.

"I see," the king replied. He was visibly disappointed, but straightened up in his chair in a dignified manner. "This is unfortunate news. I appreciate your candor, however. Surely there's one in Zarahemla who can perform this act. And, if so, we have all the more reason to quit ourselves of this place and make haste to that fine city."

At this, Ammon slowly nodded his head in an attempt to give encouragement, "That is true, your majesty. In Zarahemla, you may receive baptism and fulfill your noble desire."

"It appears that in Zarahemla we will find freedom from both physical and also spiritual bondage, then. I see no greater cause than to bring my people there."

Limhi turned and looked back out toward those at the banquet. He noticed the pleasing, eager looks of anticipation in their good faces. He felt a oneness and obligation to his penitent people. He was resolved to do all that he could to make things right for them.

"That is very true," he agreed with increased determination.

Chapter 21
A Bit of Wine

The next day, King Limhi sent a proclamation to all of the people that they should gather together at the foot of their temple and heed his words. All of the Nephites from both the city of Nephi and Shilom came together. This was the first time that such an assembly had been called. Limhi addressed the people with grand news.

"My people, lift up your hearts and be comforted. The time is soon at hand that we will no longer be in subjection to our enemies, the Lamanites! The Lord has finally heard our calls and has sent to us men from the north, from the land of Zarahemla, to help free us from our bondage!"

When Limhi mentioned Zarahemla, a great whispering swept through the crowd. For those who had not been able to attend the feast, this was confirmation that the grand rumor was true. News of Gideon's dismal find to the north had been widely interpreted as the downfall of Zarahemla. To now have messengers from that city there among them was a shockingly triumphant concept.

"My grandfather, Zeniff, led our people to this beautiful land. They lived in peace and prosperity for many years. We have witnessed the beauties of the land. We have also witnessed the dangers of evil and conspiring men, and the pitfalls of transgression. We allowed ourselves to be deceived and led astray from that which our inner selves told us was not right and true. We have slain the Lord's prophet and have fallen from the grace of God.

"As a result, our lives in this land are no longer peaceful. The Lamanites harass and tax us beyond hope. If we were to stay in this land, we should surely mourn out our days under their oppressive hands. Many true and valiant men have bled out their lives trying to free us. We have learned from sad experience that we cannot free ourselves by the sword!

"We have learned that we must return to our God if we are to receive our freedom. We have learned to humble ourselves and call upon the Lord for guidance. He has heard our prayers. He has sent these men to us from the land of Zarahemla. I trust that if we give heed to their words, we will be successful in returning to Zarahemla, returning to our people, and returning to our God."

Limhi turned and motioned for Ammon to stand and be recognized, "This is Ammon, the leader of these bold Nephites from the north! I wish for you to hear him!"

Ammon stood and raised his hand in acknowledgment. The people cheered at the sight of him. He waved again, with an embarrassed grin creeping across his face. He was not accustomed to such a welcome. The cheering continued for quite some time. Finally, Limhi raised his hand to silence the gathering so that Ammon could speak. When the commotion finally dimmed, Limhi nodded to Ammon.

"I am Ammon. I come from the land of Zarahemla –" Ammon was cut off by repeated cheering. As it subsided, he continued, "I want you to know that the city of Zarahemla is alive and well!" The cheering picked up again as a roar. "My men and I have been sent to find you by our king, King Mosiah II. Over the years, we have thought much of Zeniff and his brave people who sought the land of Nephi. We are proud of you and what you have accomplished. There are not many who could have survived so long in such a place." The people were hushed by the unanticipated compliment.

"Your King Limhi has asked that I tell you somewhat of Zarahemla. He believes it might be of interest to you. I will tell you briefly that we have prospered well in the land. King Benjamin, who was a young man when King Zeniff left Zarahemla, became a strong and mighty king, full of wisdom. He led our people well. He defended us against the attacks from the Lamanites. He grew to be a very old, very happy man.

"Before he died, he built a tower and stood upon it and addressed his people. He told us many wise things. He told us never to forget that one day the beloved Messiah will come and redeem all mankind. He himself, though he was king, worked in the fields and raised his own food. He taught us by example that we should serve each other. He said we cannot find happiness in any other way.

"He declared that, his son, Mosiah, was to be made king over the land. This Mosiah still lives. He is a wise and spiritual leader. We look up to him with great respect, which we feel he deserves. We consider ourselves to be a fortunate people to have such a leader. Just as you are to have a man as great as King Limhi!"

This time it was Limhi's turn to blush at an unexpected compliment. The people applauded and cheered, but only briefly. The brevity was not out of disrespect or disagreement, but because they were now so anxious to hear the remainder of Ammon's words.

"Our King Mosiah has been concerned about your welfare. He has grown increasingly curious to know how you have fared in this choice land. He asked that my men and I seek for you and see if you still live. I am pleased to know that you do! I am saddened to hear of your troubles. Perhaps it was the Lord answering your prayers who prompted King Mosiah to send us here to help! We will meet with your king and his wise counselors. We will find a way to free you! We will find a way to help you live in peace once more! That is why we came and that is what we will do!"

The people again cheered their visitors from the north. They looked to them more as saviors than as visitors. Hope had been restored and the people's enthusiasm was greater than it had been in months. Limhi stepped forward to address the citizens again.

"Now, go home! Go to your flocks! Go to your fields! We will work this through and we will let you know when we have the plan!"

*****

King Limhi and his advisors were assembled in the throne room discussing strategy. They were intent on discovering a feasible strategy for relieving themselves of their bondage. Various plans were presented and rejected. Ammon listened intently to them as they were put forth.

Finally, he spoke, "Your majesty, I appreciate the ingenuity of your many advisors. But, I have to say that in the end, the only clear salvation for your society will be to take yourselves, your belongings, flocks, herds, provisions and so forth and leave this place. The Lamanites are simply too numerous for you to contend with and too ferocious for you to ever hope to live again in peace in this land."

"I fear you are correct, Ammon," Limhi conceded. "But, how do we get these people out of here? The Lamanites have placed guards round about the city, particularly between Shilom and Nephi."

Gideon had remained silent throughout much of the deliberation. He rose and walked toward the king to be recognized. He bowed respectfully and then related his thoughts.

"Oh king, you have listened to my words many times as we have contended with our brethren, the Lamanites," he began. "Now, oh king, if you have not found me to be an unprofitable servant, or if you have listened to my words in any degree, and they have been of service to you, even so I would that you would listen to my words at this time. I will be your servant and deliver this people out of bondage."

"Gideon, your words have indeed been a source of wisdom," Limhi replied. "You may speak."

"The Lamanites expect us to attempt something again," Gideon said. "They have placed a greater number of guards to watch our main gate. But, we have a lesser gate, seldom used, on the back wall, on the back side of the city. The Lamanites who guard this gate often become drunk during the night. We should send a secret proclamation among all the people that they should gather together their flocks, herds and provisions, that they may drive them into the wilderness by night through this back pass.

"When we are ready, I will go and pay the last tribute of wine to the Lamanites. I will ensure that this is our most powerful wine. They will drink it and they will become drunk. We should then be able to pass through the secret pass on the left of them when they are drunken and asleep. We can then circle around the land of Shilom and gather our people from that city as well."

"Gideon," Limhi replied. "That is the most sound suggestion we have heard so far. Are there any opposed to this?"

No one raised a dissenting voice.

"I believe Gideon's plan is sound," Ammon offered.

"So be it," Limhi declared. "Let the word be sent. We will follow Gideon's plan."

*****

The night was warm. The gentle breeze was laced with the fragrant aroma of wild flowers in full bloom. Limhi looked over his people eagerly huddled together and hushing their children. Their faces shown in the darkness with tremendous anticipation mingled with fear of the unknown. Limhi watched them for a moment, enjoying a final look at his people.

His eyes drifted upward at the buildings themselves. They were poorly lit, as orders had been given to have minimal torches ablaze, lest it raise suspicions. Limhi could make out the silhouette of the central temple. Near its side was the tower Noah had built so many years ago.

Limhi's thoughts and imagination drifted back to Zeniff and his exuberance in leading his people to the land of promise; the land of their fathers; the land of their inheritance. The people were so eager and vibrant then. What a time! What a day it must have been for those who first arrived in the land of Nephi to settle in with their loved ones.

What a change had been wrought upon them over the years. Hopes had faded. Bliss was forgotten. Survival became an uncertainty. Such a tragedy of ideals had befallen them. The thoughts hurt the monarch's heart. He felt overly responsible for their dire condition. If only he had been more –

Limhi was shaken from his thoughts by a solitary figure approaching him from the right. It was Gideon. He had two large flasks of wine that were tied together by a long rope that rested on the crook of his neck and allowed the flasks to drape down on either side of his shoulders.

"I am all set, sir," Gideon declared. "This should not take more than an hour or so. I suspect we will still need at least that much time to gather everyone."

"Many of them are here already," Limhi acknowledged. "But I agree, the stragglers will take the better part of two hours to be prepared. Go and take care to do well."

"Yes, sir. You can count on me, your majesty."

Gideon bowed with respect and turned away. He had a bit of an eager spring to his gait. At this moment, he knew that the hopes and safety of an entire society rested on his shoulders, both literally and figuratively. He took care to keep his liquid burdens from spilling as he hurried away. His soul thrilled at the opportunity to play such a key role in preserving his people. He approached the main, southern gate. The Nephite guards opened it for him, without questioning him. His mission was well known to all.

Gideon walked through the gate. It was closed behind him, leaving the anxious Nephites to hope and pray that he would be successful. The torches placed in the iron holders mounted on the outside of the city wall gave him inconstant lighting. Even without it, he knew where the Lamanite guards were stationed. He approached them without hesitation. They saw him coming and looked up from their posts.

"What have you there, Nephite?" the wider of the two guards demanded.

"I bring the nightly ration," Gideon explained.

"It's about time!" the shorter of the two exclaimed. "Must we wait all night?!"

The man grabbed a flask from Gideon, even as he tried to untie it from the other. The man was clearly eager and impatient to consume his rightful share. This pleased Gideon. He took care, however, to conceal his pleasure beneath a stoic expression. The second guard was not to be left out. "Hand it over!"

Both guards opened their flasks and began to guzzle their rations away.

"Is there anything more you require?" Gideon asked subserviently.

The two nearly ignored him in their eager gulping of the fragrant liquid.

"Yes. You can wait here for us to finish, to see if we require more!" the first guard retorted.

"Very well," Gideon stated calmly.

"This is actually quite good," the second guard commented with a touch of surprise.

"It seems you lazy Nephites finally made something worth drinking," the first guard added.

The leather flasks were large, not as large as their appetites, but slightly larger than their tolerance. The two staggered under the weight of the high potency of the specially selected liquids. Both men were determined to drain their flasks. They began to sway and to slur their speech. Gideon watched their eyes glaze over.

"Thish ish definitely better than that other shtuff we got yesterday," the second guard managed to comment.

"Yesh – mush – better," the first guard got out at length, with a great deal of pauses between his words.

"I'm glad to hear that," Gideon said. "We made it for a very special occasion."

"A shpecial occasshion? How nische. Wash ish sho shpecial?" the taller guard said, barely keeping his eyes open.

"It's the night we bid you and your foul brethren farewell," Gideon said, smiling.

The guard was perplexed at Gideon's words and attempted to stand upright at them. The other guard fell to the ground before Gideon finished his sentence.

"Wash do you mean, bid farewell?" the guard stammered. "We are not – going – anywhere!"

"Possibly not, but we are."

"Not sho long ash I am here!" the guard objected, trying to pull himself into a threatening stance. He swayed from side to side and leaned so far forward he nearly lost his balance.

"I do not think you will be here for much longer," Gideon replied, undeterred. "At least not consciously."

"Wash do you mean, Nephite? Shpeak plainly!" the guard continued to sway as he stood facing Gideon. He could no longer hold his eyes open, however, and attempted a threatening posture and glare with his eyes melted shut.

"I think I have done all the talking I need to," Gideon replied. "And, now it is time for you to have a seat."

Gideon gave the man a gentle push. He flopped to the ground, and laid there unmoving. Gideon looked at the two unconscious guards who were blissfully unaware of the world around them. Wine dripped from the corners of their mouths. He nudged them both, one at a time, with the tip of his sandal. Neither one moved. He kicked the first one enough to rouse a sleeping man. His arm flopped to one side, but otherwise there was no recognition of the contact.

The first phase of the plan was now a success. Gideon hustled over to the gate and knocked loudly.

"Open up! It's time to go!" he called in.

The door opened and several eager Nephites peered out through the gate.

"Is it working? Are they out?" they asked.

"Yes, yes, it worked just as planned. They had no chance to alert the guards in the southern fields. But, we don't have much time to move so many. We must move quickly if we are to get everyone out!" Gideon warned.

Ammon and the others were already in gear. They understood all too well the need for haste and their judgment was not clouded with the eagerness and worry which overshadowed some of the city's long-term inhabitants. Limhi had divided the city into groups and placed Ammon and his men over them. The groups began to pour out of the city gate.

Micah was among the first group. He paused as he got to Gideon. "Thank you, thank you so much for watching over my family," Gideon told him as he clasped his hands firmly.

"It's a small favor for a good friend," Micah replied. Hannah and Simon were huddled with Micah. Hannah was gravely pregnant. It would be a long walk for her.

"Gideon, do be careful," Hannah coaxed, being careful to keep her voice low.

"I will. You just get on ahead and take good care of yourself and Simon. I will catch up as quickly as I can." He gave her a warm kiss and a quick embrace and urged her onward.

Gideon stayed behind and watched them leave. More families quickly and quietly fled the city. They nodded their greetings and thanks to Gideon. He urged them to hurry and keep quiet. He watched as the full entourage streamed out with their families, herds, and belongings. He imagined the feelings welling up within him were much the same as those Moses must have experienced when he led the Exodus from Egypt.

When the last group left, Gideon peered into the city through the gate. It was quiet, empty, dark, and a touch eerie. He watched for a moment as ghostly memories swirled before his eyes. His gaze went down a particular street that led beyond the buildings to the city square, far to the north. He remembered a very busy day when he had accidentally bumped into a pretty, young woman and caused her to spill her wares. It seemed like a very long time ago.

Who knew when the next Nephite would view this city, if ever, he wondered. He pulled the great back gate closed, watching the view diminish as he did so. With it also vanished the hopes and dreams of thousands of Nephites who would never be able to call the Land of Nephi home.

With the gate secured, he turned and hurriedly caught up with the group that had traveled ahead of him. They moved as quickly as they could. It was not easy, particularly for those with little children. They had wisely spread the youngest children among many families, rather than letting families watch after all of their own children. By spreading the children around, men, or older boys, could help speed their flight by carrying children not necessarily related to them.

It was not long before they approached the far, eastern side of Shilom. They traveled without torches, to avoid being detected. Few could have noticed them in the darkness of the field. As they came within a few dozen yards of Shilom, Ammon signaled for the people to be extra silent. The front group began to slow down, which inevitably allowed the straggling groups to catch up with them. As they began to bunch up, Ammon motioned for them to keep moving.

"You just have to keep especially quiet!" he urged. "But, keep moving!"

He worked his way forward with stealth. He was within two dozen feet of the city when he saw the sign. The gate opened and a single torch arched back and forth outside it three times. Amaleki had succeeded. His wine was equally potent. The people were ready. Ammon gave a hoarse, hushed shout, "Come!"

Amaleki and the people began to pour out of the city and merge with the people from Nephi as they too marched northward. Shilom's border came within a hundred yards of the jungle on its northern side. It was not long before the Nephites were all hidden within the rainforest's fringes, cutting their way to freedom. Each vine seemed like a tangible shackle being sliced in half.

They traveled with minimal light. Only those at the very front had lit their torches. They held them aloft to allow those with swords to hack away at the vines and brush as they cut their way through the jungle. The rest of the fugitive society followed in darkness, trying to remain as quiet as possible. The parents had been careful to explain the need for silence in their journey, particularly on this first night. The older children understood it better than the younger ones and proved to be a tremendous help.

Perhaps their trickiest endeavor was in keeping their flocks and herds together and reasonably silent. They previous day, they had gathered all of the animals to housing that was on the planned pathway between Nephi and Shilom. This way they could gather the animals quickly once the journey had begun. This movement and confining of the animals was a dangerous feat, for if the Lamanites had taken notice, it could have been a signal that something was afoot.

To keep suspicions low, they had herded the animals to the area in stages, throughout the day. Bit by bit, they eventually gathered the majority of their animals into the area, with the final bunch being herded in just as the sun set.

To lessen the amount of noise the animals would make on the journey, they had removed all of the bells and metal neck or leg shackles from the animals. This, too, was done throughout the day. They had taken every possible precaution with the animals, but could do nothing about the animals' temperament than to pray.

They took the concept of praying that their animals would obey and follow in extreme silence, very seriously. Family prayers at dinner that night included heartfelt and sincere prayers that the Lamanites would remain drunk and the animals would be silent. Perhaps it would seem silly to an outsider, to pray for such things, but these people knew that their very lives depended on it. They prayed with great faith.

Now, they were seeing the answer to those prayers. The animals moved in an almost eerie silence. They trudged forward as if herded by angels. Many of the larger animals were burdened with the people's belongings, and a few carried children upon their backs. The animals accepted their burdens without complaint or delay. In fact, the willingness of the animals worked as a testament to many of the Nephites that the Lord was truly watching out for them. It gave them hope that they were actually going to make it out of bondage.

The now mobile society of fugitives pressed forward over awkward territory trying to make good distance. They pressed on for a space of at least two hours. Gideon stayed in the rear, ever looking backward to keep a steady vigil on whether or not they were being followed. So far into the journey, there were no signs of pursuit. Still, they could afford to take no chances. This was the people's final hope for any sort of peace.

Ammon finally gave word to halt and rest. The Nephites were leery, but also weary, so they agreed. The mothers and children were especially relieved. He made it known that they could not rest long. He gave encouragement to those he could as he made his way to the back of the long line of refugees. Finally, he made his way to Gideon.

"Any sign of them?" he asked.

"No, sir, none," Gideon replied.

"Apparently that wine is really doing the trick," Ammon replied.

"Either that or it's the people's prayers," Gideon added.

"It's probably both. At any rate, we need to get as much distance between us and Nephi as we can before morning. I believe it's time for the second portion of our plan."

"I agree. We should keep moving."

"I will tell Amaleki."

"Good luck. And see you soon."

The two shook hands and Ammon made his way back toward the front. About halfway there he stopped and met briefly with Amaleki and Hem.

"Any sign of them?" Amaleki asked.

"No, none. It appears all is going well. It's time to part."

"Understood. We will do our best."

"Hem," Ammon said, "you will need to keep our rearward watch now."

"Will do," he replied eagerly. "You just lead the way."

"Yes, sir," Ammon smiled and moved forward to get the line going.

Ammon's half of the people were soon on their way again, keeping the same northerly direction. Amaleki let them move on a dozen paces or so, watching them disappear into the night. When they were nearly gone, he turned to his own flock of Nephites.

"All right," he said, "It's time to get moving. Remember, be very careful during the first few yards!"

The people nearest him nodded and passed the word on back through their ranks. The whole group began to follow Amaleki as he headed off the main trail at a ninety degree angle to the east of Ammon's trail. It took several minutes before his half of the people had disappeared into the jungle with Gideon and Helem at their tail.

Once the people were securely on their way, Gideon and Helem stopped and propped up several vines, logs and bushes, effectively concealing the point where their trail now diverged from Ammon's. Ammon's group purposely left a powerful tell-tale sign of their passing in the hopes that the Lamanites would wholly overlook the tracks that Gideon and Helem now attempted to conceal.

Both groups continued through the night for well over an hour. By now, they were so deep into the jungle that fear of being sighted had diminished significantly. Ammon gave the order to light torches. Though they had begun to grow accustomed to their blackened march, the children appreciated the light. The flickering flames danced between the trees and vines, awakening their imagination of strange animals and beings. Their greatest fear by far, however, was the thought of seeing a Lamanite staring back at them through the trees.

Ammon purposely veered his group slightly to the east. The turn remained very gradual and stopped once Ammon felt certain they were traveling directly east. He held their course eastward at this point. They continued for another hour then stopped to rest. The rest was highly welcome. The need for sleep was taking its toll on many of the adults, as well as the children.

While they sat, there was a sudden start among the people. They sat up alert as one of the children shouted out that he had heard voices. Some began to panic with concern that the Lamanites had caught up to them. Ammon rose to hush their fears.

"Settle down people! Everything is just fine! Stay where you are!"

The voices and sounds of jungle travel grew louder and louder. Ammon continued to settle the people down. Finally, a sword could be heard hacking away at the trail even farther east than they had come.

"We are over here!" Ammon called out.

"Surely, he isn't giving us away?!" a concerned mother whispered to her neighbor.

"Hardly!" a Nephite turned and comforted the two women. "Watch!"

As Ammon continued to call out, the hacking grew louder and eventually was upon them. A voice in the jungle called back. The two seemed to know each other. Finally, they met. It was Amaleki. His sweaty, smiling face glistened in the torchlight.

"Well, fancy meeting you here! Having a bit of a rest I see, while the rest of us busy ourselves in the woods," Amaleki teased.

"It's good to see you. I have to admit, I was a little concerned as to whether or not we would be able to pull this off!" Ammon said.

"It was either this or wander forever. I chose this!" Amaleki replied. "We better keep moving, just in case."

"I agree. Our plan is almost complete," Ammon said. "We should go."

Ammon gave the signal and his front men carefully pulled the vines and bushes aside from the northern side of their trail. His people were ushered in and cautioned to tread with care as they left the main trail. As the last of Ammon's half entered the northern trail, Helem greeted Amaleki, who stood waiting his turn and allowing his people to rest.

Once they were in, Amaleki motioned for his people to follow suit. The two groups were reunited on their quest north. Gideon again brought up the rear. Once again, as the people slipped ahead, he and two others lingered behind and replaced the vines, logs and brush in such a way as to conceal their point of exit from the main path. Once they themselves retook their journey north, there was nothing left behind but two paths which joined together so well that they gave the impression of one, continuous path traveling east and west.

Ammon led King Limhi's people northward for another hour and a half. Then he gave the order to halt for the night. Many weary feet took solace in the respite. Few people bothered to even pitch their tents, allowing their fatigue to overcome them and put them into a deep, fulfilling sleep. They had only a few hours left before daylight, when they would need to press on again in earnest to maintain their lead.

Chapter 22

Trailing

Four Lamanite guards emerged from the southern woods and crossed the field. Their sandals were already damp from the dew that lingered amid the heat of the rising sun. Their footprints could be seen on the damp grass as they made their way north toward the city of Nephi. They laughed and kidded themselves as they walked. They had another day of "minding the peasants" ahead of them, and wondered what bits of teasing torment they could inflict on their captive prey.

As they grew nearer the southern wall, they could make out the shapes of two men. Approaching closer, it became evident it was the two guards that half of their party was intended to relieve.

"Look at them. Sleeping there. Pathetic!" one guard called out.

"If Laman found out, it would be their hides."

"Well, he would have to find out first, now wouldn't he?" the first guard responded with more than a hint of warning to keep the matter between themselves.

"All right, wake-up time!" the guard called to their sleeping comrades. "Time to be up and doing!"

At first nothing happened. Both guards lay there, not stirring. The foursome came closer and saw the emptied wine flasks. They smiled at each other, guessing that their comrades had enjoyed a productive night. The tallest guard gave one of the sleeping men a good kick.

"Come on! Up with you!"

The man finally stirred and rolled to a sitting position. His eyes remained shut as he slowly reached up and held his head with both hands.

"Too much excitement, eh?!" the leader of the new guards, Gilgal, called out with an intentionally loud voice.

"Whoa! Whoa! Not so loud! Have pity already!" the sitting guard moaned.

"Come on now, get up!" Gilgal said, as he kicked the other sleeping man in the side.

He stirred as well, but continued to lay on his side as he reached for his head.

"I'm up already. Leave me alone," he said.

"All right. Consider yourselves relieved. We will take it from here," Gilgal said. "Any problems in the night?"

"No, none. It was a quiet night," the sitting guard replied.

"It wasn't too quiet, though. It looks like you had some fun," one of the other guards jested.

"We only had a little," the prostrate guard said rather defensively.

"A little?!" Gilgal laughed. "Then you must not be able to hold your wine!"

"So, where are the farmers?" one of the guards asked, changing the subject. "They're usually up and doing by now."

"Yes, you are right. That's a little odd."

"You know, it's awfully quiet in there as well. Usually, we can hear them rustling about in there buying, selling and just plain talking. I don't hear anything."

"I don't think I like this. Call the guard."

"Hello! Guard! Open the gate!"

They waited, but nothing happened.

"Guard! I said, open the gate!"

Again, nothing happened.

"Open that gate now before I tear it down myself!" the guard ordered while growing increasingly angry.

The gate remained unmoved. The inner city remained as silent as a tomb. Something was definitely amiss.

"That's it. Get this gate opened!" Gilgal ordered his men.

They drew their swords and attacked the gate, cutting away at the ropes that lashed the wooden door together. Finally, they cut through and were able to pull one log out of place. It tumbled to the ground with a dull thud. A muscular Lamanite arm reached in through the gap and pulled the draw rope free, allowing the gate to be pulled open.

All six Lamanite guards were now on their feet. The tenseness of the situation brought the two drunken men into complete consciousness. The men entered the city with a touch of apprehensive curiosity. Not a soul could be seen or heard. They walked about fifty paces and detected absolutely no sounds anywhere. They noted a few houses with doors left open.

Gilgal peered in one. No one was inside. Everything of any value was gone. A flash of inspiration struck the man. He turned with an angry, concerned look on his face.

"We better get to Shilom! Hurry!"

The six guards ran out of the city, leaving the gate open. They cleared the distance to Shilom only to find two more sleeping guards. They too had drained wine flasks lying by their sides. The guards did not even attempt to wake them; instead, they attacked the city gate. Within moments the gate was opened in a fashion similar to what had been done at Nephi.

The sleeping guards stirred and asked, "What's going on? What is it?"

The others ignored them as they stormed into the city. It too was entirely devoid of people. Houses were emptied.

"What's this? What has happened?" one of the Shilom guards repeated.

"It's an escape plan, that's what it is. And on *your* watch!" Gilgal responded coldly, as he hurried out of the city with the others behind him.

The four who had slept lingered behind, rubbing their necks in anticipation of the penalty for failure. One of them broke the pause and rushed forward to join the other four guards.

"Well, we just need to catch them. How hard can that be? You can't move two entire cities without leaving a pretty distinct trail!"

"That may be, but how are eight men going to persuade that many people to follow them home again, huh?!" Gilgal bit back.

The four stopped again. Slowly, the severity of the situation was sinking in on them.

"I suggest one of you hurry back and inform King Laman that he better send his men up here while the rest of you follow me as we try to track these vermin!" Gilgal hollered back as he ran north. "I don't envy whichever of you brings him the news!" he added with contempt.

For a bit, the four stood there dumbfounded. No one wanted to volunteer. They knew that it would most likely be the last news that they would bear. They avoided looking each other in the eye, knowing their guilt.

Suddenly, one pushed another and ran to join the other guards as he hollered, "Well, you better hurry, Lemuel. If you're lucky, Laman will take pity on you if you get there quickly enough!"

The two other guards caught onto the ploy and also trotted north. Lemuel stood only a moment, then realized he had been set up.

He hollered back, "What do you mean *me*?!"

"You're the closest to Shemlon! Now hurry!" one of the other three taunted as he hurried north.

"Fine! Just fine!" Lemuel said at last. He quickly mulled over his alternatives and could come up with none. With this, he turned and made a hasty course to Shemlon to bear the formidable news.

The other seven guards continued following the matted grass that led them north, toward the jungle. It was an easy trail to follow. The point at which it joined the jungle was also impressively easy to note.

"This shouldn't be too hard!" Gilgal said.

They charged into the jungle, following the trail that had been cleared the night before. The trail led due north. They jogged at a steady pace, following the blatant path before them. A bit over an hour into their journey, they continued northward, oblivious to the vines and logs that Gideon had placed to disguise the spot at which Amaleki had led his people eastward.

The seven guards continued onward, wearying from their fast pace. They stopped to rest, panting.

"Well – they certainly – have put – a lot of distance – behind them," one of the guards commented.

"Yeah," was all a comrade could reply.

"Are you children ready yet?" Gilgal said as he stood and prepared to continue their hunt.

Soon, they were all on the run again. No one noticed that they were slowly veering east. They continued on an endless trek. They approached an area that appeared a bit odd. It was the area where the Nephites had reunited both halves of their people and turned northward again.

"Look at all of these tracks and marks," one of the guards said.

"What about them?" Gilgal asked.

"I don't know. They just look odd. Different somehow."

"Well, certainly. They probably stopped here to rest. The kids wandered around. What about it?"

"I don't know. It's just different."

At that moment, an end of one of the vines Gideon had placed to conceal their exit slipped from its perch. The vine dangled and swayed in place.

"What was that?" Gilgal asked with a start.

"A vine! What, are you afraid it was a snake?"

The guards laughed at their self-proclaimed leader.

"Very funny! All right, we should get going," he ordered.

The men hurried on their way, unwittingly entering the path Amaleki and his people had cut. They journeyed for over an hour at a quick, but slowing pace. The exertion of the chase was beginning to take its toll. They hurried their best, no one daring to let the others detect their fatigue.

"Wait a minute! What is with this?" one of the guards shouted and stopped.

They all did the same. They stood there, panting and sweating, looking before them. Their path had come to a dead end. They could see a large amount of bushes, vines and logs blocking their path.

"This doesn't make any sense!" Gilgal said. "Look around. Did they cut off to the right or left?"

The guards did a quick search through the trees. They appeared entirely undisturbed. They even back-tracked a couple dozen yards looking for some form of exit.

"What's beyond it?" one of them suggested.

"Beyond it?! Why would that matter?"

"We should just check and see."

They unsheathed their swords and gave a great whack at the nearest bush to remove it from its roots. The guard who swung the sword nearly had the sword flung from his hand. The bush flew up in the air and perched, swinging on a vine about six feet above the ground, far to his left.

"That is a bit overdoing it, isn't it?" his partner asked, "Why did you hit it so hard?"

"I didn't. That bush was just sitting there. Loose," he said with a dubious look. "This is very odd."

"What do you mean it was just sitting there?" Gilgal asked.

"See for yourself," he replied.

The guards all stepped forward and touched the other bushes. They were all loosely placed there. They quickly tossed them aside and pushed vines out of the way.

"It's as if they were hiding their trail."

"Why would they do that? We know they went this way. What good would hiding it do them?"

"I'm not sure but –"

The Lamanite cut his speculation off as the removal of a key bush revealed an unexpected opening before them.

"Wait, take a look at this!"

They quickly removed the final bushes. As they did so, they revealed a path before them. It ran perpendicular to the one they had followed.

"It's another path!" one guard said with surprise.

"No. Not another path. It's the same one we've been following all day," Gilgal said with disgust.

"What do you mean?"

"They doubled-back. We've just gone in a huge circle."

"A circle?"

"Yes, they must have veered off somewhere and we missed it."

"Missed it? We better go back and find it!"

"How? Where? They could have cut off in a different direction at any point. We've traveled all morning. That's an enormous amount of territory to retrace and look for some sign of a hidden trail. Meanwhile, they've got a night and a morning's head start on us. Even if we found their trail by evening, they would be so far ahead of us we would never catch up! They're gone. They're history!"

"You mean we're history when King Laman finds out about this."

Just then, they heard voices to their left.

"Well, maybe they're not so far away after all. Come on!"

They charged down the trail, forgetting the meagerness of their numbers as they hurried after their prey. To their surprise, they came face to face with more Lamanite soldiers.

"Why are you returning? What's your hurry?" a tall officer, named Hamoth, demanded to know.

"What - uh - we thought you were the Nephites."

"Do we *look* like Nephites?!" Hamoth said with an accusing sneer on his face.

"No, sir. It's just that we followed the trail and it led to you."

"What do you mean it led to us?"

"It circles around and comes right back to here," a guard said with disgust.

"It does now, does it? You mean you have totally lost track of the Nephites?"

"Uh - Yes, sir," Gilgal said trying to remain bold in spite of the repercussions of his words.

"Well, now," Hamoth replied. "I think the king would like to hear how you allowed this to happen. Why don't you follow these men back and explain it to him?"

Hamoth motioned to two of his tallest men. They stepped forward, holding their swords at the ready. Suddenly, the former city guards received the distinct impression that they were now being guarded themselves.

"Yes, sir," Gilgal said as he urged his men to fall into line.

The infuriated commander turned back to his own men and shouted, "Now, we'll search these woods and find those Nephites who you have somehow managed to lose!"

As he and his men followed the trail northward, the others departed southward back down the trail toward Shilom, Nephi, and, unfortunately for some, Shemlon.

Chapter 23

King Mosiah

As the days passed, the Nephites became less and less anxious about the Lamanites. Slowly it grew clear and certain that they were no longer being pursued. They had to assume that their strategy with the trails had been successful. They became so confident that on the seventh day of their journey, they rested the entire morning.

The rest was intended for the children's sakes, but it was the mothers who appreciated it most. The children continued to laugh and play. To them this entire excursion was seen as a prolonged campout. They did not have even the slightest understanding of the significance of their migration.

That particular day, more men than normal were posted on the southern end of the group. As a precaution, Ammon had ordered that their camp be set up on the northern end of a large field they had come upon at the base of a valley. They named it the Valley of Gideon in honor of the man who had made the first part of their exodus possible.

Meanwhile, Gideon and several other men doubled back over their trail a few miles to see if they could catch any signs of their pursuers. Whenever possible in their journey, they had taken advantage of the occasional fields and streams to help disguise their trail. They would veer their course by walking upstream a ways and then concealing the point at which they reentered the jungle.

On occasion, however, their course became more difficult to conceal, as several rivers contained the dreaded devil fish which would tear and eat their flesh. They would build makeshift bridges on such occasions to allow the group to cross in safety. They would tie a rope to the far end of the bridges so that the last to cross could pull it from the embankment and let the bridge float away down the river. The last thing they wanted to do was make their pursuers' journey any easier.

From the point where they had rested in the Valley of Gideon onward, they no longer feared the Lamanites. They felt certain that if they were to be overtaken, it should have happened on that day. When it did not, they were able to lay the majority of their fears aside. Their journey shifted from being a flight from their enemies to an excursion to their new homes.

Their pace grew easier, more tolerable. Still, they made good progress. As their thoughts turned toward Zarahemla, the people became increasingly curious to know more and more. The evening campfires were spent listening to Ammon and his men tell tales of their cousins to the north.

The days were spent on the move, with children and adults taking advantage of walking beside Ammon and his men, and pummeling them with additional questions.

As the days wore on, the people began to feel they knew Zarahemla already. Everyone became anxious to see it for themselves. One day it happened. Ammon, at the head of the journey, simply stopped cold in his tracks. Limhi rushed to his side, concerned. He could see a tear in Ammon's eye.

"What? What is it?" the king asked.

"We are almost there. We should be there in time for our midday meal," Ammon replied. "It is just that I did not realize just how much I missed it. I did not expect to be so affected by returning."

"I understand," Limhi said in a fatherly way. "You have been through quite a bit, and have been a tremendous help to us all. We owe you our lives."

"I have never been so grateful to be a part of any activity in my life," Ammon said, turning to the king. "Even so, the one thought that fills me the most at this time is of my children. I have a son, three daughters and a little baby boy waiting for me up there. I'm looking forward to seeing them again. And, of course, my sweet wife."

Limhi smiled. "It is good to have a family," was all he said.

Ammon was right. They rounded the final bend in the road and saw the tall walls and great city gate of Zarahemla welcoming them. The tower guard was surprised at the sight of so many people on the road. At first he feared an invasion. Then he recognized them as fellow Nephites. Finally, he recognized the lead man in particular.

"It's Ammon!" he turned and shouted into the city square. "It's Ammon! It's Ammon! He's returning with a host of Nephites! Tell the king! Ammon returns!"

As the group traversed the final yards to the city, the wall became infested with on-lookers hailing their returning friends and family. The cheering vibrated the trees and warmed the hearts of the weary, but excited, travelers. The great city gate opened to bid them welcome. They marched into and filled the city square. Gideon kept his arm around Hannah, aiding her as they walked. They smiled broadly at each other.

All around them from high up on the city wall, on the tops of buildings, and down on their level of the square, Nephites young and old cheered their welcome.

Limhi and his people smiled and wept. Several of them fell to their knees praising God and giving thanks for their deliverance. Afterward, Limhi saw where Gideon was kneeling. He made his way over to him, just as

Gideon got to his feet and was helping his wife to hers. As she got to her feet, he put his arm around his wife's shoulders, and saw his king approaching.

"I just wanted to thank you for your help," Limhi said. "I do not know if we could have made it out of Nephi without you."

"I just wanted to help our people, your majesty," Gideon said with traditional humility. "It has been my honor to serve."

"And, you have served well and honorably," Limhi added. "Your family should be proud of you." Limhi patted young Simon on the head. The boy stood in awe. Even at his young age, he knew that this was the king. He did not know what his father had done, but in his own way, he was impressed that the king was talking to him.

Limhi turned to Hannah, who nodded to the king respectfully. "You have quite a fine man for a husband," Limhi said with a smile.

"Thank you, your majesty. I know!" Hannah said with an even bigger smile.

Limhi nodded approvingly. There was a noise behind them and everyone turned to see. The great city gate was closing behind them. There was a bit of excitement across the way. The king of the northern Nephites had just entered the square. Mosiah himself came forward to welcome his brethren home from their long journey.

As he entered the city square, a hush fell upon the crowd. Nephites from both regions of the land watched him approach the new arrivals. He walked with dignity, grace, and majesty. Yet, he was clad in no finer clothing than that of his subjects. It was clear he was their king, but this was because of an inner power and discipline, not from an outward show of ostentatious behavior.

As he walked toward the group, the northern Nephites bowed their heads respectfully, then stood tall again. His passing between them caused a dipping and standing of heads and shoulders as if a slow ripple were flowing through the dense throng. Mosiah appreciated the show of respect and adulation, but did not focus his attention on it. His attention was focused on those he had come to greet. He walked directly to Ammon.

"Ammon, it is good to see you have returned safely," the great king exclaimed. "And, it appears you have brought several friends with you. I trust all is well."

Ammon knelt and bowed his head. Then he rose and addressed his beloved monarch.

"Yes, your majesty, I have returned. The Lord has been good to us. We have brought back our brethren from the land of Nephi. We found them living there under the oppressive hand of the Lamanites. Through the grace of God, we have managed to escape and have brought them here."

"Remarkable. I welcome you all!" Mosiah declared to the new citizens.

"Your majesty, I would like you to meet their leader." Ammon motioned to the man who stood beside him. "This is King Limhi. He is the grandson of Zeniff who journeyed south to find the land of our forefathers."

"Zeniff?! Then you truly have been successful! King Limhi, I welcome you to Zarahemla."

"Please, your majesty. I relinquish my crown. Please consider me as one of your loyal subjects. Consider my people to be your people. We are pleased to live under your most generous reign," Limhi replied.

"Limhi, again, I welcome you as a brother. We will feast this night in honor of you and your noble people!"

*****

King Mosiah was as good as his word. The feast had been a graciously welcome change from the provisions they had eaten while on the trail. Nearly anything would have been considered a celebration, but Mosiah ensured that the returning people felt the full hand of fellowship and honor for having braved their stay for so long in the land of their forefathers.

*****

The next day found Limhi, Gideon, Ammon and his brethren in King Mosiah's council chamber. Limhi had his servant bring the people's records forward. He referenced the many metallic plates filled with intricate engravings and related the tale of his own people and their sojourn in the land of Nephi.

Mosiah was anxious to hear all that had transpired from when Zeniff had left Zarahemla. Limhi told the entire tale of their triumphs and took care not to omit their tragedies. Mosiah's heart burned with pride at Zeniff's success, and he openly wept over Noah's transgressions and the hardships of the people.

When both kings had shared the stories of their kingdoms, Limhi paused and acquired a bit of a pensive look. Mosiah sensed that something was weighing on his mind.

"What is it, Limhi?"

"I have something. Something peculiar that I have been interested in learning more about –"

"What?"

"You recall when I told you of sending my people north to find Zarahemla."

"Yes, and you said they found a desolate land filled with bones and crumbling ruins."

"There was something more. They found a couple dozen metal plates. The plates have some sort of writing on them that I cannot decipher. I have to assume it is a record of these people. I'm filled with curiosity as to whether or not it will tell us what terrible disaster led to their downfall. I'm anxious to find someone who can translate these plates. Ammon suggested that you may be able to do this."

"Well, that is possible. It depends on many things. I would be willing to try, at least."

"I would be very anxious to find out what you can learn."

"Bring the plates and I will do what I can."

"Actually, I have the plates with me. I had my man bring them with all of the others."

"Oh? You have them here? Very well, let me gather my things and we will see what we have."

"Gather your things? What things?"

"My urim and thummim."

"What are a urim and thummim?"

"They are special tools prepared by the Lord from the beginning of time. When used by a man of faith, they can be used to decipher ancient writings."

"How did you receive these great tools?"

"Many years ago, I sent some of my men out to explore the land, in hopes of finding you and your people. They failed to do so, but instead found a land similar to that which you have described. Perhaps it was even the same land. While there, they found a large stone full of engravings. They also found the urim and thummim sealed in a stone box nearby. They brought these things back with them. I discovered the power of the tools. I found that with them I was able to translate the engravings on the stone."

"What did they say?"

"Nothing of great consequence, I'm afraid, but at the time it was quite exciting. It turned out to be a record of the people's calendar system, explaining the times and the seasons according to their reckoning. We found the calendar itself to be highly accurate."

"Interesting. But, what are these tools you keep naming?"

"The urim and thummim consists of two round, clear stones each held by a stiff strip of metal. There's a breastplate that wraps around the chest. By sliding the metal strips that hold the stones into slots, I can look through the stones at the text that needs to be interpreted while keeping my hands free to turn the plates."

"How does it work, though? Does it alter the engravings so that you see exactly what it is supposed to say?"

"I thought so at first. I put on the breastplate and looked at the engravings, but all I saw was a clouded jumble. At first I thought it was of no help."

"How did you figure them out?"

"Quite frankly, I gave it a lot of thought. I decided that if this was something of importance, the Lord would know how to manage it. So, I prayed about it. I learned that this was half of the solution. It was not enough to simply look at the engravings through the urim and thummim. I had to study them and go at it with faith. I had to have faith that the Lord would help me find the answer."

"And did you?"

"Yes, I did."

"But, you said it was just a calendar of sorts. Why would that be important?"

"Maybe that was just an exercise to prepare me for a greater work. Had I not done that, I would not know how to do this at all. Maybe this was all in preparation for interpreting whatever it is that is on those plates your men have found. The Lord prepares us for many things in ways we often do not understand."

"You speak with great wisdom. I see your meaning."

"May I see the plates now?"

"Yes," Limhi motioned to his servant to step forward. "I have them here."

The servant placed a small satchel on the table in front of Limhi. Limhi reached in and pulled out the plates. He set them on the table in front of King Mosiah. Their metal made a scraping and ringing noise against the stone surface of the table as he slid them into place.

Mosiah eyed them with interest. He leaned forward examining them. He ran his fingertips over the engravings of the first plate.

"Most peculiar markings. I have not seen any like them before. Though in some ways they are not unlike those found on that stone."

Mosiah lifted the top plate. Its one side was fastened to the other plates by three metal bands that wrapped through holes in the right side of each of the plates.

"We added the bands to keep the plates in the order we found them. We did not know for sure if they were even in any sort of order, but just in case, we decided to ensure they would stay in that order."

"A wise move."

Mosiah carefully turned to the second plate. As he did so, the others in the room could see the light glisten off the smooth back side of the first golden sheet. The engravings were only on one side of each sheet.

"Well, these markings are very similar to those on that first sheet. Very interesting."

"Can you interpret the writing?"

"No, not without the urim and thummim. Some of the markings look roughly familiar, but I cannot make out their meaning. I'm interested in doing so, however."

"As are we. Hopefully, these tell us more than the days of the week."

"I would think so," Mosiah replied with a smile. "Please bring me my urim and thummim," he requested one of his servants.

After a bit, the servant returned with the objects. Mosiah raised his arms and allowed the thummim to be placed on his chest. He held his arms up until the leather straps had been wrapped around and tied at his back. With the breastplate in place, he reached for the urim stones.

These clear stones were nearly perfectly spherical. They were each held separately by a slender, metal rod or strip. Each rod and stone was separate devices, with the rod arching gracefully around the stone, holding it securely. The other end of the rod was placed in a slot on the breastplate.

Mosiah adjusted the rods until the crystalline stones each rested directly before his eyes. He lightly tugged at the metal strips to test their security. Satisfied that they would not slip out, he slowly leaned forward to gaze at the plates through the clear stones. He flipped back to the first plate and looked at it for only a moment. Then he shut his eyes and remained motionless for quite some time, deep in thought.

All of the others in the room remained silent and still, allowing him his peace. As the moments grew longer, some in the room began to grow uneasy with a taste of impatience to know what he was doing and when he would begin his work of interpretation. This grew from their concern that his meditation was so deep that it almost appeared as if he had fallen into a state of unconsciousness.

Finally, Mosiah opened his eyes again. He stirred only slightly and looked down upon the plates once more. He appeared to scan the entire front plate fairly quickly. Then he returned to the upper right-hand corner of the plate and gazed at it for a long time. Everyone wondered what he saw.

"Interesting!" he said at last, "Most interesting!"

"What do they say? Can you make it out?"

"Yes, I can make it out now."

"What is it?"

"It appears that it is indeed the tale of the people who met a bitter end and whose remains you have witnessed."

Chapter 24
The Jaredites

Limhi, Ammon, Gideon, Amaleki and others sat in Mosiah's grand council chamber, awaiting Mosiah's interpretation of the engravings on the twenty-four metal plates that Limhi's men had found in the land of desolation. Mosiah maintained their enraptured attention as they sat respectfully awaiting his findings.

"This is apparently a very old record," Mosiah observed. "It tells of the Creation of the world and the history of a people descending down to the time of the building of the Tower of Babel."

"The Tower of Babel?!" Amaleki was surprised, and a bit embarrassed, to hear himself exclaim aloud.

Mosiah was unruffled and continued to look down at the plates as he spoke, "Yes, the Tower of Babel. Apparently, when the Lord decided to confound the peoples' languages, there was a group led by a man named Jared who prayed to the Lord that He would not confound his people's language. They were granted their desire and told that they must leave the area, lest they be overcome by the wickedness of their fellow countrymen."

"Remarkable! You can read all that?" Limhi said with excitement.

"Well, it is not really a matter of 'reading' in the traditional concept of the term. It's more a matter of gaining the impression of the idea. That is part of why it takes such concentration and faith. I gain an impression while viewing the engravings through the urim stones, and then I need to be able to express them in words you and I understand. It's a difficult process to master."

"What else does it say?" Ammon asked, hoping to return to the story itself.

"We should see," Mosiah grew pensive again, then related the following, "Jared and his brother gathered their families together as well as their closest friends and left the city. All of them were spared the curse of confused languages. They journeyed for quite some time in the wilderness. It must have been a long time, because it says that Jared's brother went off by himself and prayed to the Lord for guidance. When the Lord spoke to him, the Lord chastised him for several hours for neglecting to pray for the past four years."

"Four years without praying. It must have been quite a chastisement," Limhi remarked, remembering how long he and his own people had gone without any form of sincere prayer.

"Imagine being chastised by the Lord for several hours," Ammon commented. "That could not have been enjoyable."

"Yes, but what a powerful lesson he must have learned!" Mosiah mused.

"Why was it Jared's brother who was out doing this praying? Why was it not Jared?" Gideon asked. "Did you not say he was their leader?"

"It seems that although Jared was the leader of the people, his brother was their spiritual leader," Mosiah replied.

"What was his name?" Ammon asked.

"It's a fairly long name. It looks like 'Mahonri Moriancumer'," Mosiah said at length.

"'Mahonri Moriancumer'?" Amaleki said with the kind of look on his face that one gets in the presence of a foul odor, then added with a shrug, "I image that is why they rather referred to him as 'Jared's brother'!"

Mosiah looked at Amaleki in a serious way, effectively hiding his appreciation for the observation. Ammon nudged him and gave him a warning look. Amaleki nearly gave an excuse, but thought the better of it and remained silent.

"Please continue," Limhi requested, shifting attention back to the story.

"It seems that the people were camped on the shores of a great sea. The land was filled with all sorts of fruits, plants and game, so they called it 'Bountiful.' While they were camped there, the brother of Jared prayed to the Lord and was told that he needed to take the people across the ocean to a promised land. A land flowing with milk and honey."

"This is beginning to sound much like the story of how Nephi and his family left Jerusalem and traveled to this land," Limhi observed.

"Yes, it does," Mosiah agreed. "It is interesting how often a people can begin to believe that they are the only ones the Lord has ever favored or blessed, is it not?"

Limhi and the others caught the meaning within his words as a direct commentary on themselves and their society.

"The brother of Jared was confused at first," Mosiah continued, "stating that he had no idea of how to cross such a great sea. The Lord told him that he would instruct him in the manner of the ships that he would build."

"Ships?" Amaleki asked, "There would be more than one?"

"Yes, 'ships.' These were ships unlike any other ever built. They were narrow and pointed on either end, but grew fatter, taller, and wider toward the center. They were smooth and rounded on the top as well as the bottom. Apparently, there was no telling the top from the bottom. They were sealed tight like a dish all around and in the shape of a ball stretched out until opposite ends came to a point. Each of eight ships was to be made the length of a tree."

"How odd," Limhi commented.

"Jared's brother was also confused. He asked how they would breathe in such vessels. The Lord told them to cut a hole in the top and the bottom and to prepare plugs for the holes, so that they could stop them up when the waves crashed upon the ships. He was told that many times they would be buried in the deep like whales crossing the waters. It sounds as if they were in for a rough journey.

"The brother of Jared did all this and had his people prepare the ships. He again went high upon a hill for solitude and prayed to the Lord. The Lord asked what was wanted and he prayed for forgiveness, and said that he wanted to know what the people would do for light in the vessels as they traveled. He said that surely they were not meant to cross the seas in darkness.

"This next part here is very interesting, when you think about it. The Lord asked the brother of Jared for a recommendation, pointing out that they could not take fire in the vessels for light. That is fairly evident, lest they die from the smoke in such confined spaces. Imagine having the Lord ask you for a recommendation."

"It must have been a test," Ammon suggested.

"Oh, yes, no doubt," Mosiah said with a ponderous distant look in his eye. "I just wonder what I would have suggested." He paused to think it through.

"Well, what did the brother of Jared suggest?" Gideon asked at length.

"He did not give an immediate reply. Instead he went to work preparing sixteen stones. He found some clear rocks, probably some sort of quartz, and polished them until they were each smooth and round. Then he laid them out in front of him and prayed again. When the Lord answered and asked what the brother of Jared wanted, he said he was prepared to receive light for the vessels.

"He asked the Lord to touch each stone with his finger, saying that if He would do this, then the stones would take of His light and offer light for their journey. Marvelous!" Mosiah mused.

"Did He do it?" Hem asked, breaking his long silence.

"Yes, He did. And, oh my! –" Mosiah paused, overwhelmed at the story unfolding before his eyes.

"What is it?" Limhi asked.

Mosiah was unable to respond for a moment. He turned his head aside, pulling his eyes away from the clear stones of the urim before him. Tears welled up in his eyes. He closed them a moment and the others could see that he was trying to picture something. They assumed it was a scene from the story he had just read. At length he again looked through the urim and thummim and continued relating the tale, his voice cracking at first.

"It says here that as the Lord touched each stone, the brother of Jared actually saw the finger of the Lord and was shocked. He withdrew his face and shrank back. When the Lord asked what troubled him, he replied that he had seen the Lord's finger and was concerned. When asked why, he said it was because it was in the shape of a man's finger and he had not realized that the Lord's finger was like that of man's. The Lord replied that it's more a matter of man's finger being in the form of God's.

"The Lord then asked if the brother of Jared had seen any more than this. He said he had not and asked the Lord to show himself to him. He did so. Imagine that! He did so!" Mosiah paused again. Everyone was quiet. The king continued, "The brother of Jared must have been the first human to have seen the Lord God reveal himself in such a way! He was commended for his great faith.

"And then, hmm, oh – it says that the Lord revealed many things to Jared about the history of the world. He was commanded to write them down, but that they should be kept back and hidden from the world until after the Lord's coming." Mosiah looked up suddenly with a look of shocked concern on his face. "There are things on these plates that are not meant to be translated or revealed! Not yet at any rate!"

He sat up straight, pushing the plates away from him. A profound hush fell over all in the room and their spines tingled. This was indeed quite a remarkable find. Several of the men attempted to speak, but were not sure how to proceed or what to say. Ammon finally broke their bewildered silence.

"Without revealing or disturbing the sacred portions of the text, are you able to tell us the rest of the story? What became of the brother of Jared and his people?"

"Well put," Limhi commented.

"This is somewhat significant," Mosiah said after finally leaning back in position and examining the plates more. "It says that in addition to the sixteen stones, the Lord gave the brother of Jared two more stones. He was told that the record he should write would be sealed up and hidden and when it would be found it would be by a people who could not read it. The two stones He gave him would act as interpreters to help them understand the story."

"Why, that sounds like a reference to us!" Ammon exclaimed.

"No less," Mosiah observed.

"Imagine that," Gideon said.

Once again the men sat in a hushed silence contemplating the implications of the words Mosiah revealed to them.

"What more do you see?" Limhi asked.

"We should see. Apparently, the glowing stones worked. They put them in the ships, gathered seeds and provisions and set off for the promised land. They were at sea – oh my – they were at sea for nearly a year. When they landed, they all gathered and gave thanks to the Lord for preserving them."

"What a journey it must have been!" Limhi said.

"It is a wonder they all kept together the entire time," Amaleki mused.

"I am certain that the Lord must have ensured that they would," Ammon added.

"They began to settle the land, plant their seeds and build their homes. They were humble and god-fearing people, quick to remember the blessing of the Lord in bringing them to this promised land. They lived for many years in peace. Jared led the people in righteousness and his brother continued as their spiritual leader. As the two grew older, they recognized that their days were growing short. Jared and his brother agreed that it would be prudent to call the people together and speak of passing on the leadership of the people to the next generation.

"They gathered and discussed this with the people. The people said they wanted a king. The brother of Jared warned them that this would not be wise, for they could not guarantee that they would always be led by upright men. He said that if an evil man were to become king, it would lead to trials, iniquity, and captivity."

Mosiah looked up at Limhi. Limhi swallowed hard. "That is for certain," he said at last, thinking of his wayward father and recently-oppressed people.

Mosiah looked down again and continued interpreting the account, carefully flipping plate after plate as he did so.

"The people pressed hard. The brother of Jared continued to advise against it. He again warned that it would lead to their captivity. But, the people got Jared himself to approach his brother and convince him to support it. He did so with reluctance. Seeking a righteous man, the people asked for the brother of Jared's oldest son, Pagag, to be their king. He refused. They asked for each brother in turn. They all refused. They then asked for each of Jared's sons in succession. All refused, except one. Orihah agreed."

"There's always one," Amaleki said under his breath. "It only takes one."

"It says that Orihah was a good man, who continued to teach his people to remember the tender mercies of God and the blessings He had poured out upon them by not confounding their language and leading them to this land. The people were happy and prosperous. They began to build buildings, refine their arts, and hone their crafts.

"His son, Kib, took on the kingdom after Orihah's death. Kib was also a good king. But, he had a son named Corihor who rebelled against him. He caused a terrible strife and eventually captured his father and imprisoned him. Kib and his loyal followers lived in captivity for many years, fulfilling the brother of Jared's prophetic warning.

"Kib had a son named Shule, born in captivity. Shule grew up anxious to avenge his father. He went to the hill Ephraim and forged swords out of metal that he mined there. He gathered those who would follow him and fought Corihor at the land of Nehor. He beat Corihor, freed his people, and returned the kingdom to Kib. Kib had grown old by this time and returned the kingdom to Shule, who was crowned king. It says that Corihor repented of his ways and that Shule actually let him serve in high positions under his reign.

"It appeared that peace was coming back to the people. But, Corihor had a son named Noah who rebelled against both Shule and his father. He fought Shule and became king over the land of their first inheritance. Shule was captured and Noah planned to put him to death. The night before the execution, Shule's sons sneaked into Noah's house and slew him. They then freed Shule.

"This was not the end of the strife, however. Noah had a son named Cohor who his followers crowned king. At this point, the Jaredite nation was divided into two people. Those who followed king Shule, and those who supported king Cohor. Cohor went to battle against Shule and lost terribly. He was killed. Cohor's son, Nimrod, returned the kingdom to Shule and the kingdom and the people were reunited.

"For this, Shule showed favor to Nimrod. Meanwhile, prophets began to preach to the people calling them to repentance. The people mocked and scorned them. Shule heard of this and made a decree that the prophets were not to be harmed or hindered. Eventually, the people repented and began to prosper again throughout the remainder of Shule's reign.

"After Shule's death, his son, Omer, reigned in righteousness. His son, Jared, however, rebelled and drew many people with him to the land of Heth."

Mosiah stopped speaking. For a moment he stood in silence peering through the urim and pondering the message on the plates. He flipped the plate and looked at the next. The only sound was the clinking and scraping of the metal as he moved onto the next plate. It was not long before he flipped that one as well and went onto the next, and the next.

He seemed to be wholly engrossed in the story, forgetting the others with him. They sat anxiously, but respectfully silent, awaiting his words. He continued at this long enough to make the others begin to grow uncomfortable. They cast wordless looks to each other wondering what to do. No one wished to break protocol and remind the king of their presence, and yet there seemed to be no other way to regain his attention.

Sensing their uneasiness, Ammon motioned with his hand that all should sit silently and allow their king to finish his perusal of the records. Minutes drifted into hours as the king pored over the account. With the turn of the last plate, he sat up with a wearied expression on his face. He pulled the stones away from his eyes. As he began to unstrap the breastplate, Ammon and Amaleki came to his side and undid it for him. They placed it gingerly on the table and sat down again.

Mosiah stretched, but continued to sit, his eyes turned to the twenty-four plates. He shook his head solemnly as the account continued to play out in his mind. He looked around him slowly and saw the inquiring looks on the faces of those around him.

"I apologize for growing silent," he said at last. "It is just that I found myself being pulled into the account. Also, these records hold many things which should not be revealed at this time. I felt that it would be best if I received the whole story, rather than giving it to you piecemeal. In this way, I could also avoid disclosing things which are best kept silent."

"We understand, your majesty," Limhi replied. "What *can* you tell us?"

"What was the last thing I told you?"

"You spoke of Omer. You said he was a good king, but his son, Jared, rebelled."

"Yes. That is right. That is right," Mosiah said, musing back to that point in the history. "There was more, much more." He paused and dismally shook his head a moment before continuing. "This Jared who rebelled against his father, the king, caused a war and captured his father. Omer's other sons raised an army and freed their father and won back the kingdom. Jared was depressed over losing the kingdom. His daughter came to him with a plan for regaining it.

"She offered to dance for a man named Akish. She told her father that if she pleased Akish, he would want to marry her. If so, then Jared should tell Akish that the marriage would occur only under the condition that Akish deliver to him Omer's head.

"The dance was performed and everything went as planned. Akish agreed to the foul pact. He returned to his home and made a secret covenant with his household to support him in this evil deed. It was the beginning of many such evil covenants among their people.

"Omer was warned in a dream to leave. He took his household with him far off to the western shores of the land. Jared still had what he wanted, for the kingdom was now his. It was a short-lived victory, however. While Jared sat giving audience on his throne, Akish had him killed and took over the kingdom himself."

"Akish killed his father-in-law?!" Ammon asked in disbelief. "What of his wife, Jared's daughter? Surely she would have known!"

"Yes, surely," Mosiah agreed. "The record says nothing of that, but perhaps this was her way of becoming queen. It goes on to say that Akish became so mistrusting that he had his eldest son imprisoned. He starved him to death. This was the beginning of serious mistrust among his own family. Another son fled in anger and joined Omer's people in the west. The other sons eventually created such a blood feud that only 30 people survived. Because of this, Omer and his people were able to return to the kingdom without opposition, and Omer was able to regain his kingdom.

"This went on for generation after generation. There would be several generations of peace and prosperity, but then some power-hungry man would rise up and try to take over the kingdom. Or, the rightful king would forget the ways of the Lord and fall into idolatry and wickedness. Prophets would come and warn the people to repent. Sometimes the people would repent. Other times the people would slay the prophets. It was a terrible account of both prosperity and destruction.

"In the end, a prophet named Ether approached the current king, named Coriantumr. He warned Coriantumr to repent or it would lead to the total destruction of his people. He went so far as to prophesy that Coriantumr would not perish by the sword, but would live to see his people wiped out entirely and he himself would be buried by another people who would come and inherit the land.

"Coriantumr dismissed Ether's prophecies and continued to lead the people in wickedness. Ether had to go into hiding, lest he lose his life. A man named Shared raised an army and fought against Coriantumr. Shared defeated and captured Coriantumr, but Coriantumr's sons later won his freedom at the cost of instigating a massive war among the people. A curse fell upon the land in that nothing could be kept safe. If a man laid down his sword at night, by morning it would be gone. So, the people slept with their swords in hand. They also tilled and sowed their fields with a sword in one hand and a hoe in the other.

"Coriantumr eventually killed Shared in battle, but then Shared's son, Gilead, took up the fight. Coriantumr tried to lay siege against Gilead in the southern wilderness, but Gilead sneaked away and took over Coriantumr's throne while Coriantumr and his army were still away.

"Gilead's reign was short-lived when his own high priest, Lib, killed him and claimed the throne for his own. Lib and Coriantumr fought long and hard, with Coriantumr eventually killing Lib in battle. Lib's brother Shiz then took up the sword and swore vengeance upon his brother's death. He also swore he would kill Coriantumr with his own sword because he wanted to thwart Ether's prophecy that he could not be killed by a sword.

"Under the hand of Shiz, the Jaredite nation knew nothing but war for several years. The people were decimated as a society. For four years both sides gathered forces for a great and final conflict, until all of the people – every man, woman, and child – were brought together on either one side or the other.

"When the fateful day of conflict dawned, the fighting was tremendous. Both sides took on massive casualties. The fighting was so bitter and intense that there was no time to bury the dead. By night, there was a great howling and lamenting for the dead. By day, there was more fighting and strife. Coriantumr finally remembered the prophecies of Ether and had a change of heart.

"He wrote to Shiz offering to deliver up the kingdom if he would be willing to spare the people. Shiz responded that he would only consent if Coriantumr offered himself up as a prisoner so that Shiz himself could kill him. Coriantumr refused to accept this. They mounted a final assault over a period of several days.

"At the end of each day, they noted that fewer and fewer men were still standing. By this time, all of the women and children had been slaughtered in battle. A people who once numbered in the millions shrank down to thousands, and then hundreds. Eventually, there were only a few dozen on both sides of the war. Shiz and his men chased Coriantumr and his men, intent on wiping them out. On the final day of battle, Shiz and Coriantumr were all who remained.

"They fought vigorously until their strength failed them. They both collapsed from exhaustion. Coriantumr rose first, leaned on his sword to rest and then smote off the head of Shiz. Shiz's decapitated body struggled to rise and gain breath, then toppled over sideways, finally dead. Coriantumr then fainted from the loss of blood.

"At this point, the Lord told the prophet Ether to come out from his hiding place and see the destruction of the people and engrave the account on the records which you found. His final words are those of lamentation for a once great people. He said that he did not know what would become of him, but he was also not concerned so long as he would be given rest in the kingdom of his Lord."

When King Mosiah finished his account, the room remained silent for quite some time, while these warriors, explorers, and leaders pondered the impact of the words. Limhi's head hung down as he compared the lust for power which had destroyed an entire nation to the actions of his own father. Ammon attempted to comment, but each time he went to speak, the words seemed inadequate.

It was the ever-enthusiastic Amaleki, now uncharacteristically somber, who spoke up with awe, "An entire nation done in by man's lust for power! So many lives needlessly lost! What a senseless tragedy!"

"Yes," Mosiah agreed. "I suppose there's something for us to learn from this."

"There certainly is! Watch out who you have for your king!" Amaleki said without thinking. He paused with an awkward look of embarrassment flashing across his face. "No offense, your majesty!"

"None taken, Amaleki. I understand your meaning entirely, and it's completely accurate." Mosiah stood and began to pace slowly, his hand tugging on his chin. "This gives me something to ponder," he said. "Something to ponder –" Mosiah's voice tapered into silence as his thoughts drifted off to considering what he should do with regards to making a future choice for his own successor. He knew that his choice would be largely influenced by the lessons learned from this tragic record, not to mention Limhi's tale of his people's plight.

Chapter 25

Sightings

"'Comb the woods! Comb the woods! Find Limhi and his men!' he says. Great. Wonderful. What a wonderful order," the Lamanite soldier muttered under his breath.

His head was bowed and he watched the ground in front of him as he walked, making sure that the soldier's foot ahead of him managed to pull free from the hold the gray mud had on it before he put his own foot down into the slurpy mire. Water poured down onto the trees, bathed the leaves, funneled down onto his head, and rolled down his face in a constant stream. His fellow soldiers were spared nothing from the deluge.

The soldier's sarcastic moan could not be heard over the thunderous reverberating sound of millions of plummeting drops of water. Knowing this likely added to the soldier's willingness to verbalize the bitter lament of the majority of his comrades. Otherwise, he would not dare utter ill words which might be overheard, lest they lead to a lethal reprimand.

"We've been wandering for weeks. And I *do* mean wandering!" the soldier continued, to no one in particular. "At what point do we get to go home?"

He was surprised when the man to his right responded with equal bitterness, "I don't think we could go home, even if they wanted to. From what I hear, they don't even know where Shemlon *is* anymore."

The first soldier looked over at him suddenly, flinging water from his nose and hair as he turned his head. He blinked repeatedly as he tried to look through the continuing splatters of water at his companion.

"What was that? What do you mean? What did you hear?" he had to shout to be heard over the watery din.

"I said, I heard they don't even know how to get back to Shemlon anymore!" he shouted back.

"What?! Those boneheads! How can they march us through the woods day in and day out and not bother to keep track of where we are?! They don't have a brain among them!" he bellowed, raising his voice with emotion.

As the final sentence was uttered, the downpour ended as abruptly as it had begun, creating a sudden stillness in the air. The Lamanite's rhetorical question was made unintentionally clear to many within his near vicinity. The angry man looked about him sullenly as this realization hit him. At first he cowered, hoping to let the statement pass. Then he stood tall in defense of his opinion.

"You might want to keep such thoughts silent –" a broad warrior turned and offered. He was cut off by a shout beyond him.

"What was that?!" a forward guard shouted, pointing. "It looked like something moving beyond those trees!"

"It was probably another panther."

"No. Not this time. It looked more like a person!"

"A person? What?! Where?!"

The man now had the attention of the entire company.

"There! Over there!" he pointed northwest. "See! I saw it again!"

"I saw it too! Come on!"

Without another word, the chase was on. For the first time in weeks, a legion of wander-weary Lamanite soldiers had a glimmer of purpose. They leapt into pursuit, anxious for the chase. Most of them had no idea what or who it was they were chasing. They suspected and hoped it was their Nephite prey. Nothing could relieve their tedium better than a good fight.

Within a dozen paces of the chase, the personage in the lead was positively identified as a male Nephite. Enthusiasm spread through the Lamanite horde like a bolt of lightning. They were as eager as they were alert. The Nephite had the advantage of familiarity with the terrain. He darted left and right, finding the better landfalls and avoiding the thicker brush.

The Lamanites continued their pursuit, attempting to close in on him. They attempted to split their forces and surround the man as they ran. Wet vines slapped at their faces. The rain-soaked foliage resisted their swords not completely, but much more so than during the drier days. The resistance was enough to keep the warriors from tearing through the brush fast enough to overtake their pale prey.

The tactic of a divided party was soon abandoned and the Lamanites regrouped in flight and followed the Nephite. He led them through passages of bushes and trees that were so narrow that the army had to follow virtually single file. This allowed the Nephite to flee at his own pace and not worry about being overtaken by an errant, swifter, Lamanite soldier who otherwise could have broken away from the group.

The Nephite ducked under an unusually thick vine, the thickness of a man's calf. The lead Lamanite saw him veer right and then dart suddenly left and disappear entirely, into the brush. It took them only seconds to duck the same vine and charge right, then turn left. Upon the turn, however, they saw nothing but a massive, thick, thorny bush.

The lead man stopped in his tracks. Those behind him slid to a halt, their sandaled feet digging into the fresh mud. The men farthest back knew only that the chase had halted and worked hard to keep from bumping into each other. The group stood there with their bronze chests heaving in and out, sweat mingled with rain moistened their faces and hair. Their clothes were thoroughly damp both from the recent rain, and from being swatted by branches and vines during the chase.

"Where is he? Where did he go?!" Hamoth, the chief Lamanite officer on this journey, demanded.

"I - I don't know! He was right here, I swear it!" the lead man replied. "I have no idea where he went -"

"He can't have just disappeared. Look for his tracks!" another offered.

"That would have been wise, had we not all trampled them to death," the lead man stated, pointing at the ground.

The men all looked down at their feet and saw his point. The muddy ground was covered with dozens of tracks already. It would be impossible to discern the Nephite's from their own.

"Now that we know he's out here, we're bound to find his lair."

"I'm willing to wager there's a lot more of them as well."

"We're finally getting closer. You men, spread out. We should search the area!" Hamoth ordered.

The men dutifully obeyed, fanning wide and pressing their way methodically through the brush in the general direction they had last seen the man run. They moved much more slowly, but advanced with determination. They knew it would not be long before they had the scent of his trail again. Soon, the Nephites would be found and made to pay for the weeks of inconvenience they had inflicted on them.

*****

The Nephite ran on and on, trying desperately to keep a cool head about him. He had thought that Amulon was right in moving them so far north. Surely, they had thought, they would avoid the Lamanites if they simply kept north. So much time had passed that they had begun to believe their plan was sound, and take their safety for granted. Now, that security seemed in desperate jeopardy, particularly for him.

When he ducked under the large vine, he purposely feigned right to lead them off his trail. Then he shifted left, ducked low and slid feet first under the large, thorny bush. He was fortunate to be so slender, and that the ground was so slick from the recent rain storm. Once beyond the bush, he continued pell-mell down the tree-studded hillside.

He sensed he had eluded them, but had no way of knowing for how long. He decided flight was more important than strategic analysis at the moment and raced as quickly back to camp as he could. It was only another couple hundred yards through the trees, around the hills, over the river and into a small clearing they had formed.

"Amulon! Amulon! Lamanites!" he shouted as he entered camp. "Lamanites! They're after me! Amulon!"

The moment he entered the campsite, he had the complete attention of four dozen fugitives. Amulon himself quickly exited his tent to learn the meaning of the alarm.

"What's this?" he demanded.

"Lamanites!" the banished royal priest announced, fighting to gain his breath. "I was looking for game when I was spotted by a large group of Lamanite soldiers! They gave chase, so I fled as quickly as I could!"

"And you led them right here!" Amulon said in bitter disgust. "You fool! They'll find your tracks and then find us! Your carelessness has endangered us all!"

Amulon's face was taking on a crimson color. The former priest of Noah was beginning to cower, fearing retribution.

"Amulon, if this is true," another in the party stated, "Then it's more important for us to ready ourselves than to lay blame. We need a plan of action. Quickly!"

Amulon turned his head away from the panting harbinger of bad news, but allowed his piercing eyes to linger on the man as he turned.

"You're right, of course," Amulon said. "Gather the women!"

"The women?! Why?"

"To beg for mercy, why else?!" Amulon replied with impatience. "We can't possibly defend ourselves, and they certainly aren't going to take pity on our homely faces. Our only hope is to have our wives plead for our heads. Now, get the women and send them in the direction from which our fearless friend here has just come."

No sooner had the women pulled together in a terrified group and edged their way into the trees, than the Lamanite soldiers stormed over a hill and encountered them. The Lamanites' forward charge was disrupted by confusion at seeing the women, not just women, but Lamanite women dropped to their knees, crying, sobbing, and pleading for mercy.

"What's this? Who are you?" Hamoth, the main Lamanite officer, demanded.

"Please, please, sir, spare us! Spare our husbands! We'll be your servants, if you will but spare us!" the nearest, trembling Lamanite woman begged, not daring to look her hostile assailant in the eye. She was crouched down with her face buried in the ground.

Hamoth was both troubled and puzzled by an odd sense of familiarity that swept over him. For a moment, he said nothing. He stood watching the woman repeat her pleas. The other soldiers awaited orders before continuing. The woman, sensing she was getting through, crawled forward enough to drop upon Hamoth's filthy feet and bathe them with her tears.

He was moved not just from her pleas and those of her sisters, but from a sense of familiarity. Her voice, though strained with emotion, brought back a feeling and a memory which shook his heart. He bent forward and touched her hair. She felt his touch and knew not what to expect of it.

He gently and quizzically called her by name, "Fatina?"

A chill ran through the woman's spine. Her sobbing stopped in that instant. Her body stopped its vibrations. She remained still for the briefest of moments. Her tears ceased. Slowly, she looked up toward her would-be captor. Her long, black hair had fallen forward and stuck to the mud of his feet. It pulled away as she looked upward. She slowly pulled her mud-streaked hair from her face with fingertips from both hands as she looked for the man's eyes high above her.

"Father?" she asked.

"Fatina?" he repeated. "Is that you?"

"Father!" she shouted with unanticipated rapture.

She jumped up as he began to bend down toward her. She wrapped her arms around his neck, nearly knocking him off balance. She kissed him repeatedly on the neck and cheeks as she repeated over and over, "Father! It's you! It's you! It's you!"

Hamoth was overwhelmed with emotion at finally finding his long-lost daughter. So many years had passed.

"Fatina!" he said nearly bursting into tears. "Your mother and I had given up hope! You're alive! You're alive! Wait until your mother finds out! She has missed you terribly!"

The two embraced as father and daughter, too long separated. None of the soldiers faulted their senior officer for an uncharacteristic show of emotion. He had grown rigid over the years. Now they understood why. His shell fled from his emotions, as for an instant he was much younger and the woman was again the girl he had helped raise so many years ago; and who had been taken away from him so abruptly.

"I thought I would never see you again," he whispered into her ear. "I never realized how much I loved you until you were taken from us. I never really let you know."

"Oh, father, I always knew," she whispered back. "I always knew. You will always be my father."

She stopped suddenly and pulled away from her father. She took a step back, straightened again, but kept her head bowed slightly. With a hand she brushed her hair away from her face.

"But, I'm not a little girl anymore," she said. "I'm a woman now. A wife. I have a husband whom I love. And, I beg you to spare us. Please, let us live."

Hamoth looked incredulously back at his daughter. His mind was transported back to the present. He saw how she had matured. She was indeed a woman now. She had dignity and grace. Then, he remembered his errand.

"Let you live?" he asked. "What are you people doing here?"

"We are but a few who have learned to live off of the land," she said, gesturing with a sweeping motion of her arm toward the other Lamanite women and their Nephite husbands who stood back on the fringes of the trees.

He looked around at the odd group before him. Flashes of the anger and anguish from years he had long tried to forget flooded his memory. Within, he again saw the heartache of his weeping and lamenting wife, as well as his own sense of loss. He perceived that there in the distance were the men responsible for their pain. They were outcast from two societies and now fearing for their lives.

His eyes returned to those of his daughter, long lost, but now found. Her face was more beautiful than he had managed to remember it. Her gaze was fixed and intent. It was clear she meant the words she spoke. Somehow, this vagabond band of misfits and captives had learned, over the years, to not just get along, but to love each other. He saw it in her eyes.

Somehow, she was happy. Though he had never dreamed of such an arrangement as this as he had cradled her in his arms so many years ago, he had wished her happiness. She seemed content with this odd life. "*What more could a father want?*" he wondered. "*How could I take it away?*" he asked within.

"Fatina, I sense you're doing well," he said at last. "How could I wish it to be different? You and your people will live. You will be our prisoners, but you will live. This I swear."

"And, we thank you sincerely," Amulon responded as he stepped forward from behind a tree and approached the Lamanite force. He walked up to Fatina and wrapped his arm around her waist, signaling his relationship with the Lamanite officer's daughter. "We will gladly follow you back to your land and live among you as your servants," he continued and bowed his head, hoping to have secured his position among the conquerors.

"That will be satisfactory," Hamoth responded, then inwardly added, "If we could only find our way back."

Chapter 26

Reunions

As Hamoth's men moved in to round up the encampment, Fatina approached her father. "Father, there is someone else that I think you should meet."

"Oh? Who is that?"

"Wait here. I will be right back."

Hamoth was puzzled, but did as she requested. Just as he began to mull the situation over, one of his men approached.

"Hamoth," he said. "We have now captured some Nephites, but these are clearly not the ones we've been searching for. Do you think they know where the others are?"

"No. I suspect they don't. Something tells me this group hasn't been with the main group for quite some time."

"What do we do with these, then? Do we drag them with us as we continue our search?"

"I don't know that we have much choice –"

Hamoth was interrupted by a rustling about his feet and a mother's voice. "Father, this is Rebekah." A little girl of about four years old rushed up to the warrior and wrapped her arms around his knees, offering a pint-sized bear hug. "And this is Hamoth," Fatina concluded as she nudged her six-year-old son forward. "Say hello to your grandfather, Hamoth," she said to the boy.

Her son stepped forward and reached out his hand. The senior Hamoth grasped the inside of the boy's right forearm as a token greeting. Words failed the officer and tears filled his eyes. He bent down and pulled both children to him, hugging and kissing each in turn.

"Rebekah? Hamoth? You remembered!" he managed to utter with his voice cracking.

"Yes, Father, I did. I have always remembered you and mother," Fatina said, wiping away her tears.

Still kneeling, with a child snuggled up to each shoulder and one arm wrapped around his grandson, Hamoth reached out with his other arm and beckoned Fatina to him. She rushed to him and the three generations shared a blissful reunion.

*****

"Are we ready to move on now?" Hamoth asked his junior officer.

"I believe so. These Nephite friends of yours took longer than they ought to pack," he replied.

"They are not my 'friends' as you so glibly put it," Hamoth corrected.

"Sorry. I didn't mean anything by it."

"See that you don't. Now, we should get moving."

The band of soldiers was split into two groups, flanking the outcasts from both ends. The front soldiers hacked away at the vines and brush, literally cutting their path through the jungle. The former priests of Noah attempted to keep their families together and keep their children from wandering off. The day was hot and humid. It was not long before the children were tired. Their parents did their best to keep them in line, carrying those they could, in addition to minding their belongings that were being toted by various pack animals the priests had kept.

This procession became more and more routine as the days wore on. The group made slow progress. They found game along the way, so at least their bellies stayed full. The question on everyone's lips was where they were going and when they would arrive there. It soon became evident that no distinct destination was in mind, worse still were the fears that they really were not just wandering aimlessly, but hopelessly lost. This was an awfully large wilderness to wander without an escape route.

* * * * *

"Hamoth, we must stop," his soldier recommended. "The children are nearly dead on their feet. I'm having trouble with the humidity myself. I can't remember a hotter day!"

"All right, I agree. We should rest here a while. Have some of the men check that river there for devil fish before any of the little ones wander into it."

"Certainly, sir."

The soldier turned and called to two of his comrades. The one gave word to stop and rest. Everyone obliged quite willingly and unshouldered their belongings with loud sighs of relief. The other went with the first soldier to the river's edge. They took a piece of meat out of one of the sacks of provisions. They tied it to a pole and dangled the flesh in the water. Nothing happened.

They shook the pole and wiggled the meat in the cool, attractive, slowly-flowing liquid. They caused it to splash and noise about, but nothing more happened. Several of the children scrambled up and watched with interest.

"Well, what are you waiting for? It's your turn!" the one soldier slapped the other on the shoulder.

"I know. I know. Just checking to be certain!"

The soldier holding the pole eased toward the water's edge. He held the pole in front of him, dangling the meat deeply beneath the water's surface. The gentle flow of the river pulled the meat along its path, but nothing more impacted it. The soldier gingerly placed a foot in the water.

Its cool, pacifying impact sent a shiver through his hot, sweaty body. If it were not for the hesitancy of the potential danger, this would have been quite a treat and a welcome break from their blistering journey. Still carefully dangling the meat ahead of him, he stepped into the river with both feet. He stood a moment, trying to be certain.

He placed the far end of his pole all the way under water and slowly waved it in large, submerged figure eights. Still nothing took the bait. He took a few steps forward very slowly, being certain that the meat waved around beneath the water's surface much more actively and obviously than his own feet did. If there was anything there whose attention would be caught by fresh flesh, he wanted its attention drawn as far away from him as possible.

Finally, he stood in the river over his knees. Still nothing had taken the bait or him. He sensed he was in the clear. A large sigh of relief escaped his lips and allowed him to finally enjoy the soothing effects of the water. He motioned to the camp and shouted.

"All clear! All clear!"

He had barely finished the second call when a dozen children flung themselves into the water, drenching any portion of him that was above the surface. He smiled and shook his head. Other adults made their way to the water without showing so much enthusiasm, but still eager, nevertheless.

He made his way to the bank. As he stepped out, an eager child, running at break-neck speed, shouted, "Catch me!" and leapt right at him. He had not expected this particular onslaught of youthful exuberance and though he caught the boy, he lost his balance and tumbled backward. Both he and the boy wound up immersed in the cool water. As he came up for breath and saw that the boy was all right, he decided he did not mind the unexpected baptism.

Not everyone had the opportunity to refresh themselves along the river bank, however. Hamoth's three forward scouts had other duties. They were to spy out the land and return with recommendations on where to go next. All three were now returning. They were together, which was unusual. Typically, only one would return to give a report of findings. They were also running at full speed, which was even more peculiar.

Hamoth was not the only one who paid attention to their return. Amulon also paid a keen eye and an eager ear for any news, though he hung back and attempted to remain as low key and aloof as possible. He had determined to bide his time before making his move.

"Hamoth! Hamoth!" the lead scout shouted. "Nephites! We have found Nephites!"

"Nephites?!" Hamoth exclaimed, "Where?!"

* * * * *

"In the south-eastern field!" the farmer shouted with excited fear, "There were at least three! Alma, we've been found!"

"Just three?" Alma questioned.

"Yes, sir. Just three."

"They may have been some advance scouts," Helam pointed out. "Who knows how many are in their midst?"

"Our lives are over! We can't possibly defend ourselves! What can we do?!" the excited farmer lamented to his leader.

Alma sat calmly on his judgment seat. He sensed the anxiety of his people and knew that it would not take much to turn their alarm into unfocused and utter panic. He knew that the best course he could take would be to show as little negative emotion as possible, so as to speak peace and confidence to his worried kinsmen. Besides, a sense deep within him spoke peace to his soul letting him know that things would work out for the best.

"Peace! Be at peace!" he said. "The Lord will be with us. The Lord will see us through this!"

"But, the Lamanites have found us! They're bound to attack!"

"I will go and deal with these Lamanites," Alma said. "There won't be an attack. I promise."

"How can you make such a promise? They're Lamanites! It's what they do!"

"Trust me! The Lord will be with us. Now, leave your farm for today and go back to your home. Tell your neighbors to stay in the city until I have settled this matter with our visitors from the south. Meanwhile, return to your homes and pray that the Lord will soften the hearts of these Lamanites that we may be able to continue to live in peace."

* * * * *

"Is it Limhi and his people?" Hamoth asked.

"Have we finally found them?" another officer asked with an intrigued look.

"It's difficult to say," the first scout answered. "We only saw several farmers."

"And their city," the second added.

"Their *city*?" Hamoth said with surprise.

"Yes, they have built themselves a city," the second continued.

"It's not very much, really," the third scout added. "Not from what we could see."

"A city? That could not possibly be Limhi then," Hamoth concluded. "They couldn't have built a city in such a short time."

"It did look fairly new," the first scout offered.

"New? Possibly," Hamoth responded. "But, still there is no way they could have built a city in such a short time. We haven't been trailing them *that* long."

"No, it only *seems* like that long," the second scout muttered under his breath.

"What's that?" Hamoth asked looking over at the scout, with an irritated lilt.

"Nothing, sir!" the scout said, straightening quickly as he said so and inwardly rebuking himself for having verbalized his grievance.

"Sir, if it isn't Limhi, then who is it?" a Lamanite soldier asked.

"Who? Who knows? It could be anybody. Maybe it's yet another group coming down here to try to take more of our land! At any rate, they won't get away with it so easily."

"What will we do? We cannot very well attack an entire city with our force."

"What we need to do is not let them know the size of our force. We will work our way in, and then work out the details of their capture later. Meanwhile, gather the men. Take a small group to stay with our captives. Keep these Nephites and the children and our daughters here in the jungle, while the rest of our men approach this Nephite city. We'll deal with these Nephites as warriors. The prisoners would just get in our way."

*****

Hamoth and his force emerged from the rainforest and entered the field at a steady gait. They progressed rapidly, intent on showing determination and courage. Their swords were drawn and held by powerful hands, accustomed to battle. Their faces were stern and focused on the grouping of stone and wooden buildings on the far side of the plowed, lush fields.

A solitary figure moved in the distance, working his way in a direct course to intercept them. He continued with equal determination. Alma bore no arms. Several paces behind him, three more figures emerged from the city's unwalled entryway. Helam and two others had decided to not let their leader, mentor and friend greet these hostile visitors on his own.

They met halfway across the field. Alma left his arms extended with his palms facing downward for the final few paces, as proof that he was weaponless. Hamoth glared at him with suspicion. He was particularly interested in Helam and the others, who quickly caught up and joined their leader. When Alma noticed them, he turned and indicated by a quick nod of his head and shaking of his hands that they should extend their arms as he had been so careful to do. They understood and followed suit. Alma turned back to face Hamoth as Helam and the others flanked him.

Hamoth raised his arm for his force to stop. They obeyed. For a moment, both parties stood staring at the other as if waiting for some significant act to be played out. Leaders on both sides were leery as to what the other had in mind. Alma decided to act first. He raised his hands upward, facing both palms toward his dark-skinned brothers.

"Welcome to our homes!" he announced. "We are pleased to have such fine men as yourselves join us in this land. We want nothing but peace and contentment for you and ourselves. Our city is open to you. We deliver it up to you to be our honored guests. My people are a peaceful people and we will gladly serve you while you are here!"

"Serve us?!" Hamoth asked, a bit taken off his guard. "Well, of course you will serve us! And, of course we will take this city! My men do not want trouble from you Nephites, either!"

"Nor do we intend to give you any. Please, come. Join us. We will have a feast in your honor. You have surely traveled far to come here."

"A feast?" Hamoth was intrigued.

His men could barely restrain themselves. This was certainly not the sort of welcome they had anticipated. It had been a long time since any of them had feasted, let alone sat in actual chairs. The day was certainly picking up for them.

Far back on the fringes of the jungle, a pair of Nephite eyes had managed to work their way forward enough to see the goings on. Amulon had a sense that something odd was transpiring. He watched the Nephites talk with Hamoth with keen interest.

"There's something strangely familiar about that man," he said in reference to Alma. "Something very familiar. If only I could get a closer look...."

Chapter 27

Promises

The feast was a welcome change for the foot-weary conquerors. They had wandered far too long and far too distantly for their own liking. Alma was pleased to see the degree of enthusiasm with which his captors relished the many courses of food that were laid before them. His hope was that it would soften their hearts and lend mercy to their reign.

"Alma," Hamoth spoke with a mouthful of venison, "you are a good man. And a wise one."

"Thank you."

"You were wise to not resist us! We have been on the prowl for so long, my men would have enjoyed a good fight!"

Hamoth grinned and his men laughed. Alma forced a smile and shifted uneasily in his seat. He knew his was a very precarious position. He hoped he would play his role right to secure peace for his people. He looked around at each of his new guests, trying to discern their moods and intentions.

"Seriously, Alma, I have a proposition for you," Hamoth said with a mouthful of food, and lowering his voice, hoping his men would focus on their food and own chatter.

"What is it?" Alma sensed that the key to his people's future was just about to be disclosed. He was intent on finding out what that would be.

"I want to discuss it in private. Tomorrow," Hamoth replied.

*****

Two Lamanite guards made their way across the field as quickly as they could. The full moon reflected silver light off the tall grass. They did not know if they had been seen. They only partially cared. The bundles they bore weighed them down enough that they were looking forward to unburdening themselves. As they entered the dark jungle, several men approached them eagerly, and quickly took charge of the provisions.

"What's all this?" one man asked anxiously.

"Venison! Fresh venison, killed today! Also fruits and vegetables! It's enough of a feast for all of you, I would say!"

"Great! Quick, we should get it back to the camp! I can hardly wait!" a second guard said as he sneaked a hand inside the bundle and pulled out a morsel before shouldering the overfilled pack.

It was not long before the remaining guards and the concealed Nephite priests of Noah were feasting with their wives and children. Hamoth had ordered them to all stay behind. He decided that it would be best to keep their presence secret, although he was not entirely certain why.

While the group ate, the soldiers were filled with a sense of merriment which loosened their lips a bit more than would have otherwise been prudent. Amulon decided to subtly take advantage of their good nature and learn all he could of his comrades in this unexpected city. He moved in next to a guard as closely as his caution would allow and sat down feigning interest in the food as he spoke.

"So, there are Nephites here, eh?" he asked.

"Yes, there are," a guard said in between large bites.

"How many would you say?"

"Several hundred, I suppose," the guard did not even bother to look up. His attention was more focused on looking for the little leather flask which contained the salt.

"Do they have a leader?"

"Yeah, some guy."

"What was his name?" Amulon queried.

"I didn't catch it. No, wait, yes I did. I think it was Alma."

"Alma?!" Amulon nearly stood with surprise. He caught himself and carefully concealed his emotions. He backed away and mumbled to himself. "Alma. Well, it seems we have finally found out where you went in such a hurry...."

Amulon was not yet certain what he would do about this chance meeting. He was certain that he would end up doing something significant, however. A good part of him became anxious to find out just what that would be. He knew it was bound to be interesting.

*****

The council room had been cleared on Hamoth's orders. Only he and Alma remained. Alma was not quite certain what the meaning of their private meeting was, but he was certain it held some sort of significance for both him and his people. He had noted that Hamoth was quite insistent on clearing out the room and anticipated an interesting discussion of some sort.

Hamoth circled about, pacing the floor restlessly. Alma sat eying him patiently, waiting for whatever words Hamoth was forming in his mind. Finally, Hamoth stopped still and turned, facing Alma, but looking more beyond him than straight in the eye as he spoke in a powerful, demanding tone.

"You people left the land of Nephi, correct?"

"Yes, several years ago."

"Do you know your way back?"

"Why would we want to go back? We're happy here."

"I didn't ask if you are happy! I asked if you know your way back!"

"Well, I suppose, yes, I believe we could find our way back."

"Are you certain?"

"Yes, I'm certain. Why?"

Hamoth stepped closer to Alma and lowered his voice somewhat.

"I'm not so certain we can."

"What? What do you mean?"

"I'm not so certain we can find our way back -" he stopped speaking, but continued to motion with his hands giving Alma the impression that he intended to convey a further meaning that he did not want to verbalize. He made a waving, circular motion with his right hand and nodded emphatically as he looked Alma directly in the face and then added, "You know - back." He waved his hand again.

Alma paused a moment, letting the air go silent. He watched Hamoth's expression of concealed desperation. One common trait that all men from all civilizations and societies have shared and passed through generation after generation is an inability to admit the need to ask directions. The situation was doubly worse for a wandering warrior to have to admit the need to his newest subject.

Alma suppressed a smile as he responded in an effort to curry favor and allow Hamoth to save face, "Would you be open to allowing my men to accompany your forces on their way back to the land of Nephi?"

Hamoth's face lit up, but he repressed any other signs of relief, "Why, yes, I believe that would be acceptable," he said at last.

"I would be more than happy to do so, with one provision."

"A provision?" Hamoth asked with a start.

"Yes, on the provision that afterward your men don't accompany mine when they return home."

"Not accompany -" Hamoth paused as he allowed Alma's meaning sink in. "I see," he added at last.

"Yes, I'm certain you do. We appreciate your visit and will be more than happy to return you to your land, if you will allow us to retain our own land," Alma said with an air of distinct clarity.

Hamoth thought it over. In the end, he realized that he would likely not succeed in forcing Alma to show them their way back. The only way he could possibly succeed in currying Alma's favor would be to do so willingly. Meanwhile, they could continue to occupy the city of Helam, but what good would that do them? Eventually, they would want to return home. Helam would soon prove to be a very shallow victory.

"It is agreed. You show us the way back, and I will let your men return unguarded. You may have this city to yourselves." In an attempt to belittle the deal he added, "It's only a small city after all, and not worth our bother."

* * * * *

Two dissimilar groups of people stood amidst the heavy dew that covered the grassy field. Alma, Helam and four other Nephite men listened to Hamoth and his men as they prepared to leave.

"Yes, yes, your men will return," Hamoth said, "And, I must thank you for lending them to me."

"Consider it a first of many gestures of friendship between our people," Alma said.

"Yes, well, that would be something, now wouldn't it?" Hamoth replied.

He looked at Alma and noted his sincerity. Then, to the surprise of all, he approached Alma and held out his hand to him. Alma reached out his own hand. Both men momentarily clasped the other's inner right forearm in a sign of peace. It was a rare sign of cooperation between the two troubled nations.

Hamoth let go and turned to head out. Alma waved farewell to his men and began his return to his city and his people.

The group had only barely entered the jungle, with Helam in the lead, when Hamoth raised his hand, "Halt!" he commanded. The group stopped. Helam and his men looked at each other quizzically, but no one verbalized their confusion.

"Wait here a moment!" Hamoth ordered.

"But, sir," Helam began, "Have we forgotten something?"

"'Forgotten?' No, but there's something more that we need," Hamoth said with intentional vagueness, as he stifled a smirk.

"But, what? –"

Helam did not have to wait long for his answer. Even as the words were leaving his lips he heard a group of people approaching from the north. Their arrival produced more questions than answers. The five Nephites watched as some of Hamoth's men led a group of some fifty Nephite men and Lamanite women, plus a plethora of children who apparently bore both Nephite and Lamanite blood in their veins.

"Who is that?" one of Helam's men whispered to him.

"Shh!" Helam cautioned. "I suddenly feel very uncomfortable. There's something familiar about these men. And, it's not a good feeling." He eyed them carefully, not able to put a finger on the cause of his ill feelings. He suddenly wished he could not be seen.

"All right, now we move out!" Hamoth ordered with a smile. "Helam, lead us back home!"

"Yes, sir," he said with less enthusiasm than before.

The group moved forward with Helam and his men again at the lead. They cut their way through the jungle in a southeastwardly direction. All of them exchanged looks at each other, trying to see if any of them had a clue as to the identity of their unanticipated guests. No one spoke, however. They sensed it would be best to remain silent. The sun was oppressively hot and the air was stiflingly humid that day.

*****

On the afternoon of the third day of the journey, Helam and his men again sat by their own campfire preparing their midday meal. The tallest of the unknown Nephites wandered about the camp at ease. They had noticed him speak frequently with Hamoth. They had also noted that Hamoth seemed to have a particular liking for this Nephite's children. Whoever he was, he seemed to be the leader of this mixed group who had joined them.

The Nephite wandered over to Helam's area. Helam's men were both intrigued by an opportunity to speak with him, but also apprehensive of the man. They found themselves torn between wanting to solve the mystery and wanting the man to leave them in peace. They sensed that the two desires were mutually exclusive. They also sensed that, ultimately, they wanted no dealings with this enigmatic man.

Wanted or unwanted, he wandered toward them nevertheless. He ambled up to them, inwardly reveling at the quandary that he knew he must be causing the men's minds to ponder. He did not even attempt to conceal a knowing grin.

"Hello, men," he said with a forced casual tone. "And, how are you doing today?"

"Uh, fine," Helam said apprehensively.

"Good. Good. I wouldn't want our guides to be any other way."

"Thank you." Helam and his men traded uneasy glances with each other.

"The children were commenting on how skillfully you make your way along. They asked how much farther it will be," Amulon pursued.

"We should be to Nephi within eight more days," Helam responded.

"Eight days? Splendid. Splendid. Keep up the good work then," he said as he sauntered off.

"What was that all about?" one of Helam's men asked after Amulon was out of earshot.

"Obviously, he just wanted to find out how much farther it will be," another answered.

"That, and I think he was feeling us out," Helam added. "I get the feeling I've seen him somewhere before. But where? –"

"Maybe he feels the same about us and was trying to get a better look."

"Could be. All the same, I don't know if I trust that man," Helam concluded aloud.

* * * * *

"Hamoth, you realize you can't return to your king empty handed," Amulon pointed out as he worked his way toward him.

Hamoth kept a strong gait, ignoring his son-in-law at the present. The company progressed onward at a steady pace. After a few moments, Hamoth finally broke the silence and acknowledged Amulon's point.

"What do you mean?" he asked, still looking forward.

"I'm sure you've thought this through," Amulon replied. "You've been in the wilderness for months now. Your king sent you to round up the Nephites. You can't possibly return to Shemlon without any."

Hamoth remained silent, looking forward, trudging onward. From his blank expression, it was not evident if he had even heard Amulon's comments, let alone perceived any validity in them. No one knew how his mind was furiously weighing the words.

"What's worse," Amulon continued, "Is that you found an entire city of Nephites and just left them there. You left them unguarded, unreprimanded, unescorted. What will your King Laman say about that?"

Hamoth still held his peace.

"Do you think he'll be pleased with you? You let the one group slip by. Perhaps you can get away with that one. But, how do you explain away the fact that you knowingly and purposely let the others get off? Here fate had given you the opportunity to make amends for missing the others and instead you squandered the opportunity. Your king will not be pleased."

Hamoth's lip began to move. He was on the verge of responding. But, instead, he closed his lips tightly and clenched his jaw. His fists opened and closed several times as he marched onward. He never responded.

*****

"Sir, we are almost there," Helam said as he approached the Lamanite leader. "It should be less than an hour's trek from here."

"Excellent," was all Hamoth replied.

True to Helam's word, the party emerged from the woods and entered a familiar field. On the far side of the field sat the city of Nephi. Its sturdy city gate was left ajar. There were no signs of its former inhabitants. As they made their way to the gate, they met some Lamanite guards milling about in the square. One noted the company's approach and came toward the group.

"Sir, what brings you here?" he asked.

"I was about to ask you the same," Hamoth replied. "What's all this?"

"We have taken charge of the city and are preparing it for the king's return, now that those Nephites are gone."

"I see. Is the king here?"

"No, he is still in Shemlon."

"Good."

*****

"Well, sir, we have done our part," Helam acknowledged to Hamoth. "We would like to be on our way again."

"Yes, you have done your part and done it well," Hamoth replied.

Amulon stood in the background, eying Hamoth carefully. Hamoth saw him standing beyond Helam. Amulon purposely kept within Hamoth's line of vision. Hamoth did not acknowledge him, but he saw him nonetheless. It was clear that this was the time for his fateful decision.

"With your leave, we would like to return to our families," Helam reiterated.

Hamoth's face was stern and forceful. Inside, he could not help cringe somewhat at what he sensed he had to do. Amulon nodded at him, sending silent encouragement. After a pause, Hamoth responded, slowly at first and with hesitation, "Yes, you may return –" Amulon's eyes narrowed suspiciously, as he hung on every nuance of Hamoth's actions. Then Hamoth's words picked up speed and forcefulness, "You may return to your city and my men will see to it that you return directly. They will also ensure that you and your people stay where we can keep our eyes on you!"

Amulon let a wicked grin crease his face. He nodded approvingly to Hamoth. Hamoth's eyes drifted over and noted this. He turned his gaze quickly away from him and back to Helam. He took no pleasure or pride in his decision, but now that he had voiced it, he would support it to the fullest.

"What?! What do you mean?! I thought we were to be left at peace," Helam responded with shocked frustration.

"Oh, you will be at peace, just so long as you abide by our will! Do as we say, and you and your people will have a peaceful life. Fight against us, and you will live to regret it, or perhaps not live at all."

"I see," Helam said with disgust. "And I thought we had finally met some Lamanites we could trust. I see now that there is no value in the word of a Lamanite."

Hamoth fought back the urge to utter his next words, but quickly lost the battle and let them slip out, "I never swore an oath."

"Oh, that's just fine. That makes this all right then, does it?" Helam observed with bitterness. Then he added with emphasis, "We put our trust in you."

Helam turned as Hamoth motioned for several of his men to escort them back to Alma and their homes. Hamoth ordered the rest of their group to leave the area and prepare for the final leg of their journey back to the land of Shemlon and their own homes.

Amulon moved closer to Hamoth as the procession made its way out of the city square and through the opened gate. "You have done well," he coaxed, "Your king will be well pleased."

Again Hamoth did not acknowledge Amulon directly. Instead, he bellowed an order to his men, "Move out quickly! I want to eat my next meal in my home!"

Chapter 28

Amulon

The Lamanite throne room was crowded. Everyone was eager to hear the report of the last army who had searched for the renegade Nephites. Hamoth was apprehensive, but stood stoically. He was determined to answer any questions put to him directly and accurately.

"– And where did you go after you learned the trails crossed over each other?" King Laman asked.

"We searched the first trail, watching for any signs that would show where they had cut off into the wilderness. One of my men thought that he had found another trail. We followed it at length, only to find it had been formed by a group of stray sheep –"

The room erupted in laughter. The thought of Lamanite warriors chasing sheep was just too much for many of them to picture without hilarity. Hamoth continued to stand tall, clenching his teeth, but determined to endure the moment.

"And what did you do with these sheep? Did you take them prisoner?" the king said with an irreverent smirk.

"We caught them, yes, and then ate them."

"Well, at least you didn't go hungry on your quest."

"No, sir. At least, not for the first couple of weeks."

"Where did you wander off to with your bellies full of mutton, then?"

"I'm afraid that 'wander' is a good word for it, my King. We lost the Nephites' trail and searched for it again at length. We were unable to gain sight of it or anyone else, until many weeks later when we caught sight of a Nephite. We chased the man and eventually found a group of Nephite men and their Lamanite wives and children."

"Nephite men with Lamanite wives?!" the king stood with indignation.

"Yes, great king. This was a group of Nephite men who had broken away from the other Nephites many years ago. They met and married the daughters of many of your noble Lamanite families. These men have sworn off the foolish traditions of the Nephite people and are determined to become Lamanites themselves."

"Is that so?" the king mused as he sat back down, "Interesting."

"Yes, my king. I have brought some of them with me here. They wait without the door."

"I will want to speak with them. Bring their leader in."

Hamoth nodded, turned, and then motioned to the guards by the door. Those within the room turned their attention to the door. For a moment, no one emerged, and the air hung heavy with anticipation. At last, a guard reentered the room. Behind him, Amulon strode forward as if he were a welcomed dignitary, basking in the attention. He was followed by another guard.

Amulon walked forward, ignoring the guards and spears which flanked him. He caught sight of the milling, whispering crowd, but only with his peripheral vision. From the moment he entered the room, his eyes sought out, discovered, and then held the gaze of the Lamanite king. He ensured that his face shown with the confidence he felt within.

He was brought to stand next to Hamoth. The king's guard was preempted in giving the order to kneel when Amulon suddenly collapsed to his knees, bent forward, and wholly prostrated himself on the ground with both arms laid before him in an act of total submission and deference to King Laman.

"My king! It is a lifetime of honor to be before you this day!" he said as he bowed.

King Laman was thoroughly impressed. "My, my, now this is a Nephite who understands his place in life! What is your name?"

Keeping his face toward the floor, Amulon replied, "Amulon, great king."

"Arise, Amulon, that we may speak."

Amulon raised himself to look toward the king, but remained on his knees.

"You are a Nephite – that is clear. This man says you wish to become a Lamanite. Is that true?"

Amulon looked toward Hamoth to acknowledge him for only a moment and then turned back to the king and said with forced sincerity, "Oh great king, I have lived among the Nephites for far too many years. Their hypocrisy and self-platitudes have been as bitter juices within my soul. I can not dwell among them longer. My men and I swore we would leave them and if at all possible join you and your noble people. We have taken some of your fair daughters to wife and are now raising our children in the traditions of the great Lamanite people. It is our grand desire to no longer be known as Nephites, but as Lamanites and to become your subjects."

"Very well," King Laman said, thoroughly impressed. "Very well indeed. We shall see. Such a desire should not go unfulfilled."

Laman turned his attention away from Amulon for the moment and returned to Hamoth's tale.

"So, after finding these interesting people, you returned to our fair city?"

"No, great king, not directly."

"No?"

"No, my king. We intended to, but only after exhausting ourselves of searching for Limhi and his people. In our final search we came upon a Nephite city."

"A city? Which one?"

"A new one, oh king."

"A *new* city?!"

"Yes. A new city populated by Nephites. At first we thought it was Limhi and his people. We soon learned that it was not. It was yet another group of Nephites infesting your land, my king." Hamoth bowed his head slightly after delivering this dreadful news, in hopes of emphasizing his part in helping to scour the King's land for signs of unwanted vermin such as those in the land of Helam.

"And you captured this city, I assume!"

"Yes, your majesty, we did. Once we had the city well in hand, I left guards to oversee them and then returned directly here to deliver this news and give this report," Hamoth bowed.

"You have done well, Hamoth. Very well. Although the escape of Limhi and his people has gone unhalted, it is good that we have at least captured these other traitorous Nephites. You have turned failure into success." Hamoth unintentionally glanced sideways at Amulon, who gave him a knowing nod. Amulon's advice to leave the city guarded was clearly dubiously inspired. Hamoth turned away quickly, feeling uncomfortable.

"Thank you, my king," he said with a bow.

"Now, what to do with these Nephites?" the king mused aloud. "I take it this city is even farther away than Nephi?"

"Yes, my king, nearly two week's journey northwest of that city."

"Even with moving myself and our people back into Nephi, I still doubt we have many who would be willing to dwell so far north. Especially among Nephites –"

"So, it is true. You are moving to Nephi?" Hamoth was so surprised by the confirmation of this news that he unintentionally queried his king.

"Certainly! The Nephites have left. The least we can do is take advantage of the repairs they have made to our city to the north! I intend to take full advantage of them all!"

"I see. A wise move, my king."

"Yes, quite. I'm still left with how to manage this city you have so nobly endowed upon me," the king's eyes drifted away as he began to think through this dilemma.

Amulon's ears perked up. He was beside himself with anxiety. The situation was beyond his fondest hopes. Finally, he could contain his eagerness no longer.

"My king, if I may," he stated.

King Laman turned his gaze back to his newest subject.

"Great King, I would relish such an opportunity to prove my loyalty to yourself and the Lamanite nation. If I could, please, sire, allow me to return and rule over those people."

"You would rule over Nephites?"

"Yes, your majesty."

"You would rule them as a Lamanite?"

"Certainly, your majesty."

"You would show them no special favors, but ensure that they kept within my laws?"

"Absolutely, your majesty!"

"Hamoth, do you trust that this man will be true to his word?"

Hamoth looked at Amulon. He remembered Amulon's words throughout their journey, then turned back to his king and said as a statement of fact, "I have every reason to believe that this man will rule over the Nephites as powerfully and thoroughly as any Lamanite ruler. I see no hint of his squandering any opportunity to make those people do as you would wish."

Laman nodded, "So be it. Arise. What is your name again?"

"Amulon, sire," he responded smoothly.

"Amulon, I put you in charge of these people. You have all power over them, save the authority over life and death. I reserve that power for myself. You must keep these Nephites working and living in accordance to Lamanite tradition. I will expect reports of your progress."

"It will be an honor and a pleasure, my king!" Amulon bowed low, pleased at his change of fate.

*****

"I'm afraid this is going to be a permanent arrangement, Alma," Helam said, shaking his head.

"I had really thought I could trust him," Alma lamented. "There was something in his eyes that led me to believe him –" He let his words trail off.

"I had the same feeling. In fact, I really believe he would have if it had not been for that mysterious Nephite I told you about."

"That *is* very strange. You say there were a couple dozen and they all had Lamanite wives."

"Yes."

"But, you didn't recognize them."

"No. Something seemed familiar about them, but I didn't recognize him. Of course, I didn't associate with the same caliber of people as you did. Maybe you would have known him."

"Perhaps. Perhaps not. We should just hope we can work out some favorable arrangements with whoever they send up here."

"What do you mean?"

"I don't think we will get by with just a series of guards. I think they're going to send up someone to keep an eye on us and their guards. We are too far from Nephi for them not to. At least, not if they seriously want to keep us at bay."

"I see," Helam went silent as his face took on a very concerned expression. He had a sickening feeling fill his belly. Something warned him that an ill time was approaching.

*****

Alma was right. The dreaded day finally came. It was to prove even more unfortunate than he had feared. Early one morning, a large party of Lamanites broke through the trees and entered the lush field that led to the city of Helam. They progressed at a steady, direct pace. The farmers looked up and stopped their tilling to see who it was that passed by them. Amulon and his party paid them no mind.

By the time they entered the city, Alma had been alerted to their arrival. He hurried to the council chamber and sat in the lead chair, anxious to give them audience. Word had it that the leader of the party was a Nephite. Alma suspected that it would be the same one that Helam had mentioned.

The guard at the chamber door was brushed aside by a Lamanite guard. The guard forced the door open to its fullest, then paused in front of it.

He then loudly proclaimed, "Give heed to the new king! Make way for King Amulon!"

Alma's heart skipped two beats. "*Amulon!* Surely not-!" he thought to himself with his mind racing nearly as fast as his heart.

His answer came instantaneously. Three more guards entered the room, followed by Amulon. He was decked out in the finest clothes of the

Lamanite nation, with a large cape made of monkey fur and a plumed headdress of toucan feathers. Around his biceps were the golden bands of appointed Lamanite royalty. There was no mistaking his new office.

What made Alma involuntarily shudder, was there was also no mistaking his identity. Alma looked into the new monarch's face and experienced clear and distinct recollection. Suddenly, his memory whisked him back to the days of King Noah. He saw the old throne room. He remembered all of the old priests by name, demeanor, and habit. Of them all, Amulon had been the most idolatrous. A shiver shot through his spine. For a moment his heart was overwhelmed with panic brought on by unavoidable discovery.

The new king strode forward, reeking of arrogance and pomp, basking in his moment of triumph and recognition. Helam, who stood next to Alma, turned and whispered to his mentor and leader, "That's him, Alma! That's the man I was telling you about!"

"I don't doubt it," Alma whispered in replied. "Now I see why he held back and didn't let himself be made known. It has been a long time –"

"You know him?"

"Yes, unfortunately I do. He is Amulon, King Noah's chief priest!"

"*That* Amulon! Surely not! –"

Alma did not need to reply, nor was he given the opportunity. The pompous procession had now made its way to where Alma sat. He stood quickly as they entered. The entourage came to a halt and the new king of the region eyed the city's former ruler with contempt.

"Well, Alma, we meet again!" Amulon sneered. "I see you and your rebellious followers have made a quaint little home here in the woods."

"What are you doing here, Amulon?" Alma asked.

"What am I doing here? The real question is what are you doing in my chair?" Amulon commanded his guards, without turning his gaze from Alma, "Guards, have this man removed from my throne!"

The guards responded quickly and with precision. Alma did, as well. He was standing and stepping aside even as they neared him. He could see that any resistance on his part would be futile. There was no need for putting up a token struggle that would only result in injury on his part, or his people.

While stepping aside, Alma asked, "Why have you come here?"

Amulon stepped up to his self-proclaimed throne, turned and whisked his cape over its girth and sat with pleased confidence. He placed his forearms on the armrests and patted the end of each rest with his palms. He looked down to see his body sitting in the throne, to admire the image a moment. Then he looked up at Alma.

"Why have I come? To lead a lost and fallen people, of course!"

Alma ventured a reply which he knew would have no impact, but he had to try.

"We don't consider ourselves to be either lost or fallen. In fact, we consider ourselves to be quite content. We appreciate your offer, but we would prefer to be left alone."

"Mine is not an offer, but a fact. You have a new king. Me. I expect to be obeyed," Amulon responded coolly, then bit out, "No more of your insolence!"

Amulon's face had actually reddened, and he spit as he shouted. He then waited a moment and gathered his composure. He added calmly, "Lest there be any doubt, let me advise you to not think for a moment that I don't remember who you are and how you betrayed King Noah, *Alma*." He placed extra emphasis on Alma's name, saying it slowly and loudly, so that all could hear his discernment. He used the name as a weapon that pierced Alma through the heart and wholly eliminated any false hopes of anonymity. "You and your people will soon learn what it means to serve a king."

Alma clenched his teeth. Amulon's was obviously going to be a long and painful stay.

Chapter 29

Oppression

It took only two more mighty chops to fell the tree. Its tall, slender body sliced through the surrounding trees which still stood at the edge of the rainforest. Several branches snagged and snarled on those of neighboring trees as it fell. Giving minimal resistance, they simply tore off and the tree continued its plummet to the soft, rich earth.

"That should be the last of them," Helam said in a sweat.

"I certainly hope so," Alma replied. "I think we have cleared more land for this new vineyard than we did for the first phase of the city!"

"I know sarcasm when I hear it, but in this case, I think you may be right –"

"Hey! You two!" a large Lamanite guard snarled. "Stop dawdling and get that tree stripped!"

"That man is really starting to tire me," Helam said with a touch of humor mingled with melancholy.

The guard kept his eyes on the duo and ensured they moved quickly to strip the branches and bark from the tree. When this task was completed, other men gathered the branches and bark. They tossed them into the smoldering heap of remains of other fresh cut trees. Alma and Helam hefted their long, slender log over to the crude cutting mill that had been established. Here, other hands would transform it into so many boards to be used in building the new king's winery. Over the years, little had changed in Amulon's desire for substance abuse.

The sun was setting by the time Alma and his companions were allowed to go home. This taxing regimen had already repeated itself for a series of weeks, with no end in sight. It appeared Amulon was not going to let up. As he walked, Alma wondered what could be done to ease the people's burdens. He knew the Lord would not forget them in their time of need, but how could he ensure that his fellow countrymen knew the same?

He noted something amiss from the moment he pushed open the wooden door that led into his home. His dinner sat on the table awaiting him, but there was a feeling in the air of discontent and flailing harmony. He looked about the room and caught sight of his wife. She stood off to the side, wringing her hands fretfully.

"What is it?" he asked concerned.

"It's little Alma," she replied.

"Is he hurt?! Is he ill?" the father asked with elevated concern.

"Oh, no, no. It's nothing like that!" She hesitated adding more.

"Then what?"

"It's just that other children can be so cruel -"

"It's not Amulon's son and his friends again, is it?"

"Yes, it's them," she confirmed.

"Why can they not leave him alone?"

"Well, it's not just Alma. It's the other children as well. You should know that I was talking with some of the other mothers. Josiah's mother said that she heard that Amulon and his men actually encourage this."

"What?!"

"They say it's true!" Then she added in a concerned tone, "It's not enough that they work you men until you are dead on your feet, but to encourage the children to tease and taunt each other- What sort of a man would do such a thing?"

Alma's face turned from surprise and concern to frustrated disgust. "I know exactly what type of man: Amulon. You should have seen him in King Noah's court." As his thoughts drifted back to that earlier time, his eyes took on a distant, melancholy look and his voice tapered off as he added, "How he would mercilessly tear into those who appeared before us, just to gratify his own ego in knowing that he could. Why once he -" Alma shook his head suddenly and looked back to his wife as he cut his thoughts away from that bitter period in his history to a more recent one.

"Where is little Alma now?" he asked.

"He is in his room. Probably still sitting on his bed sulking."

"I will go talk to him."

Naomi shook her head affirmatively and let Alma go and search out their son. He passed through the short hall and parted the cloth that hung across his son's doorway. As he poked his head into the room, he called out softly, "Mind if I come in?"

Little Alma said nothing. He just sat on the edge of his bed with his six-year-old head bowed down. His little hands were clasped together on his lap. The red and blue dyed blanket that covered his bed was still neatly laid across the wool-stuffed mattress. Alma the elder walked up to his son and sat beside him.

"Had a rough day, didn't you?" he asked.

His son remained silent, continuing to look down, and not yet acknowledging the presence of his father.

"Some children can be pretty mean. Can't they?" Alma tried again. "You know, you should try to ignore them. Don't let them get to you -"

His speech was cut short when tear-streaked cheeks suddenly turned upward to face him. The boy spoke with a mixture of sadness, hurt, and contempt.

"You always say that! But they just keep at it! It doesn't help! They hate me! I hate them! I wish they would just go away! Especially Hamoth. He's the worst!"

Alma looked into his son's dark brown eyes. He saw the hurt and anguish. He wished he could make it all go away, past, present and future. He wished he could not just stop the problem, but remove all memory of it from his son. Such a sweet child, he thought to himself, did not deserve such a bitter childhood.

"Alma, sometimes people just do mean things," he offered his son. "It doesn't mean they're bad people, it just means that they sometimes do bad things. And good people get hurt. You can't stop that. You have to learn to live with it and find ways of not letting it get you down. And, we should pray for them that they can learn how to do good things."

"Even Hamoth?"

"Especially Hamoth."

"I don't think anything can make Hamoth be nice!"

"Now, you don't know that! He surely wasn't born mean. Something must have made him start doing mean things. And, if that is the case, then something might be able to make him do nice things."

"Like what?"

"Well, I don't know and you don't know, but I'm certain that the Lord knows. That's why we need to pray for him, so the Lord can make whatever it is that needs to happen, happen, so he'll do nice things again."

"Do you really think that will help?"

"Oh, I'm sure of it! The Lord can do some pretty marvelous things. Helping a boy be nice would be easy for Him."

"Well, I wish he would take care of it soon!"

"Don't be rude, Alma, and remember a good part of that is up to you. If you don't pray for it, the Lord won't take care of it."

"Why not? Doesn't He know what we need?"

"Sure He does!"

"Then why doesn't he just fix things?"

"Because -" Alma paused, considering his own words. "Because sometimes we need things to be broken."

"Huh?"

"Sometimes we need to suffer bad things so that we can learn to appreciate the good things. If Hamoth were never mean to you, how would you learn to appreciate it when your other friends are nice to you? I judge that you like your nice friends even more after Hamoth has teased you, do you not?"

"Well, yes."

"You see, that is what I mean. Also, the Lord waits for us to ask Him things so we can learn to develop faith in Him. If He just always took care of everything, without our having to ask, then where is the growth in it for us? How would we learn to do things on our own? We need to do our part and try our best to fix things ourselves, then pray to the Lord that He will step in and help our efforts succeed. That way we work together. We can't solve it on our own, and the Lord helps us realize that we should not blindly expect Him to fix everything without some effort on our part. Does that make sense?"

"Sort of. I suppose."

"Well, someday it might make more sense to you. But right now, I think I know a young man who could use a hug."

Little Alma smiled. Father and son gave each other a comforting hug. Both received strength from the other. The older Alma was somewhat surprised at just how much he himself needed that hug, and to hear the words he had just spoken. Throughout his dinner and the succeeding days, he continued to hear them.

The more he pondered them, the more he realized there was a deeper wisdom in them than he had at first anticipated. He shared them with Helam as they worked side by side. The two discussed them at length, particularly how they pertained to the people's current plight.

"I think we have been making a mistake," Alma said while hoeing a furrow.

Helam dropped in several more grape seeds, "How so?" He made sure not to look up, lest to incur the wrath of the ever-watchful Lamanite guards.

"We're obeying their new laws and hoping that by playing nice, they will do the same." Alma continued to hoe as he spoke.

"Well, yes."

"They're not going to change their ways. There's no way that Amulon will let up for an instant. He's got too great a grudge, too much to prove to himself. He enjoys the power far too much. This will never end, unless we turn to the Lord for help."

"What do you propose?"

"I propose directing our people to turn their hearts to the Lord in prayer."

"They do pray. At least I pray, and I know you pray. I'm sure several others do as well."

"Yes, but I want to direct them to pray for a specific purpose. If we can unite our prayers to the Lord with singleness of heart and full faith that He will ease our burdens, I'm certain that we will receive His help."

"Alma, you know I believe the same as you. You lead the way and we will all follow you. We always have. That is why we are here!"

*****

The following Sabbath found the Nephites gathered in their stone church anxiously listening to their spiritual leader. He had preached a moving sermon on the power of prayer and the impact it had had on many people and prophets throughout the known scriptures and their own lives.

"– I tell you this with all sincerity, if we choose to follow these examples and pray for the Lord's guidance, He will make our burdens light and our hearts strong! We will endure these trials and be lifted up in the Last Day! –"

Alma's sermon was interrupted by an unexpected visitor. Amulon strode through the main door in the back of the room with the air of an arrogant landlord invading his tenants' picnic. He marched up the main aisle toward Alma. Alma stood at the pulpit now awaiting his overseer's next move.

The congregation's eyes were affixed on the new monarch whom they had grown to fear. No one dared even whisper to each other. Too many had already suffered under his hands during the purging that took place in the first weeks of his reign. His "examples" as he called them, had succeeded at driving home the point that his power was supreme.

Alma braced himself as Amulon neared his spot. He firmly held both sides of the podium's top, with his arms fully extended. He anticipated being removed by Amulon, but had decided to hold his ground as long as he could as a show of strength under pressure for his people. Whether Amulon sensed it or not, he had apparently decided not to play that game.

When he was a step or two from the podium, he looked Alma in the eye and smiled with arrogant contempt. Then he simply turned around in front of the podium and faced the congregation. The spin caused his fur-trimmed, red robe to flair outward for a moment and then fall loosely to his sides.

"Beautiful words!" he said in mock praise. "Such beautiful words." He turned momentarily toward Alma as he added, "You touch me, Alma! You really touch me!" Turning back to the congregation he continued, "But, unfortunately, your words are in deadly error. Just as they always were when you sat among King Noah's noble priests." Perhaps he thought a reminder of Alma's treacherous past would undermine the prophet's hold on this people.

At any rate, he concluded with, "But, know this one and all. There will be no such prayers! No pitiful pleas to this Being you call God! No unified effort for help! And, no such help! Anyone caught uttering such prayers will be put to DEATH! I invite anyone who doubts my words to step forward. I will show you who has control over life, death, pleasure, and pain in this city!"

Amulon slowly and menacingly scanned the congregation for anyone who dared defy his edict. No one dared; at least not outwardly. Most of the people looked down or otherwise avoided making eye contact with the traitorous monarch.

"I didn't think so. Don't any of you forget my words! I promise you I won't forget them! Nor will I show the least bit of mercy to any who do!"

With this, Amulon gave one final, insulting glare at Alma. He added loudly enough for all to hear, "And this will be the last of these meetings! Understood?!"

Alma slowly, but clearly, nodded his head affirmatively. Amulon then strode out of the meeting room as quickly as he had entered. He let the door slam shut with an echoing thud that struck the people deep into their hearts. Several jumped, startled by the noise. The congregation then breathed a collective sigh of relief that he was gone.

Alma paused, hoping somehow to regain his people's trust in deliverance. Finally, he uttered only a few short words, "Remember this, the Lord is God. He knows the thoughts of our hearts. A prayer uttered from the heart can be as equally powerful as one uttered from the lips. I know this because I have received answers to my prayers. The Lord has told me that He will be with us and He will make our burdens light. Now, go home and be faithful, not fearful. The Lord will be with us!"

*****

In spite of their perilous circumstances, the people continued to believe in Alma. They continued to believe that he had been right to defy King Noah and speak in support of Abinadi. Their hearts had been permanently touched and turned to good during his preaching by the crystalline Waters of Mormon, west of Nephi.

They felt the Lord's influence when the decision was made to leave their homes and strike out in search of a new land. They had been filled with thanksgiving for the life they had lived in this new land of Helam. While Amulon's threats frightened and distressed them, they knew that the Lord would watch over and protect them.

While they obeyed Amulon's edict to cease all verbal prayers, Amulon was to eventually learn that no tyrant could conquer the human heart. Unbeknownst to him, the people poured out prayers from their hearts. Their thoughts were continually elevated above the cares of their current plight and the deliverance which they fully expected the Lord would provide.

All the while, Alma's promise continued to hold true. The Lord did make their burdens light, to the vexation of Amulon. The more tasks he heaped upon their backs, the more they could tolerate. Amulon first attributed it to their own naiveté and sense of community. While he was at least right about the benefits the people garnered from encouraging each other, he could not possibly have understood the easing of their burdens which the Lord himself provided.

They worked as if angels themselves pulled the heavier loads. They met each unrealistic deadline he imposed on them. Crops flourished more than ever before. No one stood idle. Amulon was without means of finding even the most trivial of excuses to exact punishments on the people. They fulfilled his every decree. Moreover, they did it without complaint and even seemed content with their lives.

Nothing vexed this megalomaniac more than this. He cared not a whit for prosperity. His base desire was to downgrade and burden these people whom he loathed. His every attempt was proving in error. Meanwhile, unbeknownst to Amulon, an even more alluring course of action would present itself.

Chapter 30
Foresight

Years earlier, when King Laman succeeded his father to the throne, he was crowned as the sole sovereign over all of the lands of the Lamanites. As the years passed, his kingdom had grown to spread to many cities throughout the southern land. It included several lands or cities, such as Nephi, Shilom, and Shemlon. It even included the land where his soldiers had discovered Amulon, which they called the land of Amulon. Of particular note was that it now included the city of Helam. At this time, Helam was the only remaining city inhabited by Nephites. The others were strictly Lamanite cities.

Laman gradually found that maintaining control over a kingdom spread over several cities and lands was a taxing and arduous task. He divided his kingdom into sub-kingdoms and appointed "sub-kings" over various cities or lands. Most of these kings were his sons. Some, such as Amulon, were men he appointed to the position.

All of these kings were intended to bear in mind that he was the ultimate king of all the land. The kings had significant power, but Laman's word was the ultimate law of their land. He took his governing seriously, as well he should, lest unrest lead to his undoing.

Eventually, King Laman heard of the prosperity in the land of Helam. He was greatly impressed with what Amulon seemed to be accomplishing. He decided he wanted to learn the secrets of such great success so that it could be spread to and shared with other areas within his kingdom. He sent for Amulon.

*****

Amulon approached the great gate of the city of Nephi with confidence. His entourage of former priests bore his belongings behind him. His woven red robe with its fur trim glowed with distinction. The tower guards had seen his approach from the moment he had entered the northern clearing in the distance.

As Amulon neared the city of Nephi's main gate, it opened from within. He and all of those with him stopped, allowing the gate to open to its full extent. He suppressed his surprise when he saw King Laman himself standing on the threshold of the city. Upon seeing his most recent supreme monarch, Amulon bowed his head and knelt in deference to his ruler.

Laman smiled silently, appreciative of a Nephite who not only knew his place, but also understood Lamanite protocol. He walked forward and stopped in front of his kneeling protégé. Amulon's head remained bowed. He noted the brightly colored feathers woven into Laman's sandals.

Laman reached out his right hand and placed it on Amulon's shoulder, to raise him, as was their custom.

"Arise, Amulon. Welcome back to the city of Nephi," he said.

Amulon rose slowly and with respect.

"I thank you, my king. I appreciate this opportunity to again come into your presence."

"Come, I have prepared a feast for you," Laman stated.

"A feast? I am honored, my king," Amulon bowed again, "But, surely I don't deserve such an honor," he added with mock humility.

"That is probably true," the king said with a smile, "But, I am certain you will soon repay me this debt in full. Come!"

As he turned to head back into the city, King Laman slapped Amulon on the shoulder so hard it nearly knocked him off balance. Amulon smiled, but inwardly resented the king's jest. He turned and nodded for his own men to follow along.

The group, consisting mostly of King Noah's former priests, again returned to a city they had once called home. It was a place where they themselves had once been treated as kings. Already the place was returning to disrepair. The Lamanites that mingled about showed every sign of disinterest in the city's upkeep.

The city plaza was a shambles. Dirt-smeared walls were beginning to be covered by vines. Here and there cracks at their bases were giving way to weeds that were determined to reclaim the city for the jungle. The canopies and kiosks which once housed merchants plying their wares lay dormant. Some had fallen over and been left where they fell, their torn canvasses ignored.

The group continued through the square and toward the street that led to the main building. Amulon followed closely behind his new king. Amulon did not even bother to notice that the temple was now home to various and sundry Lamanite stores and weapons. At one point, his peripheral vision did catch sight of a large rat as it scurried to where several torn grain-sacks lay heaped against a storage bin's outer wall. It was the same bin he and his men had been looting the last time he encountered his former wife. He smirked as he recalled his final taunt.

It was not long before they were all within the grand hall. Many Lamanites were already present and even more were wandering in and boisterously seating themselves. King Laman walked to the head of the main table. He motioned with a long sweep of his arm that Amulon should continue to follow. When the great king reached the head of the table he turned around to face a large, ornately-carved chair. Two servants pulled the chair out for their monarch.

"You and your men can sit here!" Laman slowly spread his arms wide open, curling his hands and fingers outward once his arms completed their sweeping gesture. He stood with both arms fully extended and indicated the chairs to his right and left. He smiled and nodded to Amulon, who nodded in return as he and his men took their places.

"Welcome to my kingdom!" Laman said as he observed the men seat themselves.

Once the last was sitting, Laman stepped up to his seat of honor and began to sit. As he did so, the two Lamanite servants slid the chair into place to catch their royal master. Laman put his hands onto the armrests of the dark, high-backed, wooden chair. In many ways it resembled a throne, with carvings of large, graceful, long-plumed birds etched into its arch which peaked some two feet above the monarch's head.

"Now, eat!" Laman commanded.

Amulon and his men turned their attention to the wooden plates in front of them. The plates were empty, but flanked with large goblets filled to the brim with rich-smelling, dark wine. Beyond the place settings were several trays with breads and fruits. Others were filled with steaming, uncarved meats. There was no guesswork as to which tray contained the pork and which the fowls. Cooked heads and legs were still fully attached.

"We thank you most heartily!" Amulon said with calculated appreciation.

He reached for the nearest tray and pulled from it a roasted snake of moderate size. He placed it onto his plate forcing it to coil so as to fit within the confined area. He retrieved a knife from beside his plate and began to partake of this feast which was held in his honor.

The feast lost all signs of delicacy as the Lamanites literally tore into their food with enthusiasm. There was no talking for a great deal of time, as all attention seemed to be focused on consuming as much sustenance as possible. The lack of conversation did not bring silence to the hall, however. Instead, it was filled with the slurping, chomping, gulping, and tearing of food and sloppy gulping of strong, colorful drinks.

The pace continued for several minutes until swollen bellies began to beg for a slowing. Finally, Laman, still chewing on a mouthful of flesh, slapped the table with a powerful palm, declaring completion. In response, the servants ceased their continual replenishment of the foods and drinks on the various tables. Laman continued to chomp and chew on what remained in his overstuffed mouth. He reached for his goblet and took a large swig to wash down the food. He swallowed hard, trying to gain enough space in his mouth to allow himself to speak.

"Now, Amulon, do you know why I have called you here?" he said with a smile.

"I thought I did, your majesty," Amulon replied, "but, perhaps you can enlighten me."

"Maybe I can!" Laman laughed through his grease-stained lips, "Maybe I can!"

The king continued to laugh. His other dark-skinned subjects joined in the laughter. Amulon and his men joined in, simply to keep from being left out. They did not want to risk drawing any negative attention to themselves.

"Why, you are here to teach us!" Laman explained. "It's that simple!"

"Teach you?" Amulon questioned. The statement took him off guard.

"Certainly! My men tell me that in a fairly short time you have turned Helam into a powerfully rich land. I have noted the stores of tribute that come from there. I know that land can't possibly be much different from this, yet your crops seem to yield two-fold what ours do. If it's not the dirt, then it must be the people. I can only guess that it's your leadership that has brought about this bounty. This is a bounty that I want shared with the rest of my kingdom. And, I am not referring to sharing the crops. I want to know how I can make all of my people as productive as those you rule in Helam."

"I see," Amulon responded. He sat back in his chair and set his knife back down on his plate. He slowly wiped his mouth with his sleeve, concealing the thoughts that raced through his mind. He quickly recognized that he was being offered an enormous opportunity. If he chose his words and actions carefully, he would be able to go far in this new kingdom. Perhaps even as far as he had climbed under King Noah's reign.

"My king, you do me great honor," he said at last. "It pleases me to know that my actions have pleased you. I would find great interest in doing anything which will increase the glory of your kingdom."

"So, you believe you can make my other cities just as productive as Helam, then?" the king questioned.

Wholly ignorant of how the Lord had blessed and prospered Alma and his people, Amulon replied, "Of course, my king, it will be an easy thing."

"Easy?" Laman asked.

"Easy, yes, but not quick," Amulon said, catching himself, lest he set himself up against a task he could not complete.

"Do whatever you feel is needed. I will see to it that your orders are obeyed. I'm determined to see this kingdom prosper. I want you to teach my people everything they need to know to get gain."

* * * * *

Amulon was both flattered and enthusiastic about the opportunity King Laman had presented him. He saw this as a golden opportunity to elevate his status even further and climb to greater power and influence in this expansive kingdom. He established men of his choosing – men from among his priests – whom he could trust to further his objectives. As per Laman's request, he sent these men to every land in which the king had people.

They taught them to read, write, and to carry on commerce with each other. The Lamanites in the lands of Shilom, Shemlon, Nephi and throughout all of king Laman's lands began to trade with each other. They experienced a degree of prosperity which they had never before known.

What was more astounding, was that the Lamanites began to experience a degree of peace among themselves they had also never before known. The commerce among each other provided a means of authorized exchange that superseded the deceit and outright thieving that had previously occurred as a normal way of life. In many ways, the Lamanites turned from a competitive, vagabond society to one in which they aided each other's economic growth.

With calculated cunning, Amulon ensured that his priests taught the Lamanites everything they needed to know about increasing their wealth, while slyly omitting any reference to faith in God. The Lamanites remained wholly ignorant of Abinadi, or any of the other prophets. He purposely focused the Lamanites' attention on the things of the world, the riches of the earth, and the splendors of wealth.

He was well on his way to eliminating any form of spirituality from the minds and souls of the Lamanite people. The Lamanites literally did not know what they were missing. They were too pleased with their increased prosperity to lament Amulon's methods. News of his actions and progress spread throughout the extended Lamanite kingdoms, including the land of Helam.

The ever-vigilant Alma was keen to observe all of these events. He knew Amulon could not be trusted. As he caught wind of more and more details about Amulon's plan, he grew more deeply concerned. He knew that such a happening would eventually destroy the Lamanite society. When a people turned their thoughts solely to the things of the world, prosperity turned to greed, and greed would lead to corruption and conquest.

Alma knew full well that his people's lives in their new home were becoming in even greater jeopardy. He knew that they could continue to live, but they would not be able to thrive and grow. He knew that under Amulon's powerfully tyrannical hand, they would have little opportunity for further spiritual growth. On behalf of his people, he entered a strong fast and knelt before his Lord in silent, secluded prayer.

Chapter 31
Deliverance

The hot sun was high in the sky as Helam made his way down the narrow stone alleyway. He passed several homes, each with a large clay pot sitting by a wooden front door. He turned left down a remote corner, deep within the heart of the city. He had to carefully brush aside several successive rows of tapestries where the women had hung them to wait until their dyes had fully dried, so that he could pass.

No Lamanites, in fact few people, ever bothered to venture into this out-of-the-way location. He reached out and moved a red and blue tapestry and found Alma standing at the end of the alley. Alma's face broke into a wide smile and his eyes had a keen look of anticipation mingled with gratitude and relief.

"Helam, I thank you for meeting me here!" Alma said, grasping Helam by the forearm and shaking it in the traditional manner of greeting.

"This is awfully dangerous, but I could tell it's important," Helam replied.

"I know. I don't think the Lamanite guards should be able to overhear us in here."

"What did you want to discuss?"

"I have received another answer to my prayers," Alma's eyes seemed to glow.

Helam felt a tingle run through him. "What have you learned?" he asked with interest.

"The Lord has told me that He has heard our prayers. He remembers the covenant we made with Him. And – He will deliver us from our bondage!"

"Deliver us?! How? When?"

"Tonight."

"Tonight?!"

"Yes, tonight. We are to gather the people, our belongings, our flocks and herds and be gone from here before daybreak."

"Be gone? But, where will we go?"

"Zarahemla."

"Zarahemla? But, who knows the way? None of us have ever even been there!"

"The Lord will show us the way. We will need to trust Him."

"I do. I do. I'm just so surprised – and overjoyed!"

"Yes, soon life in this beautiful city will be nothing more than a distant memory. We will again be able to worship the Lord openly with our brethren in the north."

"Imagine. Zarahemla!"

"We need to spread the word quickly and quietly. Have the elders pass word through to their neighborhoods. We will probably have to tell the wives to tell their husbands as they come off of their shifts. Warn the people to not begin gathering their belongings any sooner than sunset. We don't want to raise any suspicions. Tell them that as they become ready, they should meet in the eastern field, near the lake. We must take care to keep silent, but move very quickly!"

"I understand. This is marvelous!"

"The Lord will be with us!"

The two clasped each other's arms as a token of their agreement. Alma slapped Helam's shoulder. Then they parted to make preparations.

*****

The still waters of the lake reflected a perfectly full moon. The reflection and the heavenly illumination offered considerable light to the steadily growing crowd. Families huddled together with their belongings. Others spread themselves around their flocks and herds. All of them were growing increasingly anxious to begin their journey. Perhaps the most remarkable aspect of the group was the lack of complaints or doubts. No one voiced either of these. All of them were anxious to leave this haven-turned-prison far behind them.

Many eyes turned westward back toward their city. A lone figure could be seen dashing toward them at a fast pace. He leapt over brush and through tall grass that had been matted down by the many feet and hooves which had recently made the same trek. He ran up to and through the throng. They graciously let him pass. He made his way up to Alma to give his report.

"Alma, every man, woman, and child has now left the city," Helam announced. "It's stone quiet now."

"What of the guards? Did any see you?"

"Not a one. I'm certain of it."

"How so?"

"They're all asleep. It's as if it is the sleep of death. I think it will be a long time before any of them wake again."

"Good. We will need all the time we can get. We need to make the most of the darkness we have left. Spread the word, we are moving on!"

As in the days of Moses, centuries earlier, Alma led his people out of bondage and toward a promised land of refuge. He stayed at the forefront of their march, leading their way. Several strong men flanked him on either side cutting vines and moving brush and logs aside to ease the passage of those who followed.

The long train of people, belongings and animals continued well past daybreak and on into the day. They were all anxious to put as much distance as they could between themselves and the angry horde which they knew would soon pursue them. They knew their challengers would be able to move much more quickly than they themselves could, hence there was very little complaining or requests for rest. Fathers did their best to guide and carry their children along.

Toward day's end they broke through the trees and came to a splendid valley at the base of several steep mountains. A waterfall cascaded down to a river that fed a small lake and then moved onward on its meandering race to the sea. The valley was filled with the sweet smell of multi-colored flowers.

"This looks like a good place to rest," Alma declared. "Have the people refill their water supplies and rest themselves near the lake. Water the animals downstream in the western end of the river, beyond the lake."

His orders were cheerfully received and carried out. Soon, the people were gathered around cook fires in the breathtaking valley. They named it the valley of Alma, in honor of their leader. Their meals were prepared with thankful hearts and praises. None of them could remember a more delightful meal.

Afterward, they gathered together to hear Alma. Alma directed them to remain with their families, lest any young ones wander off unaccounted for. He told them to rest well in preparation for further marching in the morning. He encouraged them that every step would bring them so much closer to Zarahemla and their freedom.

He also added another point, "We are no longer in the land of Helam. Amulon no longer has power over us. I believe it would be fitting to give thanks to our Lord and God – verbally."

The people cheered and began openly praising the Lord for delivering them. It had been a long time since they had been able to do so audibly and with such sincerity. Alma himself led the congregation of refugees in a prayer of thanksgiving. Many tears of joy were shed in addition to the thanks that were given in that prayer and several others that immediately followed it.

*****

Nearly all of the campfires had gone out. All that remained of others were smoldering coals that gave off very little light. The four guards that Alma had posted around the campsite were still alert, as they had only replaced their predecessors by a couple of hours. The morning was not far away.

All of the others in the camp slept peacefully. All of the others except one. Alma sat up suddenly. A sense of urgency streaked across his face. His body was engulfed in a sudden sweat. He quickly assembled his belongings and asked Naomi to take charge of little Alma as he hurried out to where the elders slept.

He stood in the center of them and shouted, "Awake! Awake! All of you! Wake up now! The Lord has told me that the Lamanites have arisen and are after us! We must move quickly!"

"The Lamanites! Already! They will catch us for certain!"

"No! The Lord has promised us that if we will leave this valley, He will hold them here. We will be safe, but we must leave this valley now!"

"Which way? Where are we going?" a voice in the crowd asked frantically.

Alma pointed up toward a steep ravine that narrowly cut its way between the two taller mountains. "Through there!" he said.

"Through the mountain?"

"Yes, that is the shortest route to Zarahemla!"

"But the children! The sheep! How will we make it?"

"Be of good faith. We will make it. But only if we hurry!"

By this time, the elders had scattered and were well into their task of assembling the people who were in their stewardship. Within half an hour, the rising sun cast an orange glow on the company as the first few of them began wending their way up the steep ravine. To their relief, the ravine was much wider than it had appeared from the valley floor. There was about a twelve foot climb up sharp rocks leading to it. But once there, they found a path winding its way up the center of the ravine. The path was about three paces wide. The sheep and the children were able to make their way upward with encouragement and assistance from the adults.

Alma had sent Helam to the front to lead the people up the ravine. He had told him to take them all the way through the pass and then wait until all of them had made it safely. Meanwhile, Alma chose to linger behind to ensure that all of the people still in the valley made it up to the path. Those farthest back in line grew more and more anxious for their turn to exit the valley. Alma knew his calming assurances would be needed to avert panic.

As he was about to coax them onward, he was stopped by a familiar voice at his side, "Father!" Alma turned and looked down to see his son standing there beside him with a very worried look in his eyes.

"Alma!" the busy patriarch exclaimed. "What are you doing here? You should have already gone up with your mother and Helam!"

"I'm scared, father! What's going to happen to us?"

Alma took a moment to comfort and encourage his son, "It will be fine. The Lord is with us. We just need to believe that He will always be with us. Now, please, go up the path!"

"But, I want to stay with you, father!" said the young voice. Tears were starting to well up in his big, beautiful brown eyes.

"You will be with me, Alma," the anxious father replied, "Soon, just not right now. Right now I have to help all of these people make it out of the valley before Amulon comes! Now, I need you to be very brave and climb up that hill. Run up the path and find your mother for me. She must be very worried about us. Go and tell her that I'm all right and I will be catching up with her soon. Can you do that?"

"Tell mother?"

"Yes, tell mother that I will be with her soon and that she should not worry. She needs you to help her right now. Will you do that?"

"I can help mother," little Alma decided. "I will go help her!"

"That's right," the elder Alma confirmed. "Go find mother and help her not be so afraid! I'll be there soon!"

He then gave his son a boost up the steep climb. Little Alma made it to the flat of the path and turned in triumph. He waved to his father, "I made it!" he said.

"Wonderful! Now, go find your mother!" Alma watched long enough to see that his son obeyed and ran up the path. "Thank goodness!" he said, as he turned back to look at the last of his people frantically scurrying toward the mountainside.

As he suspected, this last group was just beginning to climb the ravine when an horrific shout was heard to the southwest. It was the Lamanites. Amulon himself was leading the charge.

"Alma!" the infuriated king shouted. His deep, vexatious voice echoed through the valley. Amulon had no intention of allowing Alma to slip away, lest his position and status with King Laman also slip away.

Alma looked up and noted that his former comrade was racing across the valley at full speed, with a horde of armed men backing him up. He forced himself to turn his attention to the Nephites he was assisting. They too had seen and heard Amulon. They were near hysterics.

"He's too close! We can't make it! We're doomed!" they cried.

"Nonsense! We have plenty of time!" Alma responded in a commanding, comforting voice. "Trust in the Lord! He will direct us for our good! Now, climb! Quickly!"

The people obeyed, spreading word for those ahead that the Lamanites were on their tails and that they all needed to speed up their pace. The news eked forward like a spastic inchworm on a burning leaf. Soon, the entire throng was moving just a little more quickly than before.

Alma stayed back, pushing the last of the group up onto the steep path. Amulon was nearing the base of the mountain.

"Alma! I swear to you, this will be your last act of treason!" he shouted. "Bring those people back, or we will slaughter you all!"

Alma did not respond. He merely continued to urge his brethren forward up the path. A goat had wandered off and was now far above them on a ledge to their right. It took a misstep and knocked a small rock off its resting place. The rock tumbled down, crashing into others as it did so. None of them were large, but they sent enough dust and gravel in their wake that Amulon had to stop a moment and step back from his pursuit of Alma.

"Your goats and sheep won't stop me, Alma!" he shouted as the dust began to fade. "I will have you soon enough!"

It was only a little time, but it was enough time that Alma and the last of his people were now out of sight, hurrying up the path which ran the course of the ravine. Amulon turned and shouted to his men, threatening them to hurry to his side. He made it brutally clear that he would have their heads if they did not catch these loathsome Nephites.

Amulon was about halfway up the rocks, well on his way to the path when it happened. It was subtle at first, but quickly grew in intensity. Amulon attributed the first falling rock to simply being pulled from its place by his own might as he struggled up the climb. He ignored it and attempted to continue pushing onward and upward.

Soon, as the intensity increased, even he had to accept the fact that the earth itself was moving. The Lamanites in the valley shouted with concern and fright. Those nearest the mountain ducked their heads and tried to avoid the increasing number of boulders which now rolled and plummeted toward them.

"Get moving!" Amulon said, above the earthen din. "Get moving now, or I will draw my sword on you!"

Amulon's hand reached the plateau. He pulled himself upward, intent on reaching the path. He could almost hear Alma running ahead around the nearest bend. Just then, he heard something else. He looked straight up to see a massive rock cascading downward, directly for him.

It hit an outcropping and split in two, generating a massive plume of dust and debris. Amulon dodged left. The larger of the two halves did the same. It hit him directly in the face, stifling his panicked cry. His lifeless body tumbled backward and skidded to a halt at the base of the mountain.

The rumbling continued. More and more rocks were shaken from their rest and fell as if thrown down upon Amulon and his soldiers. Those Lamanites who still stood in the safety of the valley saw huge boulders crash down the hillside, causing them to run and dodge. Several rolled into the lake creating massive waves and plumes of water that shot up until the boulders finally ground to a halt.

Those who survived the onslaught could no longer make out the entrance to the ravine. It was permanently and undeniably blocked and lost to all future passage. The Lamanites were now without a leader or a means of pursuing their prey. They were forced to search for survivors and then eventually retreat back to their stations in Helam. Eventually, news would get back to King Laman. Word had it that he heard the account, he was less than pleased.

*****

Far ahead of the Lamanites, the Nephites also felt the trembling of the earth and heard the roar of the descending stones. Fear was their first reaction. Several of them dropped flat to the ground crying or shouting for refuge. Alma ran forward and shouted to them all, "People! People! Please, keep moving! The Lord has spoken! He said He would stop the Lamanites in the valley! He is doing it! See! Look, the stones fall behind us, not above us!"

Alma pointed directly overhead. All of the rocks and boulders stood fast, immovable. Many at first refused to look upward, shouting fearfully. First one, and then another, looked up and saw that Alma spoke truly.

"He's right!" they shouted. "See! We're still safe!"

"Certainly! The Lord will guide us home! Now hurry! Onward!" Alma commanded.

The people stood and were soon making their way farther up the ravine again. They never heard any more of the Lamanites. No one knew what had befallen them, although several could guess. By suppertime, they had made it through the ravine and were gathering on the far side of the mountain preparing their evening meals.

Talk quickly shifted from where they had been to where they were going. Many of them had questions about life in Zarahemla and what had come of their brethren who had remained in Nephi when they themselves had fled with Alma to the land of Helam. Instinctively, the people looked to

Alma for the answers. He let them know that while he did not have the answers to all of their questions, he was certain that Zarahemla was a beautiful city that was safe from the marauding and manipulating of the Lamanites, and that the people there must surely be happy.

*****

Twelve days into their journey, they came across a well-trodden road. This was a far cry better than the jungle terrain they had traversed for nearly two weeks. They had found game and water along their journey, making it a satisfyingly uneventful trek. The first to set foot on solid ground was Alma.

He raised his hands in triumph high above his head. Others soon joined him, leaping out from the soft undergrowth and lighting gratefully on the ancient highway. The cheers, congratulations, smiles and tears were enough to lead one to believe they had reached Zarahemla itself. After nearly three generations away, finding the final leg of the trail back was nearly as good to them.

As the celebration began to ebb, Helam turned to his leader, "So, Alma, which way now? Do we follow this road left or right?"

Alma smiled, "We follow it north and home. Now, let us get moving!"

Hundreds of eager feet were soon following the path north. They traveled for the better part of two hours. When rounding a bend, a cry went up from the travelers. A keen eye, toward the front of the group, had caught sight of something beautiful. The great city wall.

"Zarahemla! Zarahemla!" he shouted. "There it is!"

"I believe he's right," was all Alma replied, with an ever-increasing smile.

The entourage nearly ran the final distance. Alma worked hard to stay in the lead. A tower guard caught sight of a dirty, sweaty group storming the city. At first, he thought they were Lamanites and sounded the alarm. As soldiers, archers, and officers within the city dashed for the square and began mounting the city wall, the guard realized these were not Lamanites.

"They're Nephites!" he shouted down into the city square. "They're Nephites!"

"Nephites?" Ammon questioned. He had joined the many who were racing to the city square. "Nephites? What band of Nephites would this be?"

"Open the gate!" an officer called.

The great gate began to open, slowly at first, and then with increasing speed. As it did so, Gideon and Limhi joined Ammon in the square. They stood facing outward, anxious to learn the answer to this puzzle. The gate opened fully, revealing a tall, muscular, handsome man standing in the center of its opening. He held the tiny hand of his son, who seemed to have a look of awe mingled with pride. His right arm was wrapped around the shoulders of his smiling wife. This little family was flanked by several hundred foot-weary but ecstatically happy men, women, and children, as well as several hundred goats, sheep, and other animals.

"I wonder who these people are," Gideon mused. "Wait, is that – is that *Alma*?" Gideon asked, taking a closer look to be certain. "It is! Alma! My goodness! It's Alma!" Turning to Ammon he gave an emphatic explanation, "Ammon, *that* is Alma!" pointing with excitement.

"Alma?" Ammon asked, then recalling the tales King Limhi had told him, he gained recognition. "Alma?! Bless the Lord, it's Alma!"

Limhi and his faithful captain, Gideon, were already running forward to welcome Alma and his people. Soon, they were embracing and welcoming them to Zarahemla. The entire, mobile population was welcomed and ushered into the city proper. Their belongings were placed in the city square.

King Mosiah himself came out to greet and welcome them. "Welcome to Zarahemla, my brothers and sisters! Welcome! We must have a feast to celebrate your happy return!"

Alma beamed, "Thank you, sir. Thank you. And, praise be to God for leading us here!"

Alma knelt and bowed his head reverently to give thanks. As if on cue, his people did the same. It was as if a tide had suddenly withdrawn itself, going outward. Fathers, mothers, and children all knelt down to give thanks. King Mosiah recognized the need and did the same. All of his people followed their king's modest example. Within heartbeats, all of Zarahemla was kneeling and giving thanks to the Lord, their God, for preserving them as a people and reuniting them with the last of their long-lost brethren.

Chapter 32

Accounts

Following a magnificent feast, King Mosiah decreed that the account of the people of Alma, as well as the people of Limhi, should be made known throughout the land. A proclamation was sent forth that all who wanted to hear the tales of these peoples should gather to Zarahemla, for on the fifth day of the fourth month, an account would be given of all that had transpired from the time Zeniff had left Zarahemla until the time that both Limhi and Alma had returned with their people.

Rumors and word of these people had already spread rampantly among the people in their various villages. The opportunity to receive a true telling of these events was an exciting proposition. The curious and the anxious gathered their families and made the trek to Zarahemla. For some, it was not much of a journey as they lived nearby or within the actual city of Zarahemla. For others, it was a rather arduous endeavor as they traveled great distances across fields, over mountains, and through jungles.

Nevertheless, when the appointed day arrived, it found Zarahemla's city square virtually bursting with people. Tents had been set up with some housing small families, and other much larger tents, housing extended families. All of the tents faced towards the temple and the speaking-tower that had been erected before it. The people were anxious to hear whatever words would be spoken that day.

As was typical with such a crowd, there were various street vendors milling about plying their wares. They were as eager as the others to hear the words, but also needed to tend to their business. They called out for any who would listen, that they had food, or drink, or in some cases textiles or other wares to sell. This was an exciting time, not just for the reading of the accounts, but because of the hustle and bustle of people.

Many of these families lived on and tended to small farms in rural areas. They had not seen this many people in a very long time. For some, they had never seen such a gathering. Many of these good people could not help looking around with as much awe and wonder at the crowd as their children did. While some of them wandered about, taking in the sites, others huddled together at the openings of their tents watching the milling crowd throng past. While this was a source of amusement for some, it was more than a little intimidating to others. Mothers kept their children close, to avoid their becoming lost.

There were several familiar faces among the throng. Gideon and Hannah sat together in the entrance of their small tent. Gideon's loyal friend Micah and his family were immediately next door. They were among a few who had been granted special seating nearest to the base of the speaking tower. Next to them, a series of tents had been pitched for Ammon, Amaleki, Hem, and Ammon's other brave men who had followed Ammon on the quest to the Nephites' former homeland. Several of these men were married and had been gratefully reunited with their sweethearts, and in some cases, their small children, too.

To the right, Alma's good friend, Helam, sat with his family. Alma's beloved wife, Rachel shared the awning with them, which beat back the scorching heat from the powerful sun. Little Alma wandered about between Rachel and Helam, teasing Helam's youngest son. The little boy, Jared, decided that he had had enough of the teasing and darted away to seek refuge somewhere else. Gideon smiled as the boy crossed in front of his tent. He had been watching young Alma's escapades and saw the little lad run off even before Helam had noticed.

As Helam was getting to his feet to go after his little prodigy, Gideon had already caught up with him. He picked him up with a laugh, "And, where do you think you are going, young man?" he asked.

"Over to the tower!" Jared replied defiantly.

"Well, let's just see what your father has to say about that." Gideon held his son up high and suddenly shot him skyward. The boy sailed up at least a yard into the air with his arms flailing outward and a very concerned and surprised look in his wide eyes.

Rachel saw the look and shouted, "Gideon!" in a kind, but slightly scolding way; the way wives chide the men they love.

Once he landed in Gideon's welcoming arms, he shouted out with a smile almost bigger than his face could bear, "Do it again!"

"All right, just this once!" Gideon tossed him up even higher, while Rachel smiled and shook her head, marveling at how comfortable Gideon was with children.

Helam was standing by Gideon's side as Jared came down for a final landing. He, too, was smiling. "Thanks, Gideon. Uh, good catch!" he added with a twinkle in his eye.

Gideon put his son down and mussed his hair, "My pleasure," he said. "You have a fine son here!"

Little Jared moved over to his father's side and put his arm around his waist, but kept looking up at Gideon with a smile.

"Thank you. We kind of like him, too!" Helam said, complimenting his son in an off-handed way. He turned and walked back to his tent while

Jared excitedly asked over and over if his father had seen just how high he had gone into the air.

"That was nice," Rachel said to Gideon as he sat back down beside her. "It's good to see you're so good with children."

"Oh, thanks, he is an enjoyable little child," was all he responded, deflecting the compliment.

"No, really, I mean it's really good that you are so comfortable with children," she persisted.

"Well, they can be really fun," he clarified, wondering only slightly at why she was persisting. "You just never know what's going on in their little heads or what they'll do next."

"Yes, that's true. I suppose we'll have a lot of opportunities to find out though," she said coyly.

Gideon laughed a short burst of a laugh and said, "I suppose that's true – " Gideon suddenly cut himself off, "Say, why are you saying that? I mean, what do you mean?"

Gideon's face started to flush as it was beginning to dawn on him that this may be more than idle talk between him and his wife.

"You're not trying to tell me something are you?" he pursued.

Rachel just smiled broadly. Gideon was started to get excited. He turned to face her fully and reached out to hold both of her hands in his own. "You're not telling me that you are – that we are – that you are –" he was stumbling over his words terribly as his mind raced and Rachel continued to smile and nod at him, coaxingly. "Are we? Are we going to have a little one of our own?" he managed at last.

Rachel nodded quickly with the excited look of one who is finally able to share a grand secret with her best friend. "We're soon to have a little one in our home!" she confirmed.

"Oh, Rachel! Sweetheart! That is wonderful!" He leaned into her and hugged her warmly, almost knocking her off of her chair.

Then he leapt to his feet and shouted, "We're going to have a baby! I'm going to be a father!"

From all around them, Ammon, Micah, Hannah, Helam and others cheered and clapped. Micah came up to Gideon and gave him a bear hug of congratulations. Helam slapped him squarely on the back. In the midst of the men's boisterous celebration of the announcement, Hannah approached Rachel and calmly congratulated her, wishing her all the blessings of Heaven and extending a sincere offer to help in any way she could.

With the men still shouting, Gideon turned to Rachel and took her by both hands and began to dance with her, spinning her round and round in his excitement. Rachel laughed and enjoyed the moment. Suddenly, he

realized the dance may be a bit much for his tender sweetheart and stopped it
with a concerned look in his eye. He stepped up close to her, putting his arm
around her shoulder very gingerly, as if afraid of squeezing her too tightly.

"I'm sorry. I hope that you're all right. I didn't hurt you any, did I?
Do you need to sit? Here, sit down here again," he urged as he tried to lead
her back to her seat.

"I'm all right, Gideon. It's not like I'm going to break or anything. A
little dancing is not going to hurt me or the baby," she pointed out.

Micah watched the incident and laughed, "I was never like that!" he
said shaking his head with a smile.

"Oh, no, you certainly weren't," his wife replied. Then as she turned
to go back toward their tent, she added with a wry twinkle, "You were much
worse!"

"See, now – hey, what do you mean by that?" Micah asked, following
her back to their tent.

Gideon and Rachel passed the rest of the morning making plans for
their growing family.

* * * * *

An hour before noon, a horn was sounded. It quickly garnished the
attention of everyone within the city. A stately Nephite stepped forward on
the tower and announced the arrival of King Mosiah. Everyone grew silent as
their beloved king stepped within view. The curved, stone roof of the tower
provided protective shade to the king. There were two other men within the
recesses of the tower awaiting the time that they, too, should step forward.

King Mosiah acknowledged them both and ushered them to stand on
either side of him. "My beloved brothers and sisters!" he began. "It pleases
my heart to see your honest and sincere faces this day. Look among you and
you will see men, women, and children who are your friends; all of whom are
children of a loving God who has seen fit to reunite us once again!"

The people looked around and smiled at their neighbors.

"Through the tender loving mercies of our God, I have with me
today two men whom you should all get to know."

Mosiah turned and warmly gestured with his outstretched arm for the
man on his right to step forward. The former king, Limhi, nodded and
obliged. As he did so, he was taken aback by the spontaneous cheers that
erupted from the people who filled the square. Limhi felt humbled in the
presence of King Mosiah and was somewhat embarrassed by the
acknowledgment He slowly raised his hand to acknowledge the well-wishing
throng. A smile crept across his face as he turned his gaze from side to side,

taking in the view of the filled city square, smiling and waving, and humbly giving the people a chance to see him.

"I see that many of you recognize this good man!" Mosiah exclaimed. "That is a good thing! Very good indeed! He has quite a tale to share with all of you! But, there's another man here whom I also want you to see and know." He turned to Alma and ushered him forward.

The peaceful city again erupted with cheers and applause. The boisterous response made him feel uncomfortable. He simply considered himself to be a humble servant of the Lord. He silently smiled and bowed his head in acknowledgment of their affection. He knew that his feelings of discomfort were nothing compared to the opportunity and right that these fine people had earned to cheer and rejoice at the miraculous deliverance of the people with which their God had seen fit to bless them.

Mosiah put his hand on Alma's shoulder. Alma turned and looked at his new king. Both men smiled at each other, then Alma stepped back. Mosiah turned to Limhi and both men nodded at each other as Limhi, too, stepped back. Mosiah faced the Nephites and raised his hands to calm the crowd. It took a few moments, as everyone was on their feet with excitement.

As the din dimmed and faded, Mosiah began, "My good brothers and sisters. It pleases me almost beyond words to welcome you to Zarahemla on this fine day and for such a blessed occasion. Many of you have traveled long and far to be here today. Some of you have suffered through tremendous perils and even persecutions before being able to enjoy the sanctuary we offer in this beautiful land of Zarahemla. It's only through the blessings and mercies of our beloved God that we are united here today. I know that there are many of you who know some of the tales that can be told among you. But, there are very few – if any – who can tell the full tale of all of you fine people. Rather than let you live by rumors alone, I have invited you here and asked that Limhi and Alma share the accounts of their people with us all, that we may know and understand how well the good Lord has watched over us as a people, even when we have been spread so broadly apart. I have asked Limhi to begin a tale that Alma will conclude. Please give both of these men of God your full attention and respect."

The crowd was in a hush as Limhi again stepped forward to address the crowd. Mosiah stepped back into the recess of the tower to allow all attention to fall onto this king who had so willingly renounced his crown and sworn allegiance to him.

Limhi reached for the rail of the tower and leaned on it. He scanned the crowd of expectant faces. He bowed his head and his eyes fell on Gideon who sat with his arm around his wife, near the base of the tower. Gideon smiled and nodded approvingly. Limhi returned the smile and nodded, gathering the strength of will to begin a difficult tale.

In a loud voice that carried through the square, as it was amplified and directed by the unique design of the stone-roofed speaking tower, Limhi began, "I am Limhi, son of Noah, who was the son of Zeniff. This same Zeniff is the man who once lived here in Zarahemla. At that time there was a tremendous interest among the people to find and return to the land of our forefathers, the land from which they were forced to flee only a generation earlier, the land of Nephi. I am here to tell you this day, that Zeniff was successful. He did indeed lead many Nephites back to the land of Nephi. Through the mercies of our great God, the Lamanites took us in and allowed us to return to that wondrous land. There we did dwell and make our homes. We rebuilt the city. We rebuilt the temple. We tilled the earth and tended our flocks."

There were those among the crowded square who had traveled to Zarahemla from rural cities, towns, and dwellings who had heard only rumors of this bold telling. They were astonished to find that it was, indeed, true and that here before them stood a witness to the events that they believed too incredible to be true. Everyone continued to lean on Limhi's every word, anxious to hear his tale in full.

"For many years, we prospered in that beautiful land. The soil was rich and responded well to our efforts to farm. Grains, fruits, berries, and a host of other crops grew in abundance. Our flocks also multiplied and gave of their milk and furs. We lived a life that was joyous and blessed. We ourselves multiplied and began to spread ourselves between the city of Nephi and the city of Shilom that was nearby."

Limhi went into detail about the many prosperous activities they eagerly engaged in, there in their new home. He emphasized how thrilled they were to once again live in the land of their forefathers. He also stressed that the people remembered who had watched over and blessed them so richly and that under the righteous reign of King Zeniff, they gave thanks to their Divine Father daily.

"As we prospered," he continued, "our neighbors, the Lamanites, began to fear that we were growing too numerous. They feared that we would overrun the land and push them from their homes. They could not understand that we had no leanings to do this. My grandfather, Zeniff, only wanted to live in Nephi in love and peace with his neighbors. But, King Laman was persuaded otherwise. He led a terrible army against us. King Zeniff called upon God for protection and the Lord saw fit to be with us. We had not forgotten Him, so He did not forget us in our hour of need."

"We gathered our men and took up arms to defend our homes, our families, and our land. The fighting was intense, but we were victorious. We drove the enemy back and secured our rights to continue to live as we had lived. Sadly, many thousands of Lamanites lost their lives that day. We were fortunate, but still very sad to learn that only a couple hundred of our brethren had been slain. We buried them respectfully and with gratitude for their sacrifices."

"Under the righteous leadership of King Zeniff, our people continued to prosper. More than a dozen years passed and King Laman was called home to his Maker. His son, also named King Laman, determined that he would be the cause of ridding the land of us once and for all. He also gathered an army and led it against us. King Zeniff was by this time an old man, but he chose to again lead our people in defense of their homes and lives. Again, the Lord blessed us with victory. And, again, the Lamanites lost ten times the number of lives than we did. It grieved our hearts to bury the dead, but we were eternally grateful that the fighting was at an end and that we could again live in peace."

Limhi told more of the dealings of his people under King Zeniff. He told of their comings and goings. He told of their tilling of the earth and keeping of flocks. He told of the schooling of their children and of the learning of trades. It was pleasing for him to tell of all these positive aspects of life in the land of Nephi.

He also told of the people's sorrow when their beloved King Zeniff grew old and passed on to dwell with his fathers. Limhi's audience in the square mourned with him as he told of the end of a great man's life. Through Limhi, they felt that they had gotten to know him, too.

Limhi's account now shifted dramatically. His voice took on a much more serious tone, and his face shifted into a somewhat stern appearance as he told of his own father, King Noah. He was deeply – very deeply – ashamed of the man. However, he knew that if any lasting impact of good were to come of the trials his people had suffered, it would be painfully necessary to relate the sordid tale of the his father and his evil influence on a once-great people.

He told of Noah's lazy idolatry. He told of the mocking of the temple by turning it into a winery. He told of Noah's abolishment of the former king's noble priests and the degeneracy of choosing wicked men to fill that role. He spoke of the atrocities they performed, all in the name of "leadership" and "their rights." The people cringed to hear it. Parents were thankful that Limhi spared them too great of details in the acts of the people during King Noah's reign.

He also spoke of the coming of Abinadi. At this point, he deferred to Alma. He turned to his counterpart, and with a sweeping gesture of his arm, reached out to him. The people's gaze shifted to Alma as he stepped forward.

Alma began his portion of the tale, "I'm not proud to say that I was one of King Noah's priests."

This acknowledgment sent a series of whispers and murmurs through the crowd. After having heard of the idolatries of King Noah and his priests, this statement sent a series of particularly confused thoughts through the minds of those who had not yet heard the full tale. They were confused on this point because they had understood that Alma was a man of God. They had heard that he had broken off from the people of King Noah because of his conversion.

They had also heard pieces of the tale of Alma's miraculous journey to Zarahemla. They wondered how such a spiritual and powerful leader could have been one of these wicked, idolatrous priests. They listened intently with the expectation of hearing a curious and compelling account.

Alma continued, "I see by the looks on many of you, that because of the faithful account of this good brother here –" at this, Alma gestured to Limhi, "you feel that you fully understand what a terrible admission this is for me to make. Let me first acknowledge that your assumption is incorrect. It must be said that you CANNOT possibly understand just how wicked and evil King Noah was. I don't believe that even his son here can fully comprehend what a reprehensible and destructive influence that king and his priests had on our people. And, again, I tell you, I was one of those priests."

Alma paused a moment and let the people stare at him in silence. He felt it was important to drive this point home to their hearts and minds. They needed to understand the significance of what he was telling them, and the unique perspective that he had of the details. He also knew that this painful beginning was necessary for them to comprehend, if they were to more fully appreciate the wondrous conclusion this story held.

"I was a willing participant in the evil ways of King Noah. I supported him when I should not have. My soul has quailed at the memory of my failings. I have wept many bitter tears over these deeds." Alma paused again, as his emotions caught hold of him. He then continued, "But, the merciful God of Heaven saw fit to rescue us and our people. He sent a humble servant to us named Abinadi. This man was weak to look upon, but masterful and powerful in so many ways that I was not, for the Lord had fortified him with His Spirit and the word of truth."

"He came to us and warned the people of the evil path they were treading. He warned of the evil influence of our king and his priests. He told the people many things which were true and necessary, but the people would not hear any of it."

Alma's voice quivered a moment or two as he continued the tale of Abinadi's first mission to the people of King Noah. It then took on more strength and determination as he reiterated the prophecies and teachings of that man whom he had grown to love. The more Alma spoke, the more people grew to be impressed with Abinadi.

"But, as I said, the people, and our king, would hear nothing of these teachings. We thrust him from our city. We sent him out of our lives. We banished him from the land."

There were gasps let out from among those of the people to whom this story was news. They had erroneously assumed that it would only take one visit from a prophet for the people to turn around and mend their ways. They did not appreciate the struggle it would take to recapture the hearts of this wayward city.

"Two years passed," Alma continued. "Two whole years. And we had given no thought to repentance. Instead, we had grown worse. Abinadi came to us in disguise. He was disguised so that he could gain entrance into the city. Once within our walls, he shed his disguise and again preached boldly to us. The people were again incensed. They captured him and indignantly dragged him before the king and complained horribly against him."

"They repeated and mocked the words and prophesies which he had shared with them. Prophecies which were borne to us by the Spirit of God were spit back at us by the people, as if they were the idle tales and boasts of children. And we, we the king's priests, were offended and angered by them. We could not believe that such a wretch could be so sanctimonious as to call us, the king's priests – and the king himself – to repentance!"

"King Noah threw the man of God into prison and let him sit. It was more of a dungeon than a prison. He sat there and suffered for days, while we glutted ourselves in our pride and abominations. We dreamed up all sorts of hideous sport to make of this poor soul. It got to the point where we were eager to drag him before us and berate him. When he was brought up from the foul prison, his clothes were tattered, his hair unkempt. He reeked of the unavoidable putrid smells which permeated his cell. Several of us had difficulty withholding our scoffs and jeers that begged to leap from our ill-tempered mouths, just at the sight of him."

"Yet, he bore it all in stride. He stood with his head erect. He did not have a proud posture, but he certainly had one of dignity. I marveled at how a man so downtrodden could look so dignified. I shrugged it off as best I could, but still I also sensed something of power about him. It was a power that I could not place, for it was clearly not a physical power. I was to learn that it was something far greater than the physical."

"If his mastery was apparent when he was unceremoniously dragged before us, it was nothing compared to the moment he began to speak. We had cued up our most notorious debaters to berate and verbally defile this man. Yet, he withstood our questions – our attacks. He allowed us to question him and then turned the tables back on us. We were astounded by his bravery, his questions, his answers, his teachings, and his very spirit."

"At least, I was," Alma clarified.

"I tried to delight in the accusations of Amulon and the other priests, but I could not. I watched him speak. I heard his words. All the while, my heart burned within me. I must share with you his words."

At this, Alma went into great detail telling of the account of Abinadi. He told of the king's questions, the priests' accusations, and Abinadi's bold replies. He told of the softening of the king that was hindered by the jeers of the priests. He spoke of his futile and nearly fatal defense of Abinadi. Finally, he told of his own flight from the king's court and his seclusion in the hall of records.

"But, now my portion of the account must wait a moment. It's necessary that King Limhi continue his portion of the tale." Alma bowed and deferred to Limhi.

"Thank you, Alma. But, before I continue, I must make it clear to all that I have renounced my kingship. I have humbly, willingly, and thankfully stepped down from that sacred office and have sworn allegiance to King Mosiah. The people must have only one king, and that king must be Mosiah." Limhi bowed.

A cheering and stomping arose from the throng in vivid support of Limhi's words. This continued until everyone was on their feet in agreement. King Mosiah was forced to step forward and kindly acknowledge the proposition. He held up his hands and eventually calmed the crowd.

"I thank you all for this support. Truly, I do. But, now is not the time to speak of me. Now is the time to hear from our good brethren from the south. I beg of you to continue to listen. Limhi, please continue."

Limhi nodded and took the center of the platform once again. He told of the death of Abinadi. Tears adorned many cheeks at this. He told of Noah's wrath against Alma. He told of Gideon's wrath at Noah. At this, Gideon stirred uncomfortably. The memory still burned within him. Rachel squeezed his hand to comfort him and pull him back to the present.

Limhi told of many things. He gave a full accounting of the Lamanite attack that followed Gideon's charge against Noah, and the bold sacrifice of the Nephite daughters who pled on behalf of the people. This time, it was

Rachel who squirmed at the memory. Gideon put his arm around her shoulders and pulled her tightly to him. They looked at each other and Rachel managed a grateful, silent smile.

Limhi told of their lives within Nephi under the oppression of the Lamanite rule. He told of the reprisals of the Lamanites when Noah's renegade priests stole the Lamanite's daughters and how Gideon helped secure peace for a time. His account continued to speak of later wars and sad attempts to free themselves. He even told of the journey to a desolate land that resulted in the finding of 24 metal plates, but no better news or word on how to free themselves.

He made it clear that he and the people were made to know that the prophesies of Abinadi were being fulfilled in every detail. Their only hope of release would be through their own sincere and complete repentance and reliance on the Lord their God. He made it known that they truly believed that the coming of Ammon and his brethren was in direct answer to their prayers.

Upon his concluding remarks, he turned the time back to Alma. Alma also filled the people's ears and hearts with the tale of his own repentance, preaching and flight to freedom. The people were filled with awe and wonder as the story unfolded. They were relieved by his telling of the building of the city of Helam and their lives there. They were then terribly dismayed by the coming of Amulon and the resulting persecutions. They were equally amazed at Alma's miraculous exodus from Helam and eventual arrival in Zarahemla – a land which none of them had ever seen before.

"I wish," Alma continued, "all of you to know something of great importance. I myself was at one time one of the vilest sinners. I was enslaved with evil deeds, evil thoughts, evil power, and opportunity. I allowed myself to be subject to the devil and his tyranny. I mistook freedom of action for deeds without consequence. I learned to my bitter shame that such beliefs are lies. Each and every action I took was preceded by a choice I willingly made."

"It would be easy to claim that I had no choice," Alma clarified. "But, that would be wrong. I chose to follow a fallen man, this man Noah that we had crowned as our king. As a result, I fell, too. I squandered away my opportunities to do good for my fellow man by choosing instead the vain and fleeting pleasures of the flesh. I could have – and certainly deserved to have – lost my loving wife and family in these awful pursuits. I thank my God daily that I did not. I treasure my wife. I treasure our relationship. I treasure our son. I will be eternally grateful for her patience, her long-suffering, and her forgiving, loving nature."

Alma looked down and saw his wife staring back up at him. From the distance, he could not make out the tears that streaked down her face, but he knew that they were there. His own face was equally streaked.

"I had become a corrupt man, barely worthy of being called a son of God - I felt. Abinadi, and the Spirit of God that he brought into my life, made me see with clarity - for the first time in my life - the shortcomings of my soul. No, not of my soul, but of my wanton desires and shortsighted whims. I had betrayed the Spirit within me. I had pushed it aside and for the first time, I had realized this."

"Upon this realization, I felt unworthy, unwanted, vulnerable, wretched. I felt distanced from a God I did not yet know. I felt unworthy to be in His presence or even on His earth. I wished the rocks and hills to fall on me and cover my deeds for eternity. I did not dare consider that I could turn to Him for help - when I needed it most. I did not dare to pray - when I knew that prayer held my only hope of salvation."

"Yet, I could not shake from my mind the words of Abinadi. He spoke of a Savior - a loving Savior - who would give His life for all mankind. Something deep within me knew that that would include me, as well, though I dared not believe it. I have never experienced anything in my life so difficult as the beginnings of my heartfelt prayer to God. I felt that for one such as I to even mention His name - to dare to call on Him for help - to bring attention to myself and my condition - was nothing short of blasphemy. And, yet, I say again, that I forced myself to do as Abinadi had directed. I prayed all the harder."

"The feelings that came over me were not as immediate as one might think. They were gradual, but they were also very real. I was so caught up in my own cries and desperation that at first I could not notice the calming, healing influence of His Spirit that was being poured out so lovingly upon me. When I finally took notice, it was nothing short of miraculous to feel and bask in His love and forgiveness. I knew above all else that God is real. That He loves and cares about even a wretch such as I. I became determined to share His word and will with all mankind."

"I stand before you this day as His witness. I tell you with all sincerity of heart and clarity of mind that He lives, and what is more, He loves us - each and every one of us. If He can forgive one so brutally evil as I had become, and can condescend to forgive one so caught up in the evils of this world as I had been, then I testify that He can equally forgive you of your trespasses. I exhort each of you to take hold of this and move forward with faith!"

Alma's impassioned testimony deeply moved all of those who heard it. The spirit of his words and the Spirit of the Lord fell on the people with unforgettable power. The people knew without a doubt that they were listening to the words of a man of God. They knew that he was inspired. They knew that he had a power from on high to do great deeds and to teach the lessons of eternity. They also knew that as testimony of this, it was only the divine guidance of God that had managed to get these fine people to this noble city.

All of the Nephite people were filled with overpowering emotions. As they thought of the tender mercies their Lord had shown to the people, they were filled with thanksgiving and joy. But, as they thought of the evils perpetuated on one another by men who should have been their brethren, they were filled with sadness and loss for those who had gone astray, as well as for the trials their brethren had endured. In the end, they were pleased beyond measure that they were now reunited and that all of the wanderers had found their way home.

Upon the conclusion of all accounts, King Mosiah again stepped forward. He was among those who were deeply impressed by the words of both these men, but in particular, the final testimony of Alma. It took him a moment to speak.

When he finally regained that ability, he addressed the assembly, "My good people! My brothers and my sisters, I believe that there are many things to be learned from the accounts we have heard this day. Many of you are witnesses to these deeds and acts."

He reached out his arms and slowed waved them outward gesturing to the people in the square. Many men and women nodded in acknowledgment Some hugged each other with tears in their eyes and thanks on their lips.

"We must always remember these things. We must remember the impact of evil among us. Leaders, fathers, mothers, children, all of us must strive to set worthy examples for those around us. We must remember to be bold and despise that which is evil and stop it before it takes root among us. Always cry to the Lord for strength and lend of your strength to your fellow citizens, so that we can remember to whom we must look for our redemption.

"I have thought and prayed long and hard about this next matter. I am certain that if you do the same, you will come to agree with what I have been taught of God. And, it is this: we need a spiritual leader. We need a man who knows how to lead us in righteousness. We need a man who seeks not the honors of men, but simply wishes to do the will of God. I believe – no, I know – we have found such a man in Alma."

"As I said, I have prayed for guidance in this matter. I have received a witness that this is so. I have asked Alma if he will be willing to serve as the spiritual leader of this people. He has humbly agreed. I ask all of you to support him in this. Go to God in prayer and seek your own witness of this act, and then do all that you feel you can to support him in helping us all."

A great cry of "Hosanna!" leapt up and echoed throughout the city.

Chapter 33

Decisions

Mosiah waited. He knew it was best to simply wait and give his people a moment to express themselves gleefully, than to try to interrupt the rejoicing of this excited throng of Nephites. When the cheering subsided, he looked down at the many, eager faces that peered back up at him. For a moment, he was too moved to speak. He was moved as much by the love and warmth he felt from the hundreds and thousands who were encamped below him as he was by Alma's testimony.

"My dear, beloved brothers and sisters," he said at last. He chose those words carefully and sincerely, hoping to convey the love he felt within his heart. "My beloved people. I am thankful beyond words that you have had the opportunity to hear these words this day. I have been fortunate to have already heard these tales of faith and struggle. Hearing them again has touched my heart as deeply as it did the first time. I believe you can now understand why I called you here to hear these words for yourselves."

Gideon, who had come there feeling that he knew the events as well as anyone, if not better, found himself nodding his head in fervent agreement. Hannah sat by his side, tears streamed down her pretty face. Gideon looked at her and tried to speak to her, but he could feel his emotions welling up from deep within him. He knew that if he tried to speak, they would get the better of him and his voice would crack and his words would come out in thankful sobs. He held his peace and gave her a smile and hugged her tightly then looked back up at the tower.

"It is one thing to hear of the tender mercies of a loving God," Mosiah continued, "It is quite another to hear a direct witness to such marvelous events tell of them. My own heart aches for the many who have suffered and even died because of the vain foolishness of mankind. Yet, it leaps for joy when I marvel upon the blessings that can come of being unified in the faith of God."

"We have many choices to make, my people. For one, we must decide to accept these fine brethren back into our fold, back into our lands, back into our homes, and in our hearts. They have been granted temporary residences, but what say you now, shall we make space enough for this people to permanently move into our cities and lands?"

If the cheering was great before, it was nothing like that which erupted from the city square at that moment. People were standing and jumping and waving their arms and clapping and shouting. Several had thrown their head coverings into the air. Birds in the surrounding jungle were startled from their nests and took flight. Men and women hugged their neighbors with wide and firm embraces. The people were truly one in mind and heart.

"It warms my heart to see your acceptance and generosity." Mosiah beamed. "No king has ever served a more delightsome people. We will make space in our hearts and our cities for these fine people – all of them!"

Mosiah continued to survey the throng, basking in the moment. All about him he saw pleasant faces lit up by a love for their neighbors. They were not individuals caught up in their own affairs, but a unified people – a grand family of man. Who knew how long such feelings of welcome and oneness would last? At the moment, it did not matter. He was enjoying this brief time with his people.

After a few more words, he finally concluded, "Now it is time that those of us who have homes, to return to them. It is my prayer that you find all well there upon your return. Those of you who are seeking homes and lands, please stay a little longer. We will work to find you places where you can dwell and be happy. May God be with and watch over you all, in all you do and say!"

With that, he waved a final farewell and ended the ceremony. He stepped back within the shaded recess of the speaking tower and turned to see Alma and Limhi. Limhi's head was reverently, almost meekly, bowed. Mosiah put a warm, fatherly hand on his shoulder.

"Good Limhi, I thank you for coming and sharing all that you have shared with us," Mosiah said. You are a good man. King Zeniff would have been proud of you!"

At this, Limhi looked up quickly, with a start. This was an unexpected and hitherto unrealized fulfillment of a longing that Limhi had subconsciously held. He looked at Mosiah with searching eyes. Mosiah smiled back and nodded reassuringly. "I would have to say that he would be very proud of you, indeed."

"Thank you, your majesty!" Limhi replied. "I truly appreciate that," was all he could think to say.

It had not dawned on him until Mosiah spoke those words that he truly had a longing for the affection – no, also the acceptance – of his grandfather. Zeniff was a man whom he could only remember from his youth. What he could remember was that Zeniff was kindly, soft-spoken, white-haired, and loving. He was a far cry from Limhi's father, Noah.

In most ways, the two men were complete opposites. He now realized that as his detest for his own father's actions and behavior had grown into loathing, he had developed a longing for the presence of his grandfather.

He had not been able to place the longing into so many words, though. It was just a wish for something better for himself and his people.

He had been so caught up in the affairs of trying to free them from Lamanite oppression, that he had thought that his longing was simply for that freedom. He now realized it was more than that. He suddenly wished he were a little boy again – at least for a moment – and could give his beloved grandfather one more hug, one more kiss on the cheek, and tell him just one more time how much he loved and respected the great man. And, he realized just how much he wanted to be able to walk in his footsteps to be more like him, and – yes – to please him.

"I thank you most deeply," Limhi added to Mosiah, bowing low, still at a loss for words.

Mosiah nodded again and turned to Alma. "Alma, I was touched by your account. I have heard it before, yes, but I was deeply moved. You have a spirit about you that is almost tangible. I feel it when you speak. I feel it even now as we stand here. You are a great man, a great man of God."

"I am but a humble servant of the Almighty," Alma replied with a bow of his head.

"Yes, you certainly are," the king observed. "Our people will be greatly blessed to have you serve them and lead them back to our God. I cannot tell you how thankful I am that you have returned; that both of you have come back to the fold, along with your brothers and sisters. This is a great day for the Nephite nation!"

As the men turned in preparation to descend from the tower, Alma reached over and put his hand on Limhi's arm to give him reassurance. Standing at the exit he said, "I also appreciated hearing your words. I had wondered what had become of those we left behind. My mind was often troubled for your welfare, but my heart told me that all would be well. It sounds like it was not easy, but in the end it was well."

"Yes, you are correct," Limhi agreed.

They began again to leave the tower, when Limhi paused. "Alma," he said.

Alma stopped and turned back, "Yes?"

"I wonder if you could do me – do my people – a great service?"

"Certainly, if it is in my power. I would be honored."

"You spoke of baptizing your people in the Waters of Mormon."

"Yes?"

"My people – I – have not been baptized. When Ammon and his brethren came, I asked them if they could baptize us. Ammon said that he could not. I still – I still wish to be baptized. I wish to leave my sins behind and covenant with God that I will serve Him all my days. I wish to show my willingness to humbly obey Him. I know that many of my people wish the same. Can you – will you do this for us? Are you able to baptize us?"

"I am touched," Alma replied. "As I said, it will be an honor to perform this most sacred ordinance for you and your people. Thank you for asking me."

* * * * *

Below in the square, there was still a great deal of rejoicing. Men and women looked to each other and clasped hands. Some embraced. While tents were being disassembled, many words of welcome were spoken between strangers. There were even invitations extended and directions given to places or homes which were known to be vacant. The assimilation of the societies was indeed sincere and heartfelt.

Ammon walked over to Gideon, "Well, Gideon, it looks like you and your people have found homes – or at least soon will. It pleases me to have played a small role in helping your people return to Zarahemla."

"Small role?!" Gideon exclaimed with a smile. "We would still be wandering the jungles, or worse, if it were not for you and your good brethren! We are eternally in your debt." Gideon bowed sincerely.

"No, no you are not. I was just glad to have found you," he replied. "It has been, perhaps, the greatest thing I have had the good fortune to have been a part of." Ammon was most genuine and inwardly reflective with these words. He added, "So, will you and your friends move into Zarahemla proper or will you choose instead a farm or town nearby? We have room for several new homes in my neighborhood. I would be honored to have you take residence there."

"I appreciate the offer," Gideon replied. "Truly, I do. But, we have somewhere else in mind, don't we sweetheart?" Gideon turned to Hannah who walked up beside him. He put his arm around her as he spoke these words.

Hannah smiled and nodded. Looking up to Gideon, she replied, "Yes, we certainly do."

"Where, may I ask, is that?" Ammon asked with interest.

Gideon got excited at this and was eager to tell. "Do you remember that valley – the one we stayed in – it was a few day's journey from here? – " the more he said, the faster he spoke.

"Whoa! Not so fast!" Ammon teased. "Yes, I believe I know the valley you mean. It had a small lake that was fed by a mountain river, did it not?"

"Yes! That's the one!" Gideon exclaimed. "I have never seen a more beautiful valley! Nor have I ever felt the Spirit more strongly in a place - until today, of course. Hannah and I were both taken by it. When we prayed that night before retiring, we gave thanks for the Lord's guiding hand in our lives. For His bringing us together. For His bringing us out of bondage. And, for the hopes we could now enjoy of a bright future together. We were filled with His loving spirit. It was a very special experience for us both. One that we will never forget. We have talked about it at length, and we would like to make that wondrous place our home."

Ammon looked at the two. He could see how much they loved each other. They were good people. He was impressed by their spirit and eagerness. He rejoiced inwardly at the opportunity it had been to render them the services which he had.

"It sounds wonderful!" he said.

"It is, and it will be!" Gideon said. "Ammon, please join us." Gideon added.

"Yes, come and bring your family and friends," Hannah coaxed.

"Leave Zarahemla and move there?" Ammon mused.

"Yes, we can build a new city," Gideon said. "We can till new farms and plant new crops. It will be a grand place. You will see, and you will love it."

"This is very tempting," Ammon said. He considered long and hard for a moment. He had grown to really enjoy Gideon's company. He knew he would miss him when he left. "Who else would be going?"

"All who wish to, are more than welcome!" Gideon swept his outstretched arm widely, indicating the entire populace. "We have actually mentioned this to King Limhi."

"You have?" Ammon was intrigued. "What did he say?"

"He asked if he could join us," Hannah replied.

"I was a little surprised," Gideon confessed, "but, not too terribly. He is a good man. He loves his people. He has been under tremendous pressures. I think he is actually looking forward to living among them as one of them. We told him we would be delighted and honored to have him come. He said he was actually looking forward to tilling the ground with his own hands. I think he meant it, too."

"I believe he probably did," Ammon acknowledged. "And, I believe I will probably take you up on your offer!"

"Wonderful! It will be so good to have you with us!" Gideon said.

"Yes! This will be great!" Hannah added.

"We will be telling and inviting all the others, as well," Gideon added. "We are not trying to exclude anyone, nor do we expect everyone to come. This is not meant to be a private city. Just a peaceful one!"

*****

A crisp, beautiful morning found Limhi, Alma, and a host of Limhi's people gathered by the waters of the river Sidon. They had dug a small pool to the one side and allowed the flowing waters to cascade into and fill the pool. Traces of mud were just settling and revealing the purity of the water. The sun had just completed an impressive rise above the horizon. Its rays made the jungle foliage shine. The scent of many flowers curled and flowed in the gentle breeze. Birds chirped gleefully in the trees.

Limhi stood by Alma's side. They had conversed while the diggers made the temporary font for the many souls who had followed Limhi. Alma had told Limhi of his plans to build permanent baptismal fonts within the city proper.

"That will be a great thing for the Nephite nation, Alma," Limhi replied. "But, I have to admit, it will be difficult to improve upon the beauty of nature that we have before us. It is as if God Himself were smiling upon us from Above."

"I will agree with that," Alma acknowledged. "It would not surprise me at all to know that He is. This is a wonderful thing you have agreed to do, Limhi. You and your good people have suffered much, but I sense that your suffering has led you to understand the importance of the covenant you are about to undertake."

"Yes, it certainly has," Limhi agreed. "I do not expect life to suddenly get easier because of this, but I do believe it will help put my soul to rest. It is good for the soul to knowingly do those things which God has decreed."

"You are a wise man, indeed," Alma observed. "Are you ready?"

"Certainly!" was the former king's reply.

Alma and Limhi waded into the pool. The water was warm. The people reverently gathered around. The river Sidon continued to stream past them giving off a steady gurgling that had a calming effect. Alma stepped beside Limhi and held out his left arm. Limhi grasped it firmly and humbly stood, allowing Alma complete control of the ordinance. Alma raised his right arm to the square and in a firm, strong voice called Limhi by name and announced the baptismal prayer. Then, he gently, but completely, submersed the former sovereign underneath the water.

As Limhi came up from the water, a bright, angelic smile spread across his face. His whole being was filled with the Spirit. He knew a joy like none he had ever known before. As he looked at Alma, Alma saw that his face was beaming with love and power. Limhi praised God and wept for joy. He spoke of great things that his people would do and his immense thanksgiving for finally – finally – being able to enter into this sacred and lasting covenant with God.

Gideon reached out a steady hand and took hold of Limhi's. He helped his former king, and current friend, out of the cleansing baptismal waters. As Gideon wrapped his fingers around the Limhi's forearm, he was surprised to feel the warmth of Limhi. It impressed him that it was not just the warmth of his body, but must have been the warmth of his very soul.

Limhi exited the pool and stood facing Gideon. Still holding his one arm, he put his other hand on Gideon's shoulder. The two men faced each other. Gideon remained silent, expectantly awaiting what Limhi might say.

"The good Lord be with you, Gideon!" Limhi extolled. "And, with your family! This is a great day, Gideon. It is a great day indeed!"

It's doubtful that any man had ever been so eager and so purely thankful for partaking in an ordinance as Limhi was that day. He stood by and acted as a witness as his people – one by one – entered the waters of baptism with Alma. And, one by one, they each came forth out of the waters, praising God and giving thanks for their safety and their salvation.

All of their struggles, hardships, fears, woes, and trials were put far behind them. They looked back to what they knew of Abinadi and his preaching. They praised his very name for having the courage to do as God had directed and finally bring to them the Gospel which they, at that time, were too blind to see. Now they embraced it fully and completely. Now they were filled to overflowing with love and thankfulness. Now their eyes were fully opened and they wished that Abinadi could see what great things he had done for his people.

They sensed that – somehow – he knew.

Settling In

Those who had journeyed to Zarahemla returned to their homes. They took with them the stories of the marvelous, triumphant, and also tragic events that had transpired among their brethren. Those fathers and mothers who had been most impressed would repeat the tales many times to their children. They would use them as models for their children's behavior and choices for many years to come.

Mosiah continued to reign over his people in righteousness. Not all that transpired under his reign was happy and good, but he did his best to seek the Lord's guidance and will in all that he decreed. He was greatly impressed and moved by the tales of King Zeniff, King Noah, King Limhi, King Amulon, Alma, as well as the record of the kings of the Jaredites. The impact of so many examples of both good and bad kings would have a profound and lasting impact on him and would be the impetus behind monumental decision he would one day make.

Alma continued to serve out the remainder of his life as the spiritual leader – the prophet – of the Nephite nation. He established seven branches of their church within the walls of the city of Zarahemla alone. He set up teachers to teach the people, and spent his days ensuring that these teachers taught the pure teachings of God. He also became the official record keeper of the people. Alma spent the remainder of his days establishing churches and watching over their affairs, and meticulously recording the developing saga of the Nephite people upon the metal plates which he preserved.

Gideon, and many of those who had traveled north with him and Limhi, settled in the valley that they named "Gideon." They built a modest city, which they also named "Gideon." The people did this out of love and respect for a humble man who did great things to save and preserve his nation. They put their greatest trust in God, and sought to both serve and understand Him all their days. Gideon, who had been a great military leader and an inspiration and advisor to the king, took on a new emphasis in his life.

Perhaps it was having seen what he had seen in his days; perhaps it was hearing the words of Alma. Perhaps it was feeling the Spirit of the Lord touch his heart; or, perhaps it was becoming a father that made him take stock of his life and decide to become a spiritual leader. Maybe it was a combination of all of these things and much more. At any rate, he spent the remainder of his days living the life of a spiritual guide and teacher for the people. He touched lives in many ways for many years. He never stopped standing for truth and righteousness under any circumstance.

Under the direction and leadership of great men such as Gideon, Alma, and King Mosiah, the Nephite nation prospered – for a time.

Chapter Notes

A general note about this book is that this is an adaptation of a portion of the *Book of Mormon*. As such, an attempt has been made to stay true to the original text where possible. There are many places where text has been taken verbatim from the original source and others where it has been paraphrased. Some unnamed characters from the original source have been given names, while other characters have been created fresh. Some events have been consolidated, while others have been elaborated on, or created from scratch. All of this has been done for the purpose of enabling the telling of the story in this format. This was not done in an attempt to improve on the original source.

The author highly recommends that readers of this work read the original text found in *The Book of Mormon* in order to gain the full impact of, and appreciation for, that account. It is taken from the portion of the book known as Mosiah 7 through Alma 1. The following notes summarize comments about the various chapters of this work, including commentary regarding which portions of the story came from the original text found in *The Book of Mormon* and which events have been fabricated. They also give dates for when events occurred and references for where the original text for the storyline can be found.

The author wishes to note that the dates listed in these chapter notes coincide with the estimated dates listed in the original source material according to the chapters and verses from the original source that have been used in the various chapters of this new work. In the course of converting the events from the original source into this format, some of the events have been altered such that the dates listed in the original source do not necessarily line up with the events as they have been depicted in this work. The author accepts full responsibility for the date discrepancies he has introduced into his work.

Chapter 1 Notes:
124 BC. This chapter based on: Mosiah 7:1-7.
Under the commission of King Mosiah, of Zarahemla, Ammon leads a group of sixteen men southward to find the Land of Nephi, and to determine what has become of a people that had been led down there by a man named Zeniff, several years previous. The men find the Land of Nephi, but their advance party – including Ammon – is captured and thrown into prison by other Nephites.

The journey of Ammon's party southward and their subsequent finding of the city of Nephi are somewhat perplexing when viewed by the standpoint of Ammon's men. It's clear that Ammon and his men did not know the exact location of the city of Nephi. It was a city which his forefather's had left, but which he and his comrades had never seen. The original text stated that, "they knew not the course they should travel in the wilderness to go up to the land of Lehi-Nephi; therefore they wandered many days in the wilderness, even forty days did they wander" (Mosiah 7:4).

That they found the city at all is somewhat of a miracle. Basically, they traveled south and "wandered." The terrain was likely thick jungles, similar to what is in the Yucatan Peninsula today, which is difficult to navigate. Getting lost, even then, was not unheard of as was manifested later by the Lamanite guards who got so lost in the wilderness that they needed Alma's people to guide them back to Nephi (Mosiah 23:36). These were men who lived in the area. Imagine the difficulty of people coming down from up north. To describe them as "wandering" is probably an extremely accurate description. And yet, they made it.

Another interesting aspect of their honing in on Nephi is the potential quandary over why they managed to go there instead of to the city of Shilom. According to the original text, Ammon journeyed from the north to Nephi in the south. It also says that Shilom was north of Nephi. If this is the case, it could be wondered how or why Ammon's party missed Shilom and found Nephi instead, as it's clear from the text that when they arrived in the area, they came off of a hill and approached Nephi before being captured by the king's guards.

There were many potential ways that this could have been depicted. It could have been that Shilom was so much smaller than Nephi that one look would tell them that Nephi was the city to be targeted. It could have been that Shilom was in ruins and Nephi was not. It could have been that somehow they could not see Shilom from their vantage point. It could have been that as they looked down toward Nephi, their eyes caught hold of Limhi and his guards and they hurried over to meet them before they slipped back into their city. It could have even been the case that they did indeed go to Shilom first, and then to Nephi.

Very little about this is written in the original text. It simply reads, "And when they had wandered forty days they came to a hill, which is north of the land of Shilom, and there they pitched their tents. And Ammon took three of his brethren, and their names were Amaleki, Helem, and Hem, and they went down into the land of Nephi. And behold, they met the king of the people who were in the land of Nephi, and in the land of Shilom; and they were surrounded by the king's guard, and were taken, and were bound, and were committed to prison" (Mosiah 7: 5-7).

A final note on the terrain deals with how the *Book of Mormon* consistently refers to traveling from the land of Zarahemla to the land of Nephi as going "up" to Nephi and "down" to Zarahemla. Modern scholars and archeologists are becoming more and more convinced that Zarahemla was somewhere on the northeastern end of the Yucatan peninsula and Nephi was farther inland of that peninsula. While the mountains that cut through that peninsula pale in comparison to the majestic Rocky Mountains of the American West, they do exist and the land of Nephi was quite likely located "up" within them. While we, today, think of going "up north" and "down south," in this area they would travel "up south" and "down north," because of the literal shift in elevation associated with such journeys.

Chapter 2 Notes:
121 BC. This chapter based on: Mosiah 7:8-11
Ammon and his men spend some miserable days in prison and are brought before an angry Nephite king. The king identifies himself as King Limhi, a descendent of King Zeniff who had left Zarahemla to resettle in the Land of Nephi, a land which the Nephites had fled some years earlier due to Lamanite aggressions. He demands that Ammon explain who they are and why they are in his land.

Pertaining to the name of the city or land of Nephi, it should be noted that the proper name of both the city and the land was "Lehi-Nephi." It was named after both the patriarch, Lehi, of the main Book of Mormon people who sailed to the New World from the Old World, and his faithful son, Nephi. When they arrived in the New World, they had built a settlement near to where they landed. After the death of Lehi, troubles with the Lamanites grew so intense that Nephi moved all who would follow him farther inland. Actually, the direction of their journey is not clearly stated, but one assumption is that they had landed on the western shores of the New World, and that they then moved inland and northward.

Nephi himself not only oversaw the building of a great city in this new area, but he taught the people how to build buildings, plant farms, make furniture and otherwise create a city in which they could dwell in peace and comfort. The crowning achievement for their city was the temple which Nephi had them build. He said, "I did construct it after the manner of the temple of Solomon save it were not built of so many precious things; for they were not to be found upon the land, wherefore, it could not be built like unto Solomon's temple. But the manner of the construction was like unto the temple of Solomon; and the workmanship thereof was exceedingly fine" (II Nephi 5:16).

The land of Nephi, as it's often called, was a sought after homeland for both the Nephites and the Lamanites. Both societies wanted to lay claim to the land, much like the city of Jerusalem is claimed and sought after by Jews and Muslims alike, today. The Nephites referred to it as "the land of their first inheritance." Although they abandoned the land of Nephi for a time, returning to it, claiming it, and living it remained a recurring theme among them. The area became the focal point of discord between the Lamanites and Nephites.

Upon their arrival in Nephi, Ammon and his brethren must have been terribly shocked and dismayed at their rough treatment. Later chapters will reveal the cause of their horrid reception to the point that it will be clear why things transpired as they did and why these strangers were so reviled by the people of this city.

Chapter 3 Notes:
121 BC. This chapter based on: Mosiah 7:12-33; Chapter 8
Ammon explains that they have come from Zarahemla looking for these people. Limhi is pleased beyond words, frees the men, and bids Ammon to gather his other men so that they may have a feast. During the feast, Limhi has Ammon tell the history of the people in Zarahemla. Limhi alludes to the fact that he and his people are in bondage to the Lamanites. Ammon asks him to explain how this has come about.

It is difficult to imagine the relief and joy Limhi felt when he learned that Ammon was from the city of Zarahemla. It was not just a matter of meeting a kindred spirit, or a fellow Nephite. His exultation can only be understood after a careful study of the events which led up to Limhi meeting Ammon. The succeeding chapters attempt to lay out the details which put his reaction into perspective.

The section in the *Book of Mormon* from which this chapter was based, went into greater detail during the discussion between Limhi and Ammon at the feast. In that setting, Limhi asked Ammon about his translation skills, as he was particularly keen on having some ancient inscriptions deciphered. Their discussion went into relatively lengthy and interesting terms on the merits of prophets and seers and the marvels of the gift of translation. This poignant discussion was left out of this chapter as it's of a sacred nature and is best left to the manner in which it is laid out in the original source material.

Chapter 4 Notes:
200 BC. This chapter based on: Mosiah 9:1-2
The story reverts to Zeniff's tale of spying on the Land of Nephi with a band of Nephites. An argument ensues over whether or not to attack the Lamanite-controlled city. The Nephites kill their brethren and return to Zarahemla dejected. Zeniff reports to king Mosiah that he believes the Lamanites would allow them to live in that land. Upon further consideration, king Mosiah grants Zeniff permission to take whoever would like to go with him back to try to resettle in the Land of Nephi.

The original source made it clear that Zeniff spent time in the city of Nephi as a spy. It says, "I, Zeniff, having been taught in all the language of the Nephites, and having had a knowledge of the land of Nephi, or of the land of our fathers' first inheritance, and having been sent as a spy among the Lamanites that I might spy out their forces, that our army might come upon them and destroy them -- but when I saw that which was good among them I was desirous that they should not be destroyed." (Mosiah 9:1)

There are several aspects of Zeniff's spying that are left unclear. It is not known how long he was spying on the Lamanites. Clearly, there was a large party waiting for his report in the nearby wilderness, but it's not known if he was sent to the city alone, or if others were in his group. It's also unclear as to what sort of spying he did. Did he sit in the bushes at the top of a hill and peer at Nephi from a distance, or did he walk through its city gates and enter the city directly? It seems that for him to have seen "that which was good among them," he must have had some up close, first-hand observations of the city and its people.

It seems odd to think that a fair-skinned Nephite could walk into a city of dark-skinned Lamanites undetected. However, it must be remembered that when King Mosiah vacated the city of Nephi years earlier, there were Nephites who chose to remain behind. The original source material says that Mosiah took with him "as many as would hearken unto the voice of the Lord" (Omni 12). It can be assumed that there were Nephites who lingered behind who chose to not hearken to the voice of the Lord.

If such was the case, there could have been Nephites still living in Nephi when Zeniff went there as a spy. Thus, he could have managed to mingle unnoticed within the city gates. It's also assumable that those Nephites who lingered behind in the days of King Mosiah, who chose to not hearken to the voice of the Lord, were not good people and may have decided to blend with and support the cause of the Lamanites.

Another unknown about Zeniff's first trip to Nephi is how many people were in this party that was waiting for Zeniff's report. It must have been a sizable number because the leader of their party – who is unnamed in the original text – seemed to feel he had sufficient numbers to go down to the city and attack it. It says, "that our army might come upon them and destroy them" and that Zeniff was desirous "that our ruler should make a treaty with them" (Mosiah 9:2). The implication, raised by the fact that Zeniff's disagreement with his "ruler" led to a mini-civil war in which "father fought against father, and brother against brother" (Mosiah 9:2), is that Zeniff was trying to stop an immediate attack on Nephi, and not that he was trying to stop his ruler from returning to Zarahemla to gather more forces and then return to attack Nephi at a later date. Zeniff's group was more than an advance party of scouts, but an "army" that had the self-perceived potential of winning a battle to take unquestioned control of the city and the land of Nephi.

It's also possible that Zeniff went with an advance group to initially observe the city of Nephi. If so, he may have been sent into the city while his "ruler" returned to Zarahemla and gathered his substantial force. Zeniff (and any men that may have been with him) may have spent considerable time in the city of Nephi, spying on the people, and waiting for the day that he should return and report his findings to the "ruler" of the army.

It is further possible that Zeniff only spent a few hours, or even a few minutes, in the city. That may have been enough time for him to see that there were indeed good people down among the others.

Chapter 5 Notes:
200 BC. This chapter based on: Mosiah 9:3-7
Zeniff leads his people back to the Land of Nephi. He secludes them in the jungle while he successfully negotiates with King Laman, who agrees to vacate the city for the Nephites' return. King Laman even agrees to share of his food with the weary travelers, while he and his people prepare to leave the dilapidated buildings in which they had been living.

The agreement of King Laman to simply vacate the land of Nephi and allow Zeniff and his people to move into the land is a marvelous wonder. Throughout the Lamanite-Nephite history, bloody wars and battles had been fought, and would continue to be fought in succeeding years, over territorial claim of cities, lands, and various other "rights." It's a curious thing that, in this case, the Lamanites simply chose to move out and let the Nephites move in, especially since they must have known how much the Nephites wanted to move into that particular area.

One quickly-rejected theory was that the Lamanites were not occupying the land and therefore would not miss the vacant buildings. This theory dies when one reads that King Laman, "commanded that his people should depart out of the land" (Mosiah 9:7). They could not have departed out of the land if they were not in some way actively occupying the land. The original source does not emphatically state that King Laman himself was living in the city of Nephi. It does say Zeniff's group "pitched our tents in the place where our brethren were slain, which was near to the land of our fathers. [i.e. the hill overlooking the land of Nephi.] And it came to pass that I went again with four of my men into the city, in unto the king" (Mosiah 9:4-5). This seems to imply that the Lamanite king himself was actually at the city of Nephi at the time Zeniff arrived. Whether he was actually living there, or simply visiting or holding court at the time, is unknown.

Zeniff himself offered a theory as to why King Laman was so willing to give the land to him and his people. He said that it was, "the cunning and the craftiness of king Laman, to bring my people into bondage, that he yielded up the land that we might possess it." (Mosiah 9:10) His point was that the people of Laman, "were a lazy and an idolatrous people; therefore they were desirous to bring us into bondage, that they might glut themselves with the labors of our hands; yea, that they might feast themselves upon the flocks of our fields" (Mosiah 9:12).

In other words, allowing Zeniff's people to move into the land was a ruse used to bring them there, and then force them to produce goods for the Lamanites. The Lamanites would receive these goods through forced taxation.

Limhi echoed this same opinion. He said that Zeniff was "deceived by the cunning and craftiness of king Laman, who having entered into a treaty with king Zeniff, and having yielded up into his hands the possessions of a part of the land, or even the city of Lehi-Nephi, and the city of Shilom; and the land round about -- And all this he did, for the sole purpose of bringing this people into subjection or into bondage. And behold, we at this time do pay tribute to the king of the Lamanites, to the amount of one half of our corn, and our barley, and even all our grain of every kind, and one half of the increase of our flocks and our herds; and even one half of all we have or possess the king of the Lamanites doth exact of us, or our lives" (Mosiah 7:21-22).

This indeed may have been the case. However, as will be seen in later chapters, king Laman was a very patient trickster, because it seems that he did not attempt to put the Nephites into any form of bondage until they had been in the land for a considerable amount of time. Zeniff wrote that "after we had dwelt in the land for the space of twelve years that king Laman began to grow uneasy, lest by any means my people should wax strong in the land, and that they could not overpower them and bring them into bondage"

(Mosiah 9:11). Since he wrote of Laman's concern over being able to "bring" them into bondage, they must not have actually been in bondage at that period of time. Instead, it indicated that Laman wanted to make sure that he still had the ability to overpower the Nephites and bring them into bondage – which was an ability he was to learn that he did not, in fact, still possess. But, such notes relate to events in later chapters.

For the sake of telling the story in this format, the decision was made to depict the city as seldom-used, dilapidated, and of little interest to the Lamanites who felt it was better to simply move to a land that they preferred, rather than bother to continue to live in a city that interested them very little. Right or wrong, the concept of profiteering off of the Nephites is alluded to, but is not the main reason for their willingness to relinquish the city, in this novel.

Chapter 6 Notes:

200-160 BC. This chapter based on: Mosiah 9:8-19; 10:1-22

Zeniff's people elect him to be their king. They restore the buildings throughout the city, including the temple. They tend highly successful farms and generally prosper. After many years, the Lamanites grow leery of the Nephites' success. They attack in a vain attempt to subdue the Nephites. Zeniff's forces are victorious. Many years later, king Laman dies, and his son, also named king Laman leads the Lamanites on another failed attack on the Nephites. Zeniff, now an old man, ends his record looking back on his accomplishments with satisfaction.

The characters of Raehab, who was King Laman's advisor, and his son, Jobadesh, are fictional characters invented to depict what might have occurred between apostate Nephites who stayed behind, and lived with the Lamanites. The events surrounding these characters were also contrived, but influenced by events portrayed in the *Book of Mormon.*

Zeniff wrote that, "after we had dwelt in the land for the space of twelve years that king Laman began to grow uneasy, lest by any means my people should wax strong in the land, and that they could not overpower them and bring them into bondage... king Laman began to stir up his people that they should contend with my people" (Mosiah 9:11, 13). Whether king Laman chose of his own volition to become uneasy, or if he had advisors who convinced him to become uneasy, is not clearly stated. The Lamanite king's growing misgivings are reminiscent of the Pharaoh's concerns over the Hebrews in ancient Egypt.

A study of the original source material causes one to conclude that Zeniff seems to have been a very idealistic man. He had a sincere desire to return his people to their roots. In this case, it was the land of their first inheritance. In his early days, he seems to have sincerely liked, or at least respected, the Lamanites. He literally fought to protect them from what he felt was a wrongful sneak-attack when he and a large party of Nephites first spied out the land of Nephi.

He probably took pride in the fact that he had succeeded in returning the Nephites to their homeland, and that they had managed to live in peace there, defending themselves at times, but living in peace generally. He probably went to his grave a contented man, able to look back on his accomplishments and contributions with a sense of gratitude and healthy, inner pride. He would probably have also been shocked to learn that his decision for a successor to his own throne would prove to be perhaps the single worst decision any Nephite leader would ever make.

Chapter 7 Notes:
160-148 BC. This chapter based on: Mosiah 11:1-29; 12:1-17
Upon Zeniff's death, his son, Noah, has succeeded him to the throne. Noah is an idolatrous man whose immoral behavior has spread throughout the society. A prophet named Abinadi warns the people and the king to repent and is cast out. He returns two years later with a similar message and is caught and taken before King Noah, who throws him into prison.

A great amount of space and detail could have been written in this novel depicting Noah's idolatrous atrocities of what he did and how he encouraged his people to follow suit. Several chapters could have been spent with vivid examples of base behavior. However, the world is already too full of such destructive tripe. Giving such text more visibility is unwarranted, unproductive, and potentially harmful. Instead, the approach taken here was to quickly and succinctly make it clear that Noah and his henchmen were simply evil apostates who perverted the sacred offices which they claimed to hold as priests and king.

Noah was quite likely not as obese as he is depicted in this novel. Later, he contended with Gideon with a sword and climbed a high tower. He must have been somewhat physically fit to have succeeded in these endeavors. However, the author appreciates the well-known depiction Arnold Friberg produced of Noah in a painting in which Abinadi confronted Noah, and decided to follow suit. Additionally, Noah was such a tyrant who brought such lasting and generational repetitious evil to the Nephite society, that he deserves the mockery of being depicted as he has been in this novel.

There is a passage in the original source that has been the cause of mirth for countless Book of Mormon students. Mosiah 12:1 states, "And it came to pass that after the space of two years that Abinadi came among them in disguise, that they knew him not, and began to prophesy among them, saying: Thus has the Lord commanded me, saying -- Abinadi, go and prophesy unto this my people." The humor in this passage is based on Abinadi coming "in disguise," but then proceeding to state his own name as soon as he began to preach. In short, he seemed to have blown his cover.

This novel has attempted to clarify that one theory for why this was so, was that he only needed the disguise long enough to be granted admittance into the city. Once he was within the walls, he no longer needed the disguise, nor did he need to remain anonymous. In fact, he probably counted on being taken captive so that he could preach to the king and his priests directly. He would have known that any large-scale change of heart for the city would have to come from the top down. He probably also knew that this was a one-way trip, because his chances of survival were slim, at best. And yet, he was prepared and willing to go.

One unanswered question is, "Where did Abinadi come from?" There are several possible answers to this. He could have come from the neighboring city of Shilom. He could have come from Zarahemla. He could even have come from the city of Nephi, having viewed the decline of his own city firsthand. His city of origin is ultimately insignificant. What was significant was his message. It was pertinent to the people and leaders of the city of Nephi. It remains pertinent to the people and leaders of many lands today.

Chapter 8 Notes:

148 BC. This chapter based on: Mosiah 12:17-37, Chapters 13-17

Noah's priests conspire to question Abinadi so that they can find reason to accuse him. They bring him before them, but find that he is more than a match for their sly tactics. He chastises them and prophesies ill against them and the people, unless they repent and believe in the Messiah of which he teaches them. Alma, one of Noah's priests, believes Abinadi's words and speaks up for him, but Noah sends Alma away, planning to kill him. Alma manages to escape and go into hiding. Abinadi is taken and put to death by burning at the stake.

The early drafts of this chapter contained highly condensed snippets of Abinadi's preaching before King Noah. The original speech is best read in its entirety in the original source. It is both sacred and profound. It's also quite impressive when taken in the context of the situation in which it was given. Abinadi may not have known that it would be his last sermon, but he surely should have had a good idea that it was quite possible that it would be. He was clear, bold, unapologetic, and spot on in his analysis and delivery.

While the author highly recommends readers should turn to the original source material to receive the full impact and spirit behind Abinadi's words, the decision was made to include more segments of Abinadi's speech in this chapter than had been originally included. Out of respect for the abilities of a great man, much of Abinadi's dialog in this chapter is taken verbatim from the original text.

The scene in which Abinadi causes a spear that is being used to threaten him to burst, has no basis in any knowable facts. However, in the original text, at one point Abinadi declared, "Ye see that ye have not power to slay me, therefore I finish my message" (Mosiah 13:7). There is nothing in the original text that clearly explains why or how it was that the priests and guards lacked the power to kill Abinadi. In actuality, it was probably due to the power of the Spirit that permeated the room as Abinadi spoke.

The bursting of the spear was depicted to give the reader a more tangible picture of the power which accompanied this great man of God. If faith can move mountains, then surely Abinadi could have used his faith to prevent a premature stop to his preaching, in a manner similar to that which was depicted in this chapter.

Chapter 9 Notes:
148 BC. This chapter based on: Mosiah 17:4; 18:1
Alma has spent days hiding in the record chamber, where he recorded the words of Abinadi. He leaves in time to see Abinadi's death. He flees into the wilderness, stopping far away by a pool of water. He considers his behavior in light of Abinadi's teachings, does some soul-searching, which leads to very sincere repentance. He realizes he needs to pick up the torch after Abinadi and returns to Nephi where he finds some old friends, including his wife, who are trying to decide what to do next. They have a heartfelt reunion during which Alma apologizes profusely for his past behavior.

It's not known precisely where Alma immediately went when he fled the throne room. Clearly, he knew his life was in danger and he needed to be careful. It is known that at some point he went to the area known as the Waters of Mormon and hid in a thicket of small trees (Mosiah 18:5). It's also known that he recorded the words of Abinadi and then later preached those words to others (Mosiah 17:4; 18:1). If Alma recorded Abinadi's words prior to preaching them, it's doubtful that he recorded them while at the Waters of Mormon, unless he took writing implements with him as he dashed out of the king's presence.

The record says that Alma "fled from before them and hid himself that they found him not. And he being concealed for many days did write all the words which Abinadi had spoken" (Mosiah 17:4). In pondering Alma's plight, the decision was made to have his first place of refuge be in the hall of records. There were several reasons for this. First, he would have easy access to writing implements. Second, it seems that, based on the behavior of King Noah and his court, the hall of records would have been a very seldom-used area. Third, it may have been counter-intuitive for the guards to think to search for Alma there. The man's life was in danger and he was fleeing from the king. The guards must have assumed that he would try to get as far away from where the king was as possible. Hence, they wouldn't think to look for him within the same building in which the king sat.

A final reason for keeping Alma in the area was to provide him the unfortunate opportunity to witness Abinadi's death first-hand. Alma had clearly become concerned about Abinadi and his welfare. He was also moved by the Spirit he felt during Abinadi's preaching. He had experienced a conversion of his soul that was prompted by the efforts of Abinadi. To see him murdered or martyred would have had a profound impact on Alma. It would surely have played a role in his realizing that he now had to carry on the Lord's work among the people. It seemed important to depict this tragic scene in a way that would allow Alma to have witnessed it.

While it's known from the original source material that Alma was married and had at least one son, whom he named Alma, it's not known at what point Alma had gotten married, or when that son had been born. It is tragic to think of Alma as having been married while a priest under King Noah, and then performing whatever horrible moral atrocities that he may have performed while in that position. However, life is rarely idealistic. Who could better preach and testify of the need for the Atonement and the tender mercies of a loving God more than one who had felt Divine forgiveness first-hand? We do know that Alma was not spotless, as the record tells us that after he fled from Noah, he "repented of his sins and iniquities" (Mosiah 18:1).

As stated, it's not known what sort of reunion Alma had with his wife, or if he was even married at that time. The events concerning Alma's wife, related to Alma by Helam and his friends, are not based on any known records. Depicting Alma married at this time seems to make this situation all the more tragic, human and poignant. The author felt it helped make Alma more human, someone a reader could try to relate to.

Chapter 10 Notes:
147-145 BC. This chapter based on: Mosiah 18:1-35; 19:1-4

Alma gathers followers back to the Waters of Mormon. Here he preaches the gospel and baptizes the believers. Meanwhile, king Noah's forces continue to try to find and stop Alma. Alma and his people permanently flee the city and strike out on their own. Gideon becomes furious with the persecutions of King Noah and declares that someone must put a stop to him and his evil ways.

The baptism of Helam and the others has been depicted much along the lines of what was recorded in the original text where it says:

> And now it came to pass that Alma took Helam, he being one of the first, and went and stood forth in the water, and cried, saying: O Lord, pour out thy Spirit upon thy servant, that he may do this work with holiness of heart.
>
> And when he had said these words, the Spirit of the Lord was upon him, and he said: Helam, I baptize thee, having authority from the Almighty God, as a testimony that ye have entered into a covenant to serve him until you are dead as to the mortal body; and may the Spirit of the Lord be poured out upon you; and may he grant unto you eternal life, through the redemption of Christ, whom he has prepared from the foundation of the world.
>
> And after Alma had said these words, both Alma and Helam were buried in the water; and they arose and came forth out of the water rejoicing, being filled with the Spirit.
>
> And again, Alma took another, and went forth a second time into the water, and baptized him according to the first, only he did not bury himself again in the water. And after this manner he did baptize every one that went forth to the place of Mormon; and they were in number about two hundred and four souls; yea, and they were baptized in the waters of Mormon, and were filled with the grace of God. (Mosiah 18:12-16)

Regarding Alma discovering when it was time to leave the land of Nephi and permanently journey into the wilderness, the original text tells us:

> But behold, it came to pass that the king, having discovered a movement among the people, sent his servants to watch them. Therefore on the day that they were assembling themselves together to hear the word of the Lord they were discovered unto the king. And now the king said that Alma was stirring up the people to rebellion against him; therefore he sent his army to destroy them.

And it came to pass that Alma and the people of the Lord were apprised of the coming of the king's army; therefore they took their tents and their families and departed into the wilderness. And they were in number about four hundred and fifty souls. (Mosiah 18:32:35)

Regarding Gideon's anger towards the king, the original text tells us:

There began to be a division among the remainder of the people. And the lesser part began to breathe out threatenings against the king, and there began to be a great contention among them. And now there was a man among them whose name was Gideon, and he being a strong man and an enemy to the king, therefore he drew his sword, and swore in his wrath that he would slay the king. (Mosiah 19:2-4)

Chapter 11 Notes:

145 BC. This chapter based on: Mosiah 23:1-24; 19:4-15

Alma and his people find a beautiful area which they settle. Gideon determines to go after king Noah. During his pursuit, he knocks down a woman named Hannah. He chases Noah up a tower, but lets Noah escape when they learn that the Lamanites are on the warpath. Noah leads the Nephites on a wanton flight into the jungle. Several men abandon their families as they flee. As the remaining Nephites are overtaken, they have their young women plead for their lives. The Lamanites spare the people and Gideon questions why they had let themselves fall like this.

There is little written that describes the relationship between Alma and the man named Helam. There are basically only two sections of the text that reference that name. The first tells us that the first convert that Alma baptized was named Helam (Mosiah 18:12-14). The second tells us that the land which Alma moved his people into, and the city they subsequently built, was named Helam (Mosiah 23:19, 20). Further references to the name "Helam" were made in reference to that land or city.

Technically, there is no authoritative connection between the man "Helam" and the land "Helam." However, it's known that "it was the custom of the people of Nephi to call their lands, and their cities, and their villages, yea, even all their small villages, after the name of him who first possessed them" (Alma 8:7). Since Helam was baptized by Alma, it's reasonable to conclude that he went with Alma to the land of Helam. Since Helam was actually the first person Alma baptized, it is reasonable to conclude that there was a strong bond between them, either prior to, or immediately following, Helam's baptism. That the land was named "Helam," makes it even more reasonable to depict Helam as the leader of the scouting party that found the land. All of these deductions, however, are merely speculation.

The scene in which Gideon tracked down and confronted King Noah was based nearly entirely on fantasy. The original text only provides these details:

> And now there was a man among them whose name was Gideon, and he being a strong man and an enemy to the king, therefore he drew his sword, and swore in his wrath that he would slay the king. And it came to pass that he fought with the king; and when the king saw that he was about to overpower him, he fled and ran and got upon the tower which was near the temple.
>
> And Gideon pursued after him and was about to get upon the tower to slay the king, and the king cast his eyes round about towards the land of Shemlon, and behold, the army of the Lamanites were within the borders of the land. And now the king cried out in the anguish of his soul, saying: Gideon, spare me, for the Lamanites are upon us, and they will destroy us; yea, they will destroy my people. And now the king was not so much concerned about his people as he was about his own life; nevertheless, Gideon did spare his life. (Mosiah 19:4-8)

That King Noah would even stop and swordfight with Gideon is an indication that he was not the obese, easily-winded character depicted in this novel. However, as stated in the notes for Chapter 7, there was a conscious decision to depict Noah in this manner. This left the quandary of how a man in Noah's condition could have outrun Gideon to the tower and then climb up high enough to spy out the Lamanites before Gideon could overtake him. Adding to the writer's dilemma is the probability that had Noah known that Gideon was going to come after him, he would have sent his guards to apprehend Gideon, thus entirely preventing a confrontation between the two men.

To overcome this self-imposed predicament, the scene was written in such a way that Noah was wary of a potential attack and made certain to have guards nearby, but not knowing who was going to attack him, he would not be able to wholly prevent the attack. Further, by placing Gideon in a position in which others obstructed him, especially Hannah, Noah managed to gain a head-start on Gideon once he realized that Gideon was after him. Even as Gideon freed himself to pursue the king, the guards at the base of the tower continued to slow him down as King Noah made his awkward ascent. All of these events and characters were invented to further the novel's storyline in this manner, while trying to stay essentially true to the original storyline.

The pursuit of the Nephites by the Lamanites, into the wilderness, was essentially based on the original source, however, no one Nephite girl, such as Esther, was named in the original text. The original text states:

> Those who tarried with their wives and their children caused that their fair daughters should stand forth and plead with the Lamanites that they would not slay them. And it came to pass that the Lamanites had compassion on them, for they were charmed with the beauty of their women. Therefore the Lamanites did spare their lives (Mosiah 19:13-15)

Chapter 12 Notes:
145 BC. This chapter based on: Mosiah 19:15-29
The Lamanites bring the Nephites back to Nephi where king Laman announces that they are basically under house arrest and will permanently pay tribute to them. Noah's son, Limhi, becomes king of the Nephites. Gideon again meets Hannah, and both decide to create a relationship. After a bit, Gideon sends men into the wilderness to find Noah and his priests. They meet a group of men who had abandoned their families and later were ashamed and killed Noah, but his priests fled before they could catch them, too.

This chapter essentially depicts the events as described in the original source material, with the exception of the interaction between Gideon and Hannah. Hannah remains a fictional character. However, Gideon did send men into the wilderness to find Noah in this manner:

> And now there was one of the sons of the king among those that were taken captive, whose name was Limhi. And now Limhi was desirous that his father should not be destroyed; nevertheless, Limhi was not ignorant of the iniquities of his father, he himself being a just man. And it came to pass that Gideon sent men into the wilderness secretly, to search for the king and those that were with him. And it came to pass that they met the people in the wilderness, all save the king and his priests. (Mosiah 19:16-18)

Chapter 13 Notes:
135 BC. This chapter based on: Mosiah 20:1-12

Amulon, the chief priest, leads the other priests in the wilderness. They happen upon an area where Lamanite girls gathered. They kidnap several and convince them to become their wives. The Lamanites go to battle with the Nephites, believing erroneously that they were the ones who kidnapped their daughters. Some Nephites find king Laman who as fallen wounded on the battlefield and determine to take him to king Limhi.

The events in this chapter are a fairly faithful adaptation of the original text. Several assumptions on logistical details and dialog had to be made, however. It was assumed, for instance, that the men waited until there was the right number of girls available for them to kidnap. Perhaps they also waited until girls of interest were gathered. It's difficult to determine what events motivated such unscrupulous and callous men.

Another enigma is why the girls eventually agreed to stay with the apostate priests. Surely there were times when they could have fled and made their ways home. It seems reasonable that at least one girl could have escaped. However, as is learned later, these girls eventually considered the men as their legitimate husbands and would even plead with other Lamanites to spare the men who had literally captured them. At some point, some odd form of attraction must have developed. This chapter offers only one possible scenario for how that may have come to be.

Chapter 14 Notes:
135 BC. This chapter based on: Mosiah 20:13-26
King Limhi questions king Laman as to the cause of their attack. Upon declaring that it was in retaliation for the kidnapping, king Limhi swears to search his people. Gideon, however, points out that it's probably the priests of Noah who had done this. Limhi agrees and explains the situation to Laman, who believes the tale. Laman agrees to stop the fighting if Limhi will take him back out to meet his people. Laman returns home and the fighting ceases.

The events in this chapter are a fairly faithful adaptation of the original text, with the exception of Limhi's thoughts regarding King Laman as the Lamanite king returned to his people. There was no indication of this in the original source. One is left to wonder what went through the minds of both monarchs at that time.

Chapter 15 Notes:
135-123 BC. This chapter based on: Mosiah 21:1-5
Limhi has the people repair their city and their morals. They begin to prosper again. Gideon and Hannah's relationship leads to marriage. The Lamanites

continue to begrudge and abuse the Nephites. The Nephites decide to go to battle against them, to seek their freedom. They fail. Gideon is nearly killed in battle.

Again, the interaction between Gideon and Hannah has been contrived. Hannah is a purely fictional character and all interaction with her throughout this novel, no matter how plausible, is a work of fiction. In addition, the depictions of Gideon in battle are also contrived. While it's known that Gideon was a captain in the Nephite army, and that the king listened to his council on occasion (Mosiah 20:17), it is not known what part he played in actual battles.

It's interesting to note that even though they needed to change their behavior to align it with the Lord, that was not the first course of action they pursued. They still tried to free themselves through fighting rather than through faith and repentance.

Chapter 16 Notes:
122 BC. This chapter based on: Mosiah 21:5-15, 25
The Nephites have lost many good men. The people mourn their losses. A man named Zoram demands to lead another attempt. Gideon cannot talk him out of it. When the attempt fails, Zoram demands to try a third time. Meanwhile, Gideon suggests to Limhi that they need to find an alternative to fighting. He suggests a scouting party be sent out to see if they can find their way back to Zarahemla. While Zoram prepares for battle, Limhi appoints Gideon to be in charge of the scouting party.

The character of Zoram is a composite of unknown characters who were likely involved in these conflicts. It must have been extremely frustrating for the people to return to battle. The original text related the battles as such:

> And now the afflictions of the Nephites were great, and there was no way that they could deliver themselves out of their hands, for the Lamanites had surrounded them on every side. And it came to pass that the people began to murmur with the king because of their afflictions; and they began to be desirous to go against them to battle. And they did afflict the king sorely with their complaints; therefore he granted unto them that they should do according to their desires. And they gathered themselves together again, and put on their armor, and went forth against the Lamanites to drive them out of their land. And it came to pass that the Lamanites did beat them, and drove them back, and slew many of them.

And now there was a great mourning and lamentation among the people of Limhi, the widow mourning for her husband, the son and the daughter mourning for their father, and the brothers for their brethren. Now there were a great many widows in the land, and they did cry mightily from day to day, for a great fear of the Lamanites had come upon them. And it came to pass that their continual cries did stir up the remainder of the people of Limhi to anger against the Lamanites; and they went again to battle. (Mosiah 21:5-11)

Chapter 17 Notes:
122 BC. This chapter based on: Mosiah 21:25; 8:7-12
While Zoram rallies his men, Gideon surreptitiously gathers men he can trust for his adventure. Hannah speaks with Gideon about her concerns, and is comforted.

The events in this chapter were basically created out of speculation as to what may have been occurring in the land of Nephi at this time. There is no indication that Gideon was the one asked by king Limhi to lead the expedition north to find Zarahemla. Gideon was a good, brave man, who was a captain in the king's army and whose opinion and insight had been and would be later followed by the king. It's not too unlikely for him to have been asked to lead the scouting party north.

Chapter 18 Notes:
122 BC. This chapter based on: Mosiah 21:25-26
Gideon leads a band of forty-three men northward through the jungle. They find a desolate, ruined city which they assume to be Zarahemla.

Of the journey north to find Zarahemla, the original text merely says:

Now king Limhi ... sent ... a small number of men to search for the land of Zarahemla; but they could not find it, and they were lost in the wilderness. Nevertheless, they did find a land which had been peopled; yea, a land which was covered with dry bones; yea, a land which had been peopled and which had been destroyed; and they ... supposed it to be the land of Zarahemla. (Mosiah 21:25-26)

It also provided this depiction of Limhi's conversation with Ammon:

And the king said unto him: Being grieved for the afflictions of my people, I caused that forty and three of my people should take

a journey into the wilderness, that thereby they might find the land of
Zarahemla, that we might appeal unto our brethren to deliver us out
of bondage.

And they were lost in the wilderness for the space of many
days, yet they were diligent, and found not the land of Zarahemla but
returned to this land, having traveled in a land among many waters,
having discovered a land which was covered with bones of men, and
of beasts, and was also covered with ruins of buildings of every kind,
having discovered a land which had been peopled with a people who
were as numerous as the hosts of Israel. (Mosiah 8:7-8)

The most significant point to ponder is that the forty-three men who
discovered this desolate land "supposed it to be the land of Zarahemla. It's
unclear why they would suppose this. There was much about this land that
was foreign to them. For example, they encountered a strange and desolate
land with the remains of weaponry they did not recognize, with tablets
containing writing they could not read.

Although they were the offspring of people who had left Zarahemla
several years previous, one has to wonder why they would think that in that
relatively short time, their language would have evolved to the point that they
could not even remotely interpret the language of those who had remained in
Zarahemla. It seems it would have made more sense for them to believe that
they had discovered a land that was not Zarahemla and that it had been
peopled by someone other than Nephites.

However, the text makes it clear that they "supposed it to be the land
of Zarahemla." Perhaps they were so discouraged, frustrated, shocked, and
tired of struggling that a massive form of pessimism that seems to permeate
human nature couldn't help but take hold of their thought process. Many
people can probably relate instances in their lives when they have
encountered a discouraged person who couldn't see a longed-for answer even
when it was right in front of them.

Instead, they cling to false, negative beliefs that force them to remain
in a downward spiral. It takes a third party or outside influence to eventually
get such people to see the world differently and realize that they are mistaken.
Such seems to be the case with Limhi's men.

Due to their belief that Zarahemla was in ruins, they were beyond any
hope of help. They couldn't fight their way to freedom and liberty, and now
they couldn't run away to sanctuary. They had nowhere to turn for peace –
other than the Lord. Surely they must have wondered how they could turn to
Him, however, when they felt so unworthy.

The incident between Micah and the jaguar is purely fictional. As with the current environment, there may have been jaguars and pudu deer in the vicinity of the journey they took, but there is no account of such an incident taking place, in the Book of Mormon.

Chapter 19 Notes:
122 BC. This chapter based on: Mosiah 21:26-27
They search the land and find nothing but bones, rotted weaponry, and an odd stone box containing metal plates with writing which they can't decipher. They bring these back to Nephi and report their findings to Limhi, who declares he wants to address the people on the morrow. Gideon finds out that Zoram's battle failed, and returns home to Hannah. They pray for deliverance.

The majority of this chapter had to be extrapolated from the few facts found in the original source material. Of the experiences in the desolate land, all that is known is learned from two references:

> And for a testimony that the things that they had said are true they have brought twenty-four plates which are filled with engravings, and they are of pure gold. And behold, also, they have brought breastplates, which are large, and they are of brass and of copper, and are perfectly sound. (Mosiah 8:9-10)
> Nevertheless, they did find a land which had been peopled; yea, a land which was covered with dry bones; yea, a land which had been peopled and which had been destroyed; and they, having supposed it to be the land of Zarahemla, returned to the land of Nephi, having arrived in the borders of the land not many days before the coming of Ammon. And they brought a record with them, even a record of the people whose bones they had found; and it was engraven on plates of ore. (Mosiah 21:26-27)

One can only imagine the hopeless desperation they felt when they saw what they thought to be Zarahemla laid waste. It was their only – and perceptively last – hope of freeing themselves from Lamanite oppression.

Chapter 20 Notes:
122 BC. This chapter based on: Mosiah 21:18-24, 28-35
Limhi addresses the people and reports on the findings of Gideon's party. Limhi makes it known that their only hope for freedom will come from God, and that they must therefore repent and become worthy of His deliverance.

The people respond appropriately and modify their lives. Meanwhile, Amulon and his cohorts are discovered raiding the city's supplies, but get away. While the people keep their eyes open for more raids, Ammon and his brethren are discovered in the land. After being thrown into prison, they are brought before Limhi. When Limhi finds out they are from Zarahemla, and that Zarahemla has not been destroyed, he is overjoyed. He finishes his account of his people to Ammon, at the feast from Chapter 3. They agree to try to find a way to successfully get the people out of Nephi and back to Zarahemla.

It is not known who suggested that the people remember the words of Abinadi and that the people begin to fast and pray for deliverance. Nor is it known how close together the third failed battle was with regards to the 43 men finding the land of desolation. It is known that after the third failed battle, the people humbled themselves:

> Yea, they went again even the third time, and suffered in the like manner; and those that were not slain returned again to the city of Nephi. And they did humble themselves even to the dust, subjecting themselves to the yoke of bondage, submitting themselves to be smitten, and to be driven to and fro, and burdened, according to the desires of their enemies. And they did humble themselves even in the depths of humility; and they did cry mightily to God; yea, even all the day long did they cry unto their God that he would deliver them out of their afflictions. (Mosiah 21:12-14)

Regarding the pilfering of the people's supplies by Amulon and his cohorts, the original text simply says:

> And he [King Limhi] caused that his people should watch the land round about, that by some means they might take those priests that fled into the wilderness, who had stolen the daughters of the Lamanites, and that had caused such a great destruction to come upon them. For they were desirous to take them that they might punish them; for they had come into the land of Nephi by night, and carried off their grain and many of their precious things; therefore they laid wait for them. (Mosiah 21:20-21)

The timing of Ammon and his men showing up as the humbled people were on the lookout for Amulon and his henchmen provides pause for pondering. One can only imagine just how the people loathed Ammon and his men as they were brought through the city under the misunderstanding of being the very men who were the cause of so much suffering and loss of life. It's a wonder that they made it to their prison alive. There's a powerful lesson here about the importance of a fair and honest trial before being declared guilty and punished accordingly, even when presumed guilty.

Chapter 21 Notes:
122 BC. This chapter based on: Mosiah 21:36; 22:1-12
Limhi again addresses the people and tells of Ammon coming from Zarahemla. He makes it clear that they must leave Nephi and return to Zarahemla with Ammon. They devise a means of escape by making the Lamanite guards drunk and sneaking out in the night and heading into the jungle to the north.

It's difficult to imagine the great relief with which Limhi and his people must have greeted Ammon and his men once they realized who they actually were. Limhi had come to understand that they had killed a prophet of God. They had committed whoredoms and iniquities. They had allowed themselves to come into bondage to the Lamanites. They had failed three times to fight their way free from Lamanite oppression.

Each time, they had lost their most valiant men. This meant that their remaining army was becoming less and less able, which, in turn, meant that they were becoming more and more certain that they would not be able to fight their way free. The only alternative they could conceive of was sneaking away to the land of Zarahemla. When their scouting party reported that Zarahemla had been destroyed, they were completely at a loss. Sadly, they viewed fasting and prayer as their LAST resort to find peace and freedom, rather than their first.

When Ammon arrived and announced not just that he came from Zarahemla, but that Zarahemla was still a strong, thriving city, Limhi must surely have seen this as the answer to his and his people's prayers. Perhaps never in history has a search party been more welcomed and warmly received.

The portion of the chapter dealing with Gideon suggesting making the Lamanite guards drunk stayed closely true to the account given in the original text.

Chapter 22 Notes:
122 BC. This chapter based on: Mosiah 22:15
Lamanite guards come to Nephi and find the other guards passed out and the city empty. They send messengers to the Lamanite king, while others take off

after the Nephites through the jungle. They become lost because of a false, circuitous trail that the Nephites have laid.

Other than knowing that the Lamanites sent guards into the wilderness to track the Nephites, and that these guards became lost, very few other details are known. The concept of the circuitous trail was devised as one theory of how the Lamanites could have gotten lost while tracking the trail of an entire city, complete with flocks and herds in tow.

The original text actually states that the Lamanites sent an "army" to pursue them, not just a scouting party:

> And now it came to pass when the Lamanites had found that the people of Limhi had departed out of the land by night, that they sent an army into the wilderness to pursue them; and after they had pursued them two days, they could no longer follow their tracks; therefore they were lost in the wilderness. (Mosiah 22:15-16)

Chapter 23 Notes:
122 BC. This chapter based on: Mosiah 22:13-14; 8:12-21
Ammon successfully leads the refugees back to Zarahemla where they are welcomed by king Mosiah. Limhi tells Mosiah of the twenty-four plates his people found in the desolate land. He asks Mosiah if it's true that he can translate them. Mosiah explains that he should be able to do it with special tools and prayer. He reviews the plates and acknowledges that they do tell the story of a people that have been destroyed.

Mosiah did indeed welcome the people of Limhi to Zarahemla, and also received the records which they bore. The precise time at which he translated the record that was on the 24 plates found by Limhi's people is not known. It's possible that he did a verbal translation at the time depicted in this and the succeeding chapter, and then did a second translation which was written down, later. Or, there may have been only one translation.

What is known from the original text is:

> And it came to pass that Mosiah received them with joy; and he also received their records, and also the records which had been found by the people of Limhi. (Mosiah 22:14)
>
> Therefore he took the records which were engraven on the plates of brass, and also the plates of Nephi, and all the things which he had kept and preserved according to the commandments of God,

after having translated and caused to be written the records which
were on the plates of gold which had been found by the people of
Limhi, which were delivered to him by the hand of Limhi; And this
he did because of the great anxiety of his people; for they were
desirous beyond measure to know concerning those people who had
been destroyed. (Mosiah 28:11-12)

Chapter 24 Notes:
122 BC. This chapter based on: Mosiah 28:11-15; 8:12-21, Ether (all)
*Limhi, Ammon, and others are permitted to gather with Mosiah as he
verbally translates the plates. The plates tell the story of a people known as
the Jaredites who fled the Old World at the time of the Tower of Babel and
settled in the New World. The once-righteous people are led into
imprisonment and persecution due to several generations of men seeking
power. The men acknowledge that unrighteous kings can have a profound
impact on society.*

It is not known who, if anyone was present while king Mosiah
translated the 24 plates. The depiction of the events in this chapter were
devised to give a feel for what it may have been like to use the Urim and
Thummim, as well as give an opportunity for key persons involved in the
finding of the plates, as well as the delivery of Limhi's people, to learn what
was on the plates.

The approach taken for relating the story of the Jaredites was a bit
unique. While an entire novel could have been written of the Jaredite's story,
it doesn't seem that it would be a very inspiring one. It had an amazing and
awe-inspiring beginning, and a bitter dismal decline for generation after
generation until nothing was left, but a land of physical and spiritual
desolation.

Amaleki's comments are perhaps many and a bit unorthodox. The
attempt here was to use him to give this a "real person's point of view" so that
the reader would appreciate that the characters in the overall story were
human, and that the story of the Jaredites impacted them then as much as it
impacts us today, if not more so.

The translation of the Jaredite saga in this way also set the stage for
making it very clear why king Mosiah later decided to NOT pass on his
crown, but instead chose to implement a system of judges. This novel should
help highlight four key events that caused Mosiah to make that decision:

1) King Limhi escaped to Zarahemla and told him of the trouble and
spiritual decline king Noah had caused.

2) Alma later arrived and reinforced the woes king Noah had caused, and added to that the afflictions king Amulon imposed.

3) He translated the record of the Jaredites and saw the problems their kings caused.

4) Additionally, he had his own experiences of having been king, in support of how his father, king Benjamin, had so eloquently admonished his people.

Putting everything into context, it is not surprising that he stepped back and decided that having a king lead the people may not be the best approach to government.

Chapter 25 Notes:
122 BC. This chapter based on: Mosiah 22:16; 23:30-34
The Lamanites have become lost in the jungle while searching for Limhi's people. They happen upon Amulon's people. Amulon and his men, who have married Lamanite daughters, successfully have their wives plead for mercy.

The party of Lamanites who became lost in the jungle while searching for Limhi was listed as an "army" in the original text. The size of that army is not given in this chapter. The Lamanite leader named "Hamoth" in this chapter is not named in the original source material. The concept of Amulon having his and his men's wives plead with the Lamanites for their lives is based on the actual account. There must have been some form of bonding between Amulon and his men and their kidnapped wives for them to have agreed to plead for their lives rather than declaring that they had been kidnapped years earlier.

The original text recorded the events in this way:

> And it came to pass that Amulon did plead with the Lamanites; and he also sent forth their wives, who were the daughters of the Lamanites, to plead with their brethren, that they should not destroy their husbands. And the Lamanites had compassion on Amulon and his brethren, and did not destroy them, because of their wives. (Mosiah 23:33-34)

Chapter 26 Notes:
122 BC. This chapter based on: Mosiah 23:25-29, 35
Hamoth, the leader of the Lamanite guards, finds out that Amulon is married to his daughter. The Lamanites take Amulon's people under guard as they continue seeking their way back to the Lamanite capital, Shemlon. They

happen upon the city that Alma and his people have built. Alma welcomes the Lamanites to a feast, while Amulon lurks back in the shadows of the jungle, suspicious of who Alma may be.

As with "Hamoth" being a created character, there is no record of the leader of the Lamanite party having any direct relationship with any of the wives of the people of Amulon. The character of Rebekah was created for the purposes of furthering the story and bringing home the sincerely deep feelings the Lamanites had for their daughters.

Modern times have revealed other unique and unfathomable coincidences which rival those depicted in this chapter. Imagine losing your daughter and eventually coming upon her, and your grandchildren, in this way. It would make for a very emotional reunion. The question remains as to whether the father would embrace his new son-in-law at the behest of his daughter, or engage him in battle.

Regarding the finding of the land of Helam, the original text merely stated:

> And Amulon and his brethren did join the Lamanites, and they were traveling in the wilderness in search of the land of Nephi when they discovered the land of Helam, which was possessed by Alma and his brethren. (Mosiah 23:35)

Chapter 27 Notes:
122 BC. This chapter based on: Mosiah 23:35-38
The feast goes well and Hamoth agrees to let Alma and his people remain free, if they will show them the way back to the Land of Nephi. Alma agrees and sends men to guide them back. On the way, Amulon discovers Alma's identity and knows him to be the fugitive priest from Noah's court who had sided with Abinadi. He convinces Hamoth to go back on his word and guard Alma's people after all.

For the purposes of furthering the story, the author decided to have Amulon linger away from the Nephites, so that he and Alma would not meet yet. Amulon would have likely recognized Alma at that point, and Alma would have certainly recognized Amulon. When they eventually do meet and spend time with each other, they clearly know each other. The question arises as to whether or not Alma would have agreed to assist the Lamanites in getting back to the Land of Nephi, had he known they were in league with Amulon. At this point, Alma was an extremely honorable man, and he may have done so. However, he would also have needed to balance the safety of his people, and may not have. But then, what would have become of their visitors? Ultimately, he may have decided to point them in the right direction.

The other reason Alma and Amulon were kept separate was that it is not known how the promise was made to Alma regarding his freedom in exchange for showing the Lamanites the way back to the land of Nephi. More importantly, it is not known why the promise was broken. The breaking of a promise was no small thing among either the Nephites or the Lamanites. There is an account in the book of Alma of Lamanites being told that the Nephites were breaking their oath and that many of the Lamanites refused to believe this. Their king became convinced that the Nephites had broken their oath by an apostate Nephite who duped him into believing him.

In this novel, this breaking of a promise was depicted in such a way as to place responsibility for the compromised morals on Amulon, an apostate Nephite. Amulon was present at some point in the journey, but in reality, it is unknown what role he played at this point in the actual account. The original text depicts the events as such:

> And it came to pass that the Lamanites promised unto Alma and his brethren, that if they would show them the way which led to the land of Nephi that they would grant unto them their lives and their liberty. But after Alma had shown them the way that led to the land of Nephi the Lamanites would not keep their promise; but they set guards round about the land of Helam, over Alma and his brethren. And the remainder of them went to the land of Nephi; and a part of them returned to the land of Helam, and also brought with them the wives and the children of the guards who had been left in the land. (Mosiah 23:36-38)

This text says that "Alma had shown them the way" back to Nephi. Whether that meant that Alma physically went with them, if he approved sending guides along with them while he remained in Helam, or, if he simply advised them on the path to take, is debatable. The novel depicts the middle option for various reasons, not the least of which involve Alma's relationship with Amulon and Amulon's potential relationship with the Lamanite king.

Chapter 28 Notes:

122 BC. This chapter based on: Mosiah 23:38-39

Amulon meets and wins the favor of king Laman and is appointed as a sub-king over the people of Alma. Amulon arrives and lets Alma know of his new position. Alma remembers Amulon all too well.

Regarding the meeting of Amulon with King Laman, all that is actually known of this encounter is the following:

> And the king of the Lamanites had granted unto Amulon that he should be a king and a ruler over his people, who were in the land of Helam; nevertheless he should have no power to do anything contrary to the will of the king of the Lamanites. (Mosiah 23:39)

Regarding Amulon's arrival in Helam and his declaration of his authority over Alma, the original text merely stated:

> And now it came to pass that Amulon began to exercise authority over Alma and his brethren...For Amulon knew Alma, that he had been one of the king's priests, and that it was he that believed the words of Abinadi and was driven out before the king, and therefore he was wroth with him; for he was subject to king Laman, yet he exercised authority over them.... (Mosiah 24:8-9)

Chapter 29 Notes:

122 BC. This chapter based on: Mosiah 24:8-15

Alma and his people live under the oppressive reign of Amulon who delights in making their lives miserable. Amulon interrupts Alma's worship service and bans prayer. Alma encourages the people to continue to remember their God. With divine assistance, their burdens are made tolerable, which infuriates Amulon.

The specific details of the scene in which Amulon interrupts Alma's worship service and threatens the people with death if they are found praying are fictitious, but the storyline is taken from the original source material. It's reminiscent of the story of Daniel in the Lions' Den.

> For Amulon knew Alma, that he had been one of the king's priests, and that it was he that believed the words of Abinadi and was driven out before the king, and therefore he was wroth with him; for he was subject to king Laman, yet he exercised authority over them, and put tasks upon them, and put task-masters over them. And it came to pass that so great were their afflictions that they began to cry mightily to God. And Amulon commanded them that they should stop their cries; and he put guards over them to watch them, that whosoever should be found calling upon God should be put to death. And Alma and his people did not raise their voices to the Lord their

God, but did pour out their hearts to him; and he did know the thoughts of their hearts. (Mosiah 24:9-12)

The details concerning Alma speaking with his son about young Hamoth taunting him are creative conjecture. It's unknown if Alma the Younger was alive at this time. The father-to-son discussion certainly was not recorded. However, the concept of Amulon encouraging his own children to torment the children of the Nephites is based on the following verse in the original record where it stated:

And now it came to pass that Amulon began to exercise authority over Alma and his brethren, and began to persecute him, and cause that his children should persecute their children. (Mosiah 24:8)

Chapter 30 Notes:
122 BC. This chapter based on: Mosiah 24:1-7
King Laman invites Amulon and the other former priests to Nephi to teach them of their ways. Amulon teaches them worldly issues and avoids any spiritual teaching. Alma remains aware of the proceedings and the evils they foreshadow.

The request of King Laman to have Amulon and his priests teach his people was based on the original source material. The same can be said for Amulon's choice to avoid teaching them anything dealing with pure religion or a faith in God. They had wholly turned their backs on God and had made a shameful mockery of the office of "priest" that they had once held. The manner in which the request was made of Amulon, has been created for the sake of this novel. The original text that covers these events is found in Mosiah 24:1-7.

The original text covers these events as follows:

And it came to pass that Amulon did gain favor in the eyes of the king of the Lamanites; therefore, the king of the Lamanites granted unto him and his brethren that they should be appointed teachers over his people, yea, even over the people who were in the land of Shemlon, and in the land of Shilom, and in the land of Amulon. For the Lamanites had taken possession of all these lands; therefore, the king of the Lamanites had appointed kings over all these lands.

And now the name of the king of the Lamanites was Laman, being called after the name of his father; and therefore he was called king Laman. And he was king over a numerous people. And he appointed teachers of the brethren of Amulon in every land which was possessed by his people; and thus the language of Nephi began to be taught among all the people of the Lamanites.

And they were a people friendly one with another; nevertheless they knew not God; neither did the brethren of Amulon teach them anything concerning the Lord their God, neither the law of Moses; nor did they teach them the words of Abinadi; But they taught them that they should keep their record, and that they might write one to another.

And thus the Lamanites began to increase in riches, and began to trade one with another and wax great, and began to be a cunning and a wise people, as to the wisdom of the world, yea, a very cunning people, delighting in all manner of wickedness and plunder, except it were among their own brethren. (Mosiah 24:1-7)

Chapter 31 Notes:
121 BC. This chapter based on: Mosiah 24:13-25
Alma meets with Helam and announces that the Lord has revealed to him that He will deliver them from their bondage. Alma leads them out of the city by night, and through the jungle. Amulon pursues them, but is unable to apprehend them. They successfully make it to Zarahemla and are welcomed by king Mosiah.

The tender mercies of a loving God who made light the burdens of a faithful group of badly persecuted people truly occurred. The details of their daily lives is not to be had, other than a brief record of the Lord promising Alma that He would make their burdens light.

And it came to pass that the voice of the Lord came to them in their afflictions, saying: Lift up your heads and be of good comfort, for I know of the covenant which ye have made unto me; and I will covenant with my people and deliver them out of bondage. And I will also ease the burdens which are put upon your shoulders, that even you cannot feel them upon your backs, even while you are in bondage; and this will I do that ye may stand as witnesses for me hereafter, and that ye may know of a surety that I, the Lord God, do visit my people in their afflictions. And now it came to pass that the burdens which were laid upon Alma and his brethren were made light; yea, the Lord did strengthen them that they could bear up their burdens with ease, and they did submit cheerfully and with patience to all the will of the Lord. (Mosiah 24:13-15)

Likewise, while we have a record of Alma leading the people to freedom, we do not know many details of their miraculous journey. We do know that God prompted Alma to get his people out of the valley of Alma and promised him that He would stop his pursuers from following any further. While the original record does not say whether or not Amulon himself was killed, it also contains no further references to Amulon after this experience. There are references to Amulonites, or the people of Amulon, but all references to Amulon as an individual cease after the Lord's promise to stop Amulon's forces in that valley.

> And Alma and his people departed into the wilderness; and when they had traveled all day they pitched their tents in a valley, and they called the valley Alma, because he led their way in the wilderness. Yea, and in the valley of Alma they poured out their thanks to God because he had been merciful unto them, and eased their burdens, and had delivered them out of bondage; for they were in bondage, and none could deliver them except it were the Lord their God.
>
> And they gave thanks to God, yea, all their men and all their women and all their children that could speak lifted their voices in the praises of their God. And now the Lord said unto Alma: Haste thee and get thou and this people out of this land, for the Lamanites have awakened and do pursue thee; therefore get thee out of this land, and I will stop the Lamanites in this valley that they come no further in pursuit of this people.
>
> And it came to pass that they departed out of the valley, and took their journey into the wilderness. And after they had been in the wilderness twelve days they arrived in the land of Zarahemla; and king Mosiah did also receive them with joy. (Mosiah 24: 20-25)

The first draft of the novel concluded essentially here with the people returning to Zarahemla. Everyone was reunited and safe again. However, early readers said they were left hanging and wanted to have a more complete resolution in which they could see more of what happened once they returned to Zarahemla. As this novel only covers a slice of a much broader story, it's necessary to have some degree of unresolved events, but the following chapters were created as a result of this request. (They could be considered as bonus material.)

Chapter 32 Notes:

121 BC. This chapter based on: Mosiah 25:1-16; Omni 13-19

Mosiah gathers all of the people to Zarahemla to hear Limhi and Alma as they relate the accounts of their people. Everyone is impressed with the mercies and divine guidance of God. Alma is sanctioned as the official leader of the Nephites' church.

The events in this chapter are based on the brief references to the people gathering to hear the accounts from Mosiah, Alma, and Limhi. The details themselves were devised to help illustrate how that gathering of people may have occurred. There is no record of Gideon and the others at the gathering, though they were surely present.

A bit of detail that is included in the original text, but was not brought out in the novel, is further detail about the people who were living in the land of Zarahemla. Prior to the period in which the novel begins, when the people of Nephi originally left the Land of Nephi and moved northward, they discovered the city of Zarahemla. This city was not built by Nephites – or Lamanites, for that matter.

Instead, it was built by yet another group of people who had fled Israel at the time that the Babylonians captured Jerusalem around 550 BC. This group was led by a man named Mulek and were known as Mulekites. They had neglected to take with them any written text, including scriptures. Over the centuries, their language became so corrupted that the Nephites could not understand them. The first king Mosiah, who was the Nephite leader who first encountered the Mulekites, had his people teach the Mulekites their language so that they could converse with them and learn their history.

The Mulekites welcomed the Nephites to live in Zarahemla with them. There is no indication in the record of conflicts between the Nephites and the Mulekites. At the time the events in this chapter take place, after Mosiah II had the people hear the histories of the people of Alma and so forth, the Mulekites decided to officially discard that name and be known henceforth as "Nephites."

Concerning the number of people living in the land of Zarahemla at the time Limhi's and Alma's people arrived in the city of Zarahemla, the record says:

Now there were not so many of the children of Nephi, or so
many of those who were descendants of Nephi, as there were of the
people of Zarahemla, who was a descendant of Mulek, and those
who came with him into the wilderness. And there were not so many
of the people of Nephi and of the people of Zarahemla as there were
of the Lamanites; yea, they were not half so numerous. And now all
the people of Nephi were assembled together, and also all the people
of Zarahemla, and they were gathered together in two bodies.
(Mosiah 25:2-4)

Here is how we learn that following the giving of the accounts of
Limhi's and Alma's people, the Mulekites – or people of Zarahemla –
decided to be known as "Nephites":

And now all the people of Zarahemla were numbered with
the Nephites, and this because the kingdom had been conferred
upon none but those who were descendants of Nephi. (Mosiah
25:13)

Chapter 33 Notes:
121 BC. This chapter based on: Mosiah 25:17; Alma 1:8; 6:7
*After concluding their accounts, Limhi asks Alma if he will baptize him and
his people. Alma is honored to accept. Gideon announces that he will move
his family to the Valley of Gideon. Others decide to settle there as well. The
leaders are grateful for Abinadi's sacrifice which led to the spiritual
conversion and physical reuniting of their society.*

The portion of this chapter that details with Limhi seeking baptism is
based on information in the original source material. The details of that event
have been devised to help illustrate how that event may have transpired. The
original text records the following:

And it came to pass that after Alma had taught the people
many things, and had made an end of speaking to them, that king
Limhi was desirous that he might be baptized; and all his people were
desirous that they might be baptized also. Therefore, Alma did go
forth into the water and did baptize them; yea, he did baptize them
after the manner he did his brethren in the waters of Mormon; yea,
and as many as he did baptize did belong to the church of God; and
this because of their belief on the words of Alma. (Mosiah 25:17-18)

The original source material goes well beyond the scope of this novel and gives information regarding Alma becoming the main leader of the church of the Nephites, or their prophet. This is an interesting point. Clearly, he was worthy and capable of becoming their prophet, but it's a curious matter as to why the people living in Zarahemla, under King Mosiah II, did not already have a prophet. Perhaps they did and he stepped aside to allow Alma to take on that role. The record does not tell us. Instead, it refers to Alma as "the founder of their church." (Mosiah 23:16)

It records Alma's commission as prophet in the following manner:

> And it came to pass that king Mosiah granted unto Alma that he might establish churches throughout all the land of Zarahemla; and gave him power to ordain priests and teachers over every church. Now this was done because there were so many people that they could not all be governed by one teacher; neither could they all hear the word of God in one assembly; Therefore they did assemble themselves together in different bodies, being called churches; every church having their priests and their teachers, and every priest preaching the word according as it was delivered to him by the mouth of Alma.
>
> And thus, notwithstanding there being many churches they were all one church, yea, even the church of God; for there was nothing preached in all the churches except it were repentance and faith in God. And now there were seven churches in the land of Zarahemla. And it came to pass that whosoever were desirous to take upon them the name of Christ, or of God, they did join the churches of God; And they were called the people of God. And the Lord did pour out his Spirit upon them, and they were blessed, and prospered in the land. (Mosiah 25:19-24)

The source material does not give us details about Gideon regarding his decision to settle in what became known as the "valley of Gideon." It did make it clear, however, that this was where he settled. It tells us that the area that Gideon settled in took on his name for both the valley and the city:

> And now it came to pass that when Alma had made these regulations he departed from them, yea, from the church which was in the city of Zarahemla, and went over upon the east of the river Sidon, into the valley of Gideon, there having been a city built, which was called the city of Gideon, which was in the valley that was called Gideon, being called after the man.... (Alma 6:7-8)

Epilogue – Settling In

The people prosper for a time. Mosiah ponders the impacts of both good and bad kings. Alma is made the leader and prophet of the church. Gideon settles in a land that takes on his name and becomes a teacher in the church there.

After King Mosiah had the records read to all the people, he appointed Alma to be the main church leader and prophet for the Nephite people. It's interesting to speculate as to who, if anyone, had been the leader of the church in Zarahemla prior to Alma's arrival. Was it the king? Was there another who was recognized as their prophet? At any rate, there is no questioning that Alma was certainly capable of being an impressive and inspired leader. He was the only known convert of Abinadi, but he went on to impact the lives of hundreds during his lifetime, and directly impacted thousands more within a generation of his life through the missionary labors of his son, Alma, and his son's friends.

Barring revelation in his earthly life, Abinadi could not have known the tremendous impact his life, efforts, teachings, and testimony were to have on the Nephite people. They had clearly gone astray in the Land of Nephi. It's unclear how they fared in Zarahemla at that time, but it's clear that Alma, Abinadi's hidden convert, was raised up and appointed the leading prophet upon his arrival there.

One man heeded a call to speak the truth to an angry people. He bore witness and sealed his testimony with his very life.

Although he witnessed Alma stand up and defend him, he also saw Alma chased from the presence of the king. Did Abinadi know that Alma was on the verge of a complete conversion, or if his objections would be muffled and stilled by the threats against him? Abinadi may have even wondered if Alma would be put to death. Regardless, Abinadi stood strong and finished delivering the message the Lord had given to him. And, that message, testimony and spirit impacted the Nephite nation for generations.

It allowed the events in the Book of Mormon to continue in a way that worthy men were able to record them, and potentially led to the ultimate preservation of the sacred records that became the Book of Mormon today. That book has now touched millions of lives. Abinadi's sacrifice remains substantial and poignant in modern times and in ways he could not have possibly imagined. The efforts of this one man, this forgotten prophet, are still bearing fruit.

Alma's first known assignment as the leader of the church in Zarahemla was to organize branches of the church, or "churches," and appoint other leaders to lead these churches. Or, as it was recorded in the Book of Mormon:

> And it came to pass that king Mosiah granted unto Alma that he might establish churches throughout all the land of Zarahemla; and gave him power to ordain priests and teachers over every church. Now this was done because there were so many people that they could not all be governed by one teacher; neither could they all hear the word of God in one assembly; Therefore they did assemble themselves together in different bodies, being called churches; every church having their priests and their teachers, and every priest preaching the word according as it was delivered to him by the mouth of Alma. (Mosiah 25:19-21)

The reference cited above states that the seven churches were "throughout all the land of Zarahemla," not that they were "in the city of Zarahemla." The initial establishments of churches may have been located not only directly within the city limits of the city of Zarahemla, but in other cities near Zarahemla and considered to be in the "land of Zarahemla." In modern terminology, we might look at this as there having been a "city of Zarahemla" that was in the "county of Zarahemla."

One of the cities in which a church was established was the new city of Gideon, in the valley of Gideon. At some point – whether it was during the lifetime of Alma or later, we do not know – Gideon, captain of the guard and advisor to the king, was appointed to be a teacher over that church.

Later, in the book of Alma, it is recorded that Gideon, as a teacher of the church, confronted an apostate who was preaching false doctrines:

> And it came to pass as he [Nehor] was going, to preach to those who believed on his word, he met a man who belonged to the church of God, yea, even one of their teachers; and he began to contend with him sharply, that he might lead away the people of the church; but the man withstood him, admonishing him with the words of God. Now the name of the man was Gideon; and it was he who was an instrument in the hands of God in delivering the people of Limhi out of bondage. (Alma 1:7-8)

That encounter is best saved for another novel.